The Devil's Madonna

Also by Sharon Potts

In Their Blood
Someone's Watching

The Devil's Madonna

A Novel

Sharon Potts

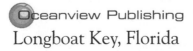
Oceanview Publishing

Longboat Key, Florida

FIRST EDITION

ISBN: 978-1-60809-049-5

Published in the United States of America by Oceanview Publishing, Longboat Key, Florida
www.oceanviewpub.com

2 4 6 8 10 9 7 5 3 1

PRINTED IN THE UNITED STATES OF AMERICA

In memory of Susi Lanner and Roy Frazier Potts

ACKNOWLEDGMENTS

It began with a tattered carton filled with crumbling scrapbooks. The yellowed newspaper articles and publicity photos told the story of my mother-in-law's glamorous career as an actress in 1930s Berlin and triggered my imagination. Though Susi Lanner's experiences have little to do with my novel's plot, I found the scrapbooks and the period evocative. I am grateful to her father, my children's great-grandfather, who lovingly compiled the scrapbooks, maintaining the legacy of his only daughter's film success.

I also want to thank my amazing sister-in-law Delia Foley for her careful, insightful reading of and excitement over early drafts of *The Devil's Madonna*. My critique partners, Christine Kling, Miriam Auerbach, and Mike Jastrzebski, gave me terrific feedback, and I am especially grateful to Neil Plakcy for sending me on the right direction with the plot and for Neil's suggestion for the book's title.

Thank you, once again to Patricia and Bob Gussin for recognizing the potential of *The Devil's Madonna*. I'm very appreciative of the enthusiastic support of the entire wonderful Oceanview team.

And while *The Devil's Madonna* was inspired by a scrapbook, my constant inspiration is my husband, Joe, who read and encouraged me through every word of every draft, and who sweetly gave me the two most awesome kids in the world.

The Devil's Madonna

I

Neil's breaths came short and quick as he rounded the curve and jogged down the dark road past houses hidden behind high hedges and bougainvillea-covered walls.

Almost home.

It was unseasonably warm for November, even by Miami Beach standards, and his T-shirt was drenched with sweat from his five-mile run. It couldn't be much after seven, since he'd headed out around six fifteen. He'd shower, grab a beer and last night's leftover Chinese food, then work on his research paper for a few hours. Give the packing and boxing a break and maybe get to bed early for a change.

The narrow sidewalks were cracked and overgrown with bushes so Neil stayed in the street. There were very few cars, just like when he was growing up. It was weird; he'd only been back a few days, but it seemed as though he'd never left. This was where he used to ride his bike, sneak over to the vacant lot by the bay to fish, hang out behind the big old banyan tree and smoke pot.

In the distance he could see an unnatural, wavering brightness coming through the windows of the neglected two-story house next door to the one where he'd spent his childhood. The movement of low-hanging palm fronds in the front yard created the illusion of an old black-and-white movie on a broken projector. He tried to process what he was seeing. The interior lights were expanding and contracting. A lot like flames.

What the hell?

He went from a jog to a sprint. The 1930s house came into blurred focus—tall columns holding up the portico, black shutters slightly askew against white stucco walls overgrown with ivy.

A shadow, backlit by the vacillating glow, appeared behind lace curtains. Neil squinted and wiped the sweat out of his eyes, trying to make out the short white hair of the old woman he knew lived there alone. Then he saw an orange glimmer. More tiny flames appeared. He slowed down. Maybe she was just lighting candles. But throughout the whole damn house?

He stopped in the street, just across from the house, and watched the flickering brightness in all of the windows. The old woman's silhouette was perfectly still. He could make out her profile—straight nose, angular jaw ending in a pointed chin, long, slender neck—like a flawless cutout for a valentine. She was holding her arm in front of her. In her hand was a long candle.

Suddenly, a blaze of orange-blue climbed the lace curtain.

Shit.

He darted across the street and banged on the door. "Mrs. Campbell. Mrs. Campbell. It's Neil. Open the door."

No answer. He didn't have time to wait to see if she would. He ran to the side of the house, unlatched the rusting gate, then pushed around the garbage cans and past the smell of rotting vegetation and cat musk. The backyard was overgrown, but the terra-cotta planters on the cracked patio were where they'd always been. He shifted the one closest to the door away from its base, and found the spare key beneath it. The dried dirt came off when he rubbed it against his shorts. He stuck the key into the door lock. It resisted, then turned.

He rushed into the house, pulling his sweaty T-shirt over his head as he made his way into the living room. "Mrs. Campbell, get back."

She seemed paralyzed, the candle clutched in her hand. The fire had spread from the lace curtains to the outer drapes and flames darted up and down the dark velvet.

He pushed her away from the window, wrapped his hands in his damp T-shirt and pulled the drapes down. The heavy curtain rod grazed his forehead before banging against the marble floor. He could feel the heat and sting of fire on his arms and chest as he smothered the burning fabric with the shirt, then stomped the last flames out with his sneakered feet.

The acrid smell of smoke and singed hair pierced his nose and lungs. He stepped away from the smoldering drapes that lay on the floor.

"Mrs. Campbell, are you okay?"

The old woman stood perfectly still, tears running down the creases in her face, her dull blue eyes wide with grief. Dozens of small candles flickered around the room—on the fireplace mantel, the built-in cupboards, and on the surface of the coffee and end tables. They cast shadows over her trembling form.

Her lips were moving, but her voice was so quiet he had to strain to hear her.

"Forgive me," he thought he heard her say. "Please forgive me."

Kali was inside one of her paintings. She could feel the caress of enveloping arms, fingers sifting through her hair, a fairy kiss on her forehead.

Somewhere, in another dimension, was the sound of ringing. Kali took in a deep breath of oil paint and turpentine. The easel was so close that she was only able to make out smudges of colors rather than defined images.

She stepped back and checked her phone. Two missed calls from Seth. Damn. It was almost eight. They were supposed to meet at his parents' for dinner.

Kali threw off her paint-spattered smock, changed into a short yellow dress over her faded denim leggings, and raced out of her studio to her car, texting as she went, *On my way.*

She knew she was driving too fast, but wasn't that the point of the four-door Volvo? Seth had insisted she replace her two-seater with the battle tank when they learned that Kali was pregnant, but she still missed her candy-apple-red Miata, which she'd bought herself ten years before when she graduated from college and got her first job as an illustrator.

Her nose itched and she rubbed it, not surprised to feel a dab of dried paint.

The traffic slowed. Kali hit the brakes as she got embroiled with cars heading for Aventura Mall. It was only November 9th—were people seriously already doing their Christmas shopping?

By the time she pulled her car under the grand entrance of the waterfront condo in the exclusive North Miami community where her in-laws lived, she was imagining Seth pacing outside his parents' apartment, dinner burned.

The valet held the car door open and seemed to be inspecting her as Kali climbed out. She brought her oversized satchel in front of her chest. Her body had changed in the three months of pregnancy and she wasn't sure if she was more self-conscious about her too-large breasts or her no-longer-narrow waist.

"Thanks," she said, taking the ticket from the valet.

"Sure." He gave her a crooked smile that suggested he'd noticed the breasts, not the waist.

Her phone beeped and she dug it out of her pocket. Text message from Seth. *Where r u?* She typed back. *Just got here.* Then added, *Keep nodding and smiling.*

The lobby was high ceilinged with black granite floors, gray modular sofas, and rectangular sculptures, and the air smelled vaguely of perfume and made her a little nauseated. Wasn't she supposed to be over that by this stage of her pregnancy?

She got into the waiting elevator, pressed 18, and checked out her disheveled reflection in the mirrored walls. Wisps of blonde hair had escaped from the thick braid she wore down her back. She pushed the loose strands of hair back behind her ears; this only seemed to accentuate the sharpness of her face. There were shadows under her blue eyes, and her bowed lips were skewed as though the air had been let out of one side. Even her nose, which she'd once considered an asset, had turned into a source of amusement for the Miller clan, who referred to it as "Kali's tiny *goyisha* nose." She spit on her finger and rubbed off a trace of paint.

The elevator came to a sliding stop, causing a fluttering in her stomach. She reached into her satchel for a saltine as she got off the elevator and practically bumped into her husband.

"Seth." Kali took a step backward.

He was only a couple of inches taller than she, about five foot six, and tightly built like a small, perfect "Ken" doll. He was still wearing the white shirt, striped burgundy tie, and navy suit pants he'd put on that morning, but she could swear there were no wrinkles in the shirt. She glanced down at her own red sneakers covered with Rorschach globs of paint.

"Thank God you're here." He ran his hand over his head. His dark hair was so closely cropped it looked lacquered on.

"Couldn't be that bad."

"Not that bad? Mom's hovering, and Dad's blackmailed me into playing golf on Sunday with some people he thinks would be good for my career. Golf, Kali."

"Oooo. That is bad."

"Don't make fun. You know I hate that scene. Small talk about football, then drinks in the locker room with all that cigar smoke. I'd much rather be home with you."

"Oh, yeah?"

"You know I would."

She had that nice feeling inside—like she was immersed in a warm honeycomb. They went down the hallway to the Millers' apartment. Close, but not quite touching. Who needed physical groping when the mental and emotional connections were so strong?

The front door was slightly ajar and a mixture of spices that were unfamiliar to Kali wafted into the hallway. At least nothing smelled burnt.

Seth was studying the door like it was a stone wall he was about to charge.

"You know, your dad's probably right about the career stuff," she said.

"Yeah." He blew out a puff of air, his lips twitching like a gerbil's. "But I wish I could just be a lawyer and not a whore."

"A lawyer that isn't a whore? Isn't that some kind of oxymoron?"

He smiled. "Thanks for the support, baby." He glanced down at Kali's abdomen. "By the way, how's Bucephalus doing?"

"Oh, lord. Please let's not name our child after a horse."

"Not just a horse. Alexander the Great's mighty horse. A name that represents strength and excellence."

"It's definitely better than Isambard—your morning suggestion. But what if it's a girl?"

"Hmmm. A girl." His eyebrows went into a squiggle above his fudge-brown eyes. "Bucephala?"

A singsong soprano voice leaked into the hallway from somewhere in the apartment. "Se-eth. Se-eth," Mrs. Miller called.

They looked at each other for a moment.

"Bucephala," Kali said. "Somehow I don't think your parents would approve."

And they both laughed.

They ate in the dining room by candlelight. The table was set with gold-rimmed china and cut crystal wine glasses—a family heirloom, Mitzi never failed to mention. Al Miller sat at the head of the table, Seth on one side of him, Kali on the other. Mitzi was in the kitchen putting final touches on the main course. Although Kali had gotten up to help several times, Mitzi kept shooing her out of the kitchen.

Al was telling Seth a story, gesturing with his hands, his grayish-blue eyes wide with excitement. He had lost most of the hair on top of his head. What remained was pure white and worn longish around his deeply tanned face.

Kali settled back against the cushioned dining chair. She felt cocooned here—a member of a real family.

From where she was sitting, she had a view of the living room, which was done in a rich palette of browns and beiges and wonderful textures—chocolaty chenille-covered sofas, silk russet throw pillows, a tweedy rug over hardwood flooring. The sliding doors to the balcony were closed, but she could see the lights of towering condos against a black sky.

Mitzi, still in the striped apron she wore over a sleeveless white camisole and pencil-thin jeans, carried a casserole dish in from the kitchen with oversized gloves. She had corded, defined arms and a head of wild, curly auburn hair, which made her look like a moppet despite her recently having turned sixty.

She set the casserole on the table. "Ta-da!" Her skin was freckled and wrinkly from too much sun, but Mitzi wouldn't consider the idea of cosmetic surgery, even though her husband was a well-regarded plastic surgeon.

"It smells so good," Kali said.

"Brisket and potato *kugel*," Mitzi said. "And the *kugel*'s vegetarian, Kali, just for you."

"*Kugel?*"

Mitzi laughed. "I keep forgetting you weren't born into it. *Kugel*. It's the Yiddish word for pudding. I guess they didn't teach you that in your conversion classes."

"No, but maybe they should have. I would have loved learning about Jewish food—especially how to cook it."

"Ha!" Al said. "Imagine—classes in *kugel* and *kneydlach*. Then everyone would want to convert to Judaism and we'd lose our exclusivity."

Kali smiled. Although Seth's parents weren't particularly religious, it was important to them that their sons marry Jewish girls so their grandchildren would be Jewish under Judaic law. Kali also didn't want her kids to be confused or torn about their religion, so she had decided to convert. Besides, after growing up with no religious beliefs, she welcomed the chance to belong somewhere.

"So what's new with our little artist?" Al asked.

"Kali's been asked to do the illustrations for another children's book," Seth said.

"How nice," Mitzi said. "I love your work. Especially those beautiful fairies and adorable cherubs. Are you going to make a mural in the nursery?"

Seth was mouthing something. *Bucephalus*. He winked.

"I'm planning to," Kali said, holding back the urge to laugh, "but I'm going to wait a while."

"Very smart," Mitzi said. "No reason to tempt the fates."

They ate and drank. Al entertained them with a story about a woman who had begged him to surgically alter her husband's face to look like George Clooney.

"Now, mind you," Al said, shoveling a forkful of brisket into his mouth, "the husband was this big, ugly clod who bore about as much resemblance to Clooney as a gorilla to a deer. So I said to the wife—"

"More sparkling cider, Kali?" Mitzi held up the bottle. The others were drinking wine.

"A little, thanks."

"And I said, ma'am, this is a complex procedure involving a great deal of discomfort and recovery time. With your husband's facial structure, I'm not sure how close I can get to Clooney. And the wife thought for a minute and says to me, 'Well, how about Schwarzenegger, then?'"

Everyone laughed, Al the loudest.

Although Seth was smiling, his eyes seemed disengaged. He was probably thinking about his trial tomorrow. Or maybe he was worrying about the golf game next Sunday. He'd loosened his tie and rolled up his shirtsleeves, exposing lean, pale arms covered with dark hair and the thin gold watch she'd given him for their first anniversary a couple of months before.

"Isn't Schwarzenegger one of your *landsmen?*" Al said to Kali.

"Excuse me?" Kali always felt awkward when they used Yiddish, like it was a secret language. "*Landsmen?* What is that?"

"There I go again. A *landsman* is someone from the same hometown. I thought I remembered someone saying your grandmother was from Austria, like Schwarzenegger."

"That's right." Kali took a sip of her cider.

"You'd never know it," Al said. "She has no accent. She must have moved here when she was a little girl."

"I don't think so. I believe she came later." Kali felt herself blush. She only had the vaguest idea of when her grandmother had moved to the United States and of the circumstances.

"Al," Mitzi said, "pour me a little wine, please."

Al reached for the wine. "Beautiful country, Austria. What part's she from?"

"I'm not quite sure." Kali noticed a splotch of turquoise paint on one of her fingernails. "She doesn't really talk about it."

A peculiar silence fell over the table. Everyone looked down at their food and concentrated on eating.

"This is terrific brisket, Mitzi." Al's voice was too cheerful. "Just like your mom used to make."

"It's her recipe."

Kali took another sip of cider. So what if her grandmother was from Austria? It wasn't like she had any involvement with the terrible things that had taken place during the war. She put her glass down, grazing the side of a serving dish.

Everyone looked up at the tinkle of breaking glass.

"Oh no. Your good crystal."

"Are you okay?" Seth said. "You didn't cut yourself, did you?"

Al reached for Kali's hand and turned it over in his. "She's fine. No cuts."

"I'm really sorry," Kali said.

"It's nothing," her mother-in-law said. "No big deal."

"It's just a glass, Mom," Seth said.

"I said it was no big deal."

Kali felt her phone vibrate in the pocket of her dress. She ignored it, the moment too awkward for her to check the caller ID.

Seth looked at her, eyebrows in a squiggle.

Her phone stopped, but a few seconds later began vibrating again.

Mitzi was picking up the pieces of glass from the table, putting them on a plate.

"Isn't that your phone, dear?" Al asked.

"Yes."

"Well, go ahead and answer it."

Kali slipped it out, glancing at a number she didn't recognize. "Hello," she said. "Yes, this is she."

She listened to the voice at the other end. "What?" Kali's stomach did a somersault. "You're sure it's nothing serious?"

Seth and his parents were watching her, his parents with concern, Seth with something more like panic.

"Yes. I know where it is. I'll be there as soon as I can." Kali closed the phone and bit down on her lower lip.

"What's wrong?" Mitzi asked.

Kali pushed out her chair and stood. "Seth, we need to go. That was the hospital. My grandmother."

"Oh dear." Mitzi brought her hands to her face.

"She's okay," Kali said. "But she almost burned her house down."

3

The students streamed through the hallway past Javier Guzman, hurrying to get to their dorms or maybe grab some dinner. The column he'd chosen to stand behind partially hid Javier, but gave him a clear view of everyone as they left the classroom. He ignored the coeds with their come-on breasts and too-tight jeans and searched among the male faces for his golden boy—now a tall, muscular young man. But only grungy, slouchy, unshaven slobs emerged from the room. Javier had dressed in worn blue jeans himself knowing, despite having thirty-plus years on this crowd, that with his smooth scalp, he'd blend in as one of their professors.

The exiting students thinned out. The hallway resumed its after-the-party desolation with crumpled papers and crushed cans of Red Bull littering the concrete floor. Javier picked up the scent of lingering cigarette smoke from the ones he'd smoked before class broke, ignoring the NO SMOKING signs. His fingers twitched for another, but he'd wait until later.

He checked his watch. 9:07. Gabriel's last class. From here, Javier expected Gabriel to head over to an off-campus bar that was loose on checking IDs and have a couple of beers. No big deal, really. Gabriel was just a few months short of twenty-one. Then around eleven, eleven thirty, the boy would drive the three-year-old BMW his mother's husband had bought him back to the garden apartment he shared with two other art students.

Javier knew Gabriel's routine well. He had been monitoring him for the last three months, since Gabriel had transferred down to the University of Miami. Javier had remained in the shadows, learning the patterns, waiting for the right opportunity.

A deep female laugh came from inside the classroom. Javier

moved back behind the column, still able to watch the door. Two people emerged from the room. The young man was wearing a wrinkled shirt with rolled up sleeves and holding a large leather portfolio. Gabriel was majoring in art—an interesting coincidence. He had a strong jaw, longish straight blond hair, and massive shoulders that could have easily brought him success in football had the boy not chosen to tackle the world with a paintbrush.

Javier felt a mixture of pride and resentment, just as he always did whenever he caught a glimpse of Gabriel. Life had been unfair to Javier, often appearing in one of the devil's many guises, so that Javier had been repeatedly tricked into believing a deception. Through these missteps, he had lost his loved ones and occasionally his own way in the world. But Javier was determined not to let the devil prevail. He now knew the truth and would one day redeem himself in the eyes of those he'd failed.

The woman was talking too loudly. She was black and Oprah plump with close-cropped kinky grayish hair and gold hoop earrings. She patted Gabriel's arm. "Catch you next week, Gabe," she said, then flounced down the hallway in the opposite direction.

Javier was surprised by the fluttering in his chest. Would Gabriel see him as flabby and useless? A middle-age man who'd amounted to little despite his brilliance? Javier brought the stale air deep into his lungs. It was time for him to take action. He'd let too many years go by without intervening and he was starting to fear that the damage might be irreparable.

The young man passed him without even a glance.

"Gabriel," Javier called, stepping out from behind the column.

Gabriel stopped. Javier could see his shoulders rise, his back stiffen. Gabriel slowly turned around.

The two of them were face-to-face. They were the same height, but Gabriel still had the narrow waist and slender hips that Javier had lost twenty or so years ago.

"What do you want?" Gabriel's jaw was clenched, his eyes charcoal gray like his mother's.

"You know who I am?" Javier was surprised. Had Gabriel noticed him lurking over the years?

"Why are you here? Why don't you just leave me alone?"

"Please, Gabriel."

"My name is Gabe."

"Gabe, then. Please. I just want to talk to you. You're a man now. You can make your own decisions about things."

Gabriel pushed past him. Javier grabbed his shoulders.

"Don't touch me, you creep."

Javier jerked his hands back. "Sorry, no touching." He held his hands up in the air like he was under arrest. "How about a quick beer? Just so you hear my side."

"I know enough about your side, you goddamn bastard."

Gabriel started walking rapidly down the hallway, his sneakers pounding against the floor. Javier kept in stride with him. "I never meant to hurt her."

Gabriel stopped abruptly. His face was contorted and he was breathing hard. "You fucking liar."

It had become warm and close in the hallway, as though the air-conditioning had been turned off.

"She wouldn't listen," Javier said. "She didn't understand."

"You're a sick man. You should be locked away somewhere. Or better yet, you belong in front of a firing squad and shot."

Javier felt like a poker had been run through his insides. "You have to listen to me, Gabriel. Please. I understand you more than you know. I didn't recognize the truth, either. And then, when I finally did, it was too late for me. I don't want that to happen to you."

There was a brief moment of hesitation. It seemed to Javier that Gabriel was studying his face, looking for something recognizable.

A door slammed in the distance. Voices and laughter. A moment later, a young man and woman, arms wrapped around each other, zigzagged down the hallway too busy sticking their tongues in each other's faces to see where they were going.

Javier returned his gaze to Gabriel. "Here, take this." He pressed one of his business cards into Gabriel's hand. He felt a jolt as his finger grazed the warm hand. His first touch in twelve years. Twelve maddening years when all Javier could do was watch from a distance.

Gabriel glanced at the card, then shoved it into the front pocket of his jeans. His lips twitched downward like Javier remembered them doing before he'd burst into tears over a broken toy or some childish disappointment.

He'd gotten through to him, Javier thought, as the tightness in his gut relaxed. "You know, Gabriel. You and I used to be great friends. Remember those rollerblades I gave you for Christmas? You were eight years old and we went to a skating—"

"Stop." Gabriel held his hand in front of Javier's face. His own features were tense, once again. "My name isn't Gabriel. And we're not friends. Never will be. Do you understand? Stop following me."

"But Gabriel—"

"I said stay the fuck away from me." Gabriel started walking quickly down the hallway, past the empty classrooms.

Javier tried to keep up. He was breathing hard as he spoke. "They've filled your head with the lies of the devil. Listen to me. I'm going to find this old woman. She has a painting. It will prove they're all wrong. You'll see, you'll be proud of who you are."

But Gabriel was racing down the hallway, leaving Javier behind.

"Wait." Javier took a few running steps, then stopped, knowing he couldn't catch him this time.

He watched the young man disappear around a curve.

"I love you, Gabriel," Javier shouted. "You're my son. You'll never be able to run away from that."

4

Lillian Campbell lay on the hospital gurney surrounded by the relentless sound of beeping. Nurses and doctors rushed around her, one blending into the next. Poking, prodding, asking question after question, making her brain hurt.

Despite the oxygen plugs in her nose, she could still taste smoke and fumes. Even a thousand candles wouldn't set her free.

November 1938. Over seventy years ago, but the memories bit into her with the impact of exploding glass.

The shrill screech of the locomotive braking. Stepping off the train onto the platform in Paris, everything a steamy haze. The sting of soot as she took a deep breath, trying to settle the seismic palpitations in her chest.

She glanced into the blur of bobbing faces, not knowing whom he had sent to hunt her down, or when an assassin's bullet would find her. He could be anywhere, anyone. And she'd never see him coming.

The shove came from the left. Her scream choked like a trampled bird's last note.

"*Pardon, m'mselle,*" said the man, touching the brim of his hat.

She backed away as he continued babbling unintelligibly in French, then she turned and pushed through the jostling mob with their trunks and bundles, into the grand terminal of the Gare de l'Est. She prayed that she looked like just another young, pretty woman, perhaps seeking work or visiting family. But she knew it would be a long time before she saw dear Mama, Papa, or Joseph again. If ever.

The crowd parted for a group of dull-eyed soldiers, rifles slung over their shoulders. She lowered her gaze and burrowed her head deeper into the scarf she wore to hide her blonde curls. The cut on her chin throbbed as it rubbed against the collar of her cloth coat. Beneath the coat, she had on only a torn slip, stiff with dried blood. She was conscious of his filth on her skin. Although she had tried to scrub away his semen in the toilette at the Lehrter Bahnhof in Berlin, it seemed to cling to her like tar.

The soldiers tramped by. Khaki uniforms, garrison caps, laced boots—French, not German. Her muscles relaxed. Safe. Or was she?

She risked another glance through the crowd, afraid to meet anyone's eyes, yet desperate to know if she had been followed.

She clutched her purse against her chest. The tiny painting was still there, wrapped in a lace handkerchief. Several times she had almost thrown it away. But she knew that wouldn't change anything. With or without the painting, she was irredeemably defiled.

The crowd carried her through the vast, echoing entrance foyer. She was immersed in the din of voices, the rapping of heels against the marble floors, the garbled announcements over the loudspeakers. A dull light leaked in through the arched glass ceiling far above her. She could smell sausage, cooking oil, shoe polish. She hadn't eaten in over two days and felt faint.

She leaned against a newspaper stall. Most of the papers were in French, but there was a German edition of the *Münchner Neueste Nachrichten*.

She scanned the bold headlines. Her heart crashed against her ribcage.

Dear God!

She remembered the spittle hanging from the side of his mouth. His promise. His curse. His retribution against her.

Lillian sat up with a jerk. Beeping all around her.

The candles. What had she done?

A black male nurse was adjusting the blood pressure cuff around her arm.

"I must go home," she said.

"I understand."

"No, you don't." She clutched at his blue uniform shirt. "I must go home now. I have to stop him."

He patted her hand, like he was trying to placate a child. It infuriated her.

"But he's coming after me," she said.

"Let me just finish taking your blood pressure, then I can help you into a wheelchair."

"My granddaughter. Where is she? What's happened to her?"

"I'm sure she'll be here very soon."

Lillian looked around the large open room, at the blur of bobbing faces, suddenly feeling very small and exposed.

He could be anywhere. Anyone. And she'd never see him coming.

5

When Kali walked into the emergency room at Mount Sinai Hospital on Miami Beach, she saw only trapezoids, parallelograms, a smattering of oblongs and spheres. Then the waiting room came into focus. It was filled with despondent, drooping people sitting or stretched out on stiff-backed chairs. A couple of TVs hung from the ceilings, emitting a low rumble, which sounded like gibberish to Kali. The burnt smell of boiled-down coffee almost made her gag as unwelcome memories surfaced.

She looked around once again. Where was Seth? He said he'd be right behind her in his own car when they left the Millers' apartment, but there was no sign of him.

Kali went to the reception desk. A harried-looking man wearing a short-sleeved white shirt sat behind the desk examining a clipboard, while an attractive woman in black argued and complained. Kali got in line behind the woman, checking if there was someone else who could help her. The door to the emergency room was operated electronically, so she couldn't simply push her way in.

Kali twirled the end of her braid around her finger. Although the man on the phone had said her grandmother was fine, Kali needed to see for herself. Hadn't everyone reassured her when her mom had been rushed to the hospital? A *little car accident. Don't worry. Everything will be okay.*

"We've been here forty-five minutes," said the woman in black. "And you let three other people who came after us go in."

The wide doors to the emergency room opened and a man in scrubs walked into the waiting area. *Now,* Kali thought. She darted around the woman in black, past the man in scrubs, and through the doors just before they closed.

She found herself in the midst of a strong antiseptic smell, frowning faces, intermittent beeping, and disembodied voices. For an instant she was thirteen again, overwhelmed by panic. *Mommy,* she almost cried out. She took a deep breath. Everything would be fine. Her grandmother was fine. Her hand went to her abdomen. Fine.

The nurses' station was in the center of the large, open area, surrounded by small alcoves separated by curtains. People lying on gurneys were scattered haphazardly in any available open space, as though there was a shortage of treatment rooms. The scene reminded her of the Paul Klee painting—*Twittering Machine.* Kali tried to get the attention of one of the nurses, but they all appeared to be busy. She scanned the room. Seated in a wheelchair in the far corner was a frail woman wrapped in a white hospital blanket. Her grandmother.

Kali hurried toward her. "Lillian."

Her grandmother's hands were in her lap, worrying the edge of the blanket, her skin looking as soft as crushed velvet.

"Are you okay?" Kali asked.

Lillian looked up at Kali, tension in her deep-set blue eyes. Her short white hair was pushed back from her face, accentuating her high cheekbones and chiseled chin. She was ninety-three, but still beautiful.

"I have to go home."

"We'll leave in a minute. Are you feeling all right?"

"Yes, yes. Tell them to let me go. They don't listen to me."

A slender, black man wearing a blue nurse's uniform and clogs sashayed over to them. He held a clipboard with some papers against his chest. "That's not quite so, Mrs. Campbell. I've listened to everything you said."

"I'll take you home now, Lillian," Kali said.

"I'm sorry," said the nurse. "And you are?"

"Kali Miller. Mrs. Campbell's granddaughter."

He pursed his lips. "You called her Lillian."

"That's right." It was what she'd called her grandmother since her mother died.

"So you're the missing granddaughter."

"I wasn't missing. I got here as soon as I heard."

"Just giving you your grandmother's perspective."

Lillian perked up. "There's nothing wrong with my perspective."

"Of course not, Mrs. Campbell." The nurse raised his eyebrows and gestured with his head. Kali followed him to a supply cabinet a short distance away. A machine beeped loudly behind them, but none of the nurses paid any attention.

"Is she okay?" Kali said.

He spoke in a low voice. "There was some concern about smoke inhalation, but she's fine. The doctor cleared her to leave."

"What exactly happened?"

"Apparently she was lighting candles and things got away from her. Someone called 911. The fire department came and an ambulance brought your grandmother here. He leaned closer to Kali. "Just so you know, she's freaking out that someone's going to break into her house while she's away. Has she ever been burglarized?"

"Not that I'm aware of."

"Probably just paranoia, then," the nurse said. "Happens to lots of older people. Your grandmother lives alone?"

Kali nodded.

"You know, she could have killed herself."

Kali glanced over at Lillian, whose eyes were darting around the room like a skittish bird's.

"Do you have other relatives who can help?"

Kali shook her head. "There's only me."

"Well, it's not safe for her to stay alone."

"I understand."

"Here are her discharge papers." The nurse pointed to the instructions. "She should see her own physician for follow-up." He started walking away. "And you might want to thank the man who rescued her," he called over his shoulder.

What man, she wanted to ask? But the nurse was already on the other side of the nurses' station.

❧

Lillian's eyes were closed when Kali returned to her, but her lips were moving silently. How she had aged in the last few years. Why hadn't Kali noticed? But the truth was, Kali had been denying the changes and the obvious signs of deterioration. Because once her grandmother was gone, Kali would lose her last connection to her roots.

Kali touched the blanket on Lillian's shoulders. "Ready to go?"

She opened her eyes. "I've been ready for a long time."

Kali took the handles on the wheelchair and pushed, glancing around to see if Seth had arrived.

A guy wearing gym shorts and sneakers was gingerly getting up from the edge of a bed in one of the alcoves, blinking as though to clear his eyes. He was long and lean like a stretched-out taffy bar, with mussed black hair, several days' beard growth, and a bruise on his high forehead. His chest, forearms, and hands, except for his fingers, were wrapped in bandages.

There was something familiar about his cleft chin and gray eyes. Familiar, but incomplete. Eyeglasses. Kali pictured the face with tortoise-shell frames, remembering how she'd look down from her bedroom window and see him adjusting those glasses as he stood partially hidden by the poinciana tree waiting for her.

"Neil Rabin," she said, stopping in front of the alcove.

His eyes met hers. He didn't seem surprised to see her. "Kali Sullivan."

Her heart hiccupped. Other than her mother, Neil was the only one who pronounced her name so that it sounded like the dog—"collie." Everyone else called her "Kaylee."

"Wait. That's not right," he said. "Not Sullivan. I heard you're married."

"That's right. It's Miller now." She subconsciously touched her abdomen. Her pregnant body felt conspicuous in her short yellow dress and form-fitting leggings.

But Neil didn't seem to register Kali's discomfort or condition as he knelt slowly in front of Lillian's wheelchair. "You okay, Mrs. Campbell?"

"I'm fine. I just need to get home." She scowled at the bandages on Neil's chest and arms. "What happened to you?"

"I'm okay. Just a few little burns."

"Oh, God," Kali said. "You were the one who saved her?"

He stood back up, grimacing a little. "I was out for a run. I saw flickering lights, then one of the drapes caught fire."

Kali was about to ask how he'd gotten into the house, but was afraid that might trigger her grandmother's paranoia. "Well, thank you so much for rescuing her," Kali said instead.

"Glad I could help."

The large door to the ER opened and several men from fire rescue came in wheeling a gurney with a woman in a neck brace.

"Are you staying with your mom?" Kali asked.

"Actually, Mom's in assisted living. She has Alzheimer's. I'm at the house, packing up so we can sell it."

"I'm so sorry. I had no idea. Your mom was always so, so—" Kali was at a loss. So nice to me, she wanted to say.

A voice over the loudspeaker was requesting a doctor to come to the nurses' station.

"Let's go, Kali," Lillian said. "I have to get home."

"Okay, we're going." Kali took hold of the wheelchair handles. "What about you?" she asked Neil. "Do you need a ride?"

"I'll walk. It isn't far."

The room was cold, too cold, and Kali wished she had something to cover herself with. "I can drive you."

"Kali."

She turned toward Seth's voice. He was working his way around the gurney with the woman in the neck brace.

"Here you are. They certainly don't make it easy to get in here." Seth pulled on his open shirt collar, further loosening his tie. He took in Lillian in the wheelchair. "Is she okay?"

"My hearing's perfect," said Lillian. "And I'm even able to speak for myself."

"Of course you are." Seth gave her a forced smile. "I just got worried when I saw the wheelchair. How are you?"

"Fine. Why does everyone keep asking me that? Would you please just take me home?"

Seth looked at Kali and frowned.

"I'm driving my grandmother. And Neil. Neil lives next door. He saved her from the fire."

"Really? You're a regular hero."

"Hardly," Neil said.

"No, seriously. You are. Thank you. We appreciate it. I'm Seth Miller, by the way. Kali's husband." Seth extended his hand to shake Neil's.

Neil held up his two bandaged ones, wiggling his exposed fingers. "Sorry."

Seth laughed. "Well, why don't we get out of here? You take your grandmother, Kali, and Neil can come with me."

Neil caught Kali's eye, then looked away quickly. "That would be great," he said. "Thanks."

6

The first thing Kali noticed when she opened the front door of her grandmother's house was the smell—smoke, candle wax, and something caustic, like burned fabric. She turned on the light, then took Lillian's arm. Her grandmother stiffened like a tense cat as they stepped into the foyer.

Although Kali had lived here for five years after her mother died, it had never felt like home. She'd been a guest, a tolerated visitor to a pristine museum. Nothing was comfortable or natural. The curved walls of the circular foyer opened up to a formal living room to the right, a large, rarely used dining room to the left. Straight ahead was a winding staircase with a wrought iron banister. The white marble floor, which had yellowed with age, was covered with footprints and crushed red flowers from the poinciana tree. It looked like a herd of men in boots had tramped through the house.

Her grandmother was looking around wildly. "Who's been here?"

"Firemen. They had to put out the fire."

"No one else? You're sure?"

"Maybe the police."

Lillian's arms were wrapped around herself as she stared at the gilded entranceway table against the wall near the living room. "How stupid of me."

"Would you like me to help you up to bed?"

"I don't need help. This is my house."

"Fine. Whatever you say."

Lillian went over to the entranceway table. A dozen small glass tumblers containing burnt-down candles were reflected in the mottled mirror above the table. "So stupid of me," she muttered.

"Why'd you light so many candles?"

Her grandmother didn't seem to hear her. She looked back at the front door. "You're sure no one else was here?"

"Neil Rabin was. You remember; he helped you."

Her grandmother pressed her hand against her chest. "No one else? You're sure?"

"Why? Do you think someone was here? Is anything missing?"

Lillian's eyes went from the front door to the staircase to the dirty marble floor to the narrow hallway that led to the kitchen.

Paranoia, the nurse had said. Happens to lots of older people.

"Lock the door," Lillian said, then she went slowly up the stairs, closing her bedroom door behind her.

Kali leaned against the arched doorway that opened to the living room and tried not to inhale the acrid, burnt air. This was one of the rooms that had been off-limits when Kali was a child. Even though she'd occasionally sat in here as an adult, years of conditioning were irrepressible. She stepped into the smoky room, fighting down a wave of nausea. The overstuffed rose-colored Queen Anne sofa and cut-velvet wingback chairs were arranged on a patterned Oriental rug like props for a royal family portrait, just as they'd always been. But the carved cherrywood tables, fireplace mantel, and other surfaces were all covered with dozens and dozens of candles.

Kali touched a blackened wick. *Yahrzeit Memorial Candle*, the label on the glass read. These were used in remembrance of a dead relative, Kali had learned in her Judaism conversion class. But what was Lillian doing with them? She wasn't Jewish. In fact, she had no religious affiliation, as far as Kali knew. It nagged at her. There was so much about her grandmother she didn't know, a past that Lillian refused to talk about.

And then there was the question of why had she lit so many candles? The nurse at the hospital had been right—her grandmother could have killed herself.

There was a light knock on the front door. Kali started at the sound. The tap came again, then a muffled voice. "Kali? Are you there?"

Kali went to let Seth in.

He stepped into the foyer, rubbing the back of his neck. He was still wearing his loosened tie and looked tired, like he often did when he came home late from work.

"Smoky in here," he said.

"I know."

"Is she okay?"

Kali gestured to keep his voice down. "She's in bed, hopefully sleeping."

"Good," he said in a half whisper. "Sorry it took me so long. Your neighbor needed some help. He's a bit incapacitated with those burns."

"It was nice of you to drive him. I know you have to get up early for court."

"Glad I could do something." Seth gave a little cough. "So Neil tells me you two grew up together. I hadn't known there was a 'boy-next-door' in your life." He wiggled his fingers when he said 'boy-next-door' as though he was putting it in quotes.

"He was a bit of a nerd."

"Well, he seems like a good guy. Not a lot of people would have put themselves at risk to help an old woman." He glanced into the darkened living room. "Damn. This place always reminded me of a funeral home, but it's worse than ever. Let's get out of here."

Kali pushed a strand of hair behind her ear. "I'm spending the night."

"Spending the night?"

She put her finger over her lips to hush him. "Let's go outside. I don't want to wake her."

Seth held open the front door and they stepped onto the portico. Mildew had grown over the coquina tiles, which were littered with wilted red flowers from the poinciana tree. The Doric columns were chipped and covered with spiderwebs and the house needed a paint job. It was obvious that Lillian was having a tough time maintaining the place since Kali's grandfather had died ten years before.

Seth ran his fingers through his short, dark hair. "Look, baby. I totally understand that your grandmother shouldn't be alone, but the house is full of smoke. It's not good for you or Bucephalus."

"I can't leave her by herself."

"Then let's call a nursing agency."

"It's after ten. I doubt they'd be able to send someone out at this hour. Besides, I don't want my grandmother waking up to a stranger in the house. I'm sorry, but I really need to spend the night."

He started pacing between the columns, crushing the small red petals beneath his wingtips. "It's not safe. She doesn't even have an alarm system."

"Of course it's safe. This is where I grew up, remember?"

He stopped directly in front of her. His eyes seemed to be pleading with her. "Please, Kali. I can't be alone."

She realized in the two years they'd been living together, they'd never spent a night apart. "Then stay here with me."

"Here? This is your grandmother's house. I can't stay here."

A dog barked excitedly up the street.

"She won't mind."

"I can't."

"Sure you can."

He shook his head, looking like a lost little boy.

"It's just for tonight, Seth. I'll get an aide to come tomorrow."

He took in a deep breath. "Okay. You can stay." He stood up straighter. "I'll open a few upstairs windows so you aren't breathing carcinogens all night."

"I can open them."

"No way." He wagged his finger at her. He seemed to have recovered from his brief panic attack. "Bucephalus doesn't want his mommy exerting herself."

"Bucephala. I think it's a girl."

He was smiling when they stepped back into the foyer.

"What are you grinning about?"

"I got you to accept Bucephala."

"I haven't accepted anything."

He started toward the stairs, but his attention was caught by the candles on the entranceway table. He picked one up and turned it over in his hands. "What's your grandmother doing with these?"

"They're everywhere. Dozens of them. She apparently lit them all."

"But why *Yahrzeit* candles? These aren't decorative candles. They're supposed to be lit in memory of the dead."

"I know. I'm guessing she bought them in bulk somewhere and didn't realize the significance."

He was squeezing the tumbler.

"She didn't mean any disrespect, Seth. You know that, don't you?"

He kept looking at the candle, not meeting Kali's eyes.

"I'm sure there's some reason she did this that makes sense to her," Kali said. "Maybe she lost friends during the war."

"Jewish friends? I doubt that."

"What? Why would you say such a thing? You don't know anything about her."

"And you do?"

Kali's mouth fell open. Just like during dinner with his parents, she felt like she was being unjustly accused of something she didn't even have any knowledge of.

The tenseness went out of Seth's face. "Look, baby. I love you, but your grandmother's something else. Haven't you noticed how she acts toward me and my family? It's like we're yesterday's garbage."

"That's just how she is. It has nothing to do with you being Jewish."

"You really believe that?"

"Yes. Yes, I do."

"Then tell me, what exactly was she doing during the war? How come she never talks about it?"

"What are you implying?" Blood rushed to her face.

"Nothing. Forget it." He put the tumbler down on the entranceway table with a clatter.

They stood without talking, staring at the yellowed marble floor, Seth in his polished wingtips, Kali in her paint-spattered sneakers.

Seth was the first to take in a long breath and relax his shoulders. "I'm sorry. It's late. I'm tired. I'd better go home."

Kali nodded. A lump had formed in her throat.

Seth took a hesitant step toward her, as though he wanted to give her a hug or kiss. She wished he would.

But he turned and left the house, without even a pat for Bucephala.

7

Kali went into the kitchen. Her hands were shaking as she filled a glass with tap water, then took a couple of swallows. She wasn't sure what she was feeling. Hurt? Sadness? Anger? Concern?

Could there be any truth in Seth's accusations? No. Not possible. As remote as Lillian was, Kali couldn't believe her grandmother was capable of evil or had had any discrediting involvements during the war. Then what could be the explanation for her lighting all those candles? And why was her grandmother obsessing about a break-in? Was there something of value in the house?

Kali finished the water and put the glass in the sink, noticing the crud around the faucet. She took another look around the room. The counters were covered with piles of mail and stacks of newspapers, there were crumbs on the black-and-white-checkered-pattern linoleum, and the appliances were rust-stained. It was clear that things were running away from Lillian. Kali flipped through the mail on the counter. Some of it was opened, some still in the envelopes. A few bills, bank statements, mostly advertisements and solicitations. Nothing out of the ordinary.

She went to turn out the kitchen light, noticing that the wicker étagère that used to be against a kitchen wall had been moved so that it was completely blocking an interior door her grandmother always kept locked. Its shelves were loaded down with more newspapers, more mail, and a large bag of cat food. Kali had grown up believing the door opened to a closet, then shortly before she left for college, she found the key. She discovered a staircase, which led to two small rooms and a tiny bathroom intended as servants' quarters, but the rooms were used for storage. Until Kali had come up with another purpose. But Lillian never knew about that. So why had she blocked the door?

Kali reached behind the étagère and tested the doorknob. Locked. She wondered where her grandmother kept the key these days. But even if Kali found it, she couldn't be rummaging about the storage rooms while Lillian was home. Still, it bugged her. Was her grandmother paranoid, or was some secret from her past finally surfacing?

Kali mounted the stairs to her bedroom. A haze of smoke hovered near the ceiling around the crystal chandelier. The door to her grandparents' bedroom was closed.

She stood for a moment on the worn carpet runner that covered the wood floor outside the bedrooms. There had been a time when Kali had looked forward to coming here for Sunday family visits, enjoying her grandfather's lap in his favorite armchair, playing hide-and-seek with an imaginary friend. Even her grandmother's disapproval when Kali touched something off-limits seemed part of the game. Then Kali's mother died, and Kali came to associate the house with everything she had lost.

She flipped on the light switch in the front bedroom. She'd been up here a few times since she'd moved away for college, but she was still caught off guard by the changes. The walls, bedspread, and throw pillows were all white, just like when this had been Kali's mother's room. Kali had painted the walls tangerine and used a comforter the color of sunflowers when she lived here, but Lillian had returned everything to its original, colorless state.

The dark wood floor creaked as she stepped into the room. Candles with blackened wicks lined the windowsills and bookshelves, and a choking smell hung in the air. Seth hadn't come up here to open the windows, after all.

There was an old air-conditioning unit installed in the wall, but Kali had always preferred fresh air, even if it was warm and humid. She went to one of the casement windows and tried to turn the crank. It stuck. She applied more pressure until the window popped loose. Then she went to open the other window that also looked over the street, and the one that faced Neil's parents' house. She noticed there weren't any lights on in the Rabins' upstairs bedrooms.

A muggy breeze circulated through the bedroom, carrying the scent of night-blooming jasmine. In the chest of drawers, Kali found a stretched-out T-shirt and sweatpants that had been her favorite in high school, relieved that Lillian hadn't disposed of her old clothes. Despite the familiar oak furniture—the chest, student desk, chair, and bookcase—the room felt like a stranger's. Only the gold-framed high-school-photo portrait of Kali's mother, which still hung above the rocking chair, reminded Kali that she'd spent five years of her life here. She stood in front of it, just like she had every night before going to bed. Framed behind nonglare glass, the photo had a matte finish and the colors were gently muted. There was a barely perceptible horizontal line, which probably only Kali with her artist's eye would notice, that passed through the bodice of the off-the-shoulder dress her mother was wearing. Her mother's dark hair was in a bouffant, combed away from an angular face, and her blue eyes stared directly into Kali's. Her lips, shiny with pink lipstick, were slightly parted as though she was about to say something.

A sense of deep loss nagged at Kali. She changed into her old clothes in the bathroom, then returned to the bedroom, folding the white bedspread and placing it on the rocking chair. When Kali couldn't sleep as a girl, she would hunt around the room for hints of her mother. At first, she found no trace, no evidence that her mother had spent her childhood in this room. Except for the framed graduation photo, it was almost as though her mother hadn't existed. Then one day, Kali noticed that the camouflage-pattern contact paper on the inside of the closet door had come partially unglued. Kali pulled it away and discovered a painting of a fairy hovering over a flower. The contact paper had probably been Kali's mother's attempt at concealing her artwork from Lillian. Kali knew her grandmother's irrational dislike of art from her own experiences, so the hidden painting made complete sense to her. Kali had been careful to restick the contact paper.

It had been years since Kali had looked at her mother's painting, and she had an urgent need to see it again. She remembered the
fairy—her delicate wings, two pairs of graceful arms bent at the elbows and radiating from the torso, hands flat and open. Just like the
fairies Kali now drew. How come she'd never made the connection
before?

She opened the closet door, noticing a vague smell of fresh paint,
and ran her fingers over the white latex finish on the inside of the
door. The camouflage contact paper was gone. Her mother's painting was gone. Gone. She felt a weakness in her limbs, as though she'd
just been told her mother was dead.

Kali turned off the light and climbed into bed. The sheets and
pillowcase smelled musty. She remembered her mother standing at
the foot of her bed in their old house, watching her, blowing her a
goodnight kiss. One day she was there, then the next, she was gone.
And there was no one to talk to about her.

Secrets. Locked doors, hidden paintings, her mother's death, and
dozens of strange candles. Maybe there was something to Seth's sus-
picions. But even if not, Kali was tired of being in the dark. She
needed to understand her roots; what made her the person she was.
Not just for herself, but for the child who was growing inside her.
And only Lillian could tell her these things. Now, before her grandmother was gone and her secrets went with her.

8

Lillian couldn't sleep. She rarely went to bed before two or three in the morning, but tonight with her granddaughter in the house, she felt like a guest in her own home. She padded across the soft rug in her bare feet, ignoring the familiar ache of arthritis in her neck and back. Ordinarily, when she was restless, she'd sit in the rocking chair in Dorothy's room, below the high school photo that Dorothy had detested, but which captured a sweetness in her daughter's blue eyes that reminded Lillian of her own mother.

The smell of smoke and burnt wax hung in the room. Someone had blown out the candles that still sat on the windowsills and tables. Lillian could have opened the windows, but she preferred breathing in the reminder of her sins.

How could she have been so stupid? All these years living a quiet, inconspicuous life, staying beneath anyone's radar, and then practically announcing herself to the world.

But maybe seventy years of guilt had become too much to bear. Maybe like the murderer in Edgar Allan Poe's *The Tell-Tale Heart*, she had no choice but to acknowledge her sins.

She thought about the shooting flames that had danced up the drapes and how they had hypnotized her. For the first time, she considered what might have happened if that Rabin boy from next door hadn't barged into the house and put out the fire. Would that have been so awful? She'd lived with her nightmare for over seventy years; when would it finally be over? Never, she knew. It would never be over.

And now, what if her foolishness made the news? What if someone had been watching and waiting for her to break? What if he had finally found her?

Oh, how she wished Harry was here to protect her, to tell her everything would be all right.

She picked up the photo of her husband that she kept on the rosewood chiffonier and sat down on the edge of the bed. The picture had been taken when Harry was in his seventies. He looked very jaunty with his cap perched at an angle over his bald head, a cigar hanging from the side of his mouth. Just like the first time they met.

December 1938. She couldn't think of that winter without feeling chilled. Although the climate in the English Channel Islands was considered mild, no matter how she bundled herself, the wind seemed to cut through her cloth coat and the scarf she draped over her head. Perhaps at another time in her life, the walk along the path down the hills from her boardinghouse to the town of St. Aubin would have been beautiful, but she had been overwhelmed with frustration and fear since arriving in Jersey weeks before. After catching a train out of Berlin that dreadful night, she had made it to Paris and into the temporary safety of the people her brother had told her to contact in an emergency. They had helped her out of France, then here to Jersey with a new name.

There was little she could do but wait for news, keeping as low a profile as possible in such a small community. Although there had been no sign that he had sent anyone to hunt her down after she'd fled Berlin, she remained alert. She knew what he was capable of and there was no way he would simply let her go.

Leli—that's how she still often thought of herself—spent her afternoons at a tea room, craving the warmth of the close bodies surrounding her as she sipped her tea.

That day, she had taken a seat against a fabric-covered wall near the back of the room, after glancing around for anyone suspicious looking. There were mostly locals, whom she recognized from other days, and a few families who appeared to be on holiday from England, but she kept to herself. She noticed that the tension from the mainland didn't seem to have touched this small village.

She ordered a pot of tea and tried not to think about the hunger pangs in her stomach. She took off her scarf and patted her hair in place. She had dyed it brown a few weeks before and wore it off her face in a severe bun. She knew that anguish had hardened her features and altered her general demeanor, as well, and it wasn't likely anyone would associate her with the pretty, vivacious, curly haired blonde she'd once been.

Leli slipped her coat onto the back of her chair and crossed her legs. She wore silk stockings and they looked flirtatiously incongruent with her plain gray wool suit. She checked her purse for money, although she already knew there was almost none left. How much longer could she continue like this? Perhaps she should sell the painting, but then she'd have nothing.

She became aware of a man approaching her table. He was wearing a tweed suit, holding his cap in front of him, and she realized he'd been sitting across the restaurant watching her since she'd come in.

"Excuse me, miss," he said with an American accent, his cigar hanging out of the side of his mouth. "Would you mind terribly if I joined you?"

He had a dashing manner, like many Americans. As though they were above the problems of the rest of the world.

She looked away from his hazel eyes and thinning brown hair, conscious of his easy good looks.

"I hate to intrude," he said, "but I would really appreciate talking to a local to get the lay of the land."

An American was safe, Leli thought. Perhaps he could even help her. She nodded at the chair across from her.

"Thank you," he said, adjusting his jacket as he sat down. "That's very kind of you." He placed his cigar in the ashtray and extended his hand. "Harry Campbell."

Leli hesitated. "Astrid Troppe." It was the name on her papers.

He looked surprised. "You aren't English?"

She shook her head.

He laughed. "I was certain you were with your china-doll skin and blue eyes. I even pictured you tending flowers in an English garden."

She picked up her teacup and took a sip. Maybe this wasn't a good idea.

The waiter came by and Harry ordered a tray of sandwiches and another pot of tea. Leli didn't protest. In fact, her empty stomach grumbled in anticipation.

He leaned back in his chair and stretched out his legs. Long American legs. Solid and strong. "So are you on vacation?" he asked. "Wait. That's not how they say it here. Holiday, they call it. Are you on holiday?"

How to answer that? What else would she be doing on the island of Jersey in the middle of winter? She nodded. "And you?"

He had a wide, toothy smile. "I'm a businessman. What you might call an enterpriser. I'm scouting out opportunities."

"For what?"

"Banking, foreign exchange, that kind of thing. But the details would probably bore you."

The waiter put a double tier of sandwiches and scones on the table and set down the teapot, jam, and cream.

Leli had to hold herself back from reaching for a scone.

"Go ahead," Harry said. "Help yourself."

He sipped his tea as he watched her slather Devonshire cream and jam on the scone and gobble it down.

"Have some sandwiches," he said. "They look awfully good."

She took one of each and ate them eagerly. It hadn't been so long ago that she turned away sweets worrying that they'd ruin her figure.

They tasted delicious, but a moment later, her stomach, unaccustomed to so much rich food, rebelled against them. She waited until the nausea passed, then ate the next sandwich more slowly.

"Astrid Troppe," he said, as though to himself. "Are you German?"

She shook her head. "Austrian."

"You speak English well."

Leli couldn't help but smile. "How could you know that? I've hardly spoken."

"I didn't. But now I do. Where did you learn English?"

"At the gymnasium, then the university. My father's a professor of languages." She clamped her mouth closed. Too much information.

He seemed to sense her discomfort. He reached for a sandwich, took it apart, and examined its contents before putting it back together, then eating it. So American.

As he chewed, he glanced around the room, studying the other customers. Then he leaned toward her, his face serious. "I have friends," he said in a soft voice. "If you need something, I know people who could help you."

The food rose in her gorge. What could he possibly have guessed about her?

"Why?" she said, finally. "Why would you want to do anything for me?"

He smiled again, but this time only with his eyes. "Because, Astrid, you're the most beautiful woman I've ever seen in my life and I believe I've fallen in love with you."

Lillian could hear a dog barking outside her bedroom window. She listened for the sound of an intruder, then relaxed. It was probably that crazy dog from next door barking for no damn reason.

She was worrying herself needlessly. Everyone who knew the truth had to be dead by now. No one was coming for her, or for her granddaughter.

They were safe.

She kissed her husband's photo and placed it on the nightstand. Dear Harry. He'd be so angry if he knew she'd almost burned herself and the house down.

She lay down against the pillows and folded her hands over her chest. The smell of candles scorched her heart.

But she was safe.

And Kali was safe.

9

Javier Guzman sat in darkness in his small home office, listening to the scratchy sound of Beethoven's *Ninth* as the 78 rpm record spun around and around on the old phonograph. Although Javier understood his son perfectly, he felt saddened by the irony of the situation. The deep hatred Gabriel had for him, just as Javier had had for his own father. After all, accepting, or even acknowledging, Javier's beliefs would forever cast Gabriel as a pariah. Until—Javier took a deep drag on his cigarette—until Javier was able to show the world that they'd gotten it all wrong.

This had been Javier's goal for many years. He had seen it as a way to make things up to Vati. To restore his father's honor and legitimacy. But now, exposing the truth was more important than ever. It was the only way Javier would be able to reclaim his son.

He leaned back in his desk chair, feeling the brass and tympani echo through his chest as he watched the lights from his computer screens glow in the darkness. Sometimes he imagined himself paddling down the River Styx, enveloped in infinite black broken by flashes of light like electrical arcs on a matrix. In the distance, he could see the looming shadow of a tall, broad-shouldered man. The bill of his cap and strong jaw were visible in profile, and the spitting lights bounced off his leather riding boots.

The image in his memory was still as powerful as the first time he'd seen his father in his uniform. Javier, a mere child, slipping from the riverside campsite in the darkness, crossing the damp grass to take a piss. He'd screamed at the unexpected vision, believing a monster had risen from the murky waters. But his father had taken the young boy in his arms and told him the story of the fallen heroes who were destined to rise again. "We live in darkness for now," his father had said, "despised by the ignorant masses, who don't know better. But one day, they will respect and revere us, just as they once did."

Had Gabriel ever experienced such reverence for Javier when he'd been a young child? If so, there was hope.

Javier put out the cigarette and lit another. The opening lyrics of "Choral" filled the room. "*O Freunde! Nicht diese Töne!*" the baritone sang. They tore at his heart. How desperately Javier wanted his son back. He had spent the last twelve years watching him grow up raised by a false father, but unable to intervene because of threats by his ex-wife to betray Javier if he ever approached the boy. Fortunately, during the years Gabriel lived in New York, and now in Miami, Javier had been able to search for the woman and the painting that had disappeared so many years ago. True—the woman had been his father's obsession, but Javier also appreciated the power of the painting to return society to the core values that had meant so much to his father and now to him. And above all else, Javier knew that if he found the woman and the painting, there would finally be closure in everything that was important to him.

He leaned forward on his chair and, just as he did every night, clicked through the computer screens glaring in the darkness of his office. Miami Beach, just like New York, was a likely place to find her and Javier was a genius at exploiting the possibilities. He had hacked into the internal communication systems and logs for local 911, fire rescue and hospitals, and read the obituaries daily, hoping for some tidbit about an elderly woman of Austrian origin. Not that he was certain she was here, or that she was still alive, for that matter. But the local populace remained one of several areas that Javier was monitoring.

He scanned the 911 calls, noting the minor incidents that probably wouldn't make the news. There were the usual heart attacks, strokes, and drug overdoses, but none involved white women over ninety.

Cymbals crashed as the music came to an end and the needle scratched blindly in the run-out groove.

In the fire rescue log, Javier noticed a report of an elderly woman on North Bay Road brought in for smoke inhalation. No details given, but possibly something to follow up on.

He leaned his chair back against the credenza and turned the record over.

10

A dog was barking wildly, jarring Kali awake. Where was she? Darkness. Sweet and sour smells. Her old room. Kali checked the time. She'd only been dozing for a few minutes. She got out of bed and looked down from her window. Through the lacey leaves of the poinciana tree, she saw a man in jeans and a button-down shirt trying to control the dog, which appeared hysterical over something in the bushes. The man's hands were wrapped in white.

"Neil," she called, before she could stop herself.

He looked up, still trying to contain the barking dog. A cat darted out of the bushes and across the street.

"Sorry," he said in a loud whisper. "That cat's driving him crazy."

"Go around back. I'm coming down."

What was she doing? But she didn't give herself time to think. She slipped on her sneakers and went down the stairs, careful not to disturb her grandmother. The house was familiar to her, even in the dark, so she didn't turn on any lights. She went through the kitchen, touching the back of a padded dinette chair, then the edge of the protruding cupboard. Her hip slammed against something hard. The damn étagère in front of the door that led to the storage rooms. She eased her way around it, then reached for the doorknob of the back door.

Kali pushed the door open. The night air was close and muggy, but she caught a whiff of the jasmine she'd smelled in her room. And then, the cutting scent of cat musk. She glanced down. One of the terra-cotta planters had been moved slightly, leaving a ring of dirt on the cracked stones of the patio. Beside the planter was a plastic dish of cat food. For as long as Kali could remember, her grandmother had been feeding stray cats.

A sound came from the far corner of the yard. Neil was standing beneath the old mahogany tree clearing off dead leaves from the corroding lawn chairs. His dog was lying quietly in the dirt.

Neil moved with a controlled grace, like an athlete. Against the darkness, his white, bandaged hands reminded her of the Invisible Man and she let out a small laugh.

The dog sat up. Neil turned. His expression changed from cautious to tentative. And then he smiled.

Kali forced herself to walk slowly across the overgrown lawn. "I'd better do that. You'll hurt your hands." She tipped one of the PVC pipe chairs forward and pushed off what she could of the damp, disintegrating leaves, staining her fingers a rust color in the process.

"Damn," Neil said. "This is a mess. Maybe we should sit somewhere else."

"I'm used to getting dirty. A hazard of my profession." She sat down on the fabric of the frame; the seat cushions were long gone.

He hesitated, then, careful of his bandages, lowered himself into the other chair. He was wearing tortoise-framed glasses, a lot like the ones he'd had as a teenager, and he no longer looked strange to her.

"So you dig ditches?" Neil rubbed the walnut-size bump on his forehead. It seemed to have gotten larger since the hospital.

"Ditches?"

"You said getting dirty's a hazard of your profession."

"I'm a freelance illustrator. Mainly children's books. But I also paint in my spare time."

"Good for you. So you didn't keep that artistic streak all bottled up."

"Nope."

"And your grandmother? She okay with it?"

"She knows I work on children's books. I don't give her any details and she doesn't ask." Kali lifted her hair off her sweaty neck. She'd taken it out of the braid when she went to bed and it hung loose on her shoulders.

Neil was studying her, a half smirk on his face like he used to get when he had a good hand at cards. He'd been a lousy gin rummy player. "I can't believe it," he said finally. "It's been what? Like fourteen years? You've hardly changed."

She folded her arms across her chest. "I've changed a lot."

"Better maybe."

The air smelled ripe. What if Seth was trying to reach her? She'd left her cell phone upstairs. How could she explain this? But what was there to explain? She was just catching up with an old friend.

Neil played with the bandage on one of his hands, wearing a focused expression.

"You know," she said, "I never would have recognized you."

He looked up, raising an eyebrow above the frame of his glasses. "Really? Because I'm pretty much the same guy."

"You look like you've been on one of those makeover shows."

He laughed. She remembered that most about him, how he laughed when she spoke, as though she was funny and clever.

"Except for the glasses no one would ever know—"

"What? That I'm a nerd?"

"Was."

"I'm still a nerd. But now I get paid to be one. I'm a history professor at UCLA."

"Good. I'm glad the egghead prevailed." Kali reached over and held her rust-stained hand out for the dog to sniff. It had one eye, but was otherwise beautiful with a shaded chestnut coat and white paws. "Your dog?"

"My mom's. A stray she picked up a couple of years ago. Some kind of German shepherd-collie mix. His name's Gizmo and he's meaner than a grizzly. Bites people if they get too close. But he seems to like you."

"Gizmo," she said.

The dog got up and rested his head on her leg so she could pet him. It was just like it used to be. How many nights had she and Neil sat beneath the old mahogany tree whispering, trying to contain their laughter so as not to awaken her grandparents? "Gizmo's not mean at all."

"I'm not sure what I'm going to do with him when I go back to L.A. No dogs allowed where I live."

Kali stopped petting. "How long will you be staying?"

"I'm on family leave for the rest of the semester, but I need to be back in January. I hope I can get the house sold by then."

"And you're here by yourself?" With the bandages, she couldn't tell if he was wearing a wedding band, but why would she even care about that?

He smiled. Nice even teeth. He'd worn braces many of the years they'd known each other. "All by myself. Never married. Not even close."

She didn't want to touch that one.

"Seth seems like a nice guy," he said.

"He is."

"I never would have thought you'd marry someone like him, though."

"What do you mean?"

Gizmo tensed as though he noticed something in the bushes.

"He just seems very, I don't know, grown up, I guess. Pinstripe suit, a real job. And you. Well, you're Kali—the Hindu goddess of external energy and change. I mean, look at you for God's sake."

She glanced down at her sweatpants, the paint-spattered red sneakers. "Seth and I really aren't that different. We like to talk about stuff, make fun of things." She scratched the remnants of a dead leaf from the arm of her chair.

"I get it. You were always a sucker for smart and witty."

"But it's more than that. Seth is ballast. He makes me feel like I belong somewhere."

Neil pushed his glasses up on his nose. "He told me you're having a baby. Congratulations."

"Thank you. We're very excited."

They were surrounded by the chirping of crickets. Neil looked up at the back of her grandmother's house where thick, blooming vines of crimson-violet bougainvillea completely obscured the windows of the storage rooms. She wondered if he was remembering that night.

"By the way, how'd you get into the house earlier?" she asked.

"The key under the terra-cotta planter. It was still there after all these years. I put it back."

"Ah."

Neil shifted forward, as though he was getting ready to leave. "So are you going to be staying with your grandmother for a while?"

"Just tonight."

"You think she'll be okay by herself?"

"I'll hire an aide to live here with her."

"She's not going to like that."

"I know."

Gizmo's ears went back. A cat darted through the bushes, and the dog began to bark.

Neil held tight to the leash. "Shit." He stood. "Gizmo, sit."

But the dog kept barking.

Kali reached for the leash to keep the pressure off Neil's hands.

"I've got him, thanks." Neil wrapped the leash around his wrists a couple of times.

Gizmo stopped barking, but continued watching the bushes, a low growl coming through his bared teeth.

"I don't know how my mom was able to walk him with all these cats," Neil said. "Well, I'd better go before he wakes your grand-mother up."

"Thanks again for helping her."

He nodded and kept going through the gate that led to the front of the house. Then he was gone.

Kali sat back against the chair frame, the exposed plastic pipe cutting into her ribs. The air was heavy and the scents of jasmine and cat musk blended in a way that made her heart ache. She glanced up at the bougainvillea-covered wall, knowing what was hidden behind the thick vines. They had called it their secret room. And she'd never told anyone, not even Seth.

11

When Kali woke up the next morning, she went downstairs to the kitchen. Lillian was sitting at the small table sipping hot tea from a chipped china cup, seemingly oblivious to the pile of newspapers that covered much of the table. She was wearing a faded housedress with a tiny floral pattern and her white hair was combed back from her face. Although it was after nine in the morning, overgrown foliage blocked the windows, making the kitchen dim. The overall effect reminded Kali of one of Degas's muted domestic scenes.

"Good morning," Kali said. "Did you sleep okay?"

Her grandmother's blue eyes were surprisingly clear, almost feverish. "Why wouldn't I sleep okay?"

"Well, good. I'm glad."

Lillian broke off a piece of the bran muffin that was on a small plate in front of her. She studied it intently, as though not interested in carrying on a conversation. The smell of burnt candles hung in the room.

Kali went to the counter, took a tea bag and a couple of sugar cubes from the metal canisters that had been there since she could remember, then poured hot water from the tea kettle into a cup. She was wearing the yellow dress and old denim leggings she'd had on yesterday. It was only Tuesday, less than twelve hours since Kali had gone to the hospital to get her grandmother, but it felt as though days had passed.

Seth had already called this morning. He sounded shy, almost embarrassed. "Sorry about last night," he'd said. "I got carried away, but I didn't mean to imply anything bad about your grandmother." Then he asked if she'd made arrangements for an aide and when she was coming home. Tonight, Kali had promised him. Unfortunately, first Kali had to broach the subject of hiring an aide with her grand-mother.

A dog barked outside and Kali's body tensed. But Neil was not on her agenda.

She brought her tea and a muffin to the table, cleared away some of the newspapers, and then sat down opposite Lillian. The table was rectangular with aluminum legs and a white Formica top marred by over fifty years of scratches and cigar burns. This was where Kali and her grandparents had eaten their meals. Rarely in the dining room.

"What about you?" Lillian said.

"What?" The question made no sense to Kali.

"I asked how you slept."

"Oh. Fine, thank you."

"I don't imagine it feels like your bed anymore."

Kali was taken aback by the statement. Lillian never talked below the surface about things. "It was a little strange," Kali said slowly. "I haven't slept here in many years."

"It used to be your mother's room."

"I know." The conversation was taking an odd turn. Of course Lillian would know that Kali was well aware it had been her mother's room.

Her grandmother looked up at the entrance to the kitchen, as though expecting someone to come in. "She was such a sweet child. So pretty with that cloud of dark hair and those blue eyes."

Kali's throat closed. Lillian never spoke about Kali's mother. In the years after she died, Kali had desperately wanted to talk about her, but was always afraid to bring up her name, concerned she'd upset her grandparents.

"She had a pretty pink pinafore with lace around the collar." Lillian touched her neck. "And such a little actress she was. Always putting on plays for me and Harry."

It bothered Kali that she didn't say "your grandfather" or "her father." It was as though Lillian thought she was talking to a stranger. But was that any different from Kali calling her grandmother by her given name?

"Her favorite was *The Wizard of Oz*. I suppose she guessed that's where I got her name." She smiled at the blank wall and shook her head as though she was watching something. "Harry used to applaud. 'Brava,' he'd say. And Dorothy would curtsey in the prettiest way, just like I'd taught her."

"You taught her to curtsey?" Kali asked, immediately sorry. Afraid she'd broken her grandmother's concentration.

"Of course. Who better than I?" And she stood up from her chair, eyes half-closed, lips parted in a small smile, and stretched her neck as she gracefully put one leg behind her, swooped forward, and extended her arms above her sides.

The gesture was practiced, yet so natural it made Kali wonder when and where she had mastered it.

"*Danke*," Lillian said in a quivering voice, as though responding to applause. "*Danke schoen*."

Kali was startled. She'd never heard Lillian speak German. With morbid fascination she watched her grandmother, recognizing the signs of senility, but at the same time riveted by this glimpse into her past.

Lillian curtsied again.

Kali clapped her hands lightly. "Brava."

"*Danke*," her grandmother said and sat back down. Something seemed to be running through her head, probably a pleasant memory, because she continued smiling. Then her face clouded over.

Kali tried to bring her back. "You were saying she enjoyed putting on plays for you and Grandpa."

Lillian looked at her and blinked a few times.

"My mother. You said she was a good little actress."

Lillian nodded.

"What else did she like to do?" All these new insights about her mother as a young girl had fresh importance to Kali now that she was having her own child.

"What's that?"

"My mother. When she was a little girl, what was she like?"

"Your mother." She seemed to be processing this. "She was so busy. All the time. Always busy—planning, thinking. She had so much energy. Sometimes it made me afraid."

"Afraid of what?"

"What she might become."

Kali's mother had died in a car accident at the age of fifty-one. She'd worked in an office job with no secret ambition that Kali ever knew of. Had Lillian stifled these things in her only child? Kali thought about the hidden painting in her closet, now gone.

"She liked to draw and paint," Kali said.

Lillian nodded. "Such beautiful pictures she made."

So she knew.

"But how could I let her?" her grandmother said.

Kali felt a surge of anger. "How couldn't you let her?"

"I was foolish. Harry told me I was being foolish, but I didn't listen." Her eyes became watery. "I couldn't take a chance. What if she made something someone recognized? Oh, I know, that doesn't make sense. But still, that's what was in my head. I was so afraid."

"Of what?"

"That someone would come and take her from me."

Kali stirred her tea. Her grandmother was clearly losing it.

"Dorothy," Lillian said. "Like in *The Wizard of Oz*. I named her that because I wanted her to live in Oz. Safe from everyone and everything."

What was Lillian talking about? Safe from whom? From what?

"And I thought if she clicked her heels, her ruby slippers would take her far away and she'd be safe." She looked at Kali suddenly, with terrible focus. "But she wasn't, was she? My poor child. She didn't stand a chance."

A shiver ran down Kali's spine. The car crash was an accident. A terrible, tragic car accident—wasn't it? "What do you mean she didn't stand a chance?"

Lillian brought her hand against her heart and looked around the kitchen like a trapped bird.

"What's going on, Lillian? Why did you light those candles? Why did you think someone might break into the house?"

Lillian shook her head and scrunched up the muffin wrapper. "I'm tired. I'm going to get some rest."

"Just a minute. We need to talk. I'm worried about you. It's not safe for you to be alone."

"Of course it is."

"You almost burned the house down."

"If I'd wanted to burn the house down, I would have burned it down."

"Please listen to me. Let me arrange for someone to stay here with you. Just for a little while. Until you're feeling more like yourself."

"I am myself." Lillian's voice was cold and precise, like the one she'd used when Kali was growing up. "And I won't have a stranger in my house."

She pushed the chair back and stood up. Then she walked out of the room, head up, shoulders back, reminding Kali of a temperamental actress storming off a movie set.

12

Javier Guzman winced at the brightness and slipped on his dark sunglasses as he strode across the oceanfront dining terrace toward the lunch guests. He hated this aspect of his work. Mingling and chatting with these people as though he cared about them. Well, sure he cared—but as a means to an end. If they only knew how much he truly despised them, these self-serving influencers of mass opinion, these distorters of the truth! This group, more than any other, had turned their parochial cause into a political juggernaut that disparaged and vilified millions of worthy, hard-working people. But these people were also the ones who would most likely lead Javier to the old woman.

The banquet manager gave Javier a smile, an acknowledgment of the business Javier had been bringing to the hotel lately.

Javier nodded back. The sun was too hot and burnt through his linen suit and the blue shirt he wore beneath it. It was his standard uniform, consistent with the role he'd created for himself as a geriatric specialist. But more important, his business-casual look appealed to this elderly crowd and conveniently hid his tattoos. Much like Superman.

A memory flashed through his mind. *Think of me as Superman*, his father had told Javier when he was a young boy. *You must never tell anyone my secret identity.* And during his adolescent years, Javier had believed his father really was Superman, disguised as a mild-mannered shopkeeper.

Superman. Javier ran a hand over his smooth scalp, feeling the slight rise at the top that made his bald head resemble the pointed end of an egg. Gabriel still had a full head of thick blond hair, like Javier once did. Like father, like son, as the expression goes. But hopefully he would be able to keep his son from making the same mistake Javier had.

Javier approached the table closest to the ocean at which a group of well-dressed women were seated. In his self-created capacity as an event coordinator for the geriatric community, he had organized the luncheon and fashion show, selecting invitees from databases of elderly females with Central European backgrounds.

"Good day, ladies." He pushed his dark glasses up on his head and turned on his Spanish accent, which he'd lost for the most part when he and his father moved from Argentina to Cincinnati many years before. Javier had discovered that this crowd had a penchant for cosmopolitan foreignness. "I've arranged a little ocean breeze for you today. I hope it's not too chilly. If it is, I can dial the wind down a little."

Most of the women smiled back, a couple of them laughed, one stared at him stone-faced. He met her eyes. A cloudy brown. She looked away, perhaps spooked by the odd teardrop-shape in one of his own green irises.

His gaze shifted from face to face around the table as he studied each woman in turn, assessing eye color, apparent age, facial structure. No matches. He wasn't surprised. His review of the attendees' vital statistics had already told him that she probably wasn't here, though he believed in confirming in person in the event of a clerical error.

He went smoothly into his planned spiel, focusing on the mannish-looking blonde with skin like a dehydrated apple, penciled-in eyebrows, and a cool manner. "Excuse me, madam." He shook his head with practiced astonishment. "I'm sure you must hear this all the time, but you bear an uncanny resemblance to Marlene Dietrich." He turned to the other women. "Don't you agree?"

They nodded and made muffled noises.

"*The Blue Angel*," said the stone-faced one. "A classic."

Javier brightened. "I love those old films myself. I'm a bit of a collector, you know." He leaned into the group and lowered his baritone voice. "In fact," he said, noting the women straining to hear him, "I heard a wonderful Austrian actress who appeared in several classic films before the War is living right here on Miami Beach."

"Before the War?" said the mannish blonde. "She must be pretty old."

There was no other reaction, no spark of recognition or concern, so Javier stepped back from the table. "Well, ladies, if there's anything I can do for you, don't hesitate to call upon me. And enjoy your event today." He gave a big smile. "*Sei gesund.*"

He checked their faces before moving on. Smiles all around, even Ms. Stoneface. "*Zie gezunt,*" she said.

Javier pulled his sunglasses down over his eyes and felt his lip twitch downward in revulsion. They always mistook his German for Yiddish, corrupting the pure as though it was their entitlement.

He retreated quickly, so they wouldn't sense his reaction.

The breeze picked up on the ocean terrace. The sky had clouded over and the turquoise water had darkened. He reached into his pocket for a cigarette, lit up, inhaled deeply, and slowly let it out.

He would finish making his rounds of the attendees, then head back to his office where he'd check his classic films website for any new orders, then follow up on the fire rescue report of the woman brought in for smoke inhalation.

He took another drag. He wondered if Gabriel had looked at the business card Javier had given him last night. Whether despite the lies and hatred Gabriel had been fed most of his life, he would be curious or interested enough to call his father. But even if not this time, Javier would persevere.

This Superman wasn't put off by a little kryptonite.

13

"I'm not sure how much longer," Kali said into her cell phone. Her legs dangled over the seawall of the vacant lot across from her grandmother's house and her sketchpad and pencils lay on the concrete ledge beside her. Overgrown trees and wild hedges covered the property, blocking her view of the street. "Maybe two or three days. I think she needs to get used to the idea of an aide gradually. I'm sure I'll be home by Friday."

"Friday?" Seth said.

She could tell from his breathing that he was pacing, probably outside the courthouse. He was on a short lunch break before he needed to return to his trial.

"Maybe Thursday."

"You need to be firm with her." He always sounded different to her when he was at work. Like he had a tough time switching out of lawyer mode.

"I won't bully her, Seth."

"I didn't say bully. This is for her own safety."

"As long as I'm staying with her, she's safe."

"And what happens if after a couple of days, she still refuses to hire an aide?"

A flock of small birds flew up from the copse of areca palms at the edge of the bay, hovered briefly over the water, then landed on the thatched roof of the boat dock of an adjacent house.

"I'm sure I can persuade her."

"You should think about getting her Baker-Acted," Seth said.

The broken edge of the seawall dug through Kali's leggings into the back of her thigh. "What are you talking about?"

"The Florida Mental Health Act of 1971. You can fill out an Ex Parte Petition for Involuntary Examination."

"Whoa. Wait. You're saying I should have my grandmother committed?"

"Not committed. Just observed for seventy-two hours. After lighting all those *Yahrzeit* candles and setting her house on fire, it's obvious she can't take care of herself. I'm sure you'll be named guardian. Then you'll be able to make the necessary arrangements for her."

It was low tide and the water was well below her, but the thick smell of decomposing vegetation rose up. "I'm not doing that, Seth."

"I can look into it for you," he said as though he hadn't heard her. "There must be a facility on Miami Beach where we can bring her."

"You're not listening. I won't do that."

"What? What do you mean you won't do that?" He sounded genuinely surprised.

"I'm not putting my grandmother in some kind of home."

"That's not what I said. Damn it, Kali. I'm trying to come up with a solution here. I'm simply suggesting that you take the appropriate legal steps so you can become her guardian and help her make the best decisions."

"I don't want to force her. Can't you understand that? Let me try to do this so she can have some dignity."

There was a long silence. A motorboat zipped across the bay, leaving spreading ripples in its wake.

"I have to get back to court."

"Please don't be angry. She's my grandmother. I'm the only one she has."

"I get that. But what I don't get is why this woman, who showed you virtually no love and affection when you were growing up, is more important than you and me and our baby."

A lone bird flew toward the thatched roof carrying a broken twig in its beak.

"Why does it have to be a choice? She's my family, too. I told you, I'll make arrangements for an aide, then I'll be home."

She could hear him taking in a deep breath. "Please, baby. I need you."

"I understand," she said in a softer voice. "I'll do what I can."

There was a moment of silence, then he said, "Okay. We'll talk later."

Kali put her phone in her pocket. Her hands clutched the rough ledge and she glanced at the sketch she was working on—the golden-haired cherub floating upward toward the beautiful fairy's open arms.

The rustling of weeds and light thumps in the vacant lot startled her. Before Kali could turn, something hard and pointy pushed against her side. She screamed.

"Gizmo," Neil called from the bushes near the street. "Damn it, Gizmo. Get over here."

Kali took a deep breath to calm herself. The dog looked back at her with his one brown eye. "Hey, boy. You startled me."

Neil strode through the tangled undergrowth toward them. He was wearing jogging shorts and a white T-shirt, his lower arms and hands still bandaged. "I'm really sorry. Gizmo literally pulled out of his collar to run to you." The dog's leash, still attached to a frayed collar, hung around Neil's neck.

"It's okay."

He squatted next to her and slipped the collar back over Gizmo's head.

Kali had reconciled Neil's longish hair and the few days' beard growth with the teenage boy she'd once known. It was as though they'd fast-forwarded through the last fourteen years.

"You're not trustworthy," Neil said to the dog, "so I'm tightening your collar a notch."

Gizmo settled down on the seawall, his warm body pressed up against Kali's. Kali had never had a pet and was surprised that she didn't mind the dog so close to her. In fact, she liked it.

"Are you up for some company?" Neil asked.

"Sure."

Neil sat down and let his lean legs drop over the wall. They were tanned and covered with dark hair that looked as soft as Gizmo's fur.

Neil glanced over at Kali's drawing. "May I?" he asked, reaching for the sketchpad.

"Sure, but it's not finished."

When they were kids, she'd always shared her artwork with him and he'd been a wonderful critic as well as one of her biggest fans. But now, as he studied the drawing, Kali felt surprisingly exposed. As though the picture revealed something of herself to him.

"Interesting. Your cherub almost looks like a fetus, except for the wings, of course. The head and torso are developed, but not the limbs."

Kali took the sketchpad away from him and turned it facedown on her lap.

"I didn't mean there's anything wrong with it. In fact, it's very good. Just unusual. I've never seen cherubim portrayed quite like that."

"Well, it's just a sketch."

"You're working on an oil, too?"

"How'd you know?"

"You seem to be using yourself for a canvas." He nodded at the paint on her leggings.

She smiled. "I rent a studio in Dania. It's a good, open space and I'm able to work better there than at home. I guess it's Dr. Jekyll–Mr. Hyde syndrome. I'm a very different person when I'm immersed in my art."

"I get that."

"My new painting. It's very special to me, but I'm not sure how others would react to it."

"Would you let me come by the studio sometime to see it?"

She took in a deep breath. "Sure."

Neil glanced back at the overgrown lot. The old banyan tree was huge now and ficus bushes and Brazilian pepper had taken over much of the area where they used to throw a Frisbee around.

"You probably don't remember," Neil said finally. "But this was the first place we ever had a real conversation."

"The day of my mother's funeral."

He nodded. "I was surprised you were wearing shorts and a T-shirt. You'd been in a dress earlier."

Kali looked down at her red sneakers dangling against the seawall. "I changed when we got back from the cemetery and I threw the dress into the trash. I thought if I made believe it hadn't happened, then she wouldn't really be dead."

"I didn't know what to talk to you about. I was embarrassed to say anything about your mom, so I asked if you liked Springsteen."

"That's right."

"And you said you saw his music in primary colors—mainly red and blue, with an occasional flash of yellow."

"You remember that?"

"I thought you were the most interesting girl I'd ever met." He pushed his glasses up on his nose. "And the saddest."

Kali wrapped her arms around her knees, the sketchpad resting against her chest like a shield.

"I used to watch you and your mom together," he said.

"What do you mean?"

"When you'd come to visit your grandparents on Sundays, I could see you from my bedroom window. Sometimes your mom would play ball with you."

"She was a terrible athlete, but she was always trying to make up for me not having a dad."

"He died when you were a baby, right?"

Kali nodded. "I don't remember him." She dug a small rock from the dirt beside the seawall and threw it into the bay. It made a tiny ripple.

"Your mom was a lot different from your grandmother."

Kali turned to look at him, surprised that he'd observed so much. "How do you mean?"

"Lillian's inscrutable, never showing any real emotion."

"Other than irritation, maybe."

He smiled. "But your mom was vivid. Her feelings seemed to run the gamut. Like a rainbow. One minute, she'd be all lightness, laughing and singing. Then, I'd see her sullen and dark, hustling you into the car."

Kali had forgotten that. How the Sunday visits often ended with her mother furious with her grandmother. Her grandfather running out to the car. *Please, Dorothy, don't go. She only wants what's best for you.* How angry her mother would be when they returned home. Sometimes she wouldn't speak to Kali for hours. And Kali blamed her grandmother for ruining everything.

"After you moved in with your grandparents," Neil continued, "I used to see you around school all the time. Kids tried to make friends with you, but you weren't interested."

"What was the point? I'd made friends at my last school and lost them all."

"And if anyone asked how you were doing, you always said you were fine."

Gizmo pressed closer against her. She could feel him panting.

"You never asked how I was doing." Kali looked down at her knees. There were a couple of smudges of turquoise paint on her denim leggings.

"I didn't have to. I knew you weren't fine."

Kali felt a tightening in her throat.

"You know, Kali, you can talk to me. I'm still a pretty good listener."

The sky had clouded up and the bay had darkened. The flock of birds rose up from the thatched roof, but seemed to be hovering in place.

"She's so damn stubborn," Kali said.

"Your grandmother won't let you hire an aide?"

Kali nodded. "And Seth doesn't understand that I need to stay with her until I work things out."

"He seems like a reasonable guy."

"He usually is. But he's being irrational about me staying here with her."

"I see." Their eyes met for an instant, then they both looked away.

"Ah, what the hell," Kali said. "I'm not being honest. Not with Seth, not with myself. It's more than concern for Lillian."

He raised an eyebrow.

"Yes, I'm worried about her putting herself in danger, but that's not why I want to stay."

"Why then?"

"I need to know who I am, Neil. Where I came from. After my dad died, my mom never made an effort to stay in touch with his parents, and now they're both dead. I have no living relatives except for Lillian. And she's finally opening up to me. Telling me things about my mom that I never knew."

"That's great."

"Is it?" Her sketchpad pressed against her abdomen and she put it down on the ledge. "Some of her ramblings are lovely. Like about my mom learning to curtsey. But then she hints at other things, darker things."

He glanced down at the sketch, at the fairy's open arms. Four arms, like Kali always drew. "You think she's hidden things from you?"

"I know she has. But I never believed there was anything truly terrible in her past."

"And now you think there may be?"

"I don't know. But good or bad, I need to understand who she is, who I am." She rested her hand on her abdomen. "My child deserves that much."

"So stay here with her."

Kali shook her head. "That's not being fair to Seth."

"How about this? You go back home, then come visit your grandmother for a few hours each day to do your bonding. I can keep an eye on her when you're not around. It'll probably irritate her that I'm checking up on her, but I'll bet she'll put up with that knowing the alternative."

"I can't ask you to do that, Neil."

"You didn't ask. I offered." He got up stiffly from the seawall, as though still hurting from his burns. "Then once she gets used to the idea of someone around her house, she'll probably be willing to have an aide." He held out his bandaged hand to help Kali. "Come on. I'll walk you back. Let's see how she reacts to the idea."

"I'm good. Thanks." Kali stood up, ignoring his hand, and brushed off the back of her dress. "Are you sure? I feel like it's an imposition."

Gizmo pulled on the leash, ready to go. "Not an imposition at all. Something you may not know is that the last few years, your grandmother had been looking in on my mom."

"My grandmother?"

Neil smiled. "Right? Who would have imagined her playing Good Samaritan? But she brought my mom dinner and checked on her in the morning. In fact," he pushed his glasses up, "your grandmother was the one who called to tell me she felt my mom couldn't manage on her own anymore."

"I had no idea. I'm glad to hear Lillian has the capacity to be kind to someone."

They got to the front door. There was a rumble of distant thunder. Kali put the key in the lock. "So I guess Lillian knows Gizmo and won't mind him visiting, either."

"I'm not so sure about that," Neil said with a laugh.

They stepped into the house. It was quiet. Kali had been gone under an hour. She'd left her grandmother in the TV room, but no sound came from there.

"Lillian," Kali called. "I'm here with Neil."

Gizmo barked.

"And Gizmo."

No answer. She expected Lillian to emerge from one of the rooms in a huff, protesting the dog.

"Maybe she went upstairs to lie down. I'll check."

Kali took running steps up the stairs. Her grandmother's bedroom door was open. The bed was made, but there was no sign of her.

Kali knocked lightly on the door and stepped into the room. "Lillian? Are you in here?"

She walked around the bed toward the bathroom. Beneath a light residue of smoke, she could smell lavender, Lillian's scent for as long as she could remember. But something wasn't right.

Her grandmother was lying on the marble floor in her faded floral housedress. Her arms were extended and her eyes closed, as though she was asleep. Her white hair was matted against her forehead with something red. Blood. There was blood everywhere.

"Oh my God." Kali dropped down beside her grandmother to check if she was breathing. "Neil," she shouted. "Call 911."

14

Her head ached. It was the opening night party. Too much schnapps. And Leli didn't even like schnapps.

"Mrs. Campbell?" A man was shouting. "Mrs. Campbell, can you hear me?"

Leli felt confused, blurry. Why did her head hurt so much?

"Lillian," a sweet voice said. "Lillian, please wake up."

Who was that? And what was stuck in her nose making it so difficult to breathe?

Voices were all around her, an irritating buzz of bees. "She's stable," said the man. "Just sleeping it off. But we're going to take some X-rays and do a CT scan. Maybe an MRI."

So much noise. Why wouldn't they go away and let her sleep? She was so tired. And her head hurt.

Too much schnapps last night. She would never drink a drop of booze again. Never.

Leli went down the crowded avenue. It was bustling with people hurrying home from work, women carrying bundles climbing onto a streetcar. A draft horse pulling a cart clopped down the street.

People stared at Leli. Probably because of her new hat with its ribbons and bow. Her blonde hair curled so nicely around the felt rim. It had been foolish to spend so much money on a hat, but she had fallen in love with it in the shop window. Besides, she'd make plenty more money this week. The show was a grand success. A dream come true. Twenty years old and on her way to stardom!

Leli turned down the alley toward the stage entrance to the theater. The avenue sounds fell away, and Leli could hear her high heels strike against the cobblestones. A cat darted past her. The street smelled like vomit and old garbage.

Leli pulled on the stage door. It stuck. She pulled again. Nothing. Then she noticed the sign plastered to the door. Cancelled, it said. The show had been cancelled.

But that was impossible. The show was a grand success. A grand success, the director had said. Hadn't the cast held a big celebration last night? She stepped away from the door to see if she was at the correct theater, but of course, she was.

Cancelled. Now what was she going to do?

An old man was coming toward her, hunched over as he balanced on his walking stick. He wore wire-rimmed glasses and had a graying goatee. His coat and hat seemed to belong to an earlier era. She stepped aside to let him pass, but he stopped and gazed at her. For an instant, he seemed vaguely familiar, as though she'd seen him somewhere before, but then realized it was highly unlikely.

"Are you all right, miss?" He spoke a soft, elegant German, like the Viennese from home. Leli hadn't acclimated to the harsh German that most people here in Berlin spoke.

She pointed to the sign on the stage door.

"Oh, my," he said. "Cancelled. What a pity. Were you in it? An actress?"

She nodded.

"Well, you're very beautiful. I'm sure there will be other shows."

"I don't think so. It had been hard enough to get a role in this one. And now—" She stopped. She couldn't believe she was telling a stranger her problems.

A gray tabby jumped from one of the trash cans and darted past them. The old man tensed and raised his walking stick.

"Are you okay?" she asked.

"Yes, yes. Of course." He dabbed at his brow, then smiled. "That horrible cat caught me by surprise is all." He reached into his overcoat and checked his gold pocket watch. "I was just heading around the block to that very nice *Konditorei* for a coffee and perhaps a piece of strudel. I'd be honored if you'd join me."

Leli shook her head. "That's very kind of you, but I'd better get going."

"Because I'm a stranger?"

He said it kindly, but she felt herself blush.

"That's very prudent, young lady." He made a little bow. "My name is Dr. Altwulf." He gave a small smile and his blue eyes twinkled. "There now, we're no longer strangers."

He was charming and not as old as Leli had originally thought—maybe fifty or sixty years old. Her father's age.

"Of course. I understand if you want to get home to your parents, or perhaps a boyfriend?" He raised an eyebrow.

"No. I have no one here. No family in Berlin."

"Come then, my dear. I'll bet you're hungry. And I'm just an old man. An artist—a painter. I teach at the university."

"My father's a professor."

"Indeed?" He held out his arm for her.

She hesitated.

"You know, my dear, that's a very striking hat."

Leli smiled and took his arm.

A sweet voice was whispering in her ear. "Please come back to me."

15

Javier Guzman pulled his car over to the side of the road next to an overgrown vacant lot, turned off the ignition, then leaned back against the headrest. It was dark on the street with little traffic, so it wasn't likely he'd be noticed, especially if he didn't linger more than a few minutes. Beethoven's *Moonlight Sonata* was playing. Javier kept the volume low so he could hear any untoward sounds coming from outside the car.

Although the sonata's rippling arpeggios usually calmed him, Javier was edgy and impatient as he studied the two-story white-columned house with its ivy-covered walls. The shutters were askew and shifting palm fronds cast giant gray claws over the cracked, flaking façade.

For a moment he was back in his childhood home in Buenos Aires, palm-frond shadows playing on the whitewashed walls, Beethoven filling the room as his father unlocked and opened the small trunk.

The hat was swathed in tissue paper and kept in a special airtight package so it wouldn't deteriorate. His father gently unwrapped it, as one might an infant at baptism.

"This was hers," his father said in a hushed voice.

The hat was made of felt and covered with ribbons and a large bow. How soft and pretty it looked. Little Javier reached out to touch it.

"No." His father slapped his hand away with a painful chop.

Javier stifled a cry and brought his throbbing hand to his mouth.

"It's not a toy." His father held its inner headband to his face and inhaled deeply, again and again. "Her scent," he said, his eyes closed. "I can hardly smell her anymore."

The pain in Javier's hand subsided as the violins gently took over the melody. He wanted to ask who she was, but was afraid of angering his father.

"Someday, Javier, I'll find her. She can't run from me forever. I'll find her and touch her and smell her, and then—"

His father sniffed the inner headband and little Javier felt a tingle in his groin, almost like his father's desire had become his own.

"Yes, Vati," Javier said to the darkness as the music swirled around him in the car. "I'll find her for you."

Javier turned his attention back to the dilapidated house. There were no lights on inside and, if Javier didn't know better, he would have believed from its rundown condition that no one had lived here for weeks, or perhaps months.

But this was where the old woman who had been treated for smoke inhalation yesterday lived. Then, earlier today, the very same woman showed up on a fresh 911 call. This time, for a stroke.

Javier had hacked into several different databases and discovered the woman, Lillian Campbell, was a widow, married to the deceased Harold Campbell, a banker. Javier's interest had been piqued when he discovered she was ninety-three. Problem was, when Javier continued digging, the information he was able to find on Mrs. Campbell was sketchy. He discovered she was formerly Lillian Breitling, born in London with a British passport, but couldn't find any photos or other details about her roots.

Probably a waste of time to investigate further. It was unlikely that she was the woman who had so consumed his father, and Javier couldn't be allocating resources to pursuing women not connected to Austria and Germany. Even if the woman was the right age. But because Javier was the kind of person who left no stone unturned, he had decided to drive by her house tonight. Maybe there'd be something of interest. Besides, he liked riding around in the dark, slowing to gaze into brightly lit rooms.

He'd developed the practice as a teenager, noticing that young women often undressed as if they didn't realize every movement was visible to someone outside their window. Javier preferred slender blondes with narrow necks and large breasts, much like his ex-wife and the woman in the photos and films his father had sequestered. It was like viewing an X-rated movie, but better. Only a piece of glass stood between them.

A car swished through a puddle of rainwater, the sound merging with the crescendo of Beethoven's liquid moonlight.

No one was home at the Campbells' tonight. Nothing to watch. Nothing to do for now.

Javier started the engine and turned up the volume. He'd drive around the block one more time, then check back.

16

Kali returned to her grandmother's house around eight. It was dark outside and she could hear cars splashing through puddles as they drove by. She didn't know when it had stopped raining since she'd been inside the hospital the entire day.

She leaned against the kitchen table feeling lightheaded. She hadn't had anything to eat since breakfast. The chipped china teacup that her grandmother had been drinking from was still on the table with the dregs from her tea. Just this morning, Kali had been sitting across from her, having the first real conversation they'd ever had. A couple of hours later, she'd almost lost her.

Kali took a bran muffin from the package on the counter and stuffed it into her mouth to quell her nausea. The tests and hospital red tape had taken hours. Lillian had had a stroke, then apparently fallen, cutting her head and bleeding everywhere. The doctors wanted to keep her for observation. But what did that mean? A day? A week? And then what?

Her cell phone rang. Seth said he'd call when he got home. He had been at his office all evening to prepare for his trial, but Kali couldn't help but wonder if he was avoiding her or her grandmother.

"Hi," she said.

"Hey. How's she doing?"

"They finally brought her to a room a little while ago. She's sleeping a lot, and when she wakes up she's not making a lot of sense." After Seth's remarks about her grandmother last night and earlier today, Kali didn't dare mention Lillian was speaking German and had no idea who Kali was.

"What did the doctor say?"

"He didn't sound worried. He said it's not unusual in an old person after a stroke."

"I guess that's good news."

"I guess."

There was that awkwardness between them, again.

"So when do you think you'll be able to leave?"

"I already left. I just got to her house."

"Her house?"

"I'm picking up a few things for her. A nightgown, robe, her hairbrush."

"You must be starving. You need to eat regular meals for the baby. Should I order in?"

Kali looked at the half-eaten muffin in her hand. "Sure." She felt a wave of sadness that he spoke about the baby instead of using one of the silly names he liked to tease her with.

"What would you like?" he asked.

"Whatever. You decide."

"Chinese? Thai? Italian?"

"I don't care."

"Okay. Chinese then. How about Szechuan-style eggplant , veggie fried—"

"Whatever you want is fine. Let me get Lillian's things together."

"Sure. Sure. But hurry. Food should be here in about a half hour."

"I'll get there as soon as I can." Kali ended the call, put her phone back in her pocket, then headed up to Lillian's bedroom. She'd pack a bag for her and go home. She and Seth would eat dinner together. He'd come up with a new ridiculous name for the baby like Sinbad or Popeye, and everything would be fine. No awkwardness. No tension.

Her sneakers padded against the marble steps. The house felt eerily empty. She shuddered and touched her abdomen, wondering if it was her hormones that were heightening her perceptions of things.

She went into her grandmother's bedroom. The smell of lavender and smoke still hung in the air. Lillian kept her nightgowns and underwear in the walk-in closet just outside the bathroom.

Kali stopped. Her hand went to her mouth as her stomach revolted. Blood from Lillian's head injury had puddled on the white marble floor. Someone had to clean it up, and there was no one but Kali.

She found a cleaning rag and a bottle of Pine-Sol and tried to imagine something else as she wiped up the mess. Red paint. That was all it was. Red paint. Jackson Pollock readying his canvas. But the tang of iron sickened her. Paint never smelled like this. She rinsed out the rag, holding her breath, then finished up the job. She needed to get out of here quickly. She gathered Lillian's things from the closet, noticing the small rectangular panel in the wall, behind which was a built-in cabinet with several narrow shelves where Lillian kept thimbles, sewing needles, and spools of thread.

Where, beneath a spool of never-used cherry-red thread on the top shelf, Lillian used to hide the key to the storage rooms. Was it still there?

Kali hesitated. Seth was waiting. But something tugged at her. An addict's need to go back and look just one more time.

She pressed the panel and it popped open. The cherry-red thread was still on the top shelf. Kali felt beneath the spool. There it was.

When she'd first found the key fourteen years before, she'd been baffled by its purpose. She'd gone around the house, checking for locked doors, and realized the key was for the closet near the back door. Opening the door and seeing the hidden storage rooms had been like discovering the secret to Ali Baba's caves. Kali began the practice of sneaking in there whenever her grandparents were out of the house, always hoping to find some secret paper or book or picture. Something that would help Kali decode her past. But she'd never found anything.

Maybe this time.

Kali took the key from the sewing cabinet, ran down the stairs and through the kitchen. She tried to push the wicker étagère away from the door that led to the storage rooms. It was weighted down with piles of newspapers and required a bit of effort for Kali to move it. Finally, it scraped against the linoleum flooring and away from the door. Kali was breathing hard as she put the key into the lock and turned it.

She felt a twitch in her abdomen and froze. Stupid. Stupid. She was crazy to be exerting herself. She waited, afraid to move or breathe. Nothing more happened. She patted her belly. "Sorry, Bucephala. No more foolish chances. I promise."

She flipped on the light and went up the creaky wooden stairs. There were no window A/C units up here and it smelled close. Each of the two rooms was barely large enough for a twin bed, a chest of drawers, and maybe a small table, and they were connected by a tiny bathroom. But no house help had ever lived in here, at least as far as Kali knew.

The first room was as she remembered it from fourteen years ago, filled so that there was barely enough space to walk around. It was a pastiche of broken and chipped chairs, an oak icebox, a Singer sewing machine, the cushions from the lawn furniture, several cans of house paint, a rickety ladder, and a folding cot. Kali touched the metal springs of the cot. But she hadn't come here to remember that one night.

She checked her cell phone again. Seth was probably starting to get worried. She'd just take a quick look around, then she'd call and let him know she was on her way.

She stepped into the other room. A study in brown and black, cubes and rectangles. Cartons were in uneven stacks against one side of the room and old-fashioned luggage was piled haphazardly in several groupings. Kali recalled going through each of the suitcases fourteen years ago, but there was a black suitcase that she wasn't sure had been here last time. She opened it and was instantly filled with sadness. It contained her grandfather's clothes, neatly folded. There was a tweed suit that she didn't recognize and a dozen or so caps. She touched a faded yellow polo shirt that had been a favorite of his. Dear Grandpa. She'd always called him Grandpa, never Harry, even when she began calling her grandmother Lillian. He'd been gone ten years, but how she still missed him. Always a cigar hanging from the side of his mouth, a cap on his head. She closed the lid on the suitcase, then clicked it shut.

She surveyed the cartons. They were all unmarked and rearranged from when she'd first examined their contents years before, so she couldn't tell what had been added or changed around. She tested the weight of one of the top cartons. Not too heavy. She took it down as thick white dust floated around her. She put the carton on the floor and opened it. The bright color of sunflowers was unexpected. Kali lifted her old quilt from the carton and buried her face in it. The smell was wrong. Musty. She put it back and closed the carton.

She slid out a battered carton from the wall. It was filled with magazines and newspapers. Probably her grandfather's. She remembered going through this box years ago. Pieces of paper disintegrated and flew up as she lifted the magazines to see if there was anything of particular interest at the bottom.

A cardboard picture the size of a baseball card fell out from between the magazines. An advertisement? But no. It appeared to be a publicity picture of a beautiful young woman with curly blonde hair. She wore a bonnet with ribbons and a large bow. The picture was artificially colorized and the woman's eyes were too blue, her cheeks and lips too red. *Leli Lenz* was printed beneath the woman's smiling face. Kali kept it out to examine later and put the magazines and newspapers back in the box.

A sound coming from downstairs startled her. She stopped and listened, remembering her grandmother's paranoia about someone breaking into the house. She heard only silence, then the creak of the old house settling itself.

She released her breath and returned to her investigation. She opened another carton, remembering its contents from last time—several large fragments of folded fabric, as though someone had intended to make curtains or a bedspread. A bit of pink and lace was sticking out from between two layers of fabric. Kali eased it out. A child's pinafore—pink with a lace collar. Just like the one Lillian had described this morning. This must have belonged to Kali's mother.

She sat down on the gritty wood floor, pressed her back against the wall, and held the dress against her face. She imagined her mother as a little girl. A cloud of dark hair, Lillian had said, and blue eyes. She liked to play at being an actress. Lillian had taught her how to curtsey.

Kali inhaled the smell of cotton and a calmness swept over her. She would take the dress home, wash it, and put it away. If she gave birth to a girl, she would dress her in the pink pinafore. And she'd tell her all about how her grandmother, Kali's mother, liked to play at being an actress. She would even teach her how to curtsey. Then she thought about the disturbing remark her grandmother had made earlier about her mother. *She didn't stand a chance.* Against whom? Kali wondered again. Why would her mother have been threatened by anyone?

She was roused by her cell phone ringing. Seth.

"Hi," she said. "Guess what I found."

"It's been over an hour," he said. "I was afraid something happened to you."

"I'm sorry. I got a little sidetracked. I—"

Someone was knocking on the door at the bottom of the stairwell.

Kali tensed. Who in the world?

"Kali?" Neil called out. "Are you up here?"

"Who's that?" Seth said in her ear. "Who's with you?"

"Kali?" Neil called again. She could hear him climbing the stairs.

"Is that the guy from next door?"

"I'm—he—I was just—"

"I see," Seth said. Then the phone went silent.

Neil came up the last few steps and stopped on the landing. His hair was damp, as though he'd just showered, and he'd changed into jeans and a button-down shirt.

He looked at Kali's face, the pile of fabric around her on the floor, the phone in her hand. "Shit. You were on with Seth?"

She nodded.

"He thought I've been up here with you?"

She took a deep breath and let it out slowly. Then she took another one.

"I'm really sorry. Your car's in the driveway. I rang the bell, but you didn't answer. Then I noticed the front door was unlocked, so I came in to make sure everything was okay."

She'd left the door unlocked? She tried to remember. She'd been so disoriented and exhausted from the day at the hospital that she wasn't functioning right.

"I hope I haven't made a mess of things for you and Seth."

"It's fine. We'll be fine. They're keeping my grandmother for observation. She had a stroke."

"They told you that before I left."

"That's right." Apparently, she still wasn't thinking clearly. Neil would know about her grandmother. He'd spent most of the afternoon and early evening with Kali at the hospital until she finally insisted he go home and take care of Gizmo.

He sat down on the floor beside her. The lack of air-conditioning was starting to get to her.

Neil looked through the doorway into the adjacent room where the folded cot was clearly visible. Was he remembering that other night? Opening the cot? Their sweaty bodies sticking to each other in the heat?

"I'd ask if you're okay," he said, "but I know you'll just say you're fine. I also know you're not."

Kali didn't want to think about Neil sitting so close to her; the smell of soap and shampoo, just like the other time.

He reached out. His bandaged hands touched the pink dress on her lap.

Kali started, then relaxed. "It was my mother's. My grandmother was just talking about how my mother used to wear it when she played at being an actress."

"That's a nice memory." He picked up the picture of the pretty woman that was lying on the floor near him. "A cigarette card?"

"What do you mean? What's a cigarette card?"

"A trading card. Years ago, cigarette manufacturers used them to stiffen the cigarette packaging and advertise their brands. People collected them. Kind of like baseball cards with bubblegum. The cigarette cards were usually pictures of important figures—sports heroes, writers, actors, and actresses." He examined it. "Who's Leli Lenz?"

"I have no idea. It was in one of the boxes."

"She resembles you."

Kali took the card from him and studied the face. "You think so? I don't." But she had an unsettled feeling, almost a longing, as she put the card next to her phone. Maybe there was a resemblance. But it was like reading your fortune. You could always interpret it the way you wanted to.

"I'd better go," she said, getting to her knees.

She put the rest of the fabric back in the carton, closed it, and shoved it back against the wall. She reached over to pick up another carton.

"Let me help you with that."

"I've got it."

But he was beside her again, smelling so good. He took the carton, stacked it, then got another one and placed it on top.

He was quite a bit taller than she and she had to lean her head back to look at him. She was sweating. Her body felt swollen, prickly.

And pregnant.

"I need to go." Then she picked up her cell phone and the cigarette card with the blonde, blue-eyed woman, and ran down the stairs.

17

It took Kali twenty-two minutes to make the drive home to Holly-wood, a ride that usually took a half hour. She noticed Seth's car missing as she pulled into the driveway of their 1950s ranch-style cottage. The smell of Chinese food hit her as soon as she opened the front door. She went into the small white kitchen. The light was on, the table set with placemats, dishes, and silverware. Three take-out containers were open on the table.

Where was he? Did he really believe something was going on be-tween her and Neil?

Kali pulled out her cell and speed dialed Seth's number. She heard his phone ringing at the other side of the house.

Thank goodness. "Seth," she called, hurrying toward the sound. "I'm so sorry."

She paused at the doorway to their bedroom. Seth's phone was on the bed. She closed her own cell and the ringing stopped.

He really was gone. Left his phone so she had no way of getting in touch with him. He'd never done this before. Maybe he just ran to the store for something. Or to his office.

She dialed his law firm's landline. After his voice mail message came on, she disconnected from the call.

She went back to the kitchen, feeling sick to her stomach. She closed the take-out containers, put them in the refrigerator, then turned out the light and went to bed.

She checked the clock on the nightstand when she heard his car pull into the driveway. After two a.m. The front door opened and closed. He came into the bedroom and she could hear him undress.

When he climbed into bed, he stayed on his side, but she could smell the alcohol and cigarette smoke come off him in waves.

She began to cry, trying not to rock the bed so he wouldn't know.

The alarm went off at six thirty, but Kali was awake. She was pretty sure she hadn't slept the entire night.

Seth turned the alarm off and went straight to the bathroom, closing the door behind him. She heard the shower water run.

The room was still dark—linen drapes pulled together over the closed blinds. Above her, the white canopy reminded her of the chuppah they'd been married beneath in the Jewish wedding ceremony. She rubbed her belly. Bucephalus or Bucephala. Whatever he wanted to call their baby was fine. She'd make breakfast. They'd talk. It was all a stupid misunderstanding.

She crossed the living room in her bare feet, and stopped. The room looked different to her, like when she saw a familiar painting in a different light or setting. But nothing had changed since yesterday.

She remembered mixing the lime-green and aqua-blue paint in order to capture the color of the ocean at dawn on the walls. She had sanded, then shellacked the Dade Pine floors so they looked natural, almost like driftwood. The canvas-covered sofas resembled cabanas at the edge of a beach. For contrast, there were accent pillows and glass vases in shades of orange like setting suns.

Kali had loved it, but Seth had seemed baffled by the result. "Aren't there too many colors?" he'd asked.

But that's how it had always been between them. She was the rainbow gypsy, Seth the black-and-white pragmatist. But they worked. Their colors worked together.

Kali went to the kitchen, made a pot of coffee, and cracked several eggs into a bowl as she listened for Seth.

She heard his footsteps in the living room, the front door opening as though he was leaving.

No.

"Seth," she called after him.

He was in a navy suit, halfway out of the house.

"Wait." She was still holding the bowl of eggs.

"I have to get to court early." He ran his hand through his short, dark hair.

"Please. Just two minutes."

He stepped back inside, leaving the door open. The warm, thick air sucked the coolness out of the house.

"What?" The muscles in his face were tight and there were shadows under his fudge-brown eyes as though he hadn't slept either.

She held out the bowl. "I can make these real quick."

"I'm not hungry."

She brought the bowl against the oversized T-shirt that she'd slept in. "Coffee, then?"

He turned his head away from her, but she was sure his eyes had teared up.

"I'm sorry about last night," she said.

He looked down at his wingtips. She couldn't see his face.

"I think you misread the situation. There's absolutely nothing going on between me and Neil."

He continued staring at his shoes, frozen in his position like a broken mannequin.

"I went to the storage rooms to try to find something that would help me understand my past. Don't you see? It's important to me for our baby's sake. And my grandmother has finally started talking to me—"

"I don't care about your grandmother or her past. What good can come out of digging up her skeletons?"

"Okay. We won't discuss her. I just want you to understand what I was doing last night. I need to know that you believe me."

His shoulders went back, as he took in a deep breath. When he lifted his head his face was red. "I believe you."

"But you didn't last night?"

He pulled the front door closed, then turned back to her. "Damn it, Kali. Why didn't you come home when you said you would? I told you I don't like being here alone."

She almost argued with him, but he looked like an injured child. "It won't happen again."

He chewed on the inside of his cheek.

"I was pretty worried about you, you know," she said. "Where'd you go?"

"For a drink."

"Alone?"

He didn't answer.

"You met someone?"

"It was only Jonathan from work. He's always asking me to grab a beer with him."

"Okay then." She knew Seth. He would never do anything to deliberately hurt her. "Can we just move on? We're both under a lot of stress, but we can't overreact to things. We have to talk when we're upset." She patted her baby belly. "For Bucephalus," she said, hoping to get a smile from him.

He stared at her abdomen. Something was going through his head, but she couldn't imagine what it was.

She took a step toward him.

He stepped back.

"Seth?" She was alarmed. "Are we all right?"

"Sure. Great." And then he smiled, but his face reminded her of a crying clown.

18

Javier Guzman lit another cigarette and took a puff as he paced in the darkened living room. The rental apartment was in one of the recently built condo towers on South Beach. Most of the apartments were owned by South American investors, big corporations, and timeshare groups. In other words, transients. No one who gave Javier a second glance. Cost him five grand a month, but money was not an issue for him. He'd put aside a comfortable nest egg back in the early nineties when he had pioneered e-mail phishing. Sadly, that career and the subsequent ones were never anything he could boast about at cocktail parties. Not that he ever attended any. But he couldn't help but wonder if things would have turned out differently with Gabriel if he'd stayed within the bounds of social acceptability. But Javier knew what the public viewed as honorable was often the lies and distortions that the devil made them believe. Lies Javier was determined to expose.

He stared at the shadows in the horizontal blinds he always kept closed. The apartment had views of the ocean and downtown Miami, but Javier hadn't moved to South Florida to enjoy the scenery. He was here for his son and to find the woman who would hopefully unite them.

He put the cigarette out in a steel ashtray that was overflowing with half-finished butts, then went into the room he used as an office and mustered his ranks of computers. There must be something else he could do to find her.

The blinds were closed in there, as well, but the six glowing computer monitors provided virtually all of the light needed in his tenebrous research chamber. The furniture, a combination of black leather, chrome, and glass, had come with the apartment, as did a couple of minimalist prints in cheap frames that hung on the walls.

Javier swiveled around in the desk chair to face the credenza. He kissed two fingers and touched them against the crumbling cover of the book he'd discovered amongst his father's things, then opened the credenza door to examine his father's old record collection. The records were badly scratched and worn. Although he had cleaned, restored, and transferred the content of the 78s to the hard-disk drive of his sound system to preserve the specific performances that his father had enjoyed, Javier occasionally treated himself to listening to the originals directly. He chose Beethoven's *Eroica*, placed it on the turntable, and lowered the needle into the groove.

The music came on with a start. Some considered the third movement light and fluffy, but Javier found it energizing.

He turned back toward the computer screens. State-of-the-art multicore processors and over eight gigabytes of memory comprised the engines in his three monstrous computers. Yes, the elaborate installation maximized Javier's search capabilities. But all the while Javier had been configuring the setup, he'd also hoped Gabriel would one day be impressed at his father's technological prowess.

Javier's personal T1 modem ensured he would never lose connectivity and could access any information he needed in an instant. Anything he cared to retain for later review or analysis was stored in one of ten massive disk drives, each with over two terabytes of available space. The setup was mirrored in the rented professional office that he also maintained, but was completely untraceable to anyone trying to track him down by IP address or any other identifier. His investigative tools unit, he was proud to say, exceeded the capabilities of most police departments. The Classic Films website was a successful business in its own right, as well as a possible magnet. It had morphed from his father's original vision, when Vati used magazine ads to sell the old movies from a little area he'd set up in the back of his photography shop. Vati always believed he'd catch her through the films, and Javier kept the business alive just in case he was right.

But it was Hailstorm that really mattered—the base from which everything would change.

Javier picked up Vati's photo from the corner of his desk. It sat beside the photo of a six-year-old Gabriel surrounded by Legos.

The third movement was over and the needle oscillated in the groove as the record turned. Javier stared at his father's strong, youthful face, remembering how Javier's adoration had turned to abhorrence. When truth and lies had become inverted and Javier could no longer tell which was which.

His heart still ached as he thought back.

At first, when eleven-year-old Javier and his father had moved from Buenos Aires to Cincinnati right after his mother died, Javier had been in a self-induced bubble. He stayed away from his classmates, not understanding their jokes or games and wanting no part of them. He missed his mother terribly. Missed her kisses when his father wasn't around to accuse her of weakening his son. Missed the sound of her footsteps and her soft humming when he lay in bed trying to fall asleep. He couldn't remember her face clearly, but he could picture her sky-blue eyes, her pale blonde hair often combed forward to hide a bruise on her cheek, her arm in a sling.

For over two years, Javier had sat in the back of the classroom, ate his lunch by himself, ignored the pointing and giggling. Because once he returned home, the world belonged to Javier and his father. He would listen to his father's stories. Promise his secret loyalty. *Superman*, Javier would think. *My father is Superman.*

Then one day, shortly before Javier turned fourteen, Superman was mortally wounded.

Javier had been confused by the changes in his body, not understanding why his arms extended way beyond his shirt cuffs or why his pants no longer covered his ankles. If ever a teacher would ask him a question, Javier's voice would crack—switching from high to low octaves in mid-word—and his classmates would laugh. Javier could still feel the humiliation.

That day, he was heading home from school when several boys

from his class blocked his way.

"Hey, freak," a pudgy, dark-haired kid named Robert said. "Is it true?"

Javier tried to get past him, but the four boys linked arms and formed a wall.

"I don't know what you're talking about." Javier's voice cracked, which made it sound like he was going to cry.

"Is it true you're a Nazi?"

Javier felt a shiver down his spine. The way Robert said the word, it sounded worse than "fuck."

"Leave me alone." Javier turned his head and looked around, hoping to run the other way. But three more boys had joined up from behind.

"My mom heard you and your father talking at the supermarket," a kid with a mouth full of braces named Barry said. "She said you were speaking German."

"So what?"

"So how do you know German if you're supposed to be from Argentina?" Barry asked. "My mom said your dad's probably hiding out. That he's probably a Nazi like Adolf Eichmann."

Nazi. It sounded so dirty.

"And what if he is?" Javier blurted out.

Javier saw their jaws drop—literally.

Just like Superman. You must never tell, his father had warned him.

And then Robert took a step closer. His face was pulsing red and his eyes looked like they were going to pop out of his head. "The Nazis are murderers. They took millions of innocent Jews and stuffed them into gas chambers to kill them."

"They burned them in ovens," a boy named Charlie said. "Millions of them. Women and children and babies."

"They didn't," Javier whispered.

"They did, freak. Don't you know anything?"

It's a lie, he wanted to say. *You have it all wrong.* But he didn't say anything. He turned, pushed past the boys, and ran. Ran and ran and ran.

That night, when his father asked him what was the matter, Javier made something up. But he couldn't erase the boys' words from his thoughts. The conviction in the way they'd spoken. Like they knew the truth and Javier's whole life had been a lie.

So Javier started going to the library where he read book after book. History books, books taught in high schools and colleges. Official books, so they had to be true, right? His father was a monster, the books screamed at him. A monster and a liar.

And Javier began staying away from home, missing dinner, ashamed of the man who had once stood so tall and strong in his uniform at the edge of the dark river.

He told Robert and Barry and Charlie and the rest of them that he'd been joking that day. The truth was he hated the Nazis, too. Not just the Nazis, but all Germans. They were all responsible for the terrible things that had happened. That the language he and his father had been speaking was Dutch, which sounds a lot like German. Dutch, like Anne Frank.

Truth and lies. Love and hate. It was the work of the devil, tricking and obfuscating, turning him against his father. And when, years later, Javier finally saw through to the truth, it was too late. He could never tell his father how sorry he was. Never get down on his knees, kiss his father's hand, and receive his father's forgiveness. Javier was destined to live in hell until he could at least do this one thing.

He looked again at the man in the photo. "I'm sorry, Vati. I promise I'll find her and the painting. I'll make sure the world knows the truth."

Javier put the photo of his father back down on his desk. Then he went to the closet and took out Vati's small trunk.

He unlocked it and carefully removed the treasures, placing them on his desk.

There was a folder of photos—mainly publicity shots. And of course, the letter. Then there were the films, the lace doilies, the heart-shaped locket, and her hat. Vati had told Javier how he'd taken these things from her apartment, just after she ran away so many years before.

Javier lifted the hat out of the trunk and removed it from the airtight plastic cover and tissue paper. He held the inner headband up to his nose and inhaled deeply.

He remembered his father standing in the shadows, Beethoven pounding in the background, her delicate hat in his large hands.

"I loved her," his father had said, running his fingers over the felt brim, as though he was caressing her cheek. "When I find her, I will kill her."

19

Kali walked through the scent of incense and vanilla in the front of the store, past the shelves of candles and tinkling wind chimes, to the back room that she used for a studio. Camilla, who owned the New Age Shop in downtown Dania, had originally held belly dancing and yoga classes in here, but couldn't make enough money to justify the cost of the space so she rented it out to Kali.

Light from four skylights bounced off the waxed blond wood floors and mirrored wall, brightening the room, and making the space an ideal studio. The incense and vanilla blended with oil paint and turpentine, and Kali felt comforted by the smell, especially after spending the last few hours inhaling hospital odors at the bedside of her semiconscious grandmother. One of the nurses, a plump motherly woman, suggested Kali take a break. That she'd call if there was a change in Lillian's condition.

Kali dropped her satchel on the desk in the corner of the room, next to her computer. She used the computer for research and maintaining business records, and the long table beside it for her "paying job." She'd already begun work on a couple of ideas for a new children's book, and several watercolor sketches were laid out on the table beneath the extra overhead lights she'd had installed.

But Kali's real passion was at the other end of the room. She slipped on a paint-stained smock as she went to the easel that held the new painting that was gradually taking form on the large canvas.

The fairy had four arms fanning out from the center of her chest. Egyptian-style arms, their rigid right angles creating an interesting contrast to the fairy's flowing dress and hair. Long blonde curls. Blue eyes.

Kali took a step back.

Blonde curls. Blue eyes.

She remembered the cigarette card picture of the blonde-haired, blue-eyed woman she'd found in the storage room last night.

She returned to her desk and dug it out of her satchel. *Leli Lenz*.

Maybe Seth didn't want to deal with the skeletons in Lillian's closet, but Kali felt a compulsive urge to find out what she could. Even if, as Kali feared, she wouldn't like what she discovered.

She booted up her computer and it groaned to life. She Googled Leli Lenz.

Several results popped up. Wikipedia, some "come-on" websites, and Facebook in German. In fact, many of the links were in German to German sites.

She clicked on the Wikipedia article. A brief biography and selected filmography listing three films made between 1935 and 1938 with German titles. The photo in the right-hand corner was the same one that was on the cigarette card.

Kali read the biography. It was very limited. Leli Lenz had a brief stage career in Berlin, then played fairly substantial supporting roles in three films. It sounded like she was on her way to becoming a major star, but then her story ended with no explanation.

There was nothing of a personal nature except—Kali's heart fluttered. It had to be a coincidence. She pushed her chair back from the computer. Or was it a coincidence?

She needed an objective person to show this to before she read too much into it. Ordinarily that would be Seth, but as of this morning, the subject of her grandmother's past had become taboo.

She looked at her cell phone. She and Neil had exchanged numbers last night, so there would be no more awkward encounters like they'd had in the storage room.

Her heart was pounding as she searched for his name and pressed Send. She thought about Seth. He told her he believed there was nothing going on between her and Neil. And there wasn't.

"Hey," Neil said in her ear.

She hesitated.

"Kali?"

"Yeah." She took a deep breath. "I was just researching Leli Lenz. I found something. Maybe I'm crazy, but—"

"Where are you?"

"In Dania. At my studio."

"I can come by. I'm not doing anything special."

She heard the door to the store open and voices. Camilla was in with a customer. So they wouldn't be alone. There was no reason for Seth to be upset. "That would be great," she said, and gave Neil the address.

Thirty minutes later, he stepped through the curtain that separated Kali's studio from the store. He had on jeans and a button-down shirt. It was probably what he wore when doing his professor thing at UCLA.

He looked around at the helter-skelter arrangement of painted canvases on the floor and those that were resting against the mirrored wall. "Well, this is better," he said.

"Better?"

"The studio. It looks like you. Organized disorder." He went over to the easel in the corner of the room. "So this is your new painting." He picked up an unopened tube of paint from the adjacent table and rolled it between his bandaged hands as he studied the painting.

He didn't speak for a long time. Kali realized she was chewing on a fingernail. She pulled her hand away from her mouth.

"It's very good," he said finally.

She felt herself relax.

"But it's also disturbing," he said.

"Disturbing?" she asked, although she'd sensed it herself.

"The fairy seems so gentle, but something about her hands—the sharpness in the way she's holding them. Well, it feels ominous." He tapped the tube of paint against the several-day-old beard on his face. "Is that the effect you're going for?"

"This may sound silly, but it's more the effect the painting's going for."

He raised an eyebrow above his glasses.

"Often when I'm painting, it seems like my hands are carrying out someone else's vision and I'm just the instrument."

"You mean like when we were kids and the plastic thingie appeared to move across the Ouija board on its own?"

"But with a Ouija board, isn't it our subconscious that moves the marker?"

He put the tube of paint back on the table. "Don't you think that's what's happening here? That your subconscious is expressing itself?"

She wanted to explain that it felt like it was coming from outside her, but that would sound ridiculous, even to Neil. "That must be it," she said instead. She left him standing by the painting and went back to her desk.

"I hope I didn't sound like I was criticizing it," Neil said, following her. "I really think it's an amazing painting."

"Thank you. And I do appreciate your reaction. Really."

"I'm flattered you trust me enough to invite me here and let me see your work." He glanced at the computer screen and the Leli Lenz card on the desk. "So you wanted to show me what you found on our mystery lady."

"It's probably just a coincidence. In fact, the more I think about it, I'm sure that's all it is. I believe Leli was an actress my grandmother admired. And it would be natural that Lillian would admire someone similar to herself, right?"

Neil pulled over a folding chair and sat down near Kali. His knee touched hers, and she felt a jolt of electricity. She rolled her chair a few inches away.

"What do you mean by similar?" he asked.

"I know my grandmother's from somewhere in Austria, and Wikipedia says that Leli Lenz was born in Vienna."

He shrugged. "Not such an earth-shattering coincidence."

"I know. But I was a little freaked out when I saw that Leli was born in 1916."

Neil cocked his head. "And?"

"So was Lillian."

Neil studied the picture on the cigarette card. "And you're think-ing your grandmother's Leli Lenz?"

"That was my first reaction. But why would she hide something like that?"

"I don't know."

"So it's probably just a coincidence. Maybe Leli was a friend of Lillian's when they were kids and she kept the card as a memento."

"Maybe." He looked at the Wikipedia article. "She was in three films."

"Yeah. And I found a website that actually sells the movies." She clicked on germanfilmsinc.net. *WELCOME TO YOUR GERMAN FILM STORE IN THE U.S.* In smaller letters, it said, *German Films Inc. is based in Ohio. Shipping will take only a few days to anyplace in the United States.*

"I was thinking about ordering the films Leli was in," Kali said. "I can't really tell from this picture if there's a resemblance to Lillian or not. Maybe I'd have a better idea from the actual films. And if it isn't Lillian, then Leli Lenz is probably a dead-end lead."

"That makes sense," Neil said.

She clicked on the "Add to cart" box near one of the Leli films in DVD Format. Then she ordered the next film, then the next. She couldn't explain the anxiety she felt as "Check out now" appeared on her screen. Like competing forces were trying to get her to order and not order the films.

She started typing her name and home address, but stopped in the middle, remembering Seth's hostile reaction to her looking into Lillian's past.

"What's wrong?" Neil asked.

"I'm not sure it's a good idea to have them sent to my house."

"Why not?"

"Seth's gotten a little weird about my grandmother. I think he's afraid of what I might find out about her."

"So he'd rather you don't even ask?"

"Something like that."

"And you? You're not afraid?"

"Maybe a little. But I have to do this. I need to know who she is. Who I am." She touched her abdomen. *Who my child will be*, she didn't add.

"Use my mom's address. Have them ship the videos there."

"Thank you." She typed in Neil's name and address of the house next door to her grandmother's. She stopped at the credit card info.

"What? Seth checks the credit card statements?"

She nodded.

He reached into his wallet and handed her his card. "Use this. You can give me the cash."

"Thanks." Kali took the card.

"Where are you planning to watch them?"

"Home, but maybe not. Could be awkward if Seth finds them."

"Change them to videocassettes and you can watch them at my mom's house. She never got a DVD player."

Kali nodded. Her grandmother also had a videocassette player, so Kali didn't have to make any decisions now.

She changed the order and entered the credit card info. Then she printed out the receipt, folded it, and put it in her satchel with the cigarette card, irrationally feeling that some force, stronger than a Ouija board, was driving the whole process.

20

Beeping, beeping, incessant beeping. Lillian wanted to plug her ears but she couldn't find her hands. Then a lovely, floral fragrance filled her lungs. Ahhh. Better. Much better.

Leli held the bouquet of flowers up to her face and inhaled deeply. They reminded her of the wildflowers she used to pick when she and her family would hike up the mountains near Baden bei Wien for a summer picnic. How she missed her parents and brother. She hadn't seen her mother and father since she'd left Vienna to become an actress three years before, in the summer of '35. Her brother had helped her get fake papers with her stage name, then had accompanied her to Berlin. The two of them had shared a small apartment on Lietzenburgerstrasse until he left unexpectedly one day. Leli had been sad and worried to find him gone, though not surprised. Joseph had warned her that his activities might require him to disappear. And although she had begged him not to do anything dangerous, her big brother had tickled her chin and told her he could take care of himself.

Leli took another deep breath of the fresh perfume, then cradled the bouquet in the crook of her arm.

Dr. Altwulf's lackey, Graeber, was watching her with an expression that always sent warning sparks down her spine. Her first impulse was to move the flowers in front of her white satin gown, blocking Graeber's view of her breasts, but instead she held her shoulders back and raised her chin. She could tell he was mesmerized as the lights from the marquee flashed on the sparkling tiara that sat in the nest of blonde curls atop her head.

"You were wonderful," Graeber said. He was young, maybe even younger than she, with thick, straight blond hair, a square jaw, and broad shoulders. He had a nice nose, broad forehead and pale green eyes, but she would never have called him handsome. There was an oblong discoloration in his right iris, like a drip of blood, and his face was often twisted in an ugly grimace that made it seem as though his features had melted.

He smiled at her and the side of his mouth drooped. "A perfect role for you."

"Thank you." She glanced around at the crowd of men and women in evening clothes who were exiting the theater and heading toward their waiting cars and limousines.

Leli had made her apologies to the film's director for being unable to attend the after party, and although he seemed unhappy about it, he had simply nodded. Of course, she was still only a supporting actress, so it wasn't absolutely necessary that she go to the party, but once she became a leading lady, Leli wasn't sure what she'd do.

"It pains him that he can't accompany you to the openings himself," Graeber said, "but he doesn't want to do anything that might compromise you or your success."

"Yes, I know. He's told me." Leli lifted the skirt of her gown off the pavement and began walking toward the street where Graeber had left the car. Her white ermine stole slipped off her shoulder revealing the dress's low-cut back.

People smiled at her, nodding in recognition. She smiled back.

"Wonderful performance, Miss Lenz," a gentleman in top hat and tails said, bowing.

"*Danke*," she said, curtseying. "*Danke schön.*"

Graeber held the car door open for her. It was a conservative, old-model black Horch. Although clean, it was practically invisible amongst the sea of brand-new, flashy roadsters and cabriolets pulled up in front of the theater.

Leli sat in the back, the flowers on her lap. The first time Graeber had accompanied her to the premiere of one of her movies, he had acted as though he expected her to sit up front with him. But she had waited by the rear door until he took the hint and opened it for her. Just because Herr Doktor Altwulf had sent Graeber as her escort didn't mean she had to like him. Maybe if Graeber didn't look at her with such an odd intensity, she would have been friendlier. After all, he wasn't that different from Leli, an artist trying to break out, with Dr. Altwulf his teacher and mentor. But Leli sensed on a visceral level that there was danger in getting too close to Graeber.

Graeber drove through the flashing lights of the theater district, then down tree-lined Unter den Lindenstrasse where the more up-scale clubs and restaurants were located. He pulled up to a burgundy awning, stopped the car, then came around to help Leli out.

"He's waiting for you," Graeber said.

"Thank you." Leli climbed out of the car, leaving the flowers on the backseat so as not to attract any additional attention when she entered the club. Dr. Altwulf preferred things that way.

The maître d' led Leli through the smoky lounge to a table that was set back in a darkened alcove. It wasn't readily visible to the other patrons, but it had a perfect view of the high-ceilinged two-tiered room, the small orchestra off to the side, a singer near the shiny black piano, and the well-dressed couples sipping cocktails at their tables or dancing too close on the parquet dance floor.

Dr. Altwulf rose as she approached, made a bow, and then kissed her hand. He was wearing an old-fashioned dinner jacket that smelled of mothballs.

"You look exquisite, my dear," he said, as the maître d' pulled out her chair and helped her arrange herself comfortably.

She draped her white stole over the back of her chair. "Thank you, Wulfie. I feel wonderful."

He sat down catty-corner to her, his walking stick resting against the edge of the linen tablecloth. He patted his graying goatee. It was a self-conscious gesture. She knew how awkward he felt being here amongst the well-heeled and sensed he was doing it for her.

"So the premiere was a success?" His blue eyes were bright behind his wire-rimmed glasses.

"The audience responded favorably."

"You're too modest. I'm sure you were sensational. Just like in the first two films."

A waiter brought over a bucket of ice and a bottle of champagne. They waited as he popped the cork, then poured the bubbling liquid into the crystal champagne flutes on the table.

Dr. Altwulf raised his glass. "To my dear Leli. Much success."

They clinked glasses and Leli took a sip. It tickled her throat, but she'd learned to love the taste of champagne. "It's as much your success, Wulfie. I never would have gotten here without you."

He shook his head, as though discounting her words. "I happen to have a friend in the entertainment ministry. Lots of people have friends. But your success is due to your talent and beauty, not because of what I did for you."

"Look who's being modest."

He smiled back at her. How lucky she'd been to meet this kind, generous man who doted on her like a precious daughter.

A waiter went by carrying a tray of pastries intended for another table. Leli strained her neck to see.

"Would you like something sweet?" Altwulf asked.

"I wish, but I can't." She patted her tummy. "Can't afford to put on even an ounce. I'm screen testing for a new film. Don't want that Susi Lanner to get the part."

"Ha. She has nothing on you, my dear."

Leli leaned back against her chair and fidgeted with the edge of her ermine stole. "I wish you'd come to the premieres with me, Wulfie."

"So do I, my dear. But I enjoy seeing your movies as just another admiring fan."

"But the premieres are so exciting."

"I'm sure they are. But we don't want people wondering what you're doing with a doddering old professor hanging on. You need to appear like an angel to your public—aloof, unattached, unattainable."

"You've said so before. And I understand. But must you always send Graeber to be my escort?"

"What? You don't like Graeber?" He looked amused.

Leli shrugged.

"But he's so young and handsome. And such a talented artist. You should see his paintings sometime."

"He's not my type." Leli didn't want to say anything negative to Dr. Altwulf about Graeber. After all, her dislike of the man was personal and she had no desire to hurt Graeber's career chances with his professor.

"You're very discreet, my dear. Another of your many charms."

She sipped her champagne and watched the couples spin across the dance floor. The singer shimmered in her tight gold dress and had a deep, throaty voice.

Leli never went out on dates anymore, which suited her. The men in the movie industry were all egotistical peacocks. Nothing like Dr. Altwulf.

She looked over at him, but his spine had stiffened and his eyes were focused on something behind her.

Leli turned her head. There was a commotion at the door. Four men in SS uniforms had entered the main room. The maître d' was issuing instructions to waiters and there was a good deal of fuss as they brought a table to the edge of the dance floor, then set it for the four Nazis.

"I hate them," Leli said under her breath.

"What's that, my dear? You hate someone?"

She had to be careful. You could never be sure what anyone's true loyalties were.

"The SS men. They're so arrogant. They think they can just barge in and have their way." She took out a cigarette from her silver case, then put it back, remembering how Wulfie disliked when she smoked.

"They have an important job to do."

"What? Enforcing foolish laws that keep people from working?"

"The laws don't seem to have hurt you, my dear."

She sipped her champagne. She was thinking about her father and the letter she'd gotten from her mother about the new restrictions at the university where he taught, but she was reluctant to reveal this to Altwulf.

"You're right, of course," she said instead. "I just question why people aren't allowed to express their beliefs just because they're contrary to Hitler's." She knew she sounded bitter, but Altwulf was smiling.

"You don't agree with what the Führer's trying to accomplish?"

"I just hate rules and restrictions."

"Of course you do, my dear. That's natural. You're young. A child doesn't like to be told to go to bed or eat his vegetables either, but that's a necessary part of the child's health and well-being."

The SS men were laughing too loudly, their voices carrying above the singer's.

Leli took another sip of champagne. "Would you tell me what you really think, Wulfie? Everyone's so afraid of speaking out. Of telling the truth. If you could design your ideal world, how would you arrange things?"

He sat back in his chair, a thoughtful expression on his face. His fingers thrummed against the tabletop.

"An ideal world." His voice was wistful. "In my ideal world, I'd be an art professor and a respected painter. And I'd be sitting in a dark, smoky nightclub sipping champagne across from the most beautiful girl in the universe."

The beeping sound began again—shrill, ugly, eternal.

21

Kali felt like a Peeping Tom watching her grandmother sleep. How exposed Lillian was—this proud, self-aware woman who never allowed anyone to see her unless she was perfectly coiffed and dressed. Yet here she was in a wrinkled hospital gown, hair disheveled, forehead bandaged, mouth open, and making tiny snoring sounds when she inhaled too deeply. Someone had taken the oxygen plugs out of her nose, which gave her a little dignity, but Lillian would be devastated if she knew anyone was seeing her like this.

Kali found a comb in the nightstand and ran it through the tangles in Lillian's shiny white hair. It seemed strange to Kali to be touching it. Her grandmother had always been aloof, just as Kali's mother had been, and Kali was suddenly aware just how much she missed having a physical connection. Ironically, now that Lillian was unable to respond to her, Kali felt closer to her than she had ever before.

Kali worked out a clump of coagulated blood. The brown crust against the silky white hair was disturbing. She removed the clot, then washed off the remaining traces of blood with a washcloth that she'd taken from the bathroom. She worked to control the revulsion she felt as the smell of blood rose.

An irritating beeping was coming from the machine that monitored her grandmother's vital signs. Her grandmother's breathing was labored; her face a mask, practically unrecognizable to Kali. There was a tiny scar on the underside of Lillian's chin that Kali had never noticed before.

Lillian's muscles relaxed and she smiled slightly, as though she was having a pleasant dream.

Kali wondered if she could smell the flowers Mitzi had brought by earlier. A beautiful arrangement of wildflowers.

Lillian's lips were moving. "*Danke,*" she seemed to be saying. "*Danke schön.*" Her face opened into a full smile, just like the other morning when she had curtseyed for Kali.

But then the smile faded. Lillian began taking labored breaths, no longer resembling the beautiful, proud woman Kali had always known, but rather looking like an old woman in a hospital waiting to die.

Kali tucked in the blanket, then stood up to leave for her studio. It was three days since she'd found Lillian lying unconscious on her bathroom floor. Although she woke up from time to time, she was either confused or frightened, and then she'd doze off again.

Lillian's face changed. "Ah, voolfee," she said, then mumbled something in German. She shook her head, as though angry, and opened her eyes.

She stared directly at Kali and began speaking in German.

"I don't understand what you're saying," Kali said. "I don't know German."

Lillian blinked a few times, looked around the room, then back at Kali. "I thought you were the singer," she said in unaccented English, though her speech was slightly slurred.

"What singer?"

Lillian seemed more alert than the other times she'd awakened. This was also the first time she'd spoken English. Kali pressed the button to alert a nurse.

"At the club. She was wearing a tight gold dress, but she had a beautiful voice. Very deep, almost like a man's."

Kali sat down on the chair beside the bed. "A nightclub?" She was wondering if her grandmother's dream had some connection to reality.

"Oh yes. One of the finest. But then—" She shook her head and took another look around. "Where am I? What is this place?"

"Mount Sinai Hospital. You fell and hit your head. Do you remember?" Kali wasn't sure if she should mention the stroke. Let the doctor deal with that.

"The flowers. I dreamt about wildflowers."

"Mitzi brought them this morning." And in case Lillian wasn't tracking, she added, "Seth's mother."

"I used to go hiking with my mother and father in the mountains near Baden bei Wien."

Kali felt a charge of excitement. Maybe Lillian would talk about her past some more. "Isn't that near Vienna?"

"Not too far."

"Well, look who's up," said the nurse standing in the doorway. "How are you feeling, Mrs. Campbell?"

"What am I doing here?"

The nurse went over to the bed, put a blood pressure cuff around Lillian's arm, blew it up, then released the air. "One twenty over sixty. Pretty good. I'll let the doctor know she's awake," she said to Kali, then removed the cuff and left the room.

Lillian was looking after the nurse. "Why do people talk like I'm not right here in the same room as they are?"

"That was rude of the nurse," Kali said. "So you were telling me about Baden bei Wien and Vienna. Is that where you grew up?"

"I hate when people treat me like I'm invisible. I'll make sure the doctor knows what I think of the service here. " She closed her eyes and lay back against the pillows. She still looked like an old woman, but a strong-willed, dignified one.

Kali couldn't help but smile. Score one for Lillian.

22

Judging from the hunger pains in his stomach, it was sometime in the evening, but with the blinds closed in his home office, Javier never knew whether it was day or night. The stainless-steel ashtray was overflowing with butts, but Javier lit another cigarette. He'd cued up the Beethoven playlist on his hard drive and Symphony No. 5 in C minor thundered in the background.

Javier had been working feverishly since the order for the three Leli Lenz films came in on Wednesday. He'd shipped the films to the Miami Beach address, noting that it was next door to the home of that old woman—Lillian Breitling-Campbell, then he began the process of learning exactly who Neil Rabin was. The order for these particular videos couldn't be a coincidence. The leading men and ladies in the three films were all different, as were the directors, so the only common element was Leli. This man had to have some connection to her.

Using his investigative tools and accessing governmental and private databases that he had successfully infiltrated, Javier found that Rabin was thirty-two and a history professor at UCLA, but had grown up here on Miami Beach. Then Javier had dug into the man's roots, learning that Rabin was an only child and had no children of his own. His mother, Susan Rabin, was still alive but currently in an assisted-living facility that specialized in Alzheimer's patients. When Javier searched further, he discovered that Neil's maternal grand-mother had been Austrian and was a Holocaust survivor.

Was it possible? But records showed that the grandmother, Gussie Stein Lowell, had been born in 1923. Javier ruled her out and investigated the other side of the family.

Neil Rabin's paternal grandmother had been born in 1915—

close enough to be a match—but in Poland. Javier had been momentarily disappointed until he recalled that sections of Poland had been part of the Austro-Hungarian Empire before 1918. So there was a good chance that this young man's paternal grandmother was the woman he was searching for. But Sophie Delanski Rabin had died in 1985. If she was dead, would her grandson know about the painting?

The idea that he may have hit a roadblock was troubling in itself, but Javier felt enormously let down that he might never get to meet the woman who had become so prominent in his life.

Leli Lenz.

He took one of the films that he'd converted to DVD format and popped it into the player, remembering the moment when the devil had led him so decisively onto the wrong path.

Since the afternoon that Javier had seen the hatred in his classmates' faces, Javier had been working diligently to win their acceptance.

Javier was a natural athlete and once muscles filled out his gawky frame, he became a bit of a hero amongst his peers. He cursed the Nazis and the Germans louder than anyone. Javier had learned his lesson. His father was a leper with a past that Javier dared not share with anyone, lest the stigma cling to Javier himself.

One night, his father came home from the photography shop he owned. "There's something I want to show you," his father said, turning off the TV that Javier had been watching.

Javier had his feet up on the coffee table in front of the couch. He was sixteen and still sweaty from the football game he'd played in that afternoon.

His father set up the film projector on the living room table and pulled down the screen he viewed his old movies on.

"This film was made in 1938," his father said. "It was the last one she was in."

"I'm not interested in your Nazi crap," Javier said.

His father turned to face him, his distorted iris a mirror image of the one in Javier's eye. Without warning, he struck Javier across the bridge of his nose.

Javier felt a burst of pain and saw a flash of light as he heard the crack of cartilage. Warm blood streamed into his mouth, over his chest.

"You'll watch and you'll listen," his father said. "And you'll learn the truth."

Perhaps it was fear of the bigger man that made Javier remain seated on the couch as blood drenched his shirt, or maybe in his subconscious Javier was hoping there would be something in these films that would bring his beloved father back to him.

His father handed him an icepack and sat down beside him. "The first time I saw her," he said, "I thought she was too beautiful to be of this world. An angel, perhaps. How could I have known she was the devil in disguise?"

His father played the film. Then another. The pain in Javier's nose throbbed. He half listened as fury and hatred for his father boiled inside him. More lies.

But Vati spoke in an awed voice about the remarkable man he had been privileged to serve. About the tiny painting and its cryptic signature. He described the work in exquisite detail—the perfection of each of her curls, the glow on her face, the grace of her miraculous arms. The beauty, its overarching significance.

Javier was struck by the idea that the woman seemed to mean even more to his father than the Movement.

When the last film reached its end, his father leaned back against the couch. He looked drained. "After she ran off," he said, "I went to her apartment and searched. I found a letter. I used it to track down her family. Her real name was Ilse Strauss. She was a fraud."

His father closed his eyes and shook his head. "We must find her and the painting," he said. "We must recover what has been stolen."

"We?" Javier stood up. His shirt was completely soaked in blood. "I don't give a shit about this woman or her painting, or any of your fucking crap."

His father sprang from the couch, his hand balled up in a fist.

"Go ahead, hit me again," the devil said, using Javier's voice. "You can't hurt me anymore. I'm out of here. I won't stay under the same roof with a sick fuck like you."

His father's hand slapped against his heart. He took a staggering step toward Javier. "Please, wait. They've lied to you."

"No. You've lied to me. You're pathetic and all I feel for you is disgust. I wish you were dead."

Javier stomped out of the room, but not before he caught the wave of desolation on his father's face, his mouth agape like a suffocating fish's. That was the last memory he had of his father.

He had packed his bags and moved into a small room in Robert's garage until he went off to college two years later. His father never bothered to look for him and Javier's wish came true. When Javier was eighteen, he got a letter notifying him that his father had died of a heart attack.

Javier did nothing. The monster was dead, some detached voice in his head whispered. The same monster that had risen from the murky waters of that river near the campsite so many years before. And when the memory of being lifted and held tightly by those strong arms tried to push its way into Javier's consciousness, Javier shut them down. The monster was dead, just like Javier had wished for. How could he have known that his mistake and youthful prayers would haunt him the rest of his life?

The film was over. Grainy black-and-white filled the screen. Leli Lenz was gone. Javier lit another cigarette, took a puff, and closed his eyes. "Oh, Vati. I'm so, so sorry I'll never be able to make it up to you."

Pathétique cried in the background.

Javier sat up straight. What was he doing? Perhaps things weren't working out as planned, but Javier was closer than he'd ever gotten before. He'd been so focused on finding the woman for his father that he hadn't been thinking clearly. After all, what was the likelihood she would still be alive at ninety-three? But the painting would have been too important for her not to have passed it on to her descendants. And it remained just as crucial to the Movement as ever.

Maybe the woman known as both Leli Lenz and Ilse Strauss was no longer attainable, but Javier could still redeem his father. And himself in his own son's eyes.

23

Kali had tried to act nonchalant when she mentioned to Seth that she was going to her grandmother's house. "To straighten up a bit before she comes home tomorrow," she'd said.

She was afraid that if he imagined her scouring floors and vacuuming, he'd intervene, using her pregnancy as an excuse. Or worse, that he'd remember the other night and imagine a secret liaison with Neil. But he had mumbled, "Fine," perhaps preoccupied by the dreaded golf game with his dad and dad's colleagues that he was heading off to.

She stopped first at the hospital to check on Lillian, who was expectedly irascible about getting out of "confinement," as she called it. Then Kali headed down Alton Road. The street was blocked off to cars so that a large group of Sunday morning bicyclists could get by. This caused a brief delay, and Kali didn't get to her grandmother's house until after ten. As she pulled into the driveway, she noticed a black sedan driving slowly down the street. It paused briefly in front of the Rabins' house, then continued on. She checked the carport. Neil's car was gone.

Good, she thought. It was probably best if he didn't come over.

She was eager to get started. Yes, she was planning on cleaning, but she also wanted to take the opportunity to explore the house without Lillian here.

First, she went through all the rooms opening the casement windows and letting in the outside air. She picked up the smell of the ocean and something clean like fabric softener. Possibly the exhaust from a neighbor's clothes dryer.

She mopped the marble floors, cleaning away the firemen's footprints, then went into the kitchen and scrubbed off the crud on the counters and appliances. She filled heavy-duty garbage bags with old newspapers and expired food from the refrigerator and cupboards. Then she went from room to room throwing away *Yahrzeit* candles, feeling oddly uncomfortable. Her recent conversion classes were still fresh in her mind. Was it sacrilegious to be disposing of the little glasses with their partially burned down wicks and wax? Or was the sacrilege in the act of a non-Jew lighting them?

She dragged the bags outside to the garbage cans, holding her breath to avoid the bite of cat musk. She noticed the black outline of dirt from where the terra-cotta planter had sat before Neil had moved it to retrieve the spare house key the night of the fire.

She wondered where he was. Perhaps visiting his mother at the nursing home.

When she got back inside, she glanced at the door behind the étagère. Neil had moved the étagère back, blocking the door.

Kali was pretty sure she'd exhausted her search of the storage rooms. The Leli Lenz cigarette card might turn out to be a good lead, but Kali was certain there was something else that would explain why Lillian had lit those candles and the secret she seemed to be keeping. The logical place to look was in Lillian's bedroom.

Kali needed to know if there was something more to her mother's death and if there was any basis to Lillian's concern that someone was trying to break into the house.

The scent of lavender drifted up, making her feel like a thief as she opened and closed each drawer in Lillian's closet, chest of drawers, and nightstands, then sifted carefully through the contents, trying to put everything back as she'd found them. There were neatly folded blouses, sweaters, underwear, and nightgowns. One drawer had things that her grandmother probably hadn't used in years— half- and full slips, several lace-trimmed handkerchiefs, and three pairs of silk stockings, probably fifty years old, still in the box they'd come in. Kali shook out the lace-trimmed handkerchiefs, noticing they were all the same except for one. It had initials embroidered on one corner. Very subtle—ivory thread on white—*H.S.* Nothing Kali recognized. She refolded the handkerchiefs and put them back.

Shoes, handbags, scarves, and dozens of hats were arranged on the closet shelves. That was odd—she'd never seen Lillian wearing a hat. But aside from clothing and accessories, there were no boxes with secret documents. None of the paper-and-memento clutter that was present in Kali's own closet. It was as though Lillian was expecting someone to go through her personal possessions and had left everything in perfect order. But in that order, there was no trace of her daughter, granddaughter, or the life she'd lived before she married. No keepsakes, photos, letters.

Kali thought about the fairy picture her mother had made in her closet, now painted over. Just like in her old bedroom across the hall, there was a sterile quality in here.

The doorbell rang. Kali closed the closet and went downstairs, wondering if it was Neil. Hoping it was.

She looked through the peephole and opened the door. Seth was facing away from her watching the street, his golf shirt stuck to his back with perspiration. A hint of cigarette smoke wafted off him and her abdomen tightened as she remembered his smell when he came home late the other night, their unsatisfactory discussion the following morning, and the awkwardness between them ever since.

"Hey," she said.

"Oh, hi." He turned toward her, looking surprised that she was standing in the doorway. "I thought I'd come by and see if you were still here."

"Is the game over already?"

"Yeah. We finished up about an hour ago, then sat around the locker room." He glanced at the street again as he stepped into the foyer. "It's weird. There's a black sedan that keeps driving past your neighbor's house, then slowing down looking at the house. He's been by twice since I got here."

Kali closed the door after them. "I think I saw the car earlier."

"Could be a realtor. It's amazing how those guys have a sixth sense for when a house is coming on the market." He looked at Kali's clothes, which she noticed were spattered with scouring powder. "Do you need help?" he asked.

"No thanks. I'm about finished."

He nodded and took in a deep breath. "I could use some water."

"There's nothing bottled, but the sink water's pretty cold."

He followed her into the kitchen and rested his hands on the back of a dinette chair as she filled a glass with tap water. "My dad and his friends are crazy," he said, taking the glass from her and drinking it down. "Thanks. Boy, I needed that. It must have been ninety on the golf course. I had a beer, but I'm sure I sweated out at least a gallon."

Kali took the glass from him and refilled it. "How'd it go?"

"Thanks." He had another sip and wiped his mouth with the back of his hand. "It was horrible. No. Worse than horrible. Nightmarish."

"Really? A golf game?"

"It's not the golf." He pulled out the chair and sat down. "It's this sense of manly fraternity. All this back pounding. I'm sure I'm all bruised."

"They were pounding your back?"

"Yeah. Congratulating me on winning my case last week."

"That doesn't sound too bad."

"I mean, they were nice enough. Especially since they all think my dad's the greatest. But most of the time they were talking about stuff I couldn't care less about. Football. Draft picks."

"Yuck." Kali and Seth had made a pact on their first date never to talk about sports, which suited Kali since she knew practically nothing about them.

"But the worst part was in the locker room. It's like some kind of time warp there. Before noon and these guys are guzzling Scotch and smoking cigars." He shook his head. "They don't even shower first, so it stank like—well, like a locker room."

Kali laughed. She was relieved that he was talking to her so naturally. That the crisis between them had apparently passed. "So you figured anything's better than the locker room? Even cleaning Lillian's house?"

His lips twisted like he was holding back a smile. "Something like that." He glanced around the kitchen. "But it looks like you don't need me. It's all spic-and-span in here."

"For now," Kali said. "I think I'll try to persuade her to hire someone who can come and clean once a week. Just to stay on top of it."

"Good luck with that." He took another sip of water. "Have you told her about the aide?"

Kali shook her head.

"Damn, Kali. She's coming home tomorrow. When are you planning to tell her?"

"I'll find the right moment."

Seth started rubbing an imagined spot or stain on the kitchen table. "And what if she refuses to let someone stay here?"

"She can't refuse. She has no choice."

"Well, she probably thinks she does." Seth got up and went over to the étagère. Kali noticed the wicker was unraveling.

"What can she do?" she asked. "She can't live here alone. She needs a walker to get around."

He picked up a pile of magazines on the étagère and jogged the edges until they were in alignment. His back was toward her. "She might ask you to stay with her." His voice was so quiet, she could hardly hear him speak.

"She won't do that."

He didn't answer, just kept jogging the sides of the magazines against the shelf.

"And if she does, I'll tell her it isn't an option."

Seth turned to face her, holding the magazines tightly against his chest. His eyes were bloodshot, but it was probably from being in the sun for so many hours. "The other night when you didn't come home when you said you would—" He looked down at the magazines, his jaw twitching.

"What, Seth?" She took a step closer. "Did something happen? Did you—" She couldn't finish the sentence. Seth would never, ever hurt her.

He took in a long breath, but kept staring at the magazines. "I'm only good when I'm with you, do you understand that?"

"I'm not sure," she said softly.

He raised his eyes to meet hers. "I love you, Kali."

"I know you do."

"I feel whole when we're together, but when we're apart—It's hard to explain. Something happens in my brain. I get—scared."

"But that's silly. I was hardly gone the other night."

"Please, Kali. I need you to promise me you won't leave me alone again."

"I don't understand. What are you afraid of?"

"Promise me."

She looked at the étagère, the unraveling wicker.

"Promise me."

"Okay," she said, even as she sensed that somehow she was letting someone else down. "I promise."

24

Her grandmother pushed the walker along the bricked path from Kali's car in the driveway to the front of the house. She was wearing the light-gray pantsuit Kali had brought to the hospital and she took slow, uncertain steps. Kali noticed her dragging her left leg ever so slightly. Her forehead was black-and-blue where she'd hit her head when she fell, and there was a line just above her eyebrow with a dozen stitches.

Lillian brought the walker up against the portico step. She seemed to be assessing how to maneuver the contraption, then banged the palm of her hand against the handgrip. "Damn thing. How the heck is this supposed to make me independent if it doesn't go over steps?"

"I'll help." Kali lifted the front wheels up on the step while making sure her grandmother's balance wasn't upset.

She still hadn't said anything to Lillian about the nurse's aide. Kali had told the woman to come to the house around noon, after her grandmother was settled in. That would give Kali time to prepare her.

She and Lillian made it to the front door and up over the small step into the house. Kali carried the tote with her grandmother's nightgowns, robe, and slippers.

Lillian stopped in the middle of the foyer and glanced around as though she was in an unfamiliar place. Or maybe she was looking for the *Yahrzeit* candles.

"Who's been here?"

"I have. I straightened up."

"No one else?"

Kali shook her head. It felt like déjà vu. But maybe the paranoia was good. At least Lillian was mentally in the same place she'd been before the stroke.

"Good. He hasn't found me."

Kali held back her frustration. It seemed impossible to tell if her grandmother was becoming demented or whether there really was some outside threat.

"Who hasn't found you?" Kali asked.

But Lillian ignored the question as she rolled her walker to the circular staircase and looked up. "All these steps," she said, shaking her head. "How am I going to get up all these steps?"

"Don't worry about them," Kali said. "I thought for now you'd be more comfortable sleeping downstairs in the TV room."

"That's not a place to sleep."

"It's just temporary. Until you're able to manage the steps." Though Kali wasn't sure that would ever be the case. "The shower in the bathroom may be easier for you to get in and out of than your bathtub upstairs, and we can open the sofa bed."

"That sofa bed? The springs will break my back."

"We can see how comfortable it is without opening it up."

"I suppose."

Kali followed her grandmother into the living room and then through the pocket door that led to the TV room. The wheels of the walker made a soft whirring sound against the marble.

Lillian surveyed the TV room from the doorway. It had originally been a screened-in porch that was accessible from both the kitchen and the living room. Kali remembered when her grandparents had enclosed it many years before, put in a window air conditioner, and added a small bathroom. There were casement windows on two sides, but shrubs and vines kept much of the sunlight out. The terrazzo floor, a mosaic of amber and turquoise pebbles, was covered with a beige shag area rug and the sofa was pushed up against one wall.

Lillian sat down on the tufted sofa and patted the brown velvety fabric. Kali used to curl up on it to watch one program a night on the old television in the corner of the room. Her grandmother didn't approve of television, so this was the only TV in the house, and even its use had been restricted.

"I suppose this will do," Lillian said, reaching for her walker. "I'll just get some sheets, my pillow, and a blanket."

"I'll get them," Kali said, relieved. Her grandmother was being uncharacteristically cooperative. "Would you like something to eat? It's almost noon."

"No, thank you. I think I'll just rest a while." Lillian leaned her head against the back of the sofa.

Kali shook out the crocheted afghan that was lying over the arm of the sofa and was hit by the scent of lavender and wool that wafted toward her. She draped the afghan around her grandmother, then started toward the door.

"Where are you going?" Lillian sat back up, her face alarmed.

"Just upstairs to get your pillow and blanket."

"You can do that later. Would you come sit with me?"

"Of course." Kali arranged herself beside the frail old woman, close, but not quite touching.

Lillian closed her eyes, hands resting on the afghan in her lap. Despite the swollen arthritic joints, the shape of her hands and fingers were much like Kali's. "Doll's hands," Kali recalled her grandfather joking. Kali tried to remember what her mother's hands had been like.

"How are you feeling?" her grandmother asked.

"Fine."

"With the baby, I mean." Lillian opened her eyes. "Are you feeling okay?"

"I'm mostly good," Kali said a little cautiously. She had told her grandmother she was pregnant a few weeks before, when she was bursting with the news, but Lillian's reaction had been almost hostile, so Kali hadn't brought it up again. "I get morning sickness sometimes."

"Still? Aren't you finished with your first trimester?"

Kali couldn't believe Lillian was tracking this. "Yes. I just finished thirteen weeks."

"I had morning sickness with your mother. You should be over it soon. Of course I didn't know it was morning sickness. I didn't even realize I was pregnant. I was so sick with worry that I'd lost track of my time of month."

Worry? Hadn't she been safe and secure here with Kali's grandfather?

"I was always hungry, but when I ate, it just came back up." Lillian seemed to be studying her. "You're a good girl, Kali."

Kali bit down on her lip. She wished she hadn't promised Seth that she wouldn't spend any more nights here. Just tonight and maybe tomorrow would have helped her grandmother get comfortable with the aide in the house.

"I'm sure your baby will be fine."

Kali started, then realized her grandmother couldn't possibly know about what had happened.

"I didn't know what to do when I found out I was pregnant." Lillian's fingers played with the border of the afghan. "I was terrified, but not to have it? To destroy my own flesh and blood?"

"Wait. You were considering an abortion?"

Lillian didn't seem to hear her. She tugged on a loose piece of wool as she stared at the dark window. "How could I make that sacrifice when I'd already lost so much?"

"What, Lillian? What had you lost?"

Her grandmother looked like she'd been suddenly awakened.

Kali tried to ease her back. "You were telling me about when you were pregnant with my mother. That you were—" Terrified? Was that really how her grandmother had felt? "Scared," Kali said instead. "You were telling me you were a little scared."

Her grandmother's blue eyes shifted around as she seemed to take in every detail of Kali's face. "How pretty you are. You look a lot like me when I was young." She nodded her head. "I was very worried, but everything turned out all right. I'm sure your baby will be fine."

The doorbell rang, a distant muted sound. Lillian tensed.

"It's just someone at the door," Kali said. "I'll get it."

"Probably that Rabin boy. He's okay."

Kali went through the kitchen, then down the hallway into the front foyer. It was noon, so it was probably the aide, not Neil. But Kali hadn't broken the news to her grandmother yet.

She looked through the peephole, took in the short, stocky woman in hot-pink scrubs, then opened the door.

The woman smiled. She had jet-black hair pulled back at the nape of her neck, black eyes, and flat, earthy features. "Mrs. Campbell?" she said with a Hispanic accent that Kali recognized from their phone conversation. "I'm Luisa Santos."

"Please come in. I'm Kali Miller. Mrs. Campbell is my grandmother."

Luisa rolled a small suitcase into the room and looked around at the foyer with its spiral staircase and marble floors. Kali had forgotten how impressive the house seemed to most people.

"My grandmother will be staying in a room downstairs, since she can't manage the stairs. You'll be upstairs in my old bedroom."

"She here, your grandmother? May I meet her?"

"Of course, but please give me a minute. We just got home ourselves, and I haven't had a chance to tell her about you."

The soft rolling of wheels coming from the kitchen told Kali she was too late. Her grandmother stood just outside the foyer taking in the uniformed woman and her suitcase.

"What was it you were going to tell me?" Lillian's voice had resumed its familiar chill.

Kali felt her face get hot. "This is Luisa Santos. She'll be staying with you for a little while until you're able to get around easily yourself."

"Hello, Mrs. Campbell," Luisa said with a big smile. "Nice to meet you."

Her grandmother ignored Luisa and pushed her walker over to Kali. Her blue eyes were like lumps of ice; she barely moved her lips. "Ask her to leave."

Luisa looked from the old woman to Kali. "I wait outside." She went out the front door pulling her suitcase behind her, as though she'd been in this situation before.

The door closed.

"Please, Lillian. You'll need someone to help you get things from upstairs, to help with your meals."

"You can do those things."

"I'm sorry, I can't."

"Of course you can."

"I have my own home, my husband to take care of."

Her grandmother shook her head.

"It's not forever. Just until you're better."

"Better? I'm ninety-three. Do you really think I'm going to get better?"

"Please, Lillian. Try it for a few days. Let's see how it works out."

"I thought you were listening. I won't have a stranger in my house."

"Luisa's from a reputable agency. She has wonderful references."

"She's not my flesh and blood." Lillian took a step closer to Kali. Her jaw was clenched, her nostrils flaring. "She's not my flesh and blood," she repeated, enunciating each syllable. "Only you are."

25

Lillian sat up abruptly, her heart pounding. She was on the sofa in the TV room. Someone had made it up with sheets, blanket, and a pillow. When had she changed out of her gray pantsuit into her cotton nightgown? How had it grown so dark outside?

She heard unfamiliar footsteps above her going from room to room. It was that woman, the aide who smiled too hard. The one Kali had left in the house to keep an eye on her until she got well. But why was the woman really here? Had she been sent to go through my things, she thought.

A toilet flushed. A door closed. Footfalls in the hallway.

Then silence. Where was the woman now? In the master bedroom? Was she rifling through Lillian's drawers? Her closet?

She got up from the sofa bracing herself on the walker. It was dark in the room, but she didn't need to turn on any lights. She'd lived here so long she could find her way around blindfolded. The pocket door that closed off the TV room was shut, and she jiggled it until it slid open.

She pushed the walker into the living room, straining to pick up noises from above. The fireplace chimney went through both rooms, and acted as a megaphone in transferring sounds, but Lillian heard nothing coming from her bedroom.

She walked into the dining room, which was directly beneath Dorothy's room, and listened. There it was. A drawer closing, the creak of the floorboards, a window opening.

Lillian held her hand to her heart. Violated. She felt violated. Couldn't Kali understand how devastating it was to know a stranger was touching her most private possessions, sleeping in Dorothy's bed, looking at her framed likeness?

But she didn't really blame her granddaughter. Kali was an innocent, a victim with no knowledge of her crime or the danger she might be in. How could she know, when Lillian had tried so hard to protect her?

For these past seventy years, this house had been an asylum for Lillian, for her family. And while she'd never felt completely safe, Lillian had garnered a sense of security and privacy. And now that had been invaded.

Even though Lillian was fairly certain this woman, this aide, would find nothing in the house to connect her to her past, there remained a fear that Lillian would inadvertently reveal something in her sleep. Or perhaps she had overlooked some giveaway detail, like the hidden painting in Dorothy's closet. Or in the storage rooms. But the storage rooms were blocked by the étagère and the key was tucked away in the hidden sewing cabinet. In her bedroom. Which was next to the room where the stranger slept. Upstairs, where Lillian was now unable to go.

The sounds upstairs stopped.

She rolled her walker back into the living room. This was where she'd spend the night. At least in here, she could hear if any untoward noises came from her bedroom.

The Queen Anne sofa was filled with goose feathers and she sank into the cushions and rested her head against the upholstered arm. The wingback chairs, fireplace, and built-in cupboards were all in shadows. Periodically a car went down the street, momentarily brightening the room. The walls were adorned with mirrors, brass candelabra, but there were no paintings. Lillian had sworn she'd never have a painting in her house.

The clock on the mantel ticked loudly. The satin fabric felt cool against her skin.

She heard the clopping of horses on the cobblestone streets and the glow of gaslight fell across his face.

Altwulf smiled shyly, his blue eyes sparkling behind his spectacles, his hands both resting on the top of his walking stick. "There's something I'd like to show you this evening."

Leli cocked her head. She had on a blue satin dress that showed off her legs, and a lovely summer hat with ribbons and a bow that she'd worn for a cigarette card photo. "Something I'll like?"

He took in a deep breath and patted his graying goatee. "I very much hope so." He looked around, probably for Graeber.

Leli felt revulsion when she spotted Altwulf's ubiquitous student standing near the car at the corner of the street. His mop of thick blond hair shone in the light of the lamppost, and he was holding something to his mouth. She'd come to think of Graeber as a vestigial organ that Altwulf should have had excised. But when she hinted that she'd prefer the absence of Graeber's company, Altwulf merely smiled at her as though she were a child asking for an unreasonable bedtime.

"Ah, there he is," Altwulf said.

Graeber had been waiting outside while she and Wulfie shared a bottle of wine in the rathskeller. At least Altwulf never invited Graeber to join them when they were dining or having a cocktail. That would have been intolerable. Leli couldn't stand how Graeber looked at her with his drippy eye and twisted smile.

Leli took Altwulf's arm and they walked toward the car. Graeber dropped something on the street, stepped on it, then brushed off his jacket. He quickly put on the dark glasses he always wore around Altwulf.

When they got to the car, Graeber held open the back door for Leli. She smelled cigarette smoke on him. Apparently Altwulf did, too, because he scowled at Graeber and said something Leli couldn't make out. Graeber lowered his head like a scolded dog.

The three of them sat in silence as Graeber drove. They were in an unfamiliar, somewhat shabby neighborhood, but Leli felt no apprehension. Altwulf had been her protector and a perfect gentleman for over two years and she had no reason to mistrust him.

Graeber stopped the car in front of a narrow red brick building on a treeless street and Altwulf helped Leli out. He said something to Graeber, then slammed the door.

"This way, my dear." Altwulf took her gently by the elbow and used a key to open the front door. There was no doorman, no lobby. Just a dismal hallway with a scarred wooden staircase and the stink of cooked cabbage.

Leli was confused. "Are we visiting someone?"

"I suppose you could say that."

He began climbing the stairs, using his walking stick to help him up.

"Is there no elevator?"

"I'm sorry. There isn't. But it's just one landing up from here. Can you make it all right?"

"Of course. I was worried about you."

He smiled, then patted her arm.

He stopped in front of an apartment, inserted a key in the lock, opened the door, and flicked on a light switch.

Leli stepped into a large, high-ceilinged room with draped windows on two sides. The smell of turpentine hit her first, but then as she looked around, it seemed as though she'd entered a musty antique shop or museum. The room was overfilled with sofas, chairs, area rugs, and paintings. So many paintings! The walls were covered with large and small canvases in gilded frames, reaching almost to the ceiling.

Altwulf went around the room turning on lamps.

Leli could tell that the furniture and rugs were of a high quality. She approached one of the walls of paintings and examined an oil of a winding country road lined with cottages painted in muted blues and browns. Next to it was a still life of a floral arrangement, and beyond, Leli recognized a cathedral she'd often passed in Vienna. Then she noticed an easel set up in the corner of the room, where the light through the tall windows was probably strong during the day. There was a stool in front of the easel and beside it a table with brushes and a palette of paint.

She got closer to the easel, which held a canvas with the outline of a grand edifice, then went back to the paintings on the wall. The artist's initials were the same on all the paintings. They looked like ALT.

"This is yours," she said, with sudden clarity. "Your apartment. Your studio. Your paintings."

Altwulf looked down at his old-fashioned high-top shoes.

Why was she surprised? She knew Altwulf was an art professor and he often spoke about his love of painting.

"Wulfie, these are wonderful. You're so versatile. Oils and watercolors, grand buildings and exquisite flowers."

"I'm pleased you think well of them."

He went to the sideboard and poured an amber liquid from the decanter into a couple of brandy glasses. He handed her a snifter. "To art," he said, clinking his glass against hers. "And beauty."

The brandy burned her throat.

"Your beauty," he said.

"I'm honored that you'd bring me here."

"What a kind thing to say." He patted his goatee, as though embarrassed.

She took his hand in her own. He was much older than she, but she felt great tenderness toward him. Perhaps even love. "I know you're a very private person. Thank you for sharing your work with me. Your paintings are truly amazing."

He squeezed her fingers, then released them. He seemed unable to meet her eye. "No portraits, though."

"Why is that? Don't you care for portraits?"

"Oh, I do. I just hadn't found the right subject." He lifted her chin with his fingertips. "Until now."

A thump startled her. Lillian's breath caught in her throat. Where was she? Why was it so dark?

She heard a creak of floorboards. It was coming back to her. Her house. She was in her house. With a stranger. Some stranger who had come here to discover her secret.

Lillian threw her feet over the side of the sofa and pulled herself up with her walker. She had to stop this. Had to stop it now.

She pushed herself to the stairwell, trembling and dizzy. She must get up the stairs before it was too late. She grabbed the banister with both hands and pulled her right foot up on the first step, then dragged her left foot after it. One step at a time. She lifted herself up to the next step, then the next one. She was breathless, but she had to stop the intruder.

It seemed to take forever pulling herself up the stairs, but finally she reached the top. Her heart was pounding and she wanted to sit down and rest, but she couldn't. Not yet.

Where was the woman? Was she in Lillian's bedroom? In the closet? Had she found the key?

The floorboards creaked. There was a dense shadow in the hallway.

"Mrs. Campbell," said the shadow, surprised. Then the voice changed and became stern. "What are you doing up here, Mrs. Campbell?"

"Me? What am I doing up here?"

From outside came the rumble of thunder.

Lillian flung herself against the woman, smacking her, tearing at her clothes, her face, using every ounce of strength to stop her. But the woman was too strong. She held Lillian's arms with a firm grip until all the fight seeped out and Lillian's legs folded beneath her.

"Stop," Lillian tried to shout, but it came out like a baby's whimper. And she dropped down to the cold, hard floor and began to sob.

She could hear the rain hitting the roof, as though the sky had opened up, and all the angels cried with her.

26

Kali's cheek rested against her pillow and she looked at her husband. There was a film of perspiration on his skin, beneath his matted chest hair. He was still breathing hard. This was the first time they'd made love in over a week—since before her grandmother's incident.

A flash of light filled their bedroom, then came the rumble of distant thunder.

"How you doing?" Seth whispered.

"Good. Very good."

He snuggled against her. She tensed, then relaxed.

"I'm always afraid of hurting Bucephala," he said.

"You shouldn't be."

"I know, but still. They say fetuses can hear music and sense their mother's stress. I wonder how they react to their parents having sex."

"Probably results in some interesting Freudian analysis when they're older."

"Yeah. Talk about delving deeply into the past," he said. "Can they do that though? Extricate memories from the womb?"

"I'm sure there's someone out there who says he can."

"There's always someone who makes improbable claims. What's amazing is all the people who believe it."

"Like the people in the story admiring the emperor's new clothes. It took a little boy to get them to see that the emperor wasn't wearing any."

Seth laughed. Kali felt the vibrations in his chest. This was how things were supposed to be. Easy, comfortable, laughter.

There was another flash of light and clap of thunder.

"Thank you," he whispered.

"For what?

He didn't answer. Instead, his fingers danced down Kali's back, caressed her buttocks, and squeezed. She felt him harden against her.

"So if you're sure we won't be creating a sociopath," he said, "what do you think about doing it one more time?"

She raised her mouth to meet his, but he rolled her over. His chest hair brushed against her back as he cupped her breasts. They rocked as one, picking up a rhythm, while outside the rumbling grew. The rain hit the roof and windows hard, like hundreds of rice pellets, and the white canopy undulated like a bride's veil in the wind.

"Oh, baby," Seth said, breathing hard.

A phone rang, shrill and startling.

Seth kept moving, faster and faster.

Kali's cell phone. It rang again, then again.

She felt Seth's member shrivel, then he slid off her.

"Who the hell?" he said.

Kali reached for the phone and flipped it open. "Yes?"

"Ay, *dios mio*," said a woman's frantic, angry voice. "*Loca. Es muy loca.*"

"I'm sorry," Kali said. "You have the wrong number."

"No, wait. Mrs. Kali? This is Luisa."

Kali sat up. "What is it, Luisa? Is my grandmother all right?"

Seth mumbled something, then got out of bed and headed toward the bathroom.

"All right?" Luisa said. "She crazy. She try to kill me."

"Wait. What are you saying?"

"She come up the stairs and attack me like a wild animal."

"That's impossible. My grandmother had a stroke. She can't climb stairs."

"Well, she did. I call to tell you, I don't stay there no more. Not with some crazy lady."

Kali heard Seth flush the toilet.

"Are you still there, Luisa? At my grandmother's house?"

"No. I pack my bag and go."

"So she's alone?"

Seth stood in the doorway to the bathroom, the light shining on him, his arms folded across his bare chest. He'd put his briefs on.

"I want to stay until you come," Luisa said, "but she tell me to go. 'Get out of my house,' she say."

Kali climbed out of bed. "When did you leave? How long has she been alone?"

"Just now. I call you right away when I get to my car." A clap of thunder came from overhead. "I sorry, Mrs. Kali. You seem a nice girl. I very sorry about your grandmother." She disconnected from the call.

Kali closed her phone. The rain was hitting the window in waves.

"What happened?" Seth's face was pale in the harsh bathroom light.

"I'm not sure, but the aide left." Kali dialed her grandmother's house. The phone rang and rang. "Shit." Kali closed her phone and took the cotton blouse and leggings she'd been wearing earlier from the chair in the corner of the room.

"What are you doing?"

"I have to go. My grandmother's not answering her phone."

"Wait. Call your neighbor. He can check on her."

Kali hesitated. She really wanted to see for herself, but Seth was right. Neil could easily run next door and make sure her grandmother was okay. Knowing Neil, he'd probably even stay with Lillian tonight. Then Kali could go there in the morning, after the storm had passed.

She scrolled down to Neil's name and hit his number. She listened to the phone ring.

Seth was watching her. "What's wrong?"

"Neil's not answering." She closed the phone. "I have to go." She tried to squeeze past Seth into the bathroom.

"It's not safe for you to drive in this."

"It's a Volvo. A battle tank. You said so yourself."

"Don't go, Kali."

"I don't have a choice. My grandmother's alone. I have to make sure she's okay."

"But why? I don't get it. She's never given a damn about you and you drop everything—"

"She's my flesh and blood." Those were the words Lillian had used a few hours ago.

Seth was breathing too hard, but it wasn't from the sex. He looked at the clothes in her arms with the panic of a frightened animal.

"Seth, this is an emergency."

"That's exactly what it is. An emergency. Don't leave me."

"Come with me, then. Drive me if you're worried."

He turned his face away.

"Seth? You know I don't have a choice here."

"You do have a choice." He wouldn't look her in the eye. "It's me or her."

"What? You're giving me an ultimatum? Really?" she said, raising her voice. "An ultimatum?"

He didn't answer. He went to their bed and climbed under the comforter.

The thunder rumbled.

Kali closed the door to the bathroom and braced herself against the sink.

She felt his semen running out of her.

27

The drive from Hollywood down to Miami Beach was slow and treacherous. Sheets of rain hitting the windshield made it almost impossible for Kali to see more than a few feet in front of her.

Impressionism ad absurdum. That's what she tried to concentrate on—Monet's *Water Lilies*, the details blurred almost beyond recognition. Because if she let herself acknowledge the sick feeling inside her, she might just fall apart.

She envisioned the muted colors of *Water Lilies, Poplars on the River Epte, Rouen Cathedral*. Beauty and clarity in the haziness.

But there was no clarity in Kali's mind. What was wrong with Seth? Why didn't he understand that her grandmother was old and alone? She had only Kali.

Water Lilies, Water Lilies. Think about *Water Lilies*.

He was upset, irrational. They'd talk it over and work it out. Just a minor crisis.

It's me or her.

He didn't really mean that. No, of course he didn't. They were having a baby.

Her neck, shoulders, and hands hurt from clenching the steering wheel when Kali finally pulled into her grandmother's driveway almost an hour after receiving the phone call from Luisa. The rain was still heavy and although Kali opened an umbrella when she got out of her car, the rain slashed at her, soaking her clothes and hair. She dropped the umbrella under the portico and opened the front door, half expecting to find her grandmother's twisted body in a heap at the bottom of the stairs. But except for her grandmother's walker in the front foyer, the house appeared to be as Kali had left it earlier this afternoon. "Don't worry, Mrs. Kali," Luisa had said, her hand on Lillian's shoulder. She had smiled broadly. "Mrs. Campbell and I have a great time."

Kali should have known at that moment it could never work. Lillian disliked people who smiled too hard.

She slipped off her soggy sneakers, dried her feet on the doormat, then went slowly up the steep, winding staircase, holding onto the banister. What an effort it would have been for Lillian to do this in her condition. But on top of that, something had frightened her grandmother so much that she had attacked—that was the word Luisa used—her grandmother had attacked the aide. It would have taken a surge of adrenaline for her to do that. But what could have driven Lillian to such a frenzy?

Kali stopped outside her grandmother's bedroom door and listened. The only sound in the house was of rain pounding against the roof. She quietly opened the door. It took a moment for her eyes to adjust to the darkness, then she made out her grandmother lying in bed, her head propped up against several pillows. Her mouth was open and she was breathing hard. Kali got closer to make sure Lillian wasn't in distress. She wasn't, but she seemed to be reacting to a dream.

Kali thought about Seth gasping for breath after they finished making love. His scent was still on her skin.

She closed the bedroom door and went to take a long, scalding shower.

28

It was warm and dark in Altwulf's studio. The smell of oil paint and turpentine hung in the air, burning Leli's lungs each time she inhaled.

She was breathing too hard, but Leli wasn't frightened. Wulfie was the gentlest man in the universe.

He lifted her hat off her head and rested his hand on her curls. She could feel him trembling, as though it was his first time, not just hers.

He leaned over and kissed her. The short hairs from his goatee felt like butterfly wings.

"Are you all right?" There was cognac on his breath.

"Lovely," she whispered.

One by one, he opened the buttons on the back of her dress, slid the satiny fabric down her arms and let it drop to the floor.

The only light in the room leaked in through a narrow gap between the drapes, but she could feel him studying her as she stood in only her white lace slip.

"You're so beautiful," he said.

She was shaking. He cocooned her in his arms and she buried her face against him. His jacket smelled like wool and mothballs. He took it off, opened his shirt.

"The most beautiful woman I've ever known." He pulled out her hairpins, letting her curls cascade over her shoulders.

His hands ran up and down her body. Her slip fell to the floor. He opened the garters and eased one silk stocking down her leg, kissing the inside of her thigh.

She felt weak, about to collapse.

He led her to the sofa, pressing her arms and chest into the cushions. Her brassiere came away, her panties. He was behind her, fondling her breasts with his warm hands.

"I'll try not to hurt you," he whispered.

He parted her legs, touching her where no man had ever been before. She tensed, then opened to him.

She felt him against her now, pushing from behind. His breathing came in short, raw gasps.

She buried her face against the sofa cushion, blocking the smell of paint and turpentine, trying to think about how she'd always imagined it would be—gentle caresses and sweet kisses.

He pounded into her.

She bit down so she wouldn't scream aloud.

From the pain, from the ecstasy.

Lillian woke up, her screams silent in her head.

From the pain.

29

Kali awakened a little after nine the next morning. Birds were screeching in the poinciana tree, but there was no longer the sound of rain. The air in her bedroom was muggy. Kali had left the windows open last night and fallen asleep as the storm heaved, then ebbed, around her.

She got out of bed. The cotton blouse and leggings she'd worn here were still damp, so she left them on her desk chair to dry. She found her old sweats in the bureau, brushed her disheveled hair back into a single braid, and went to check on her grandmother.

Lillian was still in a deep sleep. Kali went downstairs to make coffee. While it brewed, Kali slipped on her still soggy sneakers at the front door, then went outside to get the newspaper. It was Tuesday and several cars went by, splashing through residual puddles. Probably people on their way to work or school. Just an ordinary day for them.

She thought about Seth. If she were home, they'd be having breakfast right now. In a little while, Seth would leave for work and Kali would drive to her studio. That was their routine. Just an ordinary day.

When had life stopped being ordinary for her?

The newspaper was lying in the grass. Kali shook off the plastic wrapper, which was saturated with the early morning rain. A movement in the overgrown ficus hedges of the vacant lot across the street caught her attention—black, green, something that resembled a hand, an eye. It reminded her of Braque's disjointed cubism. Several small parrots went squawking into the sky.

That's what she must have seen in the bushes—the birds.

The front door to the Rabins' house slammed. Kali turned and saw Neil coming toward her, wearing shorts and a white T-shirt. He was home. Why hadn't he answered his phone last night?

She looked back at the hedges. They were still.

"Hey, good morning," Neil called as he approached. "I didn't expect to find you here. I just got back a couple of hours ago on the redeye. What's going on?"

"My grandmother's home from the hospital. We tried out an aide, but that didn't work out." She tugged on her braid. "Where were you?"

"I had to fly back to L.A. to clean up some pressing things at work. Sorry I didn't have a chance to tell you."

"What about Gizmo?"

"A friend agreed to keep him. But he probably won't again."

"Why? Gizmo misbehaved?"

"That's a nice way of putting it."

"Sounds like my grandmother."

He pushed his glasses up on his nose. The bump on his forehead had receded and the large bandages on his hands had been replaced with a few small Band-Aids. "So what are you going to do?"

"Stay here with her for a while."

"Is everyone okay with that?"

She knew he meant Seth. "Not really."

A car splashed past. They both watched it go down the street.

"Hell of a storm," Neil said. "Gizmo was terrified. He kept slinking off to corners, trying to dig under the carpet to hide."

Was that what Lillian had been doing? Trying to get up to her bedroom to hide? From the storm? From something else?

Kali stepped onto the portico. "I need to go inside in case she wakes up."

"Sure. If you need anything—well, you know. I'm here."

"Thanks."

Neil backed away. "By the way, those movies arrived. I started watching them when I got home a couple of hours ago."

Kali stood at the open door. "Movies?"

"You know, the cigarette card? Leli Lenz?"

"That's right. And?"

"It's pretty amaz—"

A sound came from inside the house. "She's awake," Kali said. "I need to go."

"Sure. I'll catch you later."

Kali went into the house, closing the door behind her.

"Who's that?" Lillian called from upstairs. "Who's there?"

"It's me. It's just Kali."

Then more to herself than aloud, she said, "Looks like I'm back."

30

Javier Guzman stood hidden in the jungle of hedges across from the Rabins' gray New Orleans-style house, relieved that the storm had passed. He'd spent Sunday and Monday driving past the place repeatedly, waiting for a car to appear in the carport, but the house of Neil Rabin, the man who'd ordered the three Leli Lenz films, appeared deserted.

After circling the block a few more times yesterday, Javier had finally gone home. He returned at seven this morning, leaving his car on a side street a block away. He was surprised to see a white car under the mildewed awning of the Rabins' house. He waited, hoping Rabin would appear. Javier's black shirt, slacks, shoes, and cap had become saturated from the early morning drizzle. To keep his mind off his discomfort and stiffening legs, he ran through his findings one more time.

His research trying to establish a link to Leli Lenz, aka Ilse Strauss, was only leading to frustration. After spending hours investigating Sophie Delanski Rabin, Neil Rabin's paternal grandmother, Javier had uncovered nothing promising. Quite the contrary. The records confirmed Sophie Delanski had been born just outside of Warsaw, which at no time had been part of the Austro-Hungarian Empire. Therefore a connection to Austria and subsequently Berlin seemed speculative, at best. And then to increase his disappointment, Javier learned that the entire Delanski family had moved to New York in 1925, when Sophie would have still been a little girl. So unless she had moved back to Berlin in the thirties to begin an acting career, which was highly unlikely, then this grandson of hers was a dead end. Why then had Neil Rabin ordered the Leli Lenz films?

Shortly before nine, Javier watched Neil Rabin emerge from his
house with a dog. Rabin stopped in front of the shabby, columned
white house next door. The house where Lillian Breitling-Campbell
lived—the ninety-three-year-old with the British passport. Rabin
seemed interested in the silver Volvo in the driveway and went
around to inspect it. Then, he walked out into the street, very close
to the bushes where Javier was hiding, and stared up at the second-
floor windows.

The dog growled and squirmed, but Rabin gave the leash a jerk
and told the dog to settle down, then returned to his own house.

What was so interesting to Rabin about the Breitling-Campbell
house, Javier wondered?

A few minutes later, Javier saw Rabin step out onto his second-
floor balcony and watch the white house next door.

The front door opened and a petite blonde woman in sweat
clothes came out to pick the newspaper up off the lawn. Her hair
was pulled back in a single braid. She straightened up and shook out
the rainwater from the newspaper wrapping.

Javier let out a gasp and slapped his hand over his mouth.

His involuntary movement caused the woman to turn. She
seemed to be staring directly at him, through the hedges. Just then
a flock of small parrots flew out around him and went squawking into
the sky.

Javier held his breath and remained absolutely still.

The young woman was exquisite—with large blue eyes, long
neck, angular face. Just like the woman Javier had become so familiar with in the photos and movies.

But how much more beautiful in the flesh!

Rabin strode across the front yard and called to her.

Javier's heart was pounding as he listened to their exchange,
watched their body language. He tried to clear his head and focus.
Rabin and this young woman were clearly attracted to each other, although they both went to some trouble to hide their interest.

They were talking about the young woman's grandmother, an
aide leaving, the young woman staying.

Javier felt his excitement grow. And then Rabin mentioned the films and Leli Lenz. But Javier already knew. This was it. This was the connection.

Javier had found her.

31

Kali left the newspaper on the foyer table, then brought her grandmother's walker upstairs with her. She rolled it across the worn hallway rug into her grandmother's bedroom. The covers were thrown back, the pillows indented, but no one was in the bed.

"Lillian?" Kali called softly. She went toward the bathroom, picking up a faint smell of Pine-Sol and lavender. The doors to both the walk-in closet and bathroom were wide open, but there was no sign of her grandmother.

Kali stepped back into the hallway. Where was she and how was she getting around without her walker?

Then she heard something. A low, unrecognizable melody was coming from Kali's bedroom. It sounded like a mournful dirge. From the doorway, she could see Lillian in the rocking chair. She'd turned it around so that she was facing the framed photo of Kali's mother. She rocked as she sang in a guttural language something unfamiliar. But then—Kali had never heard her grandmother sing in any language.

> Zet zhe, kinderlekh, gedenkl zhe, tayere,
> Vo sir lernt do.
> Zogt zhe nokh a mol, un take nokh a mol,
> Komets alef-o.

"Lillian?"

Her grandmother continued rocking and didn't turn or otherwise acknowledge Kali. She was wearing a nightgown the color of buttercups, but no robe.

Kali sat down on the edge of her bed, near her grandmother, but not quite close enough to touch.

The rocking chair made a soothing sound as it rolled on the wooden floorboards. Lillian closed her eyes. "She loved that song."

Kali straightened. "My mother?"

"No. My mother." Lillian opened her eyes and looked at the framed graduation photo on the wall. "Dorothy didn't know the song. I never sang it to her." She rocked back and forth. "So I'm singing it to her now."

A shiver passed through Kali. *She didn't stand a chance.*

"Except for the dark hair, Dorothy looks just like my mother," Lillian said. "The blue eyes, the sweetness around her lips. Her name was Hannah, but my father called her Hanchah. I once had a locket with both their photos, but that was a long time ago."

Her great-grandparents, gone with no tangible evidence of their existence. A strange song, a nickname, a likeness. In just a few words, Lillian had told her more about her family than Kali had ever known.

"But this picture of Dorothy. The way she's smiling. When I first saw it, oh, how my heart ached. It was like seeing my dear mother again." Lillian reached into the pocket of her nightgown and brought a tissue to her eyes. Kali couldn't recall her grandmother ever crying. Not when her only child died, not when her husband died.

Lillian blew her nose, put the tissue back in the pocket of her nightgown, then looked back at the photo as she rocked. "You know, we're all so much alike. Our eyes, the shape of our faces. My mother, me, Dorothy." Lillian stopped rocking and turned to Kali. Her eyes were red. "Even you, my little Kali."

A lump formed in Kali's throat. *My little Kali.* It had been a long time since anyone had called her that.

"That's why I kept the painting, you know. As much as I despised the artist and all the memories associated with him, the resemblance was so strong. And it was almost like he knew the truth, but of course he didn't at the time. He gave me the painting as a gift. It was small, the size of a postcard, and fit in my purse. I chose to keep it, because whenever I looked at what was supposed to be my own face, I could see my mother's."

What was Lillian talking about? Despised what artist? She couldn't be talking about the portrait of Kali's mother; it was way too big to fit inside even a large purse.

Lillian reached for Kali's hand and squeezed so tightly that it felt like her bones would break. For many years, Kali had longed for her grandmother's touch. But now, she wanted desperately to pull away.

"It was all I had of my dear parents and my past," Lillian said. "The painting and the baby. If I destroyed them, there would be nothing left. You understand, don't you? I hated them, but at the same time, I loved them." Her grandmother squeezed harder, her frustration climbing painfully through Kali's hand and up her arm.

Hated them? Loved them? "I'm sorry, Lillian. I don't understand."

Her grandmother looked at Kali, then down at their entwined fingers. She released her grip, then brought her hands into her lap, massaging one with the other.

Kali's own fingers smarted. "I'd like to understand. Tell me, what was that song you were singing? Would you sing it again?"

"What song?"

"The one you were just—"

Lillian looked around the room, suddenly alert. "Is she still here?"

"Who?"

"That woman from yesterday."

Kali leaned back against the bed on her elbows, disappointed. "You mean Luisa. No. She left."

"I heard her going through my things."

"Is that why you came upstairs?"

"Of course. I told you it isn't safe to have a stranger in the house."

"Well, she's gone now. I'll be staying here now, if that's okay with you."

"Why wouldn't it be okay? This is your house. Where you belong."

Kali got up from the bed, brought the walker into the room, and rolled it over to her grandmother. "Well, if I'm staying, there'll have to be some rules. You have to choose a floor and stay on it. I can bring your meals up, or if you prefer staying downstairs, that's fine, too. But you have to promise me you won't use the stairs again without someone helping you."

"I'll stay up here." Lillian took hold of the walker grips and pulled herself up. She pushed the walker around the bed, stopping before she reached the door. Then she looked back at the photo of Kali's mother and began to hum that same strange, wistful tune.

The rocking chair went back and forth over the wood floorboards. Back and forth, back and forth. As though someone were still sitting there and keeping time with the melody.

32

Lillian pushed the teacart away from the bed, feeling sated and a bit sleepy. She'd finished the cheese sandwich and tea that Kali brought up to her room a short while ago.

A sweet girl. Who would have guessed this generation would have inherited none of the evil of the earlier ones? Lillian had always feared the opposite. In fact, when Dorothy hadn't gotten pregnant after years of trying, Lillian had been relieved that the nightmare would end with her. But then, at the age of thirty-eight, Dorothy had conceived. Lillian had tried to persuade her not to have the baby, pointing out the likelihood of birth defects or danger to Dorothy's own health. That had only resulted in a bitter disagreement. Dorothy hadn't spoken to Lillian until months after Kali was born, punishing her mother by withholding the child and giving her that terrible name. Kali—the four-armed goddess of death. It seemed that everything Dorothy did was contrived to hurt Lillian.

But time passed and Harry had finally persuaded Dorothy to forgive her mother and bring little Kali around. And such a dear baby she was! Many times Lillian even thought it had been a good thing that Dorothy had given birth. And maybe it was.

She lay down on top of the blanket, her head against a tower of three pillows, and folded her hands across her chest. Sunshine poured in through the lace curtains. How good it felt to be back in her own bed. No disturbing hospital sounds and smells. No strangers prowling about.

Lillian closed her eyes. It was quiet in the house. Quiet was good. She wondered what Kali was doing. Had she gone to lie down in her room? How tired she must be after rushing over here in the middle of the night to take care of her grandmother. Yes. It was a good thing that Dorothy had given birth. That Lillian's parents' bloodline should continue.

When she had nothing else of them.

She began humming softly, her mother's favorite tune.

> *Oyfn pripetshik brent a fayerl,*
> *Un inshtub iz heys . . .*

The gold locket was shaped like a heart and hung from a delicate gold chain. Leli opened the heart, studying the tiny photos—her father on one side, her mother on the other. The photos were blurred, almost faded, but she could hear her mother's voice.

> *Zet zhe, kinderlekh, gedenkl zhe, tayere,*
> *Vo sir lernt do.*

Leli sat down on the cushioned chair in the corner of her furnished apartment and held the locket tightly in her hands. Sunlight poured in through the lace curtains, but her heart felt heavy.

How desperately she missed her parents and her brother. It had been two years since she'd been back to Vienna, but she didn't dare return for a visit. She was safe here in her false identity, making a successful career for herself. *Why take a chance and ruin it?* her mother had written in her last letter. *We're well and happy at your achievements.*

But were they well? The letters from her parents, sent to a postal box in Berlin, seemed to have less and less information in them and Leli sensed there were things her parents weren't telling her.

She had thought about telling Wulfie the truth. He would understand, just as he understood so much else about her. They had made love only the one time. He seemed to sense her discomfort and never pressed her for more. And despite the difference in their ages, she loved him, just as she knew he loved her.

Her parents and brother had warned her to tell no one, trust no one. But Wulfie—she was certain she could trust him.

A loud knock on the door startled her. Leli jumped up, the locket in her hand. She slipped it into her pocket and went to the door.

"Who's there?"

"Graeber. Open up. This is heavy."

Graeber? Leli never allowed men into her apartment. How did he even get into the house, past her landlady?

"Miss Lenz, please. Altwulf sent me and this damn thing weighs a ton."

He wouldn't dare pull anything inappropriate, Leli reasoned. He's too afraid of Wulfie. She unlocked and opened the door.

Leli had never seen Graeber other than immaculately dressed, but now his shirt was untucked from his pants and he wasn't wearing a jacket. He was bracing a very large wooden box between the hallway wall and his thighs. He hefted it and carried it into the apartment, looking around as though for somewhere to put it. He went directly to the small oak table where Leli ate her meals, and set it down. There were sweat stains under his arms and on the back of his shirt.

Leli got closer, taking in the burled wooden cabinet, the dials on the front. "You brought me a radio?"

Graeber pulled a handkerchief from his pants pocket and dabbed at the perspiration on his face. His blond hair was damp and separated into straight comb lines, reminding Leli of soldiers in formation.

"Dr. Altwulf was upset that you don't have one," Graeber said.

"Ah." A few days ago, Leli had mentioned to Wulfie that the radio in her apartment didn't work and she missed listening to music. "How thoughtful of him."

"Not so thoughtful that he'd carry it himself."

Leli sucked in a smile. Graeber often behaved like a sulky child. "I doubt he'd have been able to carry it up two stories," she said, trying to be nice. "Thank you for your trouble."

Graeber made a gruntlike noise. "It's a Blaupunkt. Their best model. I chose it myself."

"It's very beautiful."

"It sounds even better. Nothing like those piece of crap Volksempfaengers everyone has." He scanned the room, his pale-green eyes stopping briefly on the old radio, a Volksempfaenger, which sat on the low chest near her bed, and then continuing more slowly—

taking in the publicity photos on the chiffonier, the lace doilies on the arms of the chair and sofa, and her pretty hat with the bow and ribbons that lay on the bed next to an embroidered pillow—as though memorizing every detail.

"Well, thank you, Graeber. I can manage from here."

"My instructions were to install it properly for you." He went to the chest and unplugged the old radio, leaning closer to her bed than was necessary, as though he was trying to pick up her scent.

Leli felt oddly violated, but didn't know how to send him away without appearing rude.

Graeber lifted the Volksempfaenger. "Would you mind getting the door for me?"

Leli opened the door and pressed against it, trying to make herself as small as possible as Graeber went past her with the old radio into the hallway. His elbow grazed her bosom and she sucked in her chest.

He caught her eye and stared at her, but Leli looked away, disturbed by his distorted iris.

Graeber put the old radio down too hard and the sound resonated through the hallway.

"Thanks again." She tried to block the entrance to her apartment. "And please thank Dr. Altwulf."

"I'm not finished here." He shouldered her aside and went back into the apartment.

Leli wasn't sure what to do. Graeber was supposed to be a friend of sorts. And of course, Wulfie trusted him completely. The problem was when Graeber was near her, Leli felt like there were creepy-crawly things all over her.

She left the door slightly ajar as he carried the Blaupunkt over to the bedside chest, plugged it in, then fiddled with the dials. "Perhaps I can find some nice Beethoven for you," Graeber said.

But a cool, flippant male voice came on, delivering a speech about the importance of loyalty and community.

"Ah well, not Beethoven," Graeber said. "But I'm sure you like listening to your boss."

"Goebbels isn't my boss."

"Of course he is. Without him, your movies would never be made."

"Yes, they would. People enjoy going to the pictures for enter-tainment. It's their choice, not his."

"You're very naïve, Miss Lenz. Goebbels allows the films to lure people into the theaters so that they'll have to watch the newsreels and propaganda. They're too stupid to watch what's good for them without a little honey lubricating the process."

Leli went to change the station. Goebbels's speech was on every one.

"Ha," Graeber said. "So much for choice."

"I still have a choice." Leli flipped the dial, turning off the radio.

"Is that so?" One side of Graeber's mouth twisted downward as he grinned. "What exactly did Goebbels let you choose when you did your screen test for him on the casting couch?"

"How dare you. Get out this instant."

He lowered his eyes like a rebuked child and stared at his pol-ished shoes. "I'm sorry. I've offended you. I didn't mean to."

"I want you to leave."

"It was a joke. I know you're above such things. You're pure. An angel."

He was standing between Leli and the door.

He took a step toward her.

She backed up. Her butt touched the side of her bed. Trapped. She was trapped.

"I think you're wonderful, you know." He was looking at her like a lovesick schoolboy, but he wasn't a schoolboy. He was a powerful, grown man. "I've seen all of your movies over and over. And it's not for Goebbels's propaganda that I go." He walked toward her, a cou-ple of feet away now. His face was perspiring again. "It's to see you, Leli."

She held her breath, afraid to move.

His eyes dropped to her groin and he cocked his head. "What's this?" His arm reached out toward her.

"No!" She swatted his hand away, hurting her own, but he didn't seem to notice. He touched the pocket of her dress, then pulled something away. The gold chain from her locket had been hanging from her pocket. He brought the locket close to his face.

"Give that to me." Leli tried to control her rapid breathing.

Graeber opened the heart and studied the photos. "So this must be Mama and Papa."

Leli saw her chance. She slipped around him, no longer cornered. "I said give that to me."

He dangled the locket by its delicate chain, taunting her. "Mama and Papa. They must be very dear to you."

She pulled the locket out of his hand and the chain broke. She was frightened, but knew she mustn't show it. "Look what you've done with your silly games."

"You didn't have to grab it. I was giving it back to you."

Leli took the locket and broken chain and put it in the top drawer of the writing desk.

"I'd like you to leave now," she said.

He ran his fingers through his hair. "You won't tell, will you?"

"Get out."

"Just promise me you won't tell Altwulf."

"Fine. Please leave. I won't tell Dr. Altwulf what you said."

Graeber shook his head. "No, I mean all of it. Don't tell Altwulf that I came here. That I brought you the radio."

"I don't understand," she said. "Doesn't he know?"

Graeber took a step toward her and wrapped his finger around one of her curls. "Not if you don't tell him."

"What is it?" asked a girlish voice in the distance. "What's wrong?"

Leli shook her head to clear it. Her heart was beating too fast. What happened to Graeber? Where was she? The dream faded. She was in her bed in her house on Miami Beach. No longer a girl, but an old lady.

Lillian looked at the woman who was watching her so anxiously. "Kali," she said.

"You were shouting something."

"I'm fine. It was just a dream. A bad dream."

"I'm going out for a little while, is that okay?"

"Of course. Why wouldn't it be okay?"

"I'll be next door—at the Rabins' house. I've written my cell phone number on this piece of paper if you need me."

"Why would I need you?"

"Just in case." Her granddaughter handed her the paper. "Would you like anything? Some music? I can turn the radio on for you."

"No."

Her granddaughter's eyes widened, probably at the sharpness in Lillian's tone.

"No radio, please," Lillian said, softening her voice. "I prefer the quiet."

"I'll see you in a bit." Kali picked up the tray with the breakfast dishes and left the room.

Lillian sank back against the pillows. Quiet. Quiet was good. The horrible dream was gone. Graeber was gone. There was nothing to worry about.

33

Kali brought her grandmother's tray down to the kitchen and rinsed out the cup and plate. The walls, covered with layer over layer of glossy grayish-white paint, rose from the checkered floor and seemed to close in around her.

Not her kitchen. Not where Kali belonged. Yet here she was. Committed to taking care of a woman who, although providing food and shelter for Kali, had never given her any emotional support. Any love.

Seth had a point. Why did Kali care so much?

She glanced at her phone. No missed calls from Seth. She understood his frustration with the situation. Kali was frustrated, too. She still didn't know whether her grandmother was suffering from paranoia or her fears were real. Maybe it was some combination of both. Perhaps the old films Neil had received contained some clue, something that would help her unravel her grandmother's past from the present.

She left the house and walked across the uncut front lawn, remembering how often she'd done this when she was younger. The Rabins' house looked as though it had been transplanted from New Orleans. Its ornate balcony had always intrigued Kali, making her envision a Romeo and Juliet scenario, especially when she was a teenager.

She rang the doorbell. Gizmo began barking.

"One sec," Neil called.

It was late morning and the temperature seemed to have risen at least ten degrees since Kali had been out earlier. Her clothes stuck to her perspiring body.

Neil opened the door, holding a large book under his arm. Gizmo ran out, circled and sniffed her, wagged his tail, then went back into the house.

"Are you busy?" Kali asked.

Neil shook his head. A dust ball was lodged in his disheveled black hair. "Just boxing up some of my dad's books."

Kali resisted the urge to remove the dust with her fingers. "I wanted to see those old films, if you have time."

"Sure. Come on in."

Kali got a whiff of staleness as she stepped into the foyer and experienced a moment's nausea. How good the house used to smell years ago. Always something baking.

"Will your grandmother be okay?" Neil asked.

"I gave her my cell number if she needs me."

"Did you hide all the matches?"

"Not funny."

"I wasn't trying to be."

"I think she'll be fine. I can't sit and watch her twenty-four/seven."

"This is true." Neil went into the adjacent living room and dropped the book in a carton with others. The wallpaper was peeling away from the walls, and the wood floors, once polished to a high shine, were dull. Gizmo found a small space on the area rug that wasn't taken up by several partially filled boxes that were wedged between the shabby sofa and two club chairs. The dog watched Kali with his one good eye.

Kali noticed there were clean spaces in the dust on the shelves and tables where books and knickknacks had been. She felt a wave of empathy for Neil dismantling his childhood home, every book and object probably a source of a memory. She remembered returning to the small house where she and her mom had lived to pack up her room. There had been cartons in the living room that Lillian had filled with books and vases and little glass statuettes. Just the furniture remained, and the house no longer felt like where Kali had lived the first thirteen years of her life.

"I got most of the upstairs packing done," Neil said. "It's taking a long time."

"I'm sure it is. So much of your life is here." Kali stepped around the cartons and dog and went over to the fireplace mantel, still covered with dozens of photos. That was what she'd loved so much about coming here as a kid—the strong sense of family, which she never had at her grandparents' house.

She picked up a framed photo. Neil was around ten, a scrawny kid with oversized eyeglasses. His parents were on either side of him; his grandmother, a tiny woman with a sour expression, stood near his mother, but just outside the family grouping.

"That's the only photo we have of my grandmother," Neil said, looking over Kali's shoulder.

"Really?"

"She hated being photographed."

She hated a lot of things, Kali thought, but decided not to say. "I remember her very well," she said instead. "She was always baking."

"It was a safe outlet for her." Neil smiled. "She wasn't the friendliest person."

"I thought it was just me she disliked."

"It wasn't that she didn't like you." He pushed his glasses up on his nose. "She was just worried I would like you too much."

"What do you mean?"

"She was old school. She didn't believe Jews should socialize with non-Jews, especially boys and girls. She had a fear of intermarriage."

"I guess I understand that. It was important to Seth's parents that their sons marry Jewish girls so their kids would be Jewish. That's why I converted. But still. You and I were just teenagers when your grandmother was still alive. It wasn't like we were going to get married or anything."

"Right, but you have to remember. Grandma lived through the Holocaust. Lost her own parents and brothers. So she was hypersensitive."

Kali leaned against the arm of a club chair and brought her single braid over her shoulder. She recalled how one day she'd gone into the kitchen while Neil's grandmother was taking a cake from the oven. How Kali had been transfixed by the numbers tattooed on the old woman's arm. She had caught Kali staring and covered her arm with a towel. Kali had raced out of the kitchen, then back to her own house, feeling as though she'd somehow violated the old woman. She hadn't returned to the Rabins' house until a couple of months later, after the grandmother had died.

"My grandmother was complicated," Neil said. "In some ways, she was like Gizmo. Loving toward those she trusted, and vicious or cold toward anyone she didn't."

"Is that why she never talked to Lillian?"

Neil took the photo from Kali and scratched the bump on his forehead. "She was a good person. A wonderful grandmother, always feeding me and telling me stories. But she'd been so badly scarred that she was suspicious of everyone."

"I'm sorry, Neil. I didn't mean to come across like I was criticizing her."

"No. It's okay. It bothered me and my mom that she was so intolerant. My mom even pointed out the irony to her. That Grandma was behaving toward non-Jews the way she resented some non-Jews behaving toward our people." Neil put the photo back on the mantel and picked up one of his mother with long hair holding Neil as a toddler, dressed in a snowsuit. "My mom was always trying to make up for Grandma's rudeness."

"I remember that, too. Your mom would tell me not to mind her mother. That I shouldn't take her coldness personally."

"My mom loved you," Neil said. "She always said how sad it was—" He stopped in mid-sentence and put the photo down on the mantel. "Anyway, let's go watch the films."

"How sad what was?"

Neil looked at the half-empty bookshelves, the paintings on the wall, the photos on the mantel. "How sad it was that you didn't have a real family."

The den, which had been the Rabins' informal family gathering place, had a fireplace built into a brick wall, planked wooden floors covered with a braided area rug, and a worn L-shaped leather sofa that faced the TV. The room, like the rest of the house, had a northern feel to it, probably because Neil's parents had moved to Miami from New York when Neil was a few years old.

Neil popped a videocassette into the player beneath the TV, then sat down on the sofa near Kali. She noticed he didn't get too close, which relieved her. There was something disturbing about being alone with him.

Neil tapped the remote against his chin, as though considering something. "These films," he said.

"What?"

"I hope—" He shook his head, then pressed a button on the remote. "Never mind."

The film started up in shaky black-and-white, with the title and credits in German.

"This one came out in 1937," Neil said. "It's the first one Leli Lenz made and she has a pretty small role, but you'll see for yourself."

The film seemed to be a light comedy of manners, but it was in German and Kali couldn't make out what it was about.

Neil touched the remote again and the film sped up. "I'll just advance to Leli's scenes, so you don't have to watch the whole thing."

He stopped the film, then hit the Play button. "Here she is. Leli Lenz."

A pretty young woman with curly blonde hair and a fitted dress that came just below her knees entered the scene where two men were speaking German. Kali couldn't make out her face clearly, but she had high breasts and a narrow waist and hips.

Kali felt Neil's eyes on her, rather than on the film.

Leli moved with grace and a childlike lightness in her step. Nothing resembling the way Kali's grandmother walked.

Kali felt let down. Her grandmother probably hadn't been Leli Lenz.

The men in the scene turned and smiled at Leli. Kali still

couldn't make out her face. She chatted with the men in a soft German that was clearly flirtatious. The men laughed.

The camera came in for a close-up just as Leli sucked in her lower lip and tossed her head.

Kali felt a wave of heat, then a chill. "My God," she said softly. "Leli Lenz is my grandmother."

Neil paused the film. "I saw the resemblance in the cigarette card, but it wasn't obvious. But here—"

The film was frozen on the frame of the young woman, holding in a half smile, eyes twinkling.

Kali brought her braid around her shoulder. "She looks so much like me. My grandmother has to be remembering herself every time she sees me."

"I know."

Kali tugged on the braid. Lillian had been telling Kali about the resemblance this morning, but it was the first time she'd ever mentioned it. "I don't understand why she never said anything about the films. What was so terrible about being an actress?"

"What if she was hiding it from your grandfather? Maybe she worried that he wouldn't be interested in marrying an actress. Or that his family might disapprove."

Kali nodded slowly. "That could be it. And then, years later when it no longer mattered, it was too late to tell Grandpa the truth."

Kali looked at the frozen frame of Leli Lenz. Her grandmother as a vivacious young woman. How changed Lillian was from her youth. Or was she? Could the woman on the screen simply have been acting her part? This film still didn't tell Kali who her grandmother had really been.

Kali thought about Neil's grandmother, who had become bitter after living through the Holocaust. Kali's own grandmother had been on the other side of that experience, laughing and flirting here in the film as though she didn't have a care in the world.

Was it guilt that had shaped Lillian to become the aloof woman Kali had only known? Perhaps her grandmother had lit the dozens of *Yahrzeit* candles in the hope of assuaging her inability to save those who had suffered and perished. Or had the actress Leli Lenz had a greater role during the years of the Holocaust that Lillian was now unable to live with?

"So, what now?" Neil asked.

Kali looked again at the static face of Leli Lenz, so much like her own. The twinkling eyes, the half smile on her lips.

A skillful, deceptive actress or a happy, unscarred young woman? Only her grandmother could tell her the truth, but it seemed the more Kali dug to understand her past, the more she risked uncovering something that she wouldn't want to know.

Neil scratched behind Gizmo's ear. "Are you going to show your grandmother the films?"

Leli Lenz smiled at her enigmatically from the screen.

"I think I have to."

34

Kali crossed the lawn back to her grandmother's house, carrying the three videocassettes under her arm.

She was ambivalent about this new discovery. On the one hand, she had a history. A past she could actually see. Neil had noted the counter readings of the Leli Lenz scenes from his previous viewing, so he was able to fast-forward through each of the films, stopping whenever Leli Lenz appeared. Kali got to watch her grandmother laughing, singing, dancing a waltz, even eating an apple. Many of the gestures and mannerisms were familiar, and Neil had commented how much like Kali she seemed.

One moment, Kali had no sense of what her grandmother had been like, then in the next she not only knew her grandmother, but she knew a great deal more about herself. Or did she? Kali still wasn't convinced that her grandmother had hidden her acting career just because she feared disapproval from her husband's family. It seemed to Kali that there had to be something more. And if there was, how would her grandmother react to seeing the films?

The sun was beating down. Kali lifted her braid and wiped her neck. When she reached the portico, she noticed a black sedan pull up and park in the street in front of her grandmother's house. Kali paused to see who it was.

A completely bald, middle-aged man in a linen suit and dark sunglasses got out of the car. He signaled to Kali for her to wait a moment, took his briefcase out of the car, and walked briskly toward her. He had broad shoulders and his skull was shaped like a deformed eggplant.

"Thanks so much for waiting," he said, stopping in front of her.

He had a baritone voice with a slight Spanish accent. "Are you Miss Campbell?"

Kali shook her head, not willing to share any information. She'd been raised not to talk to strangers and to be suspicious of virtually everyone, though this man, with his briefcase, nice car, and well-cut suit didn't appear to be a threat of any kind.

"I see," he said, apparently deciding not to press her. "Well, in any event, my name is Dr. Guzman and I'm here to follow up on a Mrs. Lillian Campbell."

"Follow up?" Kali said. "What do you mean?"

He handed Kali a business card. Dr. Javier Guzman, with a number of professional designations after his name that Kali didn't recognize, was the president of Golden Years Enhancement, PC, "Specializing in the Social, Physical and Mental Well-Being of the Senior Community."

"You still haven't told me what you want," she said.

He dabbed his shiny, perspiring head with a handkerchief. Kali couldn't see his eyes behind the dark sunglasses, but noticed his nose leaned to one side as though it had been broken. "I see you're a busy young woman. I'll get to the point." He reached into his briefcase and took out some kind of report, which he began to scan. "I understand Mrs. Campbell was recently discharged from Mount Sinai after being diagnosed with a stroke. I would like to speak with her and her caregiver about outreach activities, which may be helpful to ward off depression." He smiled. His mouth curved down a little as though he'd had a stroke himself. "Of course, if she's unavailable just now, I could give you an overview and perhaps come back at a more convenient time."

"I don't think she would be interested."

He glanced at the videos Kali held under her arm. "I'm not a solicitor, miss, if that's what you're concerned about. I'm here on behalf of Mount Sinai Hospital."

"Why don't you give me your brochures, and she'll call you if she'd like to learn more?"

He moistened his lips. "I don't have brochures. We're not some general purpose company. I'm a certified geriatric specialist and psychotherapist and I work with people on a case-by-case basis, based on their individual needs. Many stroke victims are confused and sleep a great deal initially. Then they may become depressed, paranoid, occasionally even violent." He seemed to be gauging Kali's reaction. "I don't know if Mrs. Campbell has experienced any of these things, but if she has, I hope I can be of service to you. I've helped many seniors by means of positive mental, physical, and social therapy. I'm not a believer in overmedicating. I think that's a solution of convenience, rather than what's in the best interest of the patient."

Kali felt herself relaxing. What he was saying made sense. And the behavior he mentioned was just what her grandmother had been displaying.

"Good communication, healthy interaction with other seniors, an active lifestyle—these are the linchpins of our program." He dabbed at his glistening scalp again with his handkerchief.

"It sounds good, but—"

"Ah." He held up his hand, the handkerchief still in it. "I know you're busy, so I'll get out of your way now. I just wanted you to know that I'm a resource, if Mrs. Campbell needs me." He smiled. "Or if you do."

Kali held the tapes in front of her chest, suddenly self-conscious even though she couldn't see his eyes behind the dark glasses.

"Many times the families or friends of stroke victims are also under a great deal of strain." His voice softened. "May I ask—are you Mrs. Campbell's primary caregiver?"

Kali nodded.

"You're probably carrying a great deal on your shoulders. A little relief for your grandmother might be helpful for you, as well."

"I'm managing okay."

A bird flew squawking out of the poinciana tree.

Guzman glanced up, then turned back to Kali. "Well, I'm glad to hear that. But now you have my number."

"Thank you. I'll certainly hold on to your card."

"No, thank *you*, miss." He gave a little smile and turned—almost reluctantly, it seemed—toward his car.

Kali let herself into the house and put the business card on the foyer table next to the three tapes. Her conversation with Dr. Guzman reminded her of just how fragile her grandmother was. Best not to show her the films, at least for now.

She glanced again at the business card and a peculiar thought crossed her mind. How did Javier Guzman know that Mrs. Campbell was Kali's grandmother?

35

Lillian sat up in bed and held her hand over her heart. Deep breath in, slowly out. Deep breath in, slowly out. The attack was passing.

"Are you all right?" Her granddaughter was standing in the doorway to the bedroom. "You're awfully pale."

How to explain this feeling, this fear? Lillian licked her mouth. Dry.

"I'll get you some water." Kali left the room. Lillian could hear her rapid footfalls going down the stairs.

Don't run, Lillian wanted to call after her. You'll hurt the baby.

Lillian touched her own abdomen. The panic from her dream was still with her. Why was she remembering these things? Was it just that she was afraid to die with so much guilt on her head? Or had her past finally caught up with her?

When she had opened her eyes a few minutes ago, she had felt his presence. It was like the drop in barometric pressure before a hurricane. She was certain he was nearby. But how could that be? He was surely dead by now.

"Here you go." Kali handed Lillian a glass of water.

She took a few sips, then handed the glass back to Kali.

Her granddaughter was scowling as she sucked in her lower lip. She seemed to be debating saying something.

"I'm fine now," Lillian said. "Thank you."

"Would you like to walk around upstairs a bit? I think a little exercise would be good for you."

"Maybe later. I'm very tired."

Kali nodded. "The man said that's normal. I'll let you sleep."

The man? What man? Lillian tensed, then relaxed. Her granddaughter probably meant the nurse at the hospital.

Kali went to the door. "Call down if you need anything. I won't leave the house without telling you."

Lillian listened to her granddaughter going down the stairs, more slowly this time, but still with a childlike bounce. She leaned back against the pillows. Her abdomen felt bloated, just like in the dream.

She couldn't get it out of her head. It was as real to her at this moment as it had been then.

St. Aubin, Jersey, late December of 1938. The cold, sterile examining room. The harsh disinfectant smell of carbolic acid. The doctor's office with its dark paneled walls and diplomas.

"I would estimate you're three months," the doctor said, folding his hands and resting them on the large mahogany desk.

Leli tried to concentrate on the black hairs on the backs of his hands, his clean, straight fingernails. Not on what he was saying.

"You probably conceived sometime in September." The doctor handed her a piece of paper. "Here's a prescription for something that might help with your nausea, Mrs. Troppe. But it's very important that you eat properly."

Mrs. Troppe? There must be some mistake. Then she remembered. Astrid Troppe was the name she had given for her appointment.

She left the doctor's office, fumbling with her headscarf as she tried to tie it beneath her chin. The strength had been sucked out of her and her knees shook. Despite the cold afternoon air, she felt like she was going to pass out. She leaned against a lamppost.

Impossible. She couldn't be pregnant.

She took a deep breath in, then let it out slowly. Deep breath in, slowly out.

How could she not have guessed it? But she'd been so worried about Mama and Papa that she thought her missed periods and nausea were due to the stress of waiting for news that didn't come.

A woman pushed a pram up the hill, against the wind. Her cheeks were full and rosy.

Leli looked back at the doctor's office in one of the two-story painted row houses. Her own boardinghouse was almost a mile away through winding, hilly roads. But there was no one there for her.

Mama, she thought, choking back tears. Mama, help me.

But her mama couldn't help her. Leli wasn't even sure Mama was still alive.

She started walking down the sloping street toward town. It had snowed the day before and the streets were covered with a dirty slush. She had only her cloth coat and leather pumps, which provided poor traction, and she knew she must look like a drunk as she wobbled along.

She'd go to the tea shop. Maybe that nice American, Harry, would be there. He had said he wanted to help her. But surely he hadn't meant with this. There was no one who could help her with this.

She tested the word out loud.

"Pregnant. I'm pregnant."

The bile rose in her gorge. There was no time to find a lavatory. She vomited in the street.

An old woman climbing the hill stopped. "Are you all right, dear?"

The kind words caught Leli by surprise. She blinked back tears and tried to smile, as she straightened back up. "Must be catching a bug. I'll be fine. Thank you."

The old woman studied her for a moment, then continued her slow trudge upward.

Alone. Leli was all alone. Her face had broken out in a sweat and she wiped her cheeks and forehead with her headscarf. She couldn't have this child. She wouldn't have this child.

She tottered down the street. Icy water seeped into her shoes, numbing her toes, making it difficult to walk. She stopped by the stoop of a small building and opened her purse. The tiny painting was still there. She took out a couple of folded lace handkerchiefs. Just like the one around the painting, her mother had given them to her. She slipped off a shoe, wrapped one handkerchief around her toes, then put the shoe back on.

She sensed a change in the air, like a sudden drop in the air pressure. She looked back up the street. It seemed that someone had been behind her, but now there was no one. At least no one she could see.

She took off her other shoe, wrapped her toes in the other handkerchief, then put the shoe back on. She felt a presence in the alley between two houses in the street just above her.

She tried to act naturally, but her heart was pounding.

Was someone following her, or was she imagining it?

Ever since arriving in Jersey, she had been conscious of everyone around her, always on the alert for anyone inordinately interested in her. But there had been no disturbing attention, and she had almost believed she was safe.

But what if he had found her?

She began walking slowly down the slope. A truck was parked in the street. She crossed in front of it, stopping when she was no longer visible to anyone behind her. Then she took a step back and looked up the street.

She caught only a flash. Dark overcoat, broad shoulders, black hat. But in that instant, she saw the light eyes, and she knew. He was here.

Leli took off down the street, slipping and sliding as she went. How could she possibly outrun him in her heels? But she had to try.

She darted into an alleyway. She pulled on the back door to one of the buildings. Locked. She kept going and tried the next door, then the next one.

He was probably just behind her, but she dared not stop to check.

She got to the next door and pulled. It opened. She went inside, locking it behind her. Then she ran through the hallway, down a flight of stairs, and came out on another street. She looked both ways. No sign of him.

But where could she go? If he was here on Jersey, he surely knew where she lived.

A taxi was coming up the street. She signaled to it. He braked, skidding on the slush, but able to stop a couple of feet from her.

She climbed in the back.

"Where to?" the driver asked.

Leli was breathing so hard, she could barely speak. "Just drive. Away from here. Quickly."

She slumped down in her seat and went through her purse. She had very little money. But she still had the painting.

She could no longer do this alone.

The taxi was heading up, away from town.

"Please take me to the Somerville Hotel," she said.

"Certainly, miss."

It was where Harry was staying. Now, if she could only persuade Harry to help her get away from here. Quickly. Before he found her. Because there was no doubt in Leli's mind that when he did, Graeber would surely kill her.

36

Javier couldn't get the granddaughter out of his mind. The grace with which she held her head on her slender neck, the startlingly blue eyes. Stunning. No, beyond stunning.

After first seeing her early this morning, Javier had gone back over his original research on Lillian Campbell. He wanted to kick himself for his sloppiness the first time through. It had taken him several hours to learn that Lillian Breitling had been born in London in 1916, moved to Vienna as a child, then returned to England around 1938 and worked as a secretary in an international bank. It was a perfect cover to explain her meeting the American banker, Harold Campbell, and then leaving with him on the *Normandie* out of Southampton. Records showed Lillian Breitling arrived in New York in January 1939, exactly when Javier's father had lost track of Ilse Strauss in the Channel Islands.

But of course, Lillian Breitling's story was exactly that—a story, a cover. Campbell with his connections must have arranged the false identity and the British passport. By the time Lillian Breitling married Harold Campbell in New York, Ilse Strauss aka Leli Lenz aka Astrid Troppe, had effectively disappeared.

Until today.

Javier had returned to her house, this time masquerading as a geriatric specialist. He waited for the granddaughter, then made his play. He was confident he'd succeeded in establishing a bond, or at the very least, that he had created an option for her. Someone to call in time of need—a concerned, knowledgeable health-care professional ready and able to help her and her grandmother.

He leaned back against the credenza, the vision of the granddaughter branded into his mind. *Für Elise* played in the background. There was still so much more he needed to learn.

He let his desk chair spring forward and clicked through the old documents. There it was. Lillian and Harry Campbell had one child—a daughter named Dorothy, born in June 1939.

Javier froze. June 1939. Was it possible? He did the math. Not just possible, but probable based on the timing of events. The date of this daughter's birth suggested that she had been conceived in September 1938. Vati had told Javier all about the sexual encounter. How could he and his father never have realized that there might have been a child?

Javier got up and paced in the narrow space in front of his desk, trying to absorb the import of his findings. So Leli/Ilse had to have been pregnant when she left Berlin. But no one had suspected that.

He sat back down at his desk and continued clicking. More on Dorothy. She married a John Sullivan in 1972. John died in '78 of leukemia, then Dorothy in a car crash in 1990.

Javier paused, took a breath, then continued. The Sullivans had had one child in 1977. Just the one. A girl named Kali.

There it was. A granddaughter. Most likely HIS granddaughter. But how could he establish this for certain? And then he remembered the painting. Dear God. The painting was the link that could tie everything together.

His granddaughter. A living link. The implications were staggering. "Oh Vati, Vati. If only you were alive to witness this." He swiveled his chair around and picked up the old book from the top of the credenza. *Mein Kampf.* How his father had treasured this!

But Javier had to get control of himself. Without the painting, he had nothing.

He tried to light another cigarette. It shook in his trembling fingers. The flame caught. He took a deep pull, let it out slowly. The music crescendoed around him.

Stay calm. Think. He needed that painting. First, he had to get the mouse out of her hole.

But how?

He went to the closet and took out the small trunk. His fingers were steadier now as he unlocked it. He had a plan. He took out the hat, the doilies, and the gold, heart-shaped locket with its broken chain.

Start small, he thought. Let her be uncertain. Everyone will think she's going crazy. Wear her down.

Then pounce.

He held out the doilies, the lace dangling from his fingers like spiderwebs.

He was ready.

37

Kali opened her sketchpad on the kitchen table. The light wasn't particularly good with the shrubs blocking the early afternoon sun, but the acoustics were such that she'd be able to hear Lillian calling if she needed something. She lifted her head and listened. It was quiet in the house except for the hum of a window air-conditioning unit.

Her grandmother was deteriorating rapidly—speaking in German, imagining things, becoming agitated and fearful, and sleeping too much. Although that man who'd come by earlier had mentioned such symptoms, Kali wondered if Lillian's behavior was more than just the aftermath of her stroke. It was almost as though she was trying to fight off devils from her past while she still had strength.

But what devils?

Kali had a sick feeling that she knew wasn't related to her pregnancy. It more resembled the sense of loss that had enveloped her after her mother had died. And Kali had a premonition of another death. Her grandmother? Her marriage? Something else?

She rested her hand on her abdomen. At a little over three months, the tiny baby inside her was just over two inches long, weighing half an ounce. She glanced at her phone. Seth still hadn't called. Lillian had mentioned she'd almost had an abortion. Why had she even considered it? Had her grandparents also had a major argument when Lillian was pregnant?

She glanced down at her sketchpad. It was open to the drawing that Neil had remarked on when they sat on the seawall in the vacant lot. When was that? Only a week ago?

Kali tore the page out of the pad. Neil said that it resembled a fetus, and of course, now that she studied it, she realized he was right.

Large head and torso, underdeveloped arms and legs. Was she externalizing her pregnancy to her drawings? No. Kali had been making cherubim that looked like this for many years. They'd become her trademark along with beautiful fairies with their many reaching arms.

But Kali couldn't really claim the fairies as her own. They were much like the fairy her mother had once painted on the inside of her closet door.

A memory was forming in her mind.

Sitting at the kitchen table, a crayon in her hand, scribbling on a piece of paper.

"Not like that, silly," her mother had said. "Hold it like this." She demonstrated with her own crayon.

Little Kali tried, but the crayon wobbled. She hit the table with her tiny hand. "I can't do it."

"Sure you can."

Her mother placed her hand over Kali's and held it tightly, guiding the crayon over the paper.

Kali could almost feel it now. She put one hand over her other and squeezed, trying to recreate her mother's touch.

Had her mother really taken her hand or was that a wishful memory? She couldn't remember any other time her mother had held her, hugged her. Would Kali be that way with her own child?

She looked down at the paper, at the image she hadn't been conscious of drawing. A beautiful fairy was fluttering her arms and wings as a cherub floated toward her. Two of the fairy's four arms reached forward, the tips of her fingers almost touching the cherub's golden curls.

No. Kali was different from her mother and grandmother. Her child would know her mother's touch, her mother's warmth, her mother's love. No matter what happened with Seth, Kali would always be there for her child.

There was a knock at the door. Kali closed her sketchpad and went quickly to the front foyer so the knocking wouldn't disturb her grandmother.

Through the peephole she could see Seth's parents standing under the portico, too close to the door for Kali to make out if Seth was with them.

She opened the door. It was just the two of them. Kali was surprised by the surge of anger she felt at them. But maybe she was just angry with their son.

"Hi, angel," Mitzi said, her wild auburn curls bobbing over much of her freckled face. "We were in the neighborhood and wanted to drop off a few things."

Mitzi was holding a cakebox tied with a pink ribbon, and Al had two brown shopping bags labeled EPICURE, a nearby, high-end grocery store. He was wearing a golf shirt and shorts and his white hair was helter-skelter, as though he'd spent the morning on the links.

"Come in," Kali said quietly.

"Are you sure we're not disturbing your grandmother?" Mitzi asked, lowering her voice to a stage whisper. Her gaze went past Kali, up the winding staircase. Kali realized that the Millers had never been inside her grandmother's house.

"I think she's sleeping, but it's fine."

They stepped inside and Kali closed the door after them, relieved that neither of her in-laws had tried to hug her.

"We were just having lunch at Epicure and thought you might have trouble getting out to shop." Mitzi adjusted the strap on her tank top and the gold charms on her bracelet clanked against her thin, corded arm. "We brought some Danish, a couple of stuffed Cornish hens for your grandmother, vegetarian chili for you, and a few other small items.

"Thank you. That's very thoughtful of you. I'll put them in the kitchen." Kali reached for one of the shopping bags.

"Oh, no," said her father-in-law. "You lead; I'll carry."

Mitzi glanced into the living room. "Hmmm. I didn't realize she had such a formal house."

She and Al followed Kali past the dining room, through the dim hallway, then into the kitchen. It seemed to Kali that Mitzi was taking in all the details. Kali wondered if her mother-in-law noticed the residual smell of smoke, not quite masking a musty odor, like from a leak that hadn't completely dried.

Al put the shopping bags down on the table, glancing at the sketchpad, pencils, and the sketch Kali had torn out.

Kali gathered up her things and put them on the étagère beside a stack of mail.

"I see you're getting a little time for your own work," Al said.

"A little."

Mitzi began unpacking the shopping bags.

"I can do that." Kali reached around her mother-in-law.

"No, no," Mitzi said. "I've got it." She opened the door to the refrigerator and put the large glass jar filled with chili on one of the almost empty shelves. "Looks like we got here just in time."

"I haven't had a chance to shop."

"Oh, angel. I wasn't blaming you. Of course you haven't. That's why we came."

Al cleared his throat and pushed his sparse white hair back over his bald pate. He and Mitzi exchanged a look.

"Oh, what the hell," Mitzi said, slamming the refrigerator door. "That's not the real reason. The food's a ploy. Not that we wouldn't have brought it anyway."

"Kali, honey," Al said. "We're worried."

So they were here about Seth.

"I remember when Mitzi and I were first married." Al sat down on a kitchen chair. It creaked beneath his weight. "I was doing my residency and not getting much sleep. Believe me, when you're physically exhausted, it's hard to be patient and understanding." He tugged on the pink ribbon and opened the cake box. "I came home from the hospital one night and—"

"Al, Kali isn't interested in our ancient problems."

"Not our problems, per se. I'm just making the point that arguments between husbands and wives are universal. Like I was telling one of my patients the other day—"

"She doesn't care about your patients, Al." Mitzi sat down opposite her husband. There was an expression of intense concentration on her face as she studied Kali.

Kali pressed her back against the kitchen sink. The shrubs blocking the window made it too dark. Maybe she should turn on the overhead light. The room had never felt so small when Kali, her grandfather, and Lillian used to have their meals in here.

Mitzi pursed her lips and tapped them with a manicured fingernail. "We know this is a difficult time for you and Seth."

"He's certainly not the easiest person in the world," Al said, taking a bite of Danish.

"There's nothing wrong with Seth." Mitzi gave her husband an irritated look. "He's under a lot of pressure from work."

"Did he ask you to come?" Kali asked.

"Seth's very upset about the argument you had last night," Mitzi said.

"No," Al said. "He doesn't know we're here. We thought we'd give you a little relief. Maybe watch your grandmother while you and Seth go out for dinner."

The air conditioner cranked lower. Kali heard a car pass by in the street. "Look," Kali said, "I appreciate what you're both doing, but Seth and I have to work things out in our own way."

"Kali," Mitzi said, her voice so sharp that Kali jumped, banging her hip against the protruding handle on the door beneath the sink.

"I'm going to talk to you like a mother, since you don't have your own to help you see some sense. You and my son have to stop acting like a couple of stubborn idiots."

"Mitzi," Al said, "calm down."

"Oh, be quiet, Al. She needs to hear this." Mitzi's charm bracelet clanked against the tabletop. "You and Seth are having a baby. Grow up and behave like parents."

Kali opened her mouth to speak, but nothing came out. *You're not my mother*, she wanted to say. *My mother would never talk to me like this.*

Al slid the chair back and stood up. "Come on, Mitzalah. It's not for us to mix in. They have to figure it out themselves."

Mitzi ran her fingers through her curls, her hair snagging on her engagement ring. She jerked it free. "This affects us, too, you know. That's our grandchild you're carrying."

"Wait, I'm sorry," Kali said, "but this isn't my fault. I have to take care of my grandmother. Seth needs to try to be more supportive. Why are you attacking me?"

Al shook his head. "Ahhh, Kali. We're not attacking you, honey. Far from it. But you're the one who can fix this. You're stronger than Seth. Remember, you were his first real girlfriend. He doesn't always know the right things to do or say."

"So why aren't you having this conversation with him? Tell him the right things to say and do."

Al shook his head. "Because—"

Mitzi stood up, the chair screeching against the linoleum. She crossed the small space in front of the sink, arms outstretched. She rested her hands on Kali's shoulders. Kali could smell coffee and mint on her breath and turned her face away.

"Oh, Kali, Kali. You're angry with me. Don't be. I feel I can talk to you honestly, like a daughter. We love you, angel, and we want you and Seth to be happy."

Kali's throat swelled up. "I know you mean well."

Mitzi squeezed Kali's shoulders and backed away. "Come on, Al. We're not helping."

Al took in a deep breath and slowly released it as he followed his wife out of the kitchen. "By the way, Kali," he said, "Seth told us the aide didn't work out, but I can recommend other agencies or facilities where I'm sure your grandmother would be comfortable."

"That's good to know." Kali walked them through the hallway to the front foyer.

"I just want to say one last thing." Al stopped and looked directly at Kali with his intense grayish-blue eyes. "Mitzi and I think you're a wonderful girl helping out your grandmother like this. But please, take it easy. And this is the physician speaking. You're pregnant, honey. Stress isn't good for the baby."

"I'll try to remember that." Kali opened the front door. "Thanks again for the food."

Mitzi leaned over to give Kali an air kiss. Al winked at her.

She watched the two of them get into their white Lexus. Mitzi's face was framed in the window. She nodded at Kali as the car backed out of the driveway.

Kali felt let down, like the time she'd come home from a party she'd been looking forward to, after discovering her new school friends had little interest in her. For the last year, she had really believed Seth's parents had accepted her as one of their own. So why did it now seem as though it was them against her?

Because she wasn't "one of their own."

The car got to the end of the street and turned. Kali started to close the door. There was a white, shirt-sized gift box at the foot of one of the columns. Had her in-laws dropped it by accident? But why wouldn't they have noticed it was missing when they unpacked their packages?

Perhaps Neil had left it.

Kali picked up the box, brought it inside, and set it down on the entranceway table next to the Leli Lenz films and the business card from the man who'd come by earlier.

She opened the lid. There were several layers of tissue paper, which she pushed aside. She lifted out two pieces of yellowed lace.

She had no idea what to make of them. They looked like the doilies that people used many years ago to protect the fabric arms of chairs.

38

"Are they gone?"

The voice at the top of the stairs startled Kali. She looked up. Her grandmother was leaning over the banister watching her.

"Yes. They've left." Kali put the lace back in the box and replaced the lid.

"What do you have there?"

"I'll bring it up." She held the box under her arm and climbed the stairs.

Lillian was still in her buttercup nightgown, barefoot, the walker just beside her.

"Have you been standing here long?" Kali asked.

"Since they got here." Her grandmother took in a long breath. Her hair was uncombed and, with the bruise on her forehead, she looked a bit like someone from a mental hospital. "What's wrong with a formal living room?"

"Nothing. Mitzi's never been here before. It was just an observation. Do you want to go back to bed?"

"I suppose." Lillian took a step toward her bedroom.

"Your walker. You don't want to fall again."

Her grandmother stopped. She looked around her, confused. "I keep forgetting."

"It's natural." Kali pushed the walker toward her. "You're not used to it."

Kali followed Lillian into the bedroom. Her grandmother lay down on top of the blanket, resting her head against the stacked-up pillows, then closing her eyes.

Her legs were as narrow as saplings. How different from the beautifully formed legs she'd had when she was Leli Lenz. Kali debated saying something about the films, but decided it best for her to wait. Her grandmother still seemed off balance.

"Your in-laws act like nice people," Lillian said, keeping her eyes closed.

Act? Strange choice of words, Kali thought as she sat down on the edge of the bed. She rested the gift box on her lap. "Well, I think they mean well."

Now that her in-laws had left and Kali had a few minutes of distance, she really believed that. Sure, Mitzi and Al were being protective of Seth, but he was their son. The bottom line was they sincerely wanted what was best for Seth and Kali and for their grandchild.

"They're not your friends, you know," Lillian said.

"Really? Why do you say that?"

"I could tell she was snooping around, examining everything. What did she think she'd find?"

"She was just curious. She probably hasn't seen many old houses like this one."

Lillian grunted. The muscles in her face relaxed, as though she was dozing off.

Kali looked around the room, at the faded blue drapes that matched the bedspread and dressing table ruffle, remembering how, as a child, she would occasionally sneak in here. The fireplace, just above the one in the living room, had probably never been used. Kali used to play in it, imagining that the shiny brass andirons were actually gates that would keep her safe. She noticed now that they had turned a dull brown.

"So you and that husband of yours are quarreling?" Lillian asked.

So Lillian wasn't asleep. "You heard the whole conversation?" Kali asked.

"Most of it." Her grandmother kept her eyes closed. "What was the argument about?"

She had to know it had been about her. "He doesn't like when I'm away from home," Kali said.

"This is your home."

Kali glanced up at the photo of her grandfather on the rosewood chiffonier. How she missed him, but even when he was here, it had never felt like home.

"So what are you planning to do about it?" Lillian asked, opening her eyes.

"Nothing for now."

"What does that mean? You'll do something later?"

"I don't know."

Her grandmother leaned forward. The loose skin hanging from her bony arm trembled ever so slightly. "I never liked him, you know."

"I know. You haven't made much of an effort to hide it."

"Why should I? It wouldn't change anything. He's too insecure. He hovers around you like he's afraid if he looks away, you'll fly off."

"I didn't realize you were watching him so closely."

"Of course I watch him. I watch everything." Lillian waggled her forefinger at Kali. "He worries too much about what other people think, especially his parents."

Kali raised and lowered the lid on the box on her lap. "Maybe."

"In a crisis, he'd drop you like a hot potato."

Kali's fingers tightened around the box. "I don't agree with you. Seth is still my husband. No matter what happens, this baby will always be a bond between us."

"Ha." Her grandmother's laugh was chilling. "You think so?"

"What's that supposed to mean?" Kali got up from the bed. "Seth may not always do what I want him to, but I can't imagine him not loving his own child."

Lillian stared at Kali with such intensity that Kali turned her eyes away.

"Well," Lillian said, resting back against the pillows, "I hope it never comes to that. But if it does, just remember you don't need him. You don't need any of them."

Kali couldn't believe the swing in her grandmother's moods. A few hours ago Lillian had been reminiscing about her own mother and daughter, singing a melody from her childhood. Now she seemed intent on being mean and hurtful. Well, Kali had had enough of her for one session. She started toward the door.

"Is that from Seth's parents?" Lillian asked just as Kali reached the door.

Kali was momentarily baffled, then realized Lillian was talking about the gift box she was holding.

"I think Neil dropped it off. He may have come across it while he was packing up his house."

"Why would he bring it here?"

"Maybe it's something you gave his mother and he's returning it."

"Gave his mother? I never gave her anything." Lillian propped herself up. "What is it? Show me."

Kali sighed and returned to the bed. She put the box down, took off the lid, then lifted out the two yellowed pieces of lace.

Lillian's hand went to her throat. "Impossible," she mumbled. "Impossible."

"What's wrong?"

Lillian blinked several times, then held out her hands to take the doilies. The gesture reminded Kali of the sketch she'd made earlier of the fairy reaching for the cherub.

But as soon as her grandmother's fingers touched the lace, she recoiled and pushed herself deeper into the pillows. She spoke, but Kali had to strain to hear her.

"Where, where did you get these?"

"The box was under the portico."

"Neil put it there?"

"I assumed so. Why? Do you recognize the doilies?"

"Get them away from me. Quickly, take them away."

Kali picked up the box and doilies and started to leave the room again.

"No, wait. Give them to me."

Kali shook her head in frustration, but she put the box back on the bed, within Lillian's reach.

Her grandmother lifted the doilies in the air, one in each hand, like tattered lace gloves. Then she brought them up to her face and began to sob.

Kali felt exasperated. Lillian needed help. But it was becoming clear to Kali that she didn't have the skill or temperament to handle her grandmother's volatile moods by herself.

She left the room and went down the stairs. When she got to the foyer, she picked up the business card on the entranceway table.

Javier Guzman. Maybe he could help, after all.

39

Lillian's hands were still trembling. Was it simply a coincidence? She'd been thinking so much about the old days—had even seen these doilies in her mind's eye—that she had to consider the possibility her fears were getting the better of her.

After her granddaughter left her bedroom, Lillian inspected each of the doilies. The lace was yellowed, but the pattern was the same. Could they have belonged to the people next door? But they were so much like the ones Lillian's mother had given her.

She remembered the day. How excited she'd been to be leaving for Berlin. Her hair was freshly bobbed and styled in curls around her face and she had a new, very cosmopolitan traveling suit with padded shoulders and a narrow skirt. Her suitcase was open on her bed when her mother came into the room, some things tucked under her arm.

"Here, Ilse," her mother said, holding out a small embroidered pillow and lace doilies. "Take these with you."

"The apartment is furnished," Ilse said. "I won't need them."

"Take them." Her mother pushed the pillow and lace into Ilse's hands. Her mother's nose was red, as though she'd been crying. "There will be days when you'll be happy to have something from home."

Ilse didn't want to upset her mother even more. She placed the pillow in the corner of her suitcase, glancing at the pink, blue, and yellow embroidered flowers. She recalled her mother embroidering them just the other evening, sitting near the fireplace with her hoop and needle.

Ilse felt the sting of tears. She was going away, leaving her parents behind. She didn't know when she'd see them again. Ilse bit down on her lip and folded the doilies before putting them into her suitcase. The lace was fine and white, just like the ones that covered the arms of the sofa in her parents' drawing room to keep the fabric from fraying.

Her mother turned away, head down, shoulders trembling.

"Oh, Mama, please don't cry." Ilse put her arms around her mother. "I'll be fine. I'll be grand."

Her mother looked at her, blue eyes rimmed in red, her blonde hair, streaked with gray, pulled back in a tight bun. "What if they find out who you really are?"

"All my papers are in order. Joseph has made certain of that."

Her mother made a throw-away gesture with her hand. "Your brother thinks he's smarter than everyone."

Ilse gave a small smile. "He is, Mama. Joseph knows what he's doing and he has important friends. He's already arranged for me to meet some people in the theater. I'm sure I'll get a job soon, even if it's just in the chorus."

"I don't understand." Her mother began crying again. "Why can't you just be happy here? Why do you want to go away and leave your family and everyone you know?"

Ilse rubbed her mother's back. "Dear Mama. I'll be with Joseph. He'll watch over me. And if things don't work out, I promise I'll come home."

Her mother wiped her nose with her handkerchief. "And take these, too." She pressed several lace-trimmed handkerchiefs into Ilse's hand. "So you'll never forget me." Her mother's embroidered initials were just barely visible in the corners—H.S. for Hannah Strauss. Then she kissed her daughter's forehead with such intensity that Ilse believed her mother was trying to brand her with her love.

Lillian ran her fingers over the doily. That afternoon, she had boarded a train for Berlin with Joseph and became Leli Lenz. It was 1935. That was the last time she'd seen her mother, although they communicated often through the postal box Joseph had arranged in Berlin.

And then in October of 1938, Leli had received a letter from her mother. Her mother's letters were always filled with general details of their daily lives. But this one was different.

> *Conditions worse. Many restrictions. Your father afraid to go*
> *to the university or associate with his friends and colleagues. No*
> *word from Joseph in months.*
> *Remain in Berlin. Tell no one your secret.*
> *Love, Mama*

It was overcast that afternoon, and she felt the first chill of winter in the heavy air as she walked down Leipzigerstrasse to meet Wulfie. He'd suggested a café on Potsdamer Platz. Leli held her umbrella with one hand; in her other was her purse with her mother's letter. Joseph had warned her to destroy any letters from home in case her apartment was searched for some reason. Leli had always done as her brother had instructed, but first she would read each letter over and over, until it was forever in her memory. Then she burned the paper.

The street was crowded. Everyone seemed to be in a hurry as they pressed around her. How she wished she could tell Wulfie her concerns about her parents, but her mother's warning was too strong.

She reached the end of Leipzigerstrasse and the street opened up to the full grandeur of Potsdamer Platz—the elaborate hotel façades on each corner, cars, trolleys and double-decker buses all passing around the traffic light tower on the elliptical island in the middle of the intersection. She saw people rushing toward Wertheim Department Store.

A couple of cold raindrops splattered on Leli's face. She dashed across the trolley tracks, watching out for speeding bicyclists and cars.

The café was on the corner of Potsdamerstrasse and Bellevuestrasse. Once through the heavy door, she was struck by the contrast from outside. The café was overheated and the smell of cigarette smoke and perfume made her feel vaguely nauseated. The low, painted ceiling, ornate chandeliers, and reverberating noise seemed to close in on her. Leli pulled off her gloves and unbuttoned her coat as she squeezed between tightly spaced tables filled with too many people toward the back of the room. Wulfie always sat in the shadows away from the crowd.

He was already at a table partially hidden by a column, from which he had a view of anyone entering the café. He rose to greet her. He was wearing a long, outdated coat.

"Leli, my dear." He kissed her hand.

"Wulfie." She sat down next to him, and rested her umbrella against the column. On the table was a bottle of white wine and two glasses.

Wulfie patted his goatee. There was perspiration on his brow.

For a moment, with his handkerchief in front of his mouth and chin, Leli experienced a disturbing recognition that she couldn't place. But then, he wiped his brow and whatever she had imagined seeing was gone.

"I hope it's not too uncomfortably warm in here for you," he said.

"I'll be fine." She put her gloves on the table and slipped off her coat. "It's a dreadful day, isn't it?"

"Sorry to drag you out in such weather."

"You know I always love to see you."

He poured the wine into her glass. "Liebfraumilch. Very refreshing. Have a little."

She took a sip. People at the nearby tables were laughing, having a good time. She gave Wulfie a small smile, but she was thinking about her parents. Were they able to enjoy a glass of wine at a café?

Wulfie seemed to be studying her, but a reflection in his glasses kept her from seeing his eyes.

"Is everything all right, my dear?"

"It's just the weather. It's made me bad tempered." She reached into her purse for her cigarette case, then remembered Wulfie didn't like her to smoke, so she snapped her purse closed.

"Some bad news from home?" he asked.

Had he seen the letter folded in her purse? "My mother wrote me."

He raised an eyebrow. "Yes?"

"I'm worried. My father—" She took another sip of wine, then put the glass down.

He rested his warm hand over hers. "Tell me, my dear. Perhaps I can help."

Tell no one your secret.

She wanted so much to trust him.

Tell no one your secret.

She bit down on her lower lip. "I'm sure it's nothing. My father's caught a cold, that's all. But when I can't see for myself how he is, I blow things up in my mind. Imagine the worst."

"Of course. That's natural." He patted her hand and leaned back against his chair. "I'm sure he'll be fine."

She took another sip of wine, wishing it would quell the nausea she was feeling. Too hot. Too smoky. The air stank of frying oil and kraut.

Several Wehrmacht soldiers came into the café, strutting and blustering with their usual arrogance. A group of customers near them paid their check and quickly left.

Leli realized she was tapping her fingertips against the tabletop. She balled up her hand and put it in her lap. "Wulfie?"

"What is it, my dear?"

She had to talk to someone. Trust someone. "Doesn't it make you angry?"

"What?"

She'd feel him out carefully. "What's happening in Austria."

"How do you mean?" He dabbed his brow with a handkerchief.

"You're Austrian. How can you stand what they're doing to us?"

"They?" He raised an eyebrow as he folded his handkerchief and put it back in his pocket. "Us?"

"The Nazis. The Anschluss. Doesn't it bother you to see our country taken over by them?"

"What bothers me, my dear Leli, are the French, the British, the Americans. What bothers me is what *they* have done to our German dignity." He sat straighter in his chair and pushed a lock of hair away from his damp forehead. "They've broken us into pieces, thinking that will destroy our spirit. But if we behave like scared dogs, they'll only keep kicking us."

"But the Nazis are no better. Look how they're taking away innocent people's rights."

"Innocent people? You mean those who try to control us through financial and media manipulation? Or the Communists who want to eradicate our culture and heritage?"

"I'm talking about innocent people, Wulfie. Ordinary people. People who have nothing to do with politics." She heard her voice quivering. "People who just want to live their lives, but aren't allowed to."

Altwulf took a deep breath. His face relaxed. He reached across the table and squeezed her hand. "Oh, my dear Leli, are there some people you're worried about? Jews perhaps?"

Tell no one. "No," she said.

"It's all right. Everyone knows a Jew. A respected doctor, an inspiring teacher."

"I said I don't know any Jews."

He nodded, his face thoughtful. "I suppose you're disturbed about some of the harsh methods you've heard are being used to help restore our country's dignity. I understand. I don't blame you for being worried. But many times extreme actions are necessary in order to swing the pendulum back where it belongs. We must eradicate the corruption we've grown accustomed to in order to make room for the pure."

"But it's not just the corrupt that are targeted. Ordinary people's lives are being ruined. Good people."

He shook his head. "You're naïve, Leli. Look how our society has deteriorated—how our cultural life has retrogressed over the last twenty years. Everywhere we find the presence of germs, which give rise to protuberant growths that must sooner or later bring about the ruin of our culture." His hand tightened around the grip of his walking stick. "We must find a way to bring that morbid process to a halt."

What germs? What protuberant growths? He was talking abstractions while her parents were hurting, while her brother was missing. The heat made her dizzy. She wanted to go home. Rest her head on the embroidered pillow her mother had given her, kiss the lace doilies. She missed her parents more than she ever would have believed possible.

"My dear Leli. It was a bad idea coming here on such an unpleasant day. Graeber has the car nearby. We'll give you a lift home."

"Thank you. I think that would be best." She put on her coat and gloves while Wulfie paid the check. He took her arm, guiding her between the tables of noisy, gesturing people and out of the café.

It was raining large cold drops when they got outside, but she was too dazed to open her umbrella. As much as she cared for Wulfie, his outburst frightened her. She would never be able to risk opening her heart to him and telling him the truth.

The raindrops hit her cheeks. They reminded her of her mother's tears when she kissed her goodbye.

40

Javier sat at the desk in the dim office, the blinds closed behind him. He could hear street traffic from his rented third-floor space—the air brakes of a truck, honking, the siren of an emergency vehicle. He never played his beautiful Beethoven in this office he'd established as a front, not allowing anything personal about himself to be observed by clients who came by.

He wondered when the granddaughter would call. The old woman should have opened the package by now. Would she react? He was almost certain she would. And then, he'd be able to take things up to the next level.

He had spent the last couple of hours learning what he could about the granddaughter. Kali Sullivan had graduated from Vassar College with a degree in art history and currently worked as a freelance illustrator of children's books. She married a Jew named Seth Miller a little over a year ago. But how involved was this husband with his wife and her grandmother? Javier didn't relish the prospect of a layer of interference with his plans, but Kali had made no mention of him earlier and didn't wear a wedding ring.

Javier took a puff on his cigarette as he thought about her full lips, the way her breasts rose and fell.

He checked his phone to be sure the ringtone was turned up. Not much more to do but wait.

He had dropped off the package a short while ago and had watched from the bushes as the young woman stooped over, picked up the box with the doilies, then took it inside. He'd lingered, hoping that she would reappear. But she hadn't.

He was desperate to see her again. To study her mannerisms and look for other similarities to her grandfather.

A granddaughter. Out of the blue, Javier's mission had the potential to move into an entirely new dimension. Of course, the painting would still be a symbol and an inspiration, but as an irrefutable link between generations, it would bring hope and vitality to the Movement.

Yes. The potential was truly mind-boggling.

His hand rested on the mouse and with his forefinger, he clicked on the website where at one time he'd been practically a god, until his views had been declared "too extreme," according to the milquetoast administrator who had taken away Javier's power in the online organization. At first, Javier had been incensed. Too extreme? How dare these false prophets fling accusations at him? They were the ones who had kidnapped and corrupted the original manifesto.

But he—he was Javier Guzman, the visionary who had been instrumental in bringing the historic organization's website into cutting-edge readiness, expanding its reach to almost a million devoted acolytes around the world. It was Javier who had redesigned the site to consolidate and administer the activity of dozens of forums, placing cookies and beacons with which to track participants and amass a database for future use.

But Javier had become persona non grata and only had access to view the website like any of the other plebeians.

Now, as he scanned the latest posts, he felt sadness rather than the fury he'd experienced when he was first excommunicated. Posts about Jennifer Lopez, dumb fashion trends, what's the best wireless router. Was this what the organization had come to? A shopping club? A fan magazine? No wonder the Movement was viewed with disgust and disdain.

Fortunately, Javier had the wherewithal and technical savvy to create his own website, Hailstorm, which was still covered by an "Under Construction" screen but ready to go live. He went to it now. Javier had retained for himself the database of hundreds of thousands of present-day followers of the corrupted neo-Nazism. But soon Javier would return them to the core values that had been behind one of the greatest crusades of all times. He would show them the goodness and purity of National Socialism and the German people so they could be proud and hold their heads high, just as his father should have been able to do.

Just as he hoped his own son would once he understood the truth.

Javier was startled by the ring of his cell phone.

He picked up in the midst of the first ring. "Javier Guzman."

"Dr. Guzman," a clear, youngish female voice said. "This is Lillian Campbell's granddaughter. You were at my grandmother's house earlier today."

Javier tried to keep his voice neutral, though his heart was beating wildly. "Of course. How can I help you?"

"You mentioned that you have some programs that might benefit stroke victims and I wanted to learn more about them."

"I see. Have you discussed my services with your grandmother?"

"No. Actually, she's doing rather poorly. Sleeping a lot, behaving oddly."

"Oddly how?"

"I'd have to say she's being a bit paranoid."

"Not unusual."

"Right. That's what you said earlier. Anyway, I wanted to see if there was some kind of therapy or program you'd recommend."

Stay cool, he told himself. Just stay cool. He checked his watch. It was a little after three. "I suggest you and I meet, Miss Campbell."

"That's fine. It's Kali."

"Given your grandmother's paranoia, Kali, I don't think I should come to her house. Perhaps it would be best for us to meet at my office."

"Okay, but I'll have to make arrangements for someone to watch her while I'm gone. When is it convenient for you?"

"I should be able to fit you in later this afternoon, perhaps around five."

"That would be great." She sounded relieved. "I just need to see if a neighbor can come by. Can I call you back?"

"Certainly."

He closed his phone. His heart was still pounding. Soon she'd be here. He'd have to play this carefully. There was still the painting to be located and the grandmother to be dealt with.

He thought about Vati sniffing the inner band of her hat, running his finger over the felt brim.

When I find her, I will kill her.

But Javier had very different plans for the granddaughter.

41

Kali found a parking spot in the municipal lot near the address Javier Guzman had given her. His office was in a low-rise office building between Lincoln Road and the new City Hall. She stepped into the cobalt-blue, mosaic-tiled lobby with curved glass-block walls. On another day, she might have stopped to admire the art deco style, but such things had lost importance for her.

It was just before five and people were coming out of the elevator. A well-dressed woman glanced at Kali's paint-spattered sneakers, faded denim leggings, and cotton blouse, puckered from last night's rainstorm. Kali looked a mess, but other than old sweat clothes, this was the only outfit she had at her grandmother's.

The elevator emptied out and Kali stepped in. She had told her grandmother she needed to go home to pick up some things and asked if it would be okay if Neil stayed with her. Kali was surprised when her grandmother readily agreed.

The elevator seemed to take forever to get to the third floor. It finally stopped and Kali got out and went down the musty-smelling hallway to the office number on Guzman's business card. The plaque beside the door said Golden Years Enhancement, PC. Specializing in the Social, Physical and Mental Well-being of the Senior Community. Javier Guzman's name was beneath, complete with its long tail of certifications. Kali tried the doorknob. Locked. They'd agreed to meet at around five; was he not here?

She knocked on the frosted-glass window on the upper half of the door and saw a shadow moving toward her from inside.

The door opened. Kali started at the sight of the large, bald man with pale green eyes. He had a teardrop-shaped discoloration in the iris of his right eye. Without his dark sunglasses, it took her a second to realize this was the man who'd been at her grandmother's house earlier.

"Please come in," Javier Guzman said. He wore a pressed long-sleeved cornflower-blue shirt tucked into white linen slacks and his shiny scalp gleamed as though freshly polished.

"Thank you for seeing me on such short notice, Dr. Guzman."

"My pleasure."

Kali stepped inside, reassured by the orderly arrangement of Danish-modern furniture in the reception area. Magazines were all put away on a wall rack and the glass coffee table had a small dish of hard candies and no fingerprints. She caught a few magazine titles— *AARP, Retirement Living, Golden Years Travel.* She liked the no-nonsense feel of the office and the considerate touches. She'd made the right decision to come here. Guzman seemed like the kind of person who could provide order to her grandmother.

"May I get you something to drink?" he asked. "Water? A soda?"

"I'm fine, thanks."

Kali followed Javier into a small, poorly lighted office and noticed the lingering smell of cigarette smoke. She controlled the impulse to gag. Secondhand smoke was almost as bad as smoking. She hoped Guzman wouldn't light up while she was here.

"Please have a seat." Guzman gestured toward one of the two cushioned chairs in front of the desk as he went around to his own executive leather chair. One wall contained framed degrees and certifications, the other, photos of Javier Guzman posing with different dignitaries, none of whom Kali recognized. The large blond wood desk had three computer screens, no papers, and a steel ashtray. The room was lit only by the light leaking in from outside through the closed vertical blinds.

Kali sat down and glanced up. There were overhead fluorescent fixtures set in old-fashioned acoustic tiles. Why didn't Guzman turn them on? Maybe he had some kind of eye condition. That would explain the sunglasses earlier.

Guzman leaned back in his chair. "I know you're eager to get back to your grandmother, so why don't you bring me up to speed?"

She was almost certain that he'd had a Spanish accent earlier, but now his deep voice sounded like a radio announcer's, devoid of any accent.

Where to begin? Kali rubbed one of her fingernails. "Well, as you know, my grandmother had a small stroke last Monday. She has some weakness on her left side, so she's limited in getting around and has been staying upstairs in her room. I think she's a bit frustrated."

"You mentioned you're her primary caregiver; who else is helping out?"

"There's just me."

"What about your parents?"

"They're both dead."

His forehead went up, the creases converging with his bald scalp like a walrus. "Brothers or sisters?"

"I'm an only child."

"I see." He sat forward in his chair and rested his folded hands on his desk. There was a yellow stain on the top digit of his middle finger. "That's quite a burden on your shoulders. Isn't there anyone who can provide a little relief? An aunt? An uncle?"

"No. There's no one. But that's not why I'm here, Dr. Guzman. I can manage. I'm worried about my grandmother."

"Yes. You said that on the phone. Tell me what's happening. You mentioned she's sleeping a great deal and exhibiting paranoia."

Kali nodded. She decided not to say anything about the violent attack on the aide last night. "I was hoping you'd have some suggestions on how to calm her down. She's so frightened about everything lately."

"You weren't concerned when we met this morning," Guzman said. "Did something happen after that?"

"It seems like anything and everything's a trigger. This afternoon, someone left a package with lace doilies at the house and when my grandmother saw them, she freaked out."

"Doilies?" Guzman's strange green eyes were fixed on Kali and his lip twitched. "Did she say what upset her about them?"

Kali shook her head. "But she keeps returning to her past. Talking about things that don't make sense to me."

"That's certainly not unusual."

"I understand that, but something's bothering her. I wish I could get her to open up to me more."

"It sounds like she is."

"Not really. She talks in riddles or in German."

His forehead went up again. "She speaks German?"

"She lived in Austria when she was young."

"Again, it's not unusual for the elderly to begin speaking their first language. But tell me, what do you know about her past that could be disturbing her?"

"Well, I just found out she used to be an actress, though I'm not sure why that would upset her, unless she lied to my grandfather about it. But he's been dead for ten years."

"What do you mean you just found out?"

"She never talks about it, but I discovered some films she was in as a young woman."

"Interesting. Have you talked to her about them?"

"I just saw them myself. At first I thought I should show them to her, that she'd be happy to see them. Then I became worried they'd only upset her more. It's one of the things I wanted to ask you about."

He looked thoughtful as he tapped his chin with his folded hands. "I think showing her the films would be a good thing. If, as you say, she has something in her past that's bothering her, this may be a way to draw her out of her shell."

Guzman opened the top desk drawer and took out a cigarette and a silver lighter. "Do you mind if I smoke?"

"Actually, I'd prefer if you didn't."

His lip jerked downward.

She felt herself flush. "I'm sorry, but I'm pregnant and second-hand smoke isn't good for my baby."

His gaze remained fixed on her; his distorted iris looked like a broken keyhole.

"Maybe I'd better leave," she said.

"No, no, please sit." The harsh expression evaporated and he put the cigarette and lighter back in the drawer. "My apologies. I never would have guessed you were pregnant."

"I'm only three months."

He gestured toward her hand. "You aren't wearing a wedding ring."

She put her right hand over her left. "I'm an artist. I work with paints and chemicals. They don't go well with jewelry."

"I see, so you don't go by Campbell any longer?"

"No, sorry. It's Miller now."

"And isn't Mr. Miller able to help out with your grandmother?"

Kali shook her head. "No. My husband's a lawyer. He's, well—"

"Sorry. I didn't mean to pry. I'm only interested in your grand-mother's well-being." He gave her a small smile. "And yours, of course. I can see how important it is to help your grandmother get back on track and relieve the strain on you."

"So I should show her the films? Is there anything else? Will you be coming to the house to talk to her?"

"Ordinarily, I would. But since you mention paranoia, I'm con-cerned she might have an adverse reaction to such a visit."

Kali nodded. "You're right. She's very suspicious of strangers."

"But that doesn't mean I can't treat her from afar. And I cer-tainly want to be sure you're getting the support you need." He opened the top drawer again, this time taking out his BlackBerry. "Why don't you and I arrange to meet again tomorrow at about this time? You can tell me about her reaction to the films."

"I think that will be okay."

"That's right. You have to make arrangements with your neigh-bor."

Kali nodded.

"No problem. I'll put it down on my schedule. If you can't make it, give me a call."

"You haven't mentioned your fees. How does that work?"

"I charge a hundred and fifty an hour, but we run it through Medicare. I'll coordinate with the hospital so we don't have to bother your grandmother with paperwork."

"Thank you. I appreciate that."

They both stood. Guzman took Kali's arm, like he was escorting an old person or an invalid. "Well then, Mrs. Miller," he said, stressing the 'Mrs.' "I very much look forward to seeing you tomorrow and hearing how everything worked out with your grandmother and those films."

"Thanks for your time."

"My pleasure." He pointed a finger at her abdomen like a pistol and clicked his tongue. "And do take good care of that little one."

42

The sky was darkening as Kali pulled into her grandmother's driveway.

How many hours are in a day? Certainly she had been through many more than twenty-four since driving through the storm to get to her grandmother the night before. It was now six thirty in the evening. Only eighteen hours had passed since she and Seth were making love and got interrupted by the aide's phone call. Eighteen hours since Kali's life had been interrupted.

She reached across to the passenger seat, picked up the small bag with the clothes she'd taken from her house, then used her key to get inside. She set her bundle of clothes down at the foot of the stairs and glanced in the living room. Neil wasn't there, so she went to the kitchen.

He was sitting at the table, a large book open in front of him.

"Hey," she said when he looked up.

He put his finger over his lips. "She's sleeping," he mouthed. He gestured toward the back door.

Kali followed him outside. It was still light enough to see, but only just. Above the canopy of the mahogany tree, the tops of royal palms were silhouetted against white clouds in a mercury-colored sky. The effect was surreal, but majestic.

Her foot kicked a plastic dish on the cracked patio stone and the smell of cat musk hit her. She glanced down. The food and water dishes were empty. No one had been feeding the stray cats since her grandmother almost burned her house down over a week ago. She couldn't believe she hadn't thought of it when she was here on Sunday.

"Just one sec, Neil." Kali picked up the plastic dishes and went back inside. She opened the bag of dry cat food on the étagère and poured some into one dish. Then she filled the other with water and went back outside. Her grandmother had always taken care of the cats, but Kali had kept her distance from the slinky, aloof creatures. Never quite "getting" them. Or maybe it was because they seemed so much like her grandmother.

Neil was sitting on one of the PVC chairs in the shadow of the mahogany tree. He'd brought the book he'd been reading in the kitchen and was flipping through pages, using the light from his cell phone. Kali put the food dishes down near the edge of the step, then went to join him.

A truck rattled by in the street. Kali lowered herself into the fabric frame of the chair, thinking about the cushions in the storage room. Maybe she should bring them down. She glanced up at the flowering crimson bougainvillea, which blocked the storage room window, then over at Neil. He seemed engrossed in his book.

Should she tell him about what happened so many years ago? But how could that possibly help anything? She leaned back in the uncomfortable chair, the pipe cutting into her back. "I don't see them anywhere. I hope they haven't starved to death."

"What's that?" Neil looked up from the book.

"The cats. No one's fed them and they're not around. I hope they haven't starved to death."

"Would that be a loss?"

"Neil!"

"Just kidding. Gizmo's been barking at something in the bushes when we go for a walk. I'm sure it's the cats, alive and well."

Kali nodded. "Thanks for watching my grandmother. Everything okay?"

"Mmm-hmm." He pushed his glasses up on his nose.

"What? Something happened?"

"Nothing bad. First tell me how your meeting went."

"Dr. Guzman thinks I should show her the films."

"Anything else?"

"He wants me to come by again tomorrow around five to let him know how she reacted. I hate to keep relying on you, but—"

"It's fine. I can stay with her again tomorrow."

"I really appreciate it."

"No problem." He put his arm across the book. "So did you go home?"

She nodded.

"And?"

"I packed up some clothes and stuff. Seth wasn't there."

"So no confrontations."

"No. No confrontations." She lifted up her braid. "And what have you been up to? You seem pretty engrossed in that book."

He held it up. It was worn. "It's an old history book. One of my dad's. He had a collection about the Third Reich."

"And you decided to read this particular book for some reason?"

"Actually, yes." He opened the book to a page. "Have you ever heard of *Kristallnacht*?"

"Wasn't that the night a group of Nazis went around smashing Jewish shops?" She had an unsettled feeling talking about this. Like last week at Seth's parents' house.

"You're close," Neil said. "It was an anti-Jewish pogrom triggered by the assassination of a German diplomat by a Jew. *Kristallnacht* is known in English as The Night of Broken Glass, but it wasn't actually an organized Nazi attack. In fact, let me read what the Propaganda Minister Joseph Goebbels said in a speech."

He opened his cell phone and held it over the page. "The Führer has decided that . . . demonstrations should not be prepared or organized by the party, but insofar as they erupt spontaneously, they are not to be hampered." He closed the book. "Actually the assassination is thought to be a pretext for the attacks. *Kristallnacht* was part of the broader racial policy of Nazi Germany including anti-Semitism and persecution of the Jews." He sounded like the college professor he was. "There was a great deal of destruction on *Kristallnacht*. It's believed that thousands of Jews were arrested and placed

in concentration camps, their homes and businesses ransacked, synagogues destroyed. Many historians view this night as the beginning
of Hitler's Final Solution, leading to the genocide of the Holocaust."

"Why are you reading about this?"

"I've been trying to figure out why your grandmother lit all of
those candles last week. They were *Yahrzeit* candles, usually lit in
memory of Jewish relatives."

Kali had already been down this road with Seth. Was Neil also
starting to believe her grandmother was some kind of anti-Semite?
"I know that. But what does her candle lighting have to do with
Kristallnacht?"

"Do you remember what date last Monday was?"

She shook her head. She was losing track of time. Last Monday
was when she'd had dinner with Seth's family. The night the conversation about her grandmother's past had turned awkward. Kali
had broken one of her mother-in-law's good crystal glasses, then gotten the phone call from the hospital.

"Today's Tuesday, November 17th, so last Monday, when your
grandmother lit the candles, was November 9th."

He announced it like it was some obvious revelation, but Kali
had no idea what he was getting at.

"November 9th," he said, again.

"Right. I got that. So?"

"November 9th, 1938 was *Kristallnacht*."

Kali felt a knife cut across her spine. "And you think my grandmother was somehow involved?" Her voice sounded clipped and
harsh to her own ears.

"No, Kali. Of course not. She was lighting candles, not burning
crosses."

"I don't understand what you're getting at."

"Okay." Neil held his hands up. "Let me back up. You were asking if anything happened earlier. And yes, something did. I went to
check on your grandmother and she wasn't in her room. I found her
in your old bedroom. She was in the rocking chair facing your
mother's graduation picture and she was singing."

"She was doing that earlier. I heard her."

"Did you recognize the song?"

Kali shook her head.

"I'll sing it for you."

"You know it?"

Neil smiled and began to sing in a low, clear voice.

> *Oyfn pripetshik brent a fayerl,*
> *Un inshtub iz heys . . .*

She recognized the wistful melody that her grandmother had been singing. "Do you know what it means?"

He nodded.

> *In the little hearth flickers a little flame,*
> *Warmth spreads through the house . . .*

"That's pretty," Kali said, "but I don't understand why you're so excited."

"My grandmother used to sing it."

"Your grandmother? She knew German?"

"Not German." Neil leaned closer to her. She could see his eyes shining behind his glasses. "Let me sing the rest of the verse."

> *Un der rebe lernt kleyne kinderlekh*
> *Dem alef-beys.*

"I'll translate it for you," he said.

> *And the rabbi teaches little children*
> *The Hebrew alphabet.*

Kali stared at him, perplexed.

"It's a Yiddish folk song, Kali. I think your grandmother was lighting all those candles in memory of those who died in the Holocaust."

"I don't understand."

He reached over and took Kali's hand. "I'm pretty sure your grandmother's Jewish."

Jewish? Not possible. That would mean Kali had been born Jewish. How could Lillian have known that and not said something when Kali went through the conversion process?

"I don't know, Neil. Why would she have hidden that?" Kali pulled her hand out of Neil's, got up, and went over to the mahogany. She leaned against its rough bark.

Neil followed her. "It's a lot to process."

"Jewish." She shook her head and pulled off a piece of bark—black and moldy. "There's so much I don't understand. About her. About me. All these revelations suddenly surfacing. It's turning me upside-down."

"But isn't this what you wanted? To find your past?"

"But why is it all so mysterious? Why couldn't my grandmother have told me she'd once been an actress? That she's Jewish, if, in fact, she is or was."

"I think plenty of people hid their Jewish identities during the Holocaust. Then when they got to the United States they saw no point in revealing the truth. After all, there was a time in Europe the Jews felt they were safe, then along came Hitler. Who knows? Maybe your grandmother feared another Hitler might come to power in America. Better to keep her secret hidden."

Kali took a deep breath. Damp, decaying vegetation filled her lungs. It was a primal smell, like Kali imagined existed when the earth was first forming.

"You really believe it's true?" she asked. "That she's Jewish?"

"It fits, doesn't it? The *Yahrzeit* candles, the Yiddish lullaby, the need to hide her true religion if she wanted to be an actress in Berlin in the 1930s."

It had grown darker. Tiny flashes of light from fireflies appeared against the dark shrubs and reminded Kali of Whistler's painting *Nocturne in Black and Gold.*

"You realize what that means about you, if it is true? If your grandmother is Jewish?"

It meant she had an identity, a history, a past. Not one that she'd converted into, but one that she was born into. She would no longer be an impostor, a wannabe. "It means," she said softly, "that I'm the real thing."

In the darkness, his eyes glittered like the fireflies. "You've always been the real thing, Kali."

Her heart began to race, and the blood that was pounding in her ears made it impossible to think. She studied his high forehead, mussed black hair, cleft chin, intense gray eyes hidden behind his glasses.

A white cat ran across the yard.

Kali stepped back. Whatever this was with Neil, it wasn't real.

She could hear the sound of crunching as the cat chomped down on the food.

Kali slid her braid between her fingers. "But this is just speculation. I need to know for certain."

"Then ask her."

"Right. She's been hiding all these secrets for something like seventy years; you think she'd tell me, just like that?"

"It sounds like she's ready for the truth to come out."

She pictured her grandmother rocking beneath the photo-portrait of Kali's mother, sharing her memories, humming a Yiddish lullaby. Such lovely words.

> In the little hearth flickers a little flame,
> Warmth spreads through the house.

Neil was right. Her grandmother wanted the warmth of the hearth. She wanted Kali to know the truth.

43

Lillian was certain she smelled paint. She sniffed the air, trying to pick up the source. It was her imagination. It had to be.

She rolled her walker across the rug on her bedroom floor, then out into the hallway. The smell was coming from Dorothy's room. She followed it, the scent becoming stronger as she approached the closet.

But that was impossible. She had painted over the picture weeks ago, just as she had done with the others; there couldn't still be an odor. Unless it had come back to haunt her.

She opened the closet door. All white. Nothing more. She ran her fingertips over the smooth surface. She could feel the outline of an image. It was pushing its way through the outer layer of paint.

She jerked her hand away, as though she'd received a jolt of electricity, and brought her fingertips to her lips.

Please God, let this nightmare end.

She collapsed in the rocking chair and let Dorothy's eyes accuse her in the darkness. Low, mumbled sounds were coming from the backyard and Lillian tensed, then relaxed. The voices were soothing. She closed her eyes and heard her mother's lullaby.

Leli felt different this evening, almost happy. For the last few hours, while she and Wulfie strolled along the Wannsee enjoying the cool days of autumn, she had even been able to laugh. Had pushed thoughts of her parents to the back of her mind.

She stopped at the edge of the lake, holding tight to Wulfie's arm. The sun was setting. The bare, delicate branches of the trees behind them, like filigree against a golden orange sky, were mirrored in the still water. A breathtaking double image.

"You're so beautiful today," Wulfie said, stepping back from her. "There's a radiance about you."

He glanced from her to the water. The orange was darkening to pomegranate. "Two of my lovely Leli."

She reached out her arms toward him. He took her hands.

"I must paint you. Now, tonight." He looked again at her reflection in the crimson water, then pulled her against him.

She buried her face in his woolen overcoat, feeling warm and safe.

Leli's neck, back, and arms were stiff and she wanted desperately to get up and walk around, but she dared not move.

Wulfie had arranged her on the sofa in his studio, draped in a white sheet, her curls loose on her shoulders. She had been posed like this for hours, but Wulfie seemed to have lost track of time as he worked on the tiny canvas.

He had taken off his jacket and rolled up his shirtsleeves, working with an intensity she'd never seen before in him. He hunched over the canvas dabbing paint here and there, his palette in one hand, sweat glistening on his brow.

The room was lit by several lamps, one directed on the canvas, another behind Leli, burning through her back.

So hot. So stiff. And the smell of oil and turpentine was making her lightheaded.

"Please, Wulfie, may I get up and stretch?"

He looked startled at the sound of her voice, as though he hadn't realized he was painting a living being.

He glanced at the painting, then over at her.

"*Ach, Du lieber*," he said in the softest voice. He put the palette and brush down. Tears rolled down his cheeks from behind his spectacles.

"Wulfie, are you all right?"

She jumped up to go to him, clasping the sheet around her.

He held up one hand to stop her; the other covered his eyes.

"What is it?" she asked. "What's wrong? My God, you're bleeding."

"It's nothing." He turned away from her as he stuck his finger into his mouth. "Please, just give me a moment." He took out a handkerchief and wiped his eyes.

She stood on the back side of the easel. The tiny painting rested on the ledge, barely extending beyond the wood support.

Wulfie blew his nose in the handkerchief, adjusted his glasses, and patted his goatee.

"Is everything okay?" she asked.

"Everything is perfect."

"May I look?"

He nodded, bringing his hand in front of his mouth to hide a shy smile.

Leli stepped around the easel. She felt a rush of heat as she looked at the postcard-size painting.

A woman with long golden curls covering her shoulders, the draped sheet looking very much like a flowing robe.

Leli let out a tiny gasp. How much the face resembled her own mother's!

The background was pomegranate red and a brightness radiated from behind the woman like a sharp ray of light. Like a halo.

But the rest of it. Leli leaned closer.

The painting wasn't complete, but she could make out the outline of something that went far beyond a simple portrait.

She felt confused, betrayed. Was this how he saw her?

She bit her lip, trying to hold back her tears. Thinking about her parents, whom she had forgotten about today.

And she began to cry.

Wulfie took her in his arms and patted her back. "There, there, my lovely Leli. I'm so glad you feel it too."

Lillian smelled paint. She opened her eyes. She sensed a time shift, then her mind went blank. Had someone been holding her? Comforting her?

She was in the rocking chair in Dorothy's room, sitting in the darkness. She heard light footsteps climbing the stairs. For an instant, she thought it was Dorothy home from school.

Then she remembered.

44

Kali picked up the bag of clothes she'd left in the front foyer, then went slowly up the stairs, suddenly unsure about what she was planning to do. When she left Neil a few minutes ago, Kali had been eager to show her grandmother the films, expecting that once she saw them she would explain the mystery behind her secret acting career and admit to being Jewish. But now, Kali was uneasy. Hadn't she felt like this hours before getting the news that her mother was dead, or was that something she'd imagined remembering in retrospect?

But what could her grandmother possibly reveal that would be so life altering? Kali had already converted to Judaism, so knowing she was born Jewish shouldn't make a difference to anyone. And yet— There was a fluttering in her chest. She had read and studied Jewish history and culture in her conversion classes. She knew about the Diaspora—how the Jewish people had been exiled and persecuted since the beginning of time. And then, in recent years, how they had suffered unbearably during the Holocaust. And Kali had felt sadness for them.

For them. Not for herself. Because, as much as she had learned about the Jews during her studies, she never really identified with them. It was like watching an unhappy movie and crying in empathy for the characters. But you were still on the outside, an observer. Now for the first time, Kali realized everything she had learned about "them" could very likely have been about her.

But if it was true that she was Jewish, why wasn't she experiencing a sense of elation about finally belonging? Why did she have this feeling of dread?

Kali reached the top of the stairs and stopped abruptly. The person standing in the doorway of her grandparents' bedroom was very different from the daunting presence Kali had been conditioned to expect since childhood. This tiny old woman was hunched over her walker, her short, white hair combed haphazardly, a bruise on her forehead. She was dressed in slacks and a stained white blouse with its buttons misaligned.

"So many hours to pick up a few things?" Lillian asked.

Kali glanced at the bundle in her own arms, remembering that she'd told her grandmother she was going home to get some clothes. That was almost three hours ago. "Sorry. I was talking to Neil. I thought you were still sleeping."

"I haven't slept at all."

"I'm sorry to hear that. Are you hungry?"

"Starving."

Kali considered the logistics of serving her grandmother dinner, then watching the films. The only VCR and TV were downstairs. "Would you like me to bring something up, or would you rather eat in the kitchen?"

Lillian's face brightened. "Kitchen." She pushed the walker to the stairwell with surprising speed, perhaps worried Kali would change her mind.

Kali threw the bag of clothes on her bed. She felt a flurry of palpitations. It'll be fine, she told herself. Everything will be fine.

Lillian held the banister with both hands and gingerly felt for the next step with her right foot as Kali stood on the stair below ready to block if her grandmother lost her balance. Kali glanced down the steep stairwell. Although Lillian was a small woman, if she fell on Kali, she could theoretically hurl them both down the stairs. Kali tightened her grip on the banister and braced herself. She wasn't going to put her child in jeopardy for anything.

Lillian settled her right foot one step down, then slowly brought the left foot beside it. The process took close to a minute.

"That's good. Take your time."

Her grandmother sucked in her lips, a determined expression on her face. Kali noticed she was holding the railing tightly with her right hand and barely holding on with her left, which had been weakened by the stroke. She took another step, pulling her left foot down next to the right with a satisfied grunt. "Who would believe I used to be a dancer?"

Of course, Kali thought, first a dancer, then an actress. That made sense.

Lillian went down the next few steps more quickly, then stopped to catch her breath. Kali marveled at her determination to get downstairs.

It was almost eight by the time Kali settled her grandmother at the kitchen table. "Mitzi brought Cornish hens and chili," Kali said, taking the food out of the refrigerator. "What would you prefer?"

"Just a piece of bread and cheese."

"You said you're starving."

"I am."

Kali dumped the chili in a saucepan to heat and put a piece of buttered bread with a slice of Swiss cheese on a plate in front of her grandmother.

Lillian ate it all in a few bites.

The kitchen filled with the smell of spices as the chili heated. Kali poured some into two bowls and set one in front of her grandmother with a spoon.

Lillian eyed it.

"You don't have to eat it," Kali said, sitting down across from her. She lifted a spoonful of chili to her mouth and blew on it.

"Doesn't chili have meat?" Lillian asked.

"This is vegetarian."

"You should eat a little meat. Especially with the baby coming. You don't want to get anemic."

"I'm taking multiple vitamins. And kidney beans are very nutritious."

"Still," Lillian said, putting her spoon into her own bowl. She sniffed the chili, then tasted it. "Meat's important. I don't understand why you have such an aversion to it."

"So did Mom."

"Your mother was no better than you. At least when she was growing up, I'd make her eat lamb chops and hamburgers."

Kali's mother had once told Kali about the forced meat feedings and how they sickened her. She'd spit the food out in her napkin, then throw the napkin away.

"What about when you were growing up, Lillian? What did your mother make for you?"

"Oh, my mother was the most wonderful cook." She closed her eyes for a moment, then opened them. "She made the most delicious chicken with onions fried in schmaltz."

"Schmaltz?"

"You know, chicken fat."

Chicken fat. Was that unique to Jewish cooking or could it also have been used in German recipes, Kali wondered? "What else did she cook?"

"Mashed potatoes with schmaltz. Sometimes she'd put in peas and carrots."

"Sounds delicious," Kali said, though the idea of chicken fat in potatoes turned her stomach. She took another bite of chili, then put her spoon down.

"It was delicious." Lillian was smiling at something only she could see.

Kali thought about the meal Mitzi had made the other night. It seemed like the quintessential Jewish dinner. "Did your mother make *kugel?*"

"*Kugel?* Of course. Potato *kugel, lochshen kugel* with noodles she made herself and the plumpest raisins."

Kugels were uniquely Jewish, weren't they? Or could they be a German food as well?

"And she baked like an angel," her grandmother continued. "The lightest, fluffiest cakes."

"Did she teach you how?"

"Of course. I was the only daughter."

Kali felt a thump of anticipation. "But you had brothers?"

"Just Joseph. You know."

Kali didn't know. This was the first mention of her grandmother's brother. "Was he older or younger?" Kali asked.

"Much older. Five years. And so handsome, all the girls would come around looking for him."

So Kali had had a great-uncle she'd never known about. It was unlikely that at ninety-eight he'd still be alive. "Did he ever marry?"

Lillian studied her chili.

Wrong direction, Kali thought. Her grandmother was clamming up.

"Tell me about your father," Kali said. "Was he also a handsome man?"

She didn't answer. Kali was afraid she'd hit another dead end.

Then her grandmother looked up. Her eyes were red rimmed. "My father had the kindest face. A gentle face. His students worshipped him."

A new revelation. "What did he teach?"

"Languages." Lillian held out her hand and counted off on her fingers. "He spoke German, Russian, French, Polish, English." She went back to her thumb. "Yiddish."

"Yiddish?"

Her grandmother pushed the bowl of chili away. "This is tasteless. How can you eat chili without meat?" She looked angry.

"How did he know Yiddish?"

"I told you. He was a linguist. He knew all the languages. Latin, Greek, many others. I'm still hungry. Is there any more bread and cheese?"

"Sure." Kali got up and brought her grandmother another slice of bread and cheese. It was possible her great-grandfather, being a linguist, knew Yiddish without being a Jew. The old films would hopefully shake the truth loose.

They finished eating without talking, the air conditioner humming.

"Would you like to watch TV?" Kali asked.

"We could do that."

"Or we could see a film Neil gave me." Kali wondered if her grandmother could pick up on the awkwardness in her voice.

"If you want." Lillian pulled herself up using the table, and reached for her walker.

Kali followed her into the TV room, waited until she was settled comfortably on the sofa, then pushed in the first Leli Lenz cassette.

"What movie is this?" Lillian asked.

"You'll see."

The tape came on, sputtering black-and-white. Kali fast forwarded to the first Leli Lenz scene, then she hit the play button.

She watched her grandmother's face as the young, pretty actress walked into the scene where two men were speaking German.

At first, Lillian looked baffled. Then the camera went in for a close up of Leli Lenz.

"My God," her grandmother whispered, her eyes wide as she stared at the screen.

Kali paused the film.

"That's you, isn't it?"

"Oh, my God, dear God." She grabbed Kali's arm and shook it. "Where did this come from?"

"From Neil. I told you. It's okay. I know you've been hiding your career as an actress, but there's no need to anymore."

"Why does Neil have this?"

There was a tightening in Kali's chest. Maybe she shouldn't have shown her grandmother the film. Maybe it was too much for her after her stroke.

Lillian's fingers dug into Kali's arm. "Why? Why does he have this?"

"We found an old cigarette card with Leli Lenz on it. She looks a bit like me, so I ordered the films she was in."

"You ordered the films?"

"Yes."

"So why does Neil have them?"

"I had them sent to his house." She didn't want to explain about keeping them away from Seth.

"To his address? Next door?"

"That's right. Why are you so upset?"

"He's looking for me. I'm sure he's looking for me."

"Who's looking for you?"

Lillian brought her hands to her head and pulled on her hair. "You have to go away. You have to hide."

"Hide from whom? Are you afraid someone will find out you're Jewish?"

Lillian's mouth was open, but she made only tiny simpering noises.

"It's okay. There's nothing to fear. I understand you hid your Jewish identity so you could be an actress, but that was many years ago. No one cares about that anymore."

Lillian shook her head. Tears were running down her wrinkled cheeks.

"It's true, isn't it?" Kali said. "We're Jewish, aren't we?"

Her grandmother nodded.

The fluttering in Kali's chest was back. "Please don't be upset, Lillian. You're not in danger. I'm not in danger. Everything's going to be fine."

45

Her bedroom was dark, the only light coming in from a streetlamp and occasional headlights from passing cars. Kali sat in the rocking chair in front of her mother's photo-portrait.

"It's okay, Mama," she said softly. "It's a good thing. We're part of something bigger than ourselves. We belong to a people, a race. Maybe Moses was our great-great-great-great-great grandfather. Or maybe we're descended from the prophetess Deborah and we're destined to lead our people to defeat the bad guys, just as she did."

In the dimness, she could make out the half smile on her mother's face. Had her mother known she was Jewish? Had she been aware of Lillian's secrets? About being an actress? A Jew? Would the truth have made any difference to her?

Would she still be alive today?

Her cell phone rang. Seth. Finally.

"Hi," she said. "I'm so glad you called."

"Kali?" His voice was muffled, as though he was crying.

She tensed against the chair. "What's wrong?"

"I'm so sorry."

"Where are you? What's happened?"

He didn't answer. She could hear traffic noise in the background.

"Seth. Tell me where you are."

"North Miami." He took in a gasping breath. "I never meant—"

"Listen to me." She checked the time. Almost eleven. "There's that diner that stays open late. It's right between us." She gave him the address. "I'll be there in fifteen minutes."

He was breathing hard.

"Seth. Do you hear me? Meet me there. Whatever's happened, we can figure it out."

She slipped on her sneakers, ran down the stairs, and went to check on her grandmother, who was asleep in the TV room. She debated calling Neil to come over, but she didn't want to keep leaning on him. Instead, she wrote a note and left it on the foyer table in case Lillian woke up. Kali hated leaving her, but she had no choice. This time, Seth really was the emergency.

The diner only had a few customers. Kali was hit by the smell of coffee and frying oil and felt a moment's revulsion, but it passed.

Seth was at a booth in the back, near a window. Kali slid across the sticky red leatherette seat opposite him. There was an untouched cup of coffee by his folded hands, and a napkin holder, sugar packets, and a creamer at the side of the table.

His white button-down shirt was badly wrinkled and he'd taken off his tie and jacket. He raised his bloodshot eyes to meet hers. "I'm so sorry."

She could feel the pain in his voice, but she tried to stay calm. "The best thing is for you to tell me what happened. Start at the beginning."

A tired-looking waitress came by and Kali ordered a cup of decaf tea that she probably wouldn't drink. "Anything else for you?" the waitress asked Seth.

"No thanks." His attention was focused on the tabletop jukebox. He began flipping through the song titles.

Kali took a deep breath, then another. "First of all, tell me. Is anyone injured?"

He met her eyes, then turned away.

"Oh, God, Seth. What have you done?"

He raised his hand. "No. Nothing like that. I haven't hurt anyone. Not physically, at least."

"Then please tell me what's happened. You're making me think the worst."

He ran his fingers through his hair in two rapid movements. "It's about me. Something I've known, but never wanted to admit."

The waitress put a cup of hot water, a spoon, and a teabag down in front of Kali. "Anything else?"

Kali shook her head and the waitress left.

"The other night," Seth said, "when you didn't come home, I went out."

"You said you met Jonathan from work. Was that a lie?"

"I never lie to you, Kali."

The tabletop surface was thousands of tiny dots. From a distance, it looked gray, but up close you could see the dots. Just like Seurat's pointillism.

"Then what happened?"

"Jonathan. Well, he's smart and funny. He knows how to get me to lighten up when I'm worried about a trial or when the partners are coming down on me." He started flipping through the song titles again.

"So? What, then? You called him when I didn't come home and hoped he'd make you feel better?"

"Kind of like that." He stopped on a song. "I figured just a couple of drinks."

"And something more happened?" Kali felt a wave of nausea. She'd met Jonathan a couple of times. A red-headed, elfin young man who worked as a paralegal. Cute, fun. Kali liked him.

"Nothing actually happened. Jonathan said things. And I didn't want to hear them. I didn't want to admit I liked hearing them."

"But you met him again?" Kali could hear the trembling in her voice. "And then something happened?"

"Tonight. We went out for a drink after work." He cleared his throat. "We went back to his place. It was the first time for me."

Did he really just say what she thought he said? The dots on the tabletop were blurring.

"But I realized this was what was missing in my life."

Something warm was running down Kali's cheeks.

"Please don't cry. That's the part I can't stand. I don't want to hurt you."

"You don't want to hurt me?" Her voice was too loud, but she couldn't turn down the volume. "What about us? What about our baby?"

"I don't know what to do. All the rules have changed. But how can I stay with you? I'm gay. I suppose I always knew it on some level, but I didn't want to accept it."

"But we're married. We're having a baby."

He was crying, as well. "You're my best friend."

"Then what are you doing?"

"Oh, Kali." He got up from the bench seat and crossed over to her side, sliding in next to her. He put his arms around her and held her tight. They rested their heads on each other's shoulders and cried. She could feel his wracking sobs against her chest. Or maybe they were her own.

"Kali, Kali," he mumbled over and over.

She felt hot, numb. She wanted to scream, *How could you do this to me? I never want to see you again.*

But there was another voice in her head. Louder. So much louder. It reverberated through her entire body and filled her with panic.

Mommy, Mommy, don't leave me.

No. She couldn't lose him. She was having a baby. She needed her husband. She needed her family.

She gently pulled away and wiped her cheeks with a paper napkin, trying to control the shaking all over. "I understand," she said. "These things can happen. It must have been terrible for you all these years, sensing that something was wrong."

He nodded, then reached for a napkin from the aluminum container and blew his nose in it.

"It's okay," she said. "I'm okay with it, really. We'll just go back to the way things were before."

"Oh, Kali."

"Please, stop saying that."

"We can't go back. It's over. I'm not the Seth you married."

"I don't care. We can fix this. We love each other."

He shook his head. A smear of clear mucus was on his cheek like an accidental brushstroke of glaze. "It's not enough."

"What? You're saying we don't love each other?"

"Not like a husband and wife should. We love each other like friends."

"That is enough. It's more than most people."

"It's never been right between us, Kali. You know that, don't you?"

"You're my husband. I'm pregnant with your child. With Bucephala."

He covered his eyes. "She'll always be my child, but I just don't see how you and I can keep living together."

"We've got to figure it out."

He slid away from her, got up from the seat, and crossed back to the other side of the booth.

"Please, Seth."

"We hardly ever touch, Kali. It's like we're brother and sister. I understood you had intimacy issues from your grandmother, but I didn't realize what was going on inside me until tonight."

Her stomach was roiling. This couldn't be happening.

She felt his hand over hers. He gave it a gentle squeeze against the tabletop. "I do love you, Kali. Even if it's like I'd love a sister. Whatever else I was feeling, I knew that. I think I believed if you were always keeping an eye on me, I'd be okay. But now—" He shook his head. "I can't fake it. Even if it hurts you and my parents, I can't lie about who I am."

Something icy and sharp pricked her heart. No. NO. She wasn't going to let him do this to her. After her mother died, she swore, never again would she allow anyone to hurt her like that.

Kali took in a shuddering breath and wiped her cheeks.

"I'm so sorry," he said.

But Kali no longer felt his pain.

"Say something, Kali."

What was there to say? Thank you for being honest and ruining our lives?

Truth and lies. Her grandmother had lied and Kali resented that. Now, Seth was telling the truth. It didn't feel any better.

"My grandmother's Jewish."

Seth looked back at her, confused.

"You and your parents were wrong. She's not a Nazi after all."

He opened his mouth, but nothing came out.

"I know." She felt cold and flat inside. "What does that have to do with anything? Probably nothing. She's Jewish and you're gay."

Kali slid out of the booth and stood up. "And I'm still me, I guess. Or maybe not."

And she left the restaurant without waiting to hear what he was about to say.

46

Javier stood in the muggy night air across from the decrepit white house. He had returned to his hiding place in the bushes around nine p.m. He ignored his stiff back and watched the occasional brightening of the street as a car went by, the winking of the street-lamp when the leaves of a nearby tree shifted in the breeze.

Kali's silver Volvo had been parked in the driveway since he'd arrived and several lights were on in the house. He could see silhouettes moving behind lace curtains. The windows in one of the upstairs bedrooms were open. He supposed that was Kali's room and hoped she would go to the window so he could catch a glimpse of her, but she didn't. Around ten thirty, someone turned off the lights, leaving the house dark except for the glow of the streetlamp.

Javier debated his next move. Drop it off now, or wait? Wait, he decided. The later it got, the less likely neighbors would be about.

He inhaled deeply, longing for a cigarette. He was overwhelmed by the revelations of the day. Since she had come by his office earlier today and disclosed that she was pregnant, everything had become sharply clear. It was as though a bolt of lightning had cracked through to the core of the earth and glowing magma was now rising from beneath to consume all that once was.

But wasn't that the way his father had always said it would be? That the world as we know it must be destroyed to make way for the pure?

Watching her in his office, noting the subtle mannerisms in the flick of her head, the flash of her blue eyes. Picking up cues—more than a coincidence—that she was an artist, just as He had been. Javier had been left with no doubt. She was His true granddaughter.

Sacred blood flowed through her veins, pounded in her unborn child's heart. If only he could harness her power.

Kali. It was as though she herself had risen from below. It couldn't have been an accident that her mother had chosen that name. Kali, the four-armed goddess of darkness, energy, and death. Unfortunately, having met the young woman, Javier sensed principled naïveté that would resist his influence, though he desperately hoped to turn those wary blue eyes into trusting ones for him. A shiver passed through him as he thought about her slender neck, the quiver of her mouth. Yes, first he would try to make her understand. Get her to love who she was and what she represented. But if he failed, there was still her child. A child he'd be able to nurture and shape from birth. This time he would prevent the rifts that had torn him from his father and his son.

His hand tightened around the small box in his pocket. The pain of unabsolved guilt washed over him afresh, no less intense than when it had first hit him over thirty years ago. Too late to right things with his father, Javier had come to the epiphany that changed his life.

It had been an ordinary, hazy, drunken day. Javier had been at a bar with some college friends having a few beers. They were talking politics and enjoying their congenial bitching about the insipid government. Then the conversation turned to Israel and "The Chosen People." The easiness evaporated, as least for Javier. He remembered feeling irked. "Chosen People?" Who the hell chose them? And then, one of the guys called some politician a Holocaust denier and cold outrage ran through Javier's blood. Who the hell were these ignoramuses to pass judgment over things they couldn't possibly know the truth about? As though erupting from a long dormant volcano, his father's words came back to him.

We live in darkness for now, despised by the ignorant masses, who don't know better. But one day, they will respect and revere us, just as they once did.

It felt like a pointed log had been rammed through his chest as

Javier realized the depth of the damage he had done. He had been no better than these devil-deluded boors, accusing and vilifying his own father.

Javier had let out a primal battle shriek and heaved the table up on its side. The sound of crashing pitchers and shattering glass filled the room.

Everyone stared at Javier in stunned silence.

"What the fuck?" he heard someone say as he left the bar, tears rolling down his cheeks.

Javier returned to Cincinnati the next day, desperate to find something, some way to make amends for the years he'd let his father down. The lawyer who handled the estate told Javier that his father's furniture had been sold, or otherwise disposed of, but he gave Javier contact information about a small trunk that had been left in storage for him. So his father had never given up hope on him!

Javier brought the trunk to his hotel room. With trembling hands, he carefully removed the photos, films, and collection of 78 rpm records. There were the papers, hat, doilies, and locket that had belonged to her. But there was also a book. A first edition of *Mein Kampf*. Written on the title page was: *An meinen treuen Graeber*. To my loyal Graeber. It was signed simply, *A.H.*

The damp night air clung to Javier's lungs. The streetlamp cast the shadow of the poinciana tree against the ivy-covered walls of the old house. Javier squeezed the small box in his pocket. Soon, very soon now, it would all come together.

He knew exactly what the locket would mean to her.

Around eleven p.m., Javier caught the distant ringing of a phone. The sound seemed to be coming from the room he believed was Kali's bedroom. He felt a surge of that strange energy again. A few minutes later, the lights in the upstairs room came on, then a minute later, the foyer light. The front door opened. He saw Kali leave the house, lock the door, and run to her car. She pulled the Volvo out of the driveway fast and jerkily, as though in a hurry to get somewhere.

Javier's pulse accelerated as he evaluated the situation. Ilse Strauss was alone. For Kali to have left without waiting for someone to come and watch the old woman meant two things. First, whatever had pulled Kali away from the house was some kind of emergency. Second, the granddaughter probably wasn't expecting to be away for long. That meant Javier didn't have much time.

He glanced over at the Rabins' house, just in case Kali had called her neighbor and he was on his way, but the lights remained off.

Javier waited a few minutes longer. Then he crossed the street.

47

She couldn't have been dreaming. Lillian hadn't slept in days. She'd been so worried about everything, how could she possibly sleep? First the doilies appeared out of nowhere. Then her granddaughter got ahold of the old films. And now Kali knew the truth about her Jewish heritage. Everything was coming up like bloated corpses rising to the surface of a lake. So Lillian had no time for sleeping.

And yet, she kept seeing the past. Reliving the pain of every moment.

Harry's room at the Somerville Hotel was cold, and Ilse kept her hands in the pockets of her cloth coat as she paced in front of the window. The sky had turned a slushy gray. Harry had been gone for hours. Could something have happened to him? What if Graeber had followed him? Or what if Graeber was here at the hotel, waiting for her?

Harry had warned her not to leave the room, but where was he?

She looked out at the ruins of a medieval fort in St. Aubin's Bay, able to make out the silhouettes and twinkling lights of the low houses in the jutting peninsula of St. Helier. It was low tide and the fishing boats lay in the dark sand like beached whales.

Ilse rubbed her abdomen and thought about her doctor visit this morning. A beached whale. Stranded, gasping for breath. Would she ever reach water again?

A key turned in the lock. Ilse brought her hand to her mouth, stifling a cry.

Harry opened the door, crinkling his brow beneath his wool cap. "I've startled you. I'm so sorry."

He closed and locked the door behind him. "Damn, it's cold in here. Let me turn up the heat." He fiddled with the knob on the radiator and the smell of burnt dust filled the room. "That's better." He pulled the drapes closed, turned on a lamp, then came toward her with a brown paper bag. "I've brought you some food."

"I can't eat." She pushed the bag aside. "Tell me. Any news about my parents?"

"Please, Astrid." He paused and shook his head. "Ilse." He'd been using her real name since she'd told him the truth. "You must eat something. For the baby's sake."

"I'm not—"

He held the bag out toward her. "Please, Ilse. Sit down and eat, and I'll tell you what I've found out."

She took a pastry from the bag and stuffed it into her mouth as she perched on the edge of the bed. "Tell me," she said, her words muffled.

"First, there's no question we have to get out of here before he finds you. I've made arrangements. The *Normandie* is leaving from Southampton the day after tomorrow. There's a cabin reserved for us. I've been assured that your new identification papers will be ready by then. You will become Lillian Breitling with a British passport. My international banking contacts are fortunately well connected. And you won't have to worry. Anyone tracking Astrid Troppe or Ilse Strauss will lose the trail."

"But what about my parents? I can't leave until I know they're safe."

He sat down beside her on the bed, opened his overcoat, then loosened the plaid muffler around his neck. He stared at the faded carpet.

She grabbed his arm. "Have you found out something about them?"

He ran his tongue over his lips. "There's nothing you can do for them here, Ilse."

"What do you mean? What are you saying?"

"They're being held in a camp."

"I know; I told you that. They were picked up on November 9th and taken to some place called Dachau. But many of the Jews who were taken away that night have been released."

He shook his head. "It's different for your parents. They're being held as political prisoners in connection with your brother, Joseph, who's a known agitator."

"No. That's wrong. They were picked up because they're Jews. Because of me."

She began to sob. Harry held her against him and patted her back. His overcoat smelled like cigar smoke and damp wool. "I'll take you away from here. We'll figure it out in the States."

"Don't you see?" Her voice quivered. "It's all because of me. *Kristallnacht*, the destruction of the synagogues and Jewish shops, the roundup of the Jews. My parents."

"No, silly girl." He stroked her hair. "You had nothing to do with that. Some young, crazed Jewish boy shot a German diplomat. That's what triggered *Kristallnacht*. Nothing you did."

"You don't understand." She could hardly get the words out for the lump in her throat. "I did it. It was my fault. And now my parents are suffering for it, and so many others."

Lillian wiped the tears from her cheeks. Her fault. And she never saw her parents again.

She brought the blanket more tightly around her. She was in the TV room, on the uncomfortable sofa, not her own bed. And she was cold. So cold. She wished Harry were here to turn up the heat, to stroke her hair.

Someone was knocking on the front door. Who could that be? The Rabin boy at this hour? She checked the clock on the end table. A little after eleven.

Lillian listened for her granddaughter's footsteps. Nothing. She was probably sound asleep.

The knock came again, louder, urgent.

Lillian put her feet over the side of the sofa. Surely Kali would hear the noise and see who was banging on the door.

The knock again. Then again. It must be some emergency. Maybe Kali had left the house. What if it was the police?

Dear God.

Lillian got up and started walking. She staggered and fell back onto the sofa. Walker. She needed her walker.

Her hands found it. She pushed her way through the pocket door, across the living room.

The banging had stopped, but Lillian still heard the reverberation from her heart.

Kali. Please God, let Kali be safe.

In the foyer, she looked up the stairwell, hoping to see her granddaughter emerging sleepily from her bedroom.

"Kali," Lillian shouted.

No answer.

Lillian noticed a note on the foyer table. *Had to meet Seth. Back soon. Call if you need me.*

Kali's handwriting was scribbled, as though she was upset. She had signed the note and left her cell phone number. So she was out driving around. Upset. Like Dorothy had been.

Dear God. Don't let anything happen to her.

Lillian unlocked the front door and pulled it open, gasping for breath, looking around for the police officers. That's who had come to tell her about Dorothy.

No one was there.

She stepped onto the portico. "Who's there?"

No answer. The night was still and dark.

Her bare foot brushed against a small white box on the cracked coquina tile. Using the column for balance, she bent over and picked it up.

She took off the lid. Her heart was pounding, too hard, too fast.

There was a layer of tissue paper. She reached beneath it and lifted out a thin, broken chain. Hanging from it was a gold, heart-shaped locket.

She slid her fingernail into the seam and popped open the heart. Her mother and father stared up at her from their faded photos. Then she crumpled.

48

Kali was confused by what she saw as she drove toward her grand-mother's house. The front door was wide open. Beneath the portico, a low shadow lay against one of the columns.

Her grandmother?

Kali pulled the car into the driveway, turned off the ignition, jumped out of the car, slamming the door behind her, and ran across the front yard.

"Lillian? Are you okay? Lillian?"

Her grandmother was emitting a low, deep moan, as though someone dear to her had died.

Kali wrapped her arms around her frail body and helped her up. Lillian, wearing only a light nightgown, trembled against Kali. How unsubstantial she felt—thin, sharp bones covered with a layer of gos-samer skin.

"Everything's okay," Kali soothed. "We'll go inside and I'll make you some hot tea."

Her grandmother kept moaning, over and over, the same pa-thetic, toneless sound.

Kali pried her grandmother's arms from the column, and noticed she was clenching something in her hand. Kali could make out the end of a delicate gold chain. There was a small white box lying on the coquina step, but it appeared to be empty.

"Here we go. Almost inside." Kali led her grandmother into the foyer, then closed and locked the front door. The note she'd left on the foyer table was on the marble floor, suggesting that her grand-mother had read it. Why hadn't Lillian called if she was frightened?

Lillian's walker was next to the door, but Kali continued sup-porting her down the hallway and into the kitchen. She settled her grandmother on one of the chairs at the kitchen table, and went to get a blanket from the TV room. Everything in the house appeared much like Kali had left it less than an hour ago.

She wrapped the blanket around her grandmother's shoulders, put up water for tea, then sat down across from her grandmother.

The old woman was still whimpering softly, but she'd stopped making that horrible moaning sound.

"I'm sorry I left you, but it was an emergency."

Her grandmother didn't respond. No concern or curiosity about why Kali had left.

"Did you have a bad dream?"

Her grandmother shook her head. She brought her clenched fist in front of her chest and grasped it with her other hand. The end of the gold chain dangled out. Kali noticed it was broken.

Kali leaned back in her chair, drained. All she had wanted to do after leaving Seth at the diner was climb into her own bed and lie in the darkness. She still couldn't fully process the implications of what Seth had told her. All she knew was that her marriage and her life as she'd known it were over. How could she cope with her grandmother's terrors right now?

The kettle screamed. Kali got up, fixed two cups of tea with honey, and put them down on the kitchen table.

"Drink a little tea," she said as she sat back down. "You're shivering."

Her grandmother slowly unclasped her hands from her chest and set something down on the table. A gold heart-shaped locket.

Lillian picked up the cup with trembling hands and took a sip. Her deep-set blue eyes looked haunted and her high cheekbones practically pushed through her iridescent skin.

"Pretty locket. Where did it come from?"

Lillian set the cup back down on the table. She picked up the locket and brought it against her chest.

Kali was tired. So tired. She needed to think about her baby. What she was going to do without Seth. She didn't have the energy for this.

"He left it," her grandmother said.

Kali looked up. "The locket? Who left it?"

Lillian slipped her fingernail into the heart. It popped open. She held it out for Kali.

The photos were faded, but she knew instantly whom she was looking at. The gentle-looking young man, the pretty woman with high cheekbones and a smile much like the one on Kali's mother's face in the graduation portrait. "Your parents. You told me you didn't have any pictures of them. How lovely that you found this."

Her grandmother shook her head.

"What?"

"My fault," her grandmother said.

"What's your fault?"

"I told Harry. I knew as soon as I heard about that terrible night, it was because of me."

"What night?"

"They went around like crazy animals. Smashing, breaking, destroying what they could of the Jews. Everyone said it was because of the Jewish boy who shot a German diplomat, but I knew the truth the moment I heard what had happened."

Kali leaned forward across the table. The details matched what Neil had told her about *Kristallnacht*. "What truth, Lillian?"

Her grandmother raised her face. Tears were streaming down her cheeks. "He was so angry. So angry."

"Grandpa was angry with you?"

Lillian shook her head. She turned her gaze down on the dark tea in her cup. "Not Harry. The devil."

The devil?

"I knew he would come after me," Lillian said. "But I didn't realize. Never in a million years could I have realized that he would take it out on them."

"On who?"

Lillian squeezed her eyes shut as though she was experiencing an unbearable pain. "On all of them." Her voice was so soft Kali could barely hear her. "They rounded up the Jews. Took them away. Most of them, they released shortly after—at least for a while." She picked up the locket and studied the faded photos. "But not Mama and Papa. That's when I knew for certain, it was because of me."

Her grandmother believed she was responsible for *Kristallnacht*? "Is that why you lit the *Yahrzeit* candles last week?"

Her nod was almost imperceptible.

So Neil was right. For some reason, her grandmother was carrying guilt over *Kristallnacht*.

"And now he's found me."

"Who found you?"

"He's playing with me. Letting me know he knows. Trying to terrify me."

"Who is?"

"Graeber."

"Who's Graeber?"

Lillian's hand closed over the heart.

"The one who wants to destroy us."

49

"I'm concerned that she's completely lost touch with reality," the young woman said.

Javier studied her as she sat on the other side of his desk in the dim office. The granddaughter. Her hands were clenched in her lap, but he admired the slope of her neck, the gleam of her golden hair, the intensity of her blue eyes.

"She made me close the windows and check all the doors to be sure they were locked. She believes someone is after us."

"Us?" Javier raised an eyebrow.

"Yes. That's the problem. Her paranoia isn't just about herself; my grandmother believes someone's out to hurt me and my baby. At least, that was what she was ranting about last night."

"I see." Javier leaned back in his chair. His fingers thrummed against the desktop. After receiving the phone call from Kali, begging to see him this morning rather than waiting for their afternoon appointment, Javier had been in a state of frenzied anticipation. He was very close, but he had to continue his calm, concerned act.

"I'm worried," she said.

"Of course you are. But why don't we take a step back, shall we? I'd like to have a complete understanding of what's triggering your grandmother's behavior before I presume to make any recommendations."

Kali took in a deep breath and nodded. He noted that she was much more wound up than yesterday. He didn't want to take a chance that something might happen to the child.

"First, tell me," Javier said. "How are you holding up?"

"Me?"

"Yes, you. You told me you're pregnant. How is all this stress affecting you?"

Her hand went directly to her abdomen. "I'm okay."

"Because, we don't want to put the little one at risk, do we?"

She shook her head and looked down at the oversized satchel in her lap. "I appreciate your concern."

"That's one reason we need to find a solution to your grandmother's situation, and quickly."

She pushed a strand of pale blonde hair behind one of her perfectly shaped ears. Her lips were like a frightened child's—red and full and puckered ever so slightly.

"Let's see where we are." Javier sat forward and folded his hands on the desk blotter. It was fortunate the desk was between them and she couldn't see his physical reaction to her. "When you were here yesterday afternoon, you mentioned the old films your grandmother had been in. Did you have a chance to show them to her?"

"Yes."

"And?"

"She became very agitated, asking where I got them." Kali played with the strap on her satchel. "I told her I was pretty sure I understood why she had hidden her past from everyone."

"Yesterday you said you believed she'd lied to your grandfather about being an actress and was simply perpetuating the lie."

"Yes, but there's more to it." Kali looked over at the closed blinds. She had long, thick eyelashes. "My grandmother's Jewish, but she never told anyone."

Javier's heart took a bounce. How much else did she know about her grandmother's past? "You discovered that since yesterday?"

Kali nodded. "My grandmother keeps finding objects that remind her of her past. First, there were the lace doilies I told you about, then last night, she claimed someone left a locket on the doorstep."

"A locket?"

"Yes. A gold locket with photos of her parents. I'd never seen it before, so she must have lost it or had it hidden somewhere."

"So she hides things?"

"I suppose, though I've searched the house and I haven't found much."

Javier sat up straighter. "You've searched your grandmother's house?"

Kali blushed. "She's just always been so secretive about the past. I was looking for anything about my roots, my family."

"No need to apologize. It's very gratifying to go through old pictures and see what our ancestors looked like. How much we resemble them." He smiled.

She glanced away. "I didn't find any pictures. I never knew anything about my past or my ancestors until I saw my grandmother's old films, and then the locket with her parents' photos."

"I see."

"But apparently my grandmother has some hidden stash. I think she planted the locket and maybe the doilies, and then acted surprised when she found them."

"Each discovery gives her a nudge to talk about her past," Javier said. "She clearly wants the truth to come out."

"I thought so, but I'm not sure anymore. She's terrified. My neighbor's at the house watching her, but my grandmother insisted that he stay in the same room with her and bring his dog."

"His dog?"

"I guess as protection against this threat she's imagined."

The shrill sound of brakes from a passing bus pierced the office.

"Tell me more about the locket," Javier said.

"When I came home last night, she was outside the house, clinging to one of the columns, making these awful moaning sounds."

Exactly as Javier observed from his hiding place behind the hedges.

"I brought her inside, and she told me someone had left the locket, hoping to frighten her."

"What did your neighbor say happened?"

"He wasn't there."

Javier scrunched up his brow and acted perplexed. He'd been wondering why Kali had left in such a hurry last night. He needed to understand all the players and exactly what was going on in Kali's life before he proceeded. "You left your grandmother alone in the house?"

"It was an emergency."

Javier waited. The sound of honking horns from the street below filled the room.

"My husband," she said finally.

Again, Javier raised an eyebrow. "Is everything all right?"

Kali twisted the strap of the satchel around her finger and looked down. Her nose reddened, as though she was about to cry.

"I don't mean to pry. But as I told you the other day, I'm just as concerned about your well-being as your grandmother's."

Her eyes watered. She covered them and turned her face so he couldn't read it. In profile, she had the lovely grace of Leli Lenz in the films. He watched her full breasts rise and fall as she took several deep breaths.

This was going to be a pleasure, he thought. Once the grandmother was disposed of, he would take the granddaughter away somewhere, and then—

"I'm sorry," she said, taking her hand away from her face and turning to look at him. Her eyes were red rimmed, but she'd composed herself.

"No need to apologize. This is a stressful, emotional time."

"My husband wants out of our marriage." She said it in a surprisingly strong voice.

Javier felt his lower lip twitch. He brought his fingers up, as though stroking his cheek thoughtfully. "I'm sorry to hear that."

She nodded and pulled on a strand of flaxen hair. He watched her throat expand and contract as she swallowed.

"You have a lot on your shoulders. I'm glad you've come to me, Kali. At least I can be a sounding board and try to help you deal with your grandmother's situation."

"Thank you."

And she took in another deep breath, causing her beautiful breasts to tremble as she exhaled.

50

Kali got out of her car and stood outside her grandmother's house, not quite ready to go inside to deal with her. She felt raw inside and out, as though her lungs, heart, and skin had all been scorched in a raging fire. She didn't want to touch anything, or even breathe. Every movement brought pain.

She slowly took in a breath of cool, fragrant air and realized it was a gorgeous day. How was that possible? She looked up at the cloudless blue sky. The brightness of the sun sliced through her eyes. She squeezed them shut. Pain. Everything brought pain.

She heard the front door open and turned to see Neil leaving the house with Gizmo. The dog pulled its leash out of Neil's hand and ran to greet Kali, spinning around and panting, then looking up at her with his one eye. Kali leaned over and petted him, surprised that instead of hurting her hand, the soft fur soothed it.

The raw pain was all in her head.

"So how'd it go?" Neil asked, retrieving Gizmo's leash from the grass.

"Okay, I guess." Kali straightened back up.

Neil didn't press her, for which she was grateful. He was wearing a wrinkled T-shirt. Probably the one he'd slept in. She could tell she'd awakened him when she called earlier to ask if he'd watch her grandmother while she went to talk to Dr. Guzman. She'd told him about the gold locket, but nothing more.

"How's Lillian doing?" Kali asked.

"She wanted to go to her bedroom, so I carried her up the stairs and settled her in bed."

"Great. She'll probably tell me she'd prefer being back down in the TV room."

"I can carry her back down, if you'd like me to." He grinned with his even white teeth. Then he reached out and took something out of her hair. She inadvertently flinched.

He held out a red flower from the poinciana tree. "You look tired."

"I am."

"So take a nap. You're wearing yourself out."

"That's what Dr. Guzman said. He gave me a mild sedative."

"Really? But you're pregnant."

"Not for me. For Lillian. He figures if I can get her to sleep, I'll be able to take a break."

"Not a bad idea. Good luck getting her to take it, though."

"Isn't that the truth."

"If you'd like, I can sit on her and hold her mouth open while you shove the pill down her throat. Sort of like I do with Gizmo."

She smiled.

"Good. First smile I've seen on you today."

"Actually, Dr. Guzman gave me a sample in liquid form. She's not supposed to be able to taste the sedative if I mix it in hot choco-late or something."

"Try chocolate mousse, but watch out for a chalky under-taste."

Kali smiled again. They always used to quote the line from *Rose-mary's Baby* when they were kids.

"Thanks for watching her."

"No problem. Get some rest. And if you want to talk, give me a call."

She took a step toward the house, then hesitated. She hadn't told Neil anything about her meeting with Seth last night—that her marriage was over. She was afraid that he'd try to comfort her and that she'd let him. But he looked so sturdy and strong standing be-side the columned portico, his jaw set like he'd take anyone's punch for her.

"What is it?" he asked.

"I need—" The words caught in her throat. She tried again. "I need—" She shook her head. She couldn't do this now.

Neil leaned toward her, his gray eyes wide behind his glasses. "It's okay, Kali. I won't ask if you're all right, because I know you're not. Whenever you're ready, I'm here for you."

Kali nodded thanks, then went inside.

"Who's there?" her grandmother called from upstairs, her voice shrill with panic.

Tired. Kali was so tired.

"It's just me," Kali called back, locking the door behind her. "I'll be right up."

Then she went into the kitchen to fix her grandmother some hot chocolate with the sedative Dr. Guzman had given her.

51

After Kali had left his office this morning, Javier changed into a uniform stolen from a local cable company, put on a baseball cap, dark
sunglasses, and a fake beard, and drove to the old woman's house.
He parked his car a block away and walked down the cracked, tree-
lined sidewalk wearing an official-looking tool belt.

He needed to have a look around the property in daylight and
thought his chances pretty good that Kali wouldn't be out and about.
Given how exhausted she looked in his office, he was optimistic that
she'd be napping along with her grandmother, who was hopefully
doped up on the sedative he'd supplied to Kali.

Javier had considered passing along a stronger drug that would
likely have put the grandmother into a sleep she'd never wake up
from, but he didn't want her death to look suspicious and possibly
point back to him. The mild sedative would be sufficient to knock
the old woman out for a few hours so she wouldn't be listening for
noises and making a fuss if she happened to hear him.

He carefully opened the rusted gate that led to the backyard and
was hit by the stench of feral cats and decaying vegetation. The yard
was overgrown. A thick ladder of purplish-red bougainvillea grew
up the back of the house blocking the first-story windows, probably
of the kitchen, judging from its location. That was good. If Kali or
the old woman were in there, they wouldn't be able to see him.

He took a step back and followed the dense flowered vines up
to the second floor with his eyes. He could just barely make out a
couple of small windows behind the bougainvillea. He wondered
what rooms were up there. He'd already established that Kali and
her grandmother used the bedrooms that faced the street.

He wished he could see into Kali's bedroom. He imagined her

spread out naked on her bed, her full, trembling breasts shifting to the side, her pink nipples alert.

His erection pressed painfully against his pants. He thought about his father, sniffing the inner band of the hat Leli Lenz had worn. Javier understood his father's preoccupation a lot better now. It wasn't just about saving civilization. It was more personal. But soon the old woman would be out of the picture, and then—

There was a rustling in the bushes. A large gray cat, like an oversized rat, darted through the weedy dirt beneath the mahogany tree.

Disgusting creatures.

Javier readjusted his pants, then stepped over to the cracked coquina patio and examined the back door. It was locked.

The police report, about the fire set by Lillian Campbell and her rescue by Neil Rabin, said that Rabin had gone into the house through a back door, but hadn't explained how he had gotten in. Rabin had been out jogging when he noticed the flames, so it was unlikely that he had his neighbor's key on him, if he even had a key.

But Rabin and Kali were the same age, and their behavior toward each other suggested a relationship that probably went back to their youth. Many people left spare keys hidden outside their houses. Very likely, Rabin knew where the Campbells kept theirs.

Javier's eyes skimmed the likely hiding places. He slid his fingertips over the top lip of the doorjamb, then behind the shutters of the kitchen windows. Nothing. He stepped back, accidentally kicking a plastic food dish that clattered against the coquina. He froze and waited. No sound came from inside.

He studied the broken coquina tiles, but none appeared to have been lifted out recently. Then he noticed the circular pattern of dirt about an inch from one of the planters, as though it had been moved.

He smiled. How obvious. He tilted the planter and slid his fingers beneath it. They touched a small, metal object.

He took the key and put it in his pocket. Then he went out the rusting gate, down the street.

Perhaps he'd return later when it was dark. With a little luck, she'd stand near her bedroom window where he could see her.

52

Kali was strangling. She tried to pry the squeezing hands away from her throat, but they tightened around her.

She awoke with a start. Her damp T-shirt clung to her body; the top sheet and blanket had been tossed to the floor. Why was her bedroom so dim and airless? Then she remembered. Her grandmother had told her to close all the windows in the house, terrified that some bogeyman was trying to get in.

Kali got out of bed, checking the time on her cell phone. Already six in the evening. She'd been asleep for hours. She went to the window and worked the crank until the casement window popped open. She breathed in the cool, scented air and then reality hit her. She felt a wave of nausea. Seth, her marriage, her baby, her grandmother.

She looked again at her cell phone, desperately needing to talk to Neil. Was it right to burden him with her problems? But who else could she turn to?

She went to the corner of her room and sat down in the rocking chair. It was where she'd been sitting last night when Seth called. She looked up at her mother's face.

"Tell me, Mama, what should I do?"

Her mother looked back at her.

"Can I raise my child without a father?"

Her mother smiled.

"I know. Of course, I can. You did. But how lonely that was for both of us."

Her mother seemed to take a deep breath, but that was just the change in the angle of the horizontal line across her chest as Kali rocked back and forth.

"Were you always lonely, Mama, even when my father was alive? Grandma never hugged you, so you never learned to hug me. I guess that's why I don't know how to hug."

The sound of rocking filled the room.

"Tell me, Mama. When you felt lost and all alone, what did you do? Who did you turn to?"

Her mother didn't answer.

Kali got up from the chair and put her finger to the glass in front of her mother's pink, parted lips. "I'm sorry, Mama. I'm sorry I couldn't be enough for you."

Kali braided her hair, slipped into her leggings and sneakers, and went across the hallway to her grandmother's darkened bedroom. She had closed the drapes after giving Lillian the hot chocolate hours ago.

She hadn't followed Dr. Guzman's instructions and had used only a small amount of the sedative when she prepared the chocolate. Her grandmother had reluctantly drunk it, then lay back down against the pillows.

From the doorway, Kali could hear her grandmother breathing strong and even. She left the bedroom door open and went downstairs.

She rummaged through the refrigerator, weak with hunger. She put the leftover vegetarian chili in a pot to heat and tore into one of the cold pastries that Seth's parents had left.

She wondered if Seth had told them yet. Would they accept that their son was gay? They were open-minded people. Maybe they'd even get him to realize he couldn't walk out on Kali and their baby.

But was that what Kali wanted?

She spooned some chili into her mouth directly from the pot. It was hot and cold, not cooked through. She didn't care. The baby was ravenous, making her eat.

She looked again at her cell phone. Call him.

Her fingers dialed Neil's number.

He answered on the first ring. "You up?"

"Yeah."

"You slept all this time?"

"I did."

"Good. What about your grandmother?"

"She's still sleeping."

"Well, you two have been through a lot these last few days."

Kali didn't answer. She watched the chili bubbling in the pot. She turned off the gas.

"Shall I come over?"

She stared at the chili. "I'd better eat something first, then I'll meet you out back."

"I'll be waiting."

In the semidarkness, the backyard had the faded edges of an old black-and-white film.

"Hey." Neil got up from the lawn chair and held out his arms as Kali crossed the lawn toward him. She thought about what she'd just said to the photo in her bedroom, how she and her mother had never learned how to hug.

Neil wrapped his arms around her and she rested her head against his chest. His T-shirt smelled like laundry detergent, his skin like soap. She held his scent deep in her lungs like it was a balm.

"You looked like you could use a hug." Neil lifted her chin and looked down into her eyes. His thumb rubbed her cheek and she felt a cool wetness beneath his finger. She was crying.

"Whenever you're ready to talk," he said. "We've got plenty of time."

She took another deep breath. "I went to meet Seth last night."

Neil frowned.

"He . . . we—" She cleared her throat and tried again. "I guess we'll be getting divorced."

"Divorced? Why?"

"Seth is gay." She let out a small laugh. "How do you like that? I've been married to a gay man and never realized it."

"Shit, Kali."

"Anyway, Seth feels it would be unfair to me to stay married."

Neil's lower lip jutted out as he tightened his jaw. "What about you? How do you feel?"

"Hurt. Abandoned. Deceived."

"He's known for a while?"

"He suspected it, but didn't want to acknowledge it. But I feel more like I deceived myself. I wanted to believe everything was perfect, even though I should have seen it wasn't."

"Come here." Neil opened his arms.

She rested her head against his shoulder. Such a hard-soft shoulder.

"And if he decides he wants to stay married, after all, what will you do?"

"I don't know." Her hand went to her abdomen. "We're having a baby."

"So you'd stay with him? Even if you couldn't truly love each other?"

She raised her head to look into the intense gray eyes behind his glasses.

"Even if you love someone else?" he asked.

Some force, like a magnetic pull, brought their faces closer, closer. His warm breath was on her cheek. Her heart pounded in her ears, making her light-headed.

He took her face in his hands, his fingers, still healing from the burns, rough against her skin. "Please, Kali, don't go back to him. Ever."

His lips were against hers, so warm. She remembered their feel, the taste from the last time. His tongue slid into her mouth.

"Come with me," she said, breathless.

They ran across the weeds back to the house, hand in hand. She'd left the door to the storage rooms unlocked the other night, thinking she might go back searching for more of her past. Or perhaps she always knew she'd be returning with Neil.

She went up the back stairs, leaving the overhead lights off. She could hear Neil's sneakered footfalls behind her own.

She stopped in the doorway to the first room. The dim glow from the light in Neil's phone cast the room in sepia, ghostlike, as though it might disappear at any moment.

Neil put the lit phone on the floor and opened the folded cot.

Just like last time.

He pulled her toward him, took her face into his hands, and kissed her again.

Just like last time.

Kali could hardly breathe.

He lifted the T-shirt over her head and pulled off his own shirt. She leaned back against the cot, felt his whirling tongue on her chest. Cool against heat.

Just like last time.

He pulled down her leggings, caressing her abdomen, his fingertips wonderfully rough against her. He kissed the mound of her raised belly.

Not like last time.

Hot tears ran down the sides of her face into her hair and turned cold. Not his. It could have been his. Her baby needed a father.

"I love you, Kali," he whispered into her soft flesh. "I've always loved you."

She pulled his head up and brought it to her face. She kissed him until there was no breath left inside her. Then she turned her head away, gasping in the stagnant air heavy with the smells of mildew, sweat, and pheromones.

The light from his phone cast shadows around the small room— the broken chairs, icebox, sewing machine, paint cans, and the rickety ladder.

The room was as it had been the other time. When he had held her and she'd prayed he would never let her go.

He unhooked her bra, taking her nipples in his mouth, one then the other, then back again.

Oh, dear God, what was she doing?

He eased off her panties.

Yes? No? She couldn't stop him if she wanted to.

She raised her hips and felt him slip inside her. The cot creaked and thumped against the wood floor. She held him tighter, tighter.

The world was expanding, contracting. Tighter, tighter. Faster, faster. Everything was converging. She had a past. An identity. Neil. She had Neil. A father for her child. The family she'd always dreamed of.

Her breath shuddered out of her. "I love you."

He kissed her neck.

She melted against him. The smell of the musty cot wafted up, making her stomach roil. She pushed her nose against his chest, blocking the bad smell, inhaling his sweat, the scent of soap and laundry detergent. Taking him deep into her lungs, into her core.

For a long time, they lay in each other's arms. Her braid had come undone and he stroked her hair, from her scalp all the way down. He kissed her shoulder.

If only they could stay in here forever.

The light from the cell phone was growing dimmer. There were no colors in the room. Everything was disappearing.

She held him tighter. "Don't go."

"I'm not going anywhere."

"You won't leave me?"

"Never."

She remained motionless, locked in his arms. Did anything else really matter? Kali's true past? Her grandmother's secrets? Kali was tired of secrets. Of discovering the people she cared about weren't who she'd believed them to be.

She needed to tell Neil the truth. "Last time was the first time for me. I never thought that I could—"

"I know." He kissed her hair. "I feel the same way. And here we are again. It's like we've never been apart."

It wasn't what she'd been about to say. But maybe she shouldn't tell him what had happened so many years ago. What mattered was they were together now. And he was right. It was as though they'd never been apart.

She snuggled against him and her eyes rested on the old rickety ladder. It leaned against the wall just beneath an indented rectangle. A trapdoor leading to an attic.

She sat up.

"What is it?" he asked.

Kali pointed to the ceiling. "I never looked up there."

"For what?"

"Lillian's afraid someone will find something she's hidden. But I've been through the whole house and I haven't found anything. Maybe it's up there."

"Your grandmother couldn't climb up that ladder."

"Maybe she hid something there years ago, when she could."

Kali slid her T-shirt on and stepped into her panties. She went over to the door and flipped on the overhead light. It was startlingly bright.

"Ouch." Neil held his hand in front of his eyes. "Thanks for the warning." He sat up on the cot, completely naked.

Kali took in his broad shoulders, the vee of dark hair that ran down his chest over his taut stomach muscles. As she studied him, she noticed him hardening. She started toward him, then stopped. Tonight was just the beginning for them. Just as Neil had said earlier, they had plenty of time.

Instead, she went to the ladder and dragged it away from the cans of paint, closer to the trap door.

"Wait," Neil said, putting on his jeans. He took the ladder and positioned it. "I'll climb up and look."

"No. I need to."

"That's crazy."

"Please, just hold the ladder for me."

He shook his head, but held the ladder in place as Kali climbed up. She pushed on the rectangle and it popped up. She moved it aside, then went up a couple more rungs until she could put her head into the black opening. She reached inside for a light switch or pull cord, but found nothing.

"Hand me your cell phone, please."

Neil let go of the ladder, picked up the phone from the floor, and handed it to her.

Kali brought the phone into the attic. Shadows jumped around the exposed beams and rusty pipes. She choked on the damp, metallic smell.

"Anything there?"

She went up another rung, and hoisted herself into the crawl space.

"Damn it, Kali. Get out of there."

She held the phone in front of her, moving the light from side to side. Something was sticking out from behind a beam.

"I see a small carton."

"Great. Now come down and let me get it."

But she was already crawling on her belly, through the dust, past the spiderwebs.

Her fingers touched the edge of the carton. She got ahold of the side and pulled it toward her, then slid back toward the ladder.

Her feet touched the top rung, and she carefully backed down, bringing the carton to the edge of the opening.

"Please, Kali. Come down and I'll get the carton."

"I've got it. It's light. I can hand it down to you."

"Same stubborn-ass girl you've always been," he said, taking the carton from her.

She backed down the ladder, closing the cell phone, and dropping it on the cot next to the carton.

"Strange thing to seal it with," Neil said. "Looks like someone taped it up with a strip of contact paper."

Kali ran her finger over the camouflage pattern.

"You recognize it?" he asked.

"It's my mother's."

"The carton?"

"Maybe. But definitely the camouflage seal. It's what she used to cover over a painting she made on the inside of her closet door. To hide it from my grandmother."

"You think she hid this carton?"

"We'll soon see." Kali ripped the contact strip off and opened the carton. Dust drifted up and bits of disintegrated cardboard flew around the room.

Kali's heart was pounding. Secrets. More secrets. Did she really want to know what was in here?

She reached into the box. It was filled with crumpled newspaper. Her fingers touched something. She lifted out an object wrapped in plastic. She pulled off the plastic and found an old-fashioned suede handbag with worn leather straps.

Neil picked up one of the balled-up pieces of yellowed newspaper and straightened it out. "February 1940," he said. "I don't think this was your mother's."

Kali opened the clasp to the handbag and looked inside. There was a vaguely sweet smell, but except for a lace handkerchief, the handbag was empty.

"I don't get it. Why would your grandmother have gone to so much trouble to hide this?"

Kali fingered the strip of camouflage contact paper. "Maybe she hid something else and my mother found it, then resealed the carton. Maybe my grandmother doesn't even know what she hid is missing."

"But what?"

Kali shook out the lace handkerchief. It was yellowed with age. And there was something on it. What looked like smudges of white latex paint. Beneath the white paint, she could see little specks of color. She looked more closely. The colors were from oil paint forming the outline of a small rectangle. As though the handkerchief had once been wrapped around a tiny painting.

53

They stood in the dark in the small foyer by the back door. Neil kissed Kali hard on the mouth.

"I hate leaving you," he said.

She rested her forehead against his shoulder. "I know."

He lifted her chin with his fingertips and looked into her eyes. "Maybe I shouldn't go. It's not like my mom will even notice whether I'm there or not."

"She'll notice," Kali said. "Even if your mother can't show that she's aware of her surroundings, I'm sure on some level she senses your presence and it comforts her."

"I wish that were true."

"Besides, it's a special day—her birthday. You should be there to celebrate with her."

"You're one to talk. You never celebrate your birthday."

"That's different," Kali said, taking a step back. She didn't like being reminded of that.

"I'm sorry. I'm coming across as insensitive. I'm just so amazed that you and I are together again, I hate to leave you, even for a few hours."

"I'll be here when you get back."

"Yes, you will." He kissed her again. "And then you and I have forever."

He left by the back door, pulling it closed gently behind him.

She leaned against the door and locked it. Forever with Neil, she thought. A normal family for her child. She ran her tongue over her lips. They were bruised, not accustomed to kissing. She and Seth rarely kissed, and when they did, it was always cursory, butterfly kisses, like they were brother and sister or good friends. How could she not have realized there was a problem?

Kali touched her inflamed lips and tears welled up in her eyes. It was over between her and Seth, so why did she want to run to him and beg forgiveness?

But she knew why. Seth had been her best friend, and she was carrying his child. Although it had been his decision to end their marriage, Kali couldn't quite let go of the future she'd envisioned with him.

She went up the stairs, conscious of the soreness between her legs. Everything would be fine. She had never forgotten her dream of Neil as her child's father. And they loved each other. What else mattered?

She paused at the door to her grandmother's bedroom. It was after seven p.m. and she was still asleep. Kali felt a flutter of anxiety. Had the sedative been too strong for her?

Kali went to the bed and turned on the nightstand lamp. "Lillian?"

Her grandmother took a sharp breath and opened her eyes. "Dorothy?"

"No, it's me, Kali. I wanted to be sure you're okay. You've been asleep for a long time."

Lillian settled back against the pillows and closed her eyes. "I'm tired."

"Okay, but if you want anything, I'll be in my room."

Kali turned off the lamp and went to take a shower. The hot water pounded against her head, her face, her shoulders. The tension and emotional overload of the last few days steamed out of her. For the first time, she was able to think clearly.

Yes, her marriage was over, but she still had her baby, and that was more important than anything. And while the last hour with Neil seemed magical, she wasn't going to be a fool about it. She didn't have to make any decisions right now. Nothing was pressing except for Lillian's deteriorating condition. But were her grandmother's fears imagined, or could there be some significance to the lace handkerchief hidden in the purse in the attic?

Kali turned off the water and dried her body, wrapping her hair in a towel. She slipped on a robe and went into her bedroom. The air that circulated from the open windows felt cooler, as though a cold front was coming through. Kali went to the window and looked down through the poinciana leaves, half expecting to see Neil walking Gizmo, but the street was deserted.

She sat down on the edge of her bed and took the lace handkerchief out of the pocket of the T-shirt she'd been wearing. She shook it out and flattened it against the white bedspread. There were initials embroidered on one corner with ivory thread. H.S. This handkerchief was the same as the one Kali had found in her grandmother's closet. But what did *H.S.* stand for? Then Kali remembered. Lillian's mother's name was Hannah. Could this handkerchief have belonged to her? Then what had it been wrapped around?

Kali studied the rectangular outline from oil and latex paint residue. She got a ruler from her desk and measured it. $3\frac{1}{2}"$ x $4\frac{3}{4}"$, like a postcard. Hadn't her grandmother said something about a postcard-size painting she'd once kept in her purse?

The contact strip that sealed the carton suggested Kali's mother had been the last one to have opened the carton, since it was the same pattern as the camouflage paper she'd used to hide the fairy on the closet door. The fairy that Lillian had covered over with white latex—just like the paint on the handkerchief.

Kali opened her closet and ran her hand over the smooth white surface. She could almost make out the outline of the fairy's graceful head, the harp-shaped wings, the four angled arms.

Kali felt a palpitation in her chest. She was remembering something. Something that hurt whenever it touched the surface of her consciousness, so Kali always pushed it back down. But not this time. She sat on the wood floor, her head against the closet door and let the memory out.

ॐ

She remembered waking up that morning, vaguely aware of the smell of pancakes. Her mother was singing a silly rendition of *Happy Birthday*.

Kali laughed. It was her birthday. Her thirteenth birthday.

"Good morning, my beautiful teenage daughter," her mother said from the doorway. She was wearing a hot-pink sweater with her jeans. A good day. "I've made you pancakes for breakfast."

"They smell yummy."

"Yummy's not a word a teenager uses. It's more of a twelve-year-old's word. Say something like, 'They smell decadent.'"

"But they don't smell decadent," Kali giggled. "They smell yummy."

Her mother laughed. "Fine. Have it your way." She opened the curtains and blinds, letting the sunshine into the room. She glanced at the top of Kali's desk and picked up the sketch Kali had made last night before going to sleep. She looked at it for a long, long time, making Kali nervous.

"Don't you like it?"

"It's wonderful, Kali."

Kali felt lightheaded. "You really think so?"

"Yeah, I do. You have a true talent." Her mother sat down on the edge of Kali's bed. Her dark hair was pulled back in a ponytail and the blue in her eyes was the same shade as a perfect sky. She looked very serious. "I want you to promise me that you won't let anyone ever stop you from painting."

"I promise, Mommy. But I don't have to worry about Grandma. I have you."

"You certainly do." She patted Kali's leg through the blanket. "You know, when I was a little older than you, I found something that was very inspiring."

"What?"

Her mother wrinkled her brow. "A beautiful little painting. I never found out who made it though."

"Do you still have it?"

She shook her head. "But I know where it is." Then she smiled.

"What a great birthday present." She stood up from the bed. "I can get it while you're at school." The smile turned into a broad grin. "Come on, now. Your yummy pancakes are waiting."

Kali made an extravagant flourish with her arms. "You mean my decadent pancakes."

And they had both laughed.

The collar of Kali's bathrobe was wet. She wiped the tears from her cheeks and neck. Kali never saw her mother again after that morning. Never saw the present her mother had been planning to give her.

Could it have been the postcard-size painting Kali was now looking for? Her mother had told Kali she would get it while Kali was at school. And her mother had come here that afternoon. So it was probably somewhere in this house, very likely in this room.

Kali sat up and started looking through the closet, examining anyplace a thin, postcard-sized object could have been hidden. She tested the floorboards, the walls, and looked under the shelves. When she had exhausted every possibility in her closet, she went through her room. She pulled out every drawer, checking beneath and behind for something taped. She turned her mattress over, then the box spring. Nothing below and no slits where something might have been hidden inside.

Despite the coolness in the room, Kali became hot and sweaty. She took off the robe and put on a pair of shorts and a T-shirt, letting her hair loose from the towel. She got down on her hands and knees and went back and forth across the room examining every floorboard.

Nothing.

Frustrated, she sat down in the rocking chair and looked up at her mother.

"Please, Mommy. Tell me where you hid it."

Her mother just smiled.

And then Kali noticed the very slight horizontal line across her mother's dress.

"Oh, my God." Kali jumped up, leaving the rocking chair pitching wildly.

She lifted the framed photo from the wall and turned it around. There was brown paper backing glued to the edges, but the top edge had separated from the frame.

Kali pulled the backing away a little more and turned the picture upside-down. Something fell to the floor.

She picked up the postcard-size rectangle and turned it over, letting out a growl of frustration. Whatever it had been, Kali couldn't tell. Someone had painted over it with white latex paint.

54

Javier had been standing in the shadows since the sun had set. The lights in the upstairs bedrooms were off, but as he walked down the deserted street, he observed a light come on in one of the back windows that were obscured by the thick bougainvillea vines. He wondered what was in there.

At around seven, the upstairs back light went out and Javier returned to his post across the street. He saw the young man from next door leave through the rusted gate. When had he come by and what had he been doing in the house? Had Kali been with him?

Javier felt a surge in his pulse. He didn't like this Rabin guy messing with Kali.

His Kali.

Of course, that's what she was. She belonged to Javier and the Movement that she and her child would resurrect.

Javier watched a light come on in the grandmother's bedroom. A moment later, it went off and the light in Kali's bedroom came on.

He could hardly breathe as he watched the window, willing her to appear. Then, there she was, leaning out, her hair in a towel, the bathrobe falling open, revealing the curve of her breast.

Javier was breathing harder. His fingers tightened around the key in his pocket. He could go up there now, put a pillow over the old woman's face and be done with her. And then, he'd have Kali to himself.

But of course, that wouldn't work. He needed to be patient and do things the right way.

Then he would take his time with the granddaughter.

55

It was early November, but Leli could hear the cold Berlin wind pounding against the tall windows of Wulfie's studio. She shivered and took a sip of the brandy he had given her to ward off the chill in the room.

The little painting sat on an easel, the light from a lamp on the adjacent table angled to brighten it, but Leli kept averting her eyes, unwilling to take in the full image. The woman, the infant—she caught them in flashes.

"It's finished," he said, startling Leli with the nearness of his voice. "No, that's not quite right. It can never be finished. I'll never be able to achieve perfection, but it's as close as I can get. At least—" He chuckled and wrapped his arms around Leli from behind. "I had better stop before the paint gets too thick and it loses the sense of what it is."

Leli forced herself to look at the painting and realized what he was talking about. The oil paint had been applied so heavily that the figures seemed three-dimensional, practically ready to jump out of the tiny picture.

The infant's blond curls looked real, and the rosy cheeks, sweet enough to kiss. Would Leli ever have a child of her own, she wondered?

"The arms are miraculous, are they not?" he asked.

The arms. How could the man she loved have created such a thing? She looked down at his hands crossed over her chest. There was a brownish smear on his forefinger like dried blood.

"You know," he said, "for thousands of years, these arms have symbolized life, purity, and good luck."

That was true. Leli had always made that association until the last few years. Until the symbol had been hijacked and perverted. But Wulfie was old. Of course, to him the bent arms would still have positive connotations. She relaxed against him.

"I want you to have it." His warm breath sent goose bumps down her back.

"No, Wulfie. I couldn't possibly take it from you."

He tightened his arms around her and rested his chin on her shoulder. "I have the original, my own Madonna in the flesh. You keep the painting, my darling."

The expression on the woman in the painting was practically angelic, reminding Leli so much of her mother that she wanted to cry. She reached out her hand to touch the face. It had been two weeks since she had gotten a letter from her mother and Leli was consumed with anxiety. There had been no word from Joseph in months. Her fingertip came away with a pin-prick-size drop of red from the lips. The paint hadn't quite dried, but Wulfie didn't seem to notice.

He was reaching for her purse, opening it before Leli had a chance to stop him, removing the lace-trimmed handkerchief her mother had given her that Leli imprudently kept with her wherever she went.

He didn't pay attention to the initials in the corner as he shook out the white square. "I'll wrap it in this," he said, taking the tiny painting from the easel and swaddling it in the soft cloth as one might an injured finger.

She dared not argue with him as he put it into her purse, snapped the clasp shut, then placed it back on the end table.

He looked at Leli, patting his goatee, as though he was expecting her to say something.

She was conflicted. Disturbed by the odious image the arms conjured up in her mind, despite how Altwulf intended them.

But at the same time, Leli loved the tiny picture. Loved the reminder of her mother's smile, the promise in the blue eyes of the beautiful cherub on her lap.

"Leli?" Wulfie took a step toward her.

"Thank you for the painting," she said.

Then he smiled and took her into his arms. "My Madonna. You're my very own Madonna."

He undid her dress, leaving her shaking in her slip. His eyes looked different behind his wire-rimmed glasses, almost like he was seeing something other than her.

Leli brought her arms in front of her chest. It was too cold in the room, but her trembling went beyond what her skin was feeling. She loved him, so why didn't she want him to make love to her?

Wulfie pulled off his jacket, undid his pants. He was breathing quickly—low shallow breaths like a runner after a sprint.

He turned her face toward the sofa and pushed her roughly against the cushions. He pulled her slip up and ripped off her panties, scratching her skin with his nails.

"You're hurting me."

He pressed harder against her, trying to enter her. She wasn't ready. She tightened her muscles, resisting him.

He pushed harder.

Outside, the wind was pounding against the windows.

"Stop," she whimpered into the sofa cushion.

And then he thrust inside her. The pillow absorbed her scream.

He pounded into her, over and over and over.

She twisted and tried to pull away, but he was holding her too tightly.

"Please, Wulfie. Stop."

Over her shoulder, she could see his face contorted into something ugly and unrecognizable.

He pounded and pounded into her, his head whipping up and down, up and down, a lock of dark hair against his forehead, sweat running down his cheeks into his moustache, his gray beard hanging from one side of his face.

His beard hanging loose from one side of his face.

Her scream caught in her chest.

Then she let it all out.

56

Kali heard a scream. She ran from her bedroom to her grandmother's.

Lillian was sitting up in bed, frantically looking around the room.

Kali turned on the lamp. "It's okay. It's just me."

"He's here. I know he's here."

"I've locked the doors. There's no one in the house but us."

Lillian put her feet over the side of the bed and started toward her bathroom.

"Wait. Use the walker."

But Lillian ignored her and zigzagged across the room.

Kali could hear her shifting things around in her closet. She wondered if Lillian was looking for the key to the storage rooms. It was a good thing Kali had put it back in the hidden sewing cabinet.

A moment later, Lillian left the closet, turning the light off behind her. She seemed calmer.

"Is everything okay?"

"He hasn't been here, yet. He hasn't found it." She hobbled back to the bed and sat down on the edge.

"Found what?"

Lillian shook her head.

"The tiny painting you mentioned the other day?"

Lillian's eyes widened.

"Is it valuable?"

"I don't know what you're talking about."

"You said there was a painting of your mother that you kept in your purse. Is that what you're afraid someone is trying to steal from you?"

Lillian got up and went to the chiffonier. She picked up the photo of Kali's grandfather.

"I'm sorry, Harry. I miss her, too." She kissed the photo. "And I'll keep my promise."

She put the photo back on the chiffonier and got back into bed. "I'm tired."

"So you're not going to tell me?"

Lillian closed her eyes. "No. Never."

Kali took the small painting from her room and went down to the kitchen. She was furious with her grandmother for refusing to talk about it. Was that what happened with Kali's mother the day she had come here looking for the painting? Her mother had been very excited about giving it to Kali as a birthday gift. Had she found it covered in white paint and then confronted Lillian in anger? Her mother had always been volatile. Could there be any connection to her having a car accident that afternoon?

Kali turned on the kitchen light and examined the small rectangular shape. The latex paint was cracking, the surface beneath it bumpy, as though the artist had layered the original paint on heavily, which would explain the rectangular outline of oil paint on the handkerchief.

An experienced artist trying to cover over an existing oil painting permanently would first have sanded or pumiced down the original, then painted over it with lead oil ground. Latex paint doesn't adhere well to an oil-painted surface. But Lillian, if she was the one who painted over the original, wouldn't have known that, or maybe she just used what was expedient. Kali thought about the cans of latex wall paint in the storage room.

She put her fingernail into one of the cracks and chipped away some of the paint. She wished she could drive to her studio and do this properly, but she didn't want to leave Lillian alone in the house. She'd have to remove the outer layer of paint here. Her fingernails were too short, so she got a knife from the utensil drawer, started at the top left corner and went across to the right side. The paint popped away in small chips.

The background color was a pomegranate red. Then she uncovered a brightness, like a ray of light.

Kali peeled off the next section, exposing what seemed to be a white hood, then blonde curls, two arms raised and bent at an artificial angle, like in primitive Egyptian art. This must have been why Kali's mother had wanted Kali to see the painting. There was a definite resemblance to Kali's own work.

She chipped away down the center of the painting.

She gasped when she saw the face. The blue eyes, the hint of a smile. Lillian had been right. The woman in the picture looked both like Kali's mother and like her great-grandmother in the locket photo.

Whoever had made this was a talented artist. The painting was very likely quite valuable. Maybe she should wait until she got to her studio and not risk ruining it. But the content was more important to Kali than the painting's market value. She kept chipping and peeling.

More blonde curls, another pair of blue eyes. A cherub. Like the cherubim Kali painted, the head too large for its torso.

Kali stopped.

A Madonna and child. A painting with religious connotations. Was that why Lillian had painted over it? Because she was disturbed to see her Jewish mother portrayed as a Christian symbol?

Kali peeled away the next section. Two more arms held the cherub. No. That wasn't quite right. The woman's four arms radiated out from the cherub's torso, in a pinwheel formation.

The result was disturbing, unnatural. Not like the four integrated arms Kali made in her own work. These arms seemed odious, symbolic, reminding her of something she couldn't quite place.

She pushed the knife under the white paint with less care, anxious to see the artist's signature in the corner.

And there it was in a reddish brown. ALT. Unfamiliar initials.

She put the painting down and studied it from a distance.

Four white arms against a red background. And then she realized what she was seeing.

Not arms, but a big white swastika.

57

Kali went shouting up the stairs. "Wake up, Lillian. Wake up, damn you."

She turned on the nightstand lamp, knocking over a glass of water. "I'm tired of lies. I'm sick and tired of all your bullshit lies."

Her grandmother had the blanket pulled up over her mouth. She looked back at Kali with terror in her eyes. "*Gott im Himmel!* What's happened?"

Kali brandished the small painting. "Who painted this? Why do you have it?"

"Oh, my God. Where, where did you find that?" She started getting out of bed. "It's hidden. I have the key."

"No, Lillian. It wasn't in the storage room. Someone hid it in my mother's portrait. And I want to know why. Did my mother put it there? What did you tell her? Who are you really? This time, I want to know the truth."

"Hidden in her portrait?" Her eyes went to the painting in Kali's hand, then to the door. "Put it back. Quickly. He mustn't find it. He mustn't find out about you."

"Me? What are you talking about?"

Lillian lay back down against the pillows. She gasped to catch her breath, unable to speak.

Kali sat down on the edge of Lillian's bed. For some reason, she remembered the morning of her thirteenth birthday, her mother perched on Kali's bed, excited about the birthday present she was planning to bring home for Kali after school.

"You painted over it, didn't you?" Kali asked.

Lillian nodded.

"Why did you do that?"

Her grandmother stared up at the ceiling fan above her bed.

"I know my mom came here to get the painting the day she died."

Lillian started. "You know?"

"She told me there was something she was going to give me for my birthday. Something that had inspired her."

"Inspired? That's what she said? Inspired?" Lillian's jaw trembled. She sat up and reached for the tiny painting, studied it for a moment, then brought it against her chest. "Dear God."

"Please. I need to understand what this painting meant to my mother. Tell me what happened."

Lillian lay back against the pillow, the painting clenched in her hand. "I'd hidden it away in the attic. I didn't think she'd find it."

"But she did."

"Many years ago. When she was still in high school. Dorothy didn't tell me she had, but I knew. She began making drawings with four-armed women. I was horrified when I saw them and tried to make her stop. When she wouldn't, every time I found one of her drawings or paintings, I would throw it away."

Just as she'd done with Kali's pictures.

"Then," Lillian said, "Dorothy started painting on the walls."

"And you painted over them."

Her grandmother nodded. "I locked the door to the storage rooms so she wouldn't be able to get to it, but that didn't help. The image was firmly in her mind."

"If you hated the painting so much, why didn't you destroy it?"

Lillian brought the painting close to her eyes. "My mother's face. I couldn't believe he had captured my mother's face. It was all I had of her."

"But this is you in the picture. You when you were Leli Lenz." She nodded.

Kali's voice quivered. "Whose baby is this?"

"Not a real baby. One he imagined."

"Who? Who painted this, Lillian? Whose initials are these?"

"Professor Altwulf."

ALT. Altwulf.

"Who was Professor Altwulf?"

"A gentle, older man with a goatee and spectacles. An art professor, he told me. He had some connections and helped me get into
films."

"And he painted this?"

"He used to take me to his studio. It was filled with paintings.
And he was so kind, so generous. I let my heart go."

"You fell in love with this man?"

"I was a young, naïve girl. My brother Joseph had brought me to
Berlin, but then he disappeared one day and I had no one. No one
but Wulfie."

"Wulfie?"

"Professor Altwulf. I called him Wulfie. And I trusted him. Of
course, I didn't tell him the truth. My mother had warned me to tell
no one."

"Truth about what?"

"That I was really Ilse Strauss. That I was Jewish."

Ilse Strauss. A name Kali had never heard before. Her grandmother's true name, but Kali still didn't know who this woman really was.

Kali looked at the four arms shaped liked a swastika. How could
Kali's mother have found inspiration in this? And yet, if one didn't
associate the symbol with the hatred of the Holocaust, Kali's artist's
eye could appreciate the beauty in the symmetry. And these were
clearly arms, like the four arms of the goddess that Kali had been
named after. Hadn't Kali's mother once tried to explain it to her?
How symbols meant what you wanted them to. That the goddess
Kali represented the best, most positive qualities—life and goodness
and energy. That's what her mother saw in the name, despite the
death and destruction others tended to see.

"I want to know about my mother. What you told her the day she
died."

Lillian was looking at something on top of the chiffonier in the corner of the room. The photo of Kali's grandfather. "I promised Harry I wouldn't speak of it again."

"Please, Lillian. I need to know."

Her grandmother turned her faded blue eyes to Kali. Her face was gaunt, all angled bones and shadows. "Yes, you do."

A shiver ran down Kali's spine.

"Dorothy came to the house while I was out," Lillian said. "I suppose she did so deliberately, so she could find the key."

"To the storage rooms?"

Lillian nodded. She had let go of the painting and her arthritic fingers played with the edge of her blanket. The satin ribbing was frayed. "I was surprised to see Dorothy's car in the driveway. She rarely came to visit. I brought the groceries into the kitchen, calling her name. I heard footsteps coming down the storage room staircase. At first I panicked. I thought he had found me. Found the painting. That he had Dorothy up in the storage rooms and was going to hurt her. I picked up a knife."

"Who did you think found you?"

"Graeber." Lillian took hold of Kali's arm and dug her fingers in. "And now he's back. That's why you need to know this. He wants the painting and he wants you."

Kali eased her grandmother's fingers off her arm. They left a red imprint. "But it wasn't Graeber. It was my mother who was coming down from the storage rooms."

Lillian nodded. She'd brought her hand back to the blanket and her fingers pulled at the torn ribbing. "Dorothy was holding something. I could tell it was the painting." Lillian's features tensed and she looked like a furious young woman as she spoke. "Then Dorothy said, 'What did you do to my painting?'"

"Give that to me," I said. "It isn't yours."

Lillian began to sob. "She told me she wanted to give it to you as a present. And all I could think about was that I had to make Dorothy understand it was evil. That she couldn't contaminate you as well. So I told her."

Kali felt her abdomen convulse. She held herself, trying to protect her baby. "Told her what?"

But Lillian didn't seem to hear Kali. "And, after I told her, something changed in her demeanor. Instead of the horror and outrage I
was expecting, Dorothy became calm. 'I see,' she said. 'Well, I'd
better put this away.' And then Dorothy went back up to the storage room with the painting. When she came down, she locked the
storage room door, and gave me the key." Lillian shuddered. "I should
have known something was wrong. She was too composed, but I was
so relieved that the truth was finally out and that Dorothy seemed
okay with it."

Kali's heart was pounding in her ears. "What happened then?"

"Dorothy went up to her bedroom." Lillian ripped the edge of
the blanket. "I suppose she had the painting with her and that's
when she hid it in her portrait, but I didn't know that then. I never
went back to check. Perhaps I should have." She took a deep breath.
"Dorothy left the house. I heard her car pulling out of the driveway.
I still believed that everything was okay—but of course, it wasn't."

Kali knew what happened next. Her mother's car had crashed
into a giant ficus tree a few blocks away. The car had been going over
seventy miles an hour, according to the police. Her mother had died
on impact, they said. Kali's grandparents had told her it was an accident, but at some deeper level, Kali had known it couldn't have
been. Her mother had been a careful driver; she never would have
driven so fast down the neighborhood street.

"What did you tell her about the painting that upset her so
much?" Kali asked.

Lillian stared up at the ceiling fan.

"What did you tell her?"

Lillian wet her thin, dry lips with her tongue. "I told her who
painted it."

Kali glanced at the reddish brown initials in the corner. ALT.
The pounding in her ears got louder. "You said Professor Altwulf
painted it."

Lillian closed her eyes.

"Who was Altwulf?" Kali looked again at the initials in the corner of the painting again. Not ALT. The initials were AH. Her stomach did a flip-flop.

"Who was Altwulf?" Kali asked, her voice sounding shrill and foreign to herself.

"God forgive me," Lillian said. "A disguise. He wore a disguise. I didn't know. Not until that terrible day. His goatee came off and hung from his face. And then I saw."

"Who was he, Lillian?"

"He was the devil." She licked her lips. "Altwulf was Adolf Hitler."

Kali heard her grandmother speak, but the words seemed to be coming from the end of a wind tunnel.

"And Hitler was . . . he was Dorothy's real father."

A long, long wind tunnel.

"Your real grandfather."

58

Lillian heard the front door slam. She listened expectantly, caught in the déjà vu nightmare. A moment later, a car squealed out of the driveway.

Just like Dorothy.

But no. Dorothy had been unnaturally calm. Almost zombielike. Dorothy had pulled out of the driveway slowly, picking up speed as she went, as the reality of who she was hit her.

And then she crashed the car into a tree.

Please God, protect my granddaughter. Let his curse end now.

She reached for a glass of water. Her lips and mouth were so dry. But the night table was wet with spilled water, the glass on the floor.

Harry was watching her from the top of the chiffonier.

"What choice did I have, Harry? I had to tell her. She had figured out too much. And I won't be here forever. She needs to protect herself and her child from Graeber."

Lillian felt a slight weight through the blanket. Her fingertips touched the small rectangle. Kali had left the room without the painting.

It had been in Leli's purse when she fled his studio. Perhaps she should have destroyed it when she first realized she had it. But would that have changed anything?

Would Dorothy still be alive? Lillian's parents? The millions of Jews who were exterminated because of her?

No. It wasn't the painting that brought his wrath down on everyone who was tinged with her blood.

It was Leli herself.

Perhaps if she had said nothing, things would have worked out differently.

But she hadn't remained silent.

He pounded into her, tearing her open with explosive jabs, hurting her like she'd never thought possible. "Stop," Leli cried and turned to see his contorted face whipping up and down, a lock of dark hair against his forehead, sweat running down his cheeks into his moustache, his gray beard hanging loose from one side of his face.

Her scream caused him to stop abruptly. He pulled out of her, a stunned expression on his face. He touched his cheek. The fake goatee came off in his hand.

He looked at the beard, then at her with those blue, blue eyes. His lips twitched upward in a small smile. "So now you know, my Leli. I was planning to tell you soon, but now is as good a time as any."

He took a step toward her, his shirt open, pants down around his ankles. His penis hardened.

She squeezed back into the sofa, wanting to vomit. The studio was cold and the outside wind pounded against the windows.

"Don't be frightened, Liebchen. I am still the same man who loves you. Better than Professor Altwulf, though I suppose there's no need for him any longer."

He pressed the palms of his hands against the back of the sofa and leaned in to kiss her. His breath smelled foul and in the dimness, his eyes were the color of blue mold. "Don't worry, Leli. No harm will ever come to you."

She spit in his face.

He drew his head back and wiped the spittle away. "What's the matter with you?" His voice had become sharp. "Do you know how many women would give their lives for the opportunity to be fucked by me, even once?" Then his expression softened. "Don't you know what you mean to me? You're my beautiful Madonna. The only woman I've ever truly loved."

He reached out to touch her cheek and she smacked his hand away. "Don't touch me, you disgusting murderer."

His chest expanded as his penis drooped.

"You're a disgusting, perverted murderer."

"What did you call me?"

"I've heard what you've done. Kidnapping innocent people, murdering them."

"Innocent people? You mean the traitors and Jews?" He raised his voice. "And what should I do with them? Jews are the protuberant tumors in our society. They must be excised before they infest the rest of us through their leprous souls."

"Our leprous souls? Then I pray to God I've infected you with mine."

"What are you talking about? You're no Jew."

Leli covered her mouth. What had she done?

He leaned toward her, breathing too hard. Some of her spittle hung from his moustache. She felt his fingers close over her hair. He lifted her up off the sofa and flung her across the floor. She hit hard, her face banging into the leg of an end table. The room spun around her.

"Get out. Get out of my sight."

She reached for the table, pulling herself up. Her slip was torn and sticky against her raw skin.

"Get out, you Jewish whore." He kicked her and she went sprawling over the carpet, toward the door. Her chin was throbbing and something warm was running down her neck. It turned the lace on her slip red.

She grabbed her coat and purse from the chair, and crawled to the door.

He was screaming obscenities, smashing liquor bottles and glasses, knocking over lamps, the easel, his paintings along the wall.

She reached for the doorknob, pulling herself up. She got the door open, eased herself outside, her coat and purse clenched in her hand.

Almost safe, she thought as she pulled the door closed after her, but his words escaped, echoing in the narrow hallway.

"I'll get you, Jew. You and all the rest of your filthy kind. I swear I'll eradicate all of you from this earth."

Lillian held the painting tightly. November 7, 1938. She had escaped that night, leaving Berlin on the next train out.

Lillian closed her eyes in pain.

And when millions of Jews were killed in the ensuing years of the Holocaust, only Lillian knew the truth. Adolf Hitler had fulfilled his threat.

And it was all because of her.

59

Kali drove with no idea where she was going. It was raining and the windshield was blurred. The raindrops were warm and running down her cheeks. She touched her face. Not raindrops. Tears.

A dark shadow pulled in front of her. Kali swerved. Honking all around her.

Kali's heart pounded through her chest.

She slowed the car, put on her right blinker, and pulled over to the side of the road. What was she doing? Trying to kill herself? Kill her baby?

She put her head back against the seat as she caught her breath. She needed to get herself together. This was her baby inside her. Hers. She wasn't going to put it in danger.

Headlights from oncoming cars streamed by to her left. She was on the strip of parkland called Haulover Beach. To her right were palm trees and a deserted parking lot. Beyond, moonlight played on the breaking waves in the ocean. No people. Kali got out of the car. The air was briny and a breeze whipped through her hair. She leaned against a palm tree for support.

Adolf Hitler was her real grandfather.

She said it aloud over the sound of traffic and crashing waves. "Adolf Hitler is my grandfather. My grandfather was a monster."

Her knees went weak and she dropped to the ground. "Noooooo. Noooooo."

There was a pain in her abdomen, like her guts were being wrung out. She retched into the sparse grass and rocky dirt.

She tried to spit out the vile taste in her mouth, but it stuck to her tongue.

Hitler was her grandfather.

Suddenly, everything that had happened these last few days made sense to her. Her grandmother's guilt and fear that someone was stalking her, even Lillian's reference to considering an abortion many years ago. Of course, she had considered it. She'd been carrying Hitler's spawn.

And so was Kali. She touched her belly. Hitler's great-grandchild was growing within her womb.

She heard a car pull off the road onto the gravel a distance behind her. A car door slammed. Someone was walking toward her. A large man in dark clothes.

Had he followed her here? Lillian had said someone was after the painting and Kali, and Kali had assumed it had been paranoia, but that was before she knew the truth. Was it possible the man Lillian spoke about—this Graeber—was still alive? That he would want to destroy all evidence of Hitler's Jewish offspring?

The gravel crunched beneath the man's shoes.

Kali got up and ran toward her car.

The man called after her, "Hey, don't run away."

Kali climbed into her car, slamming the door after her.

She turned on the ignition and pulled into traffic, almost colliding with a speeding car in the right lane.

The scream of the other car's horn echoed in her head as she straightened her car and continued into traffic, her heart pounding. She glanced in her rearview mirror. The man was watching her, rubbing his head. He was wearing a police uniform.

Kali drove with heightened awareness, keeping to the speed limit, both hands clutching the wheel, conscious of the baby inside her. She checked the rearview mirror periodically, but realized the man Lillian feared couldn't possibly still be alive. Her grandmother was reacting to years of pent-up guilt and fear. Kali and her baby weren't in danger. No one knew their terrible secret.

No one but Kali and her grandmother.

A few minutes later, Kali pulled into a parking spot near her studio. The street was quiet. No cars driving by, no pedestrians. Kali got out her keys. The New Age store was dark. It was almost nine and Camilla usually closed up around seven.

Kali went inside, locking the door behind her and leaving the light off. She found her way past the shelves of candles, inhaling the scent of incense and vanilla as the wind chimes tinkled from the movement in the air.

Once through the drape that blocked off her studio, Kali turned on the overhead light. The brightness stung her eyes as it bounced off the pale wood floors and mirrored wall.

She sat down on the floor, folding her legs beneath her and began to cry. It was too much to hold inside, but whom could she tell? Seth used to be her best friend, her confidant, and their baby's father. But he was also a Jew. He would never accept that his child had Hitler's blood. He might even demand that Kali have an abortion.

She touched her abdomen. She would never do that. Never.

What about Neil? He seemed to know her better than she knew herself. He could be fair and objective.

She thought about lying in his arms a few hours earlier, their bodies entwined. He said he loved her. But their relationship was so new, did she really want to burden it with this awful secret?

Maybe she should just keep it to herself. Tell no one. Why not just go on as though nothing had changed?

Kali got up from the floor and went to the mirror. She touched her face as she studied her image. Except for the bluish shadows that had darkened and spread beneath her eyes, she still looked like Kali. She still was Kali. No one had to know the truth.

After all, she didn't have the impulse to kill, control, or destroy. She didn't hate anyone or any group of people.

But how could she come from this monster genetically and not share some of his traits?

She inhaled, bringing the smell of oil paint and turpentine deep into her lungs. In the mirror, she could see the reflections of several canvases on the floor, the sketches and watercolors on the table, the large painting on her easel.

Four-armed monsters and floating cherubim.

Just like his.

"Noooo," she cried as she ran to the table. "I'm not like you." She grabbed the watercolors and charcoal sketches, tearing them in half, then in half again. Turning them into tiny pieces of heads and bodies and arms. Terrible, terrible arms.

"I hate you," she screamed as she ripped. "I hate you."

She rushed to the oil paintings, digging at them with her short fingernails, but the canvases couldn't be torn. She pounded on them with her fist, spit on them. "I hate you."

She took the scissors off her desk and cut through the canvases. Cut off the arms, cut through the heads, shredded the rest.

She pulled the painting off the easel. Her masterpiece. She stabbed it with the scissors, penetrating the fairy's blue eyes. Then again, cutting through the cherub's undeveloped torso. And again, slashing through the outstretched arms. Again and again and again.

"I'm not like you. Not like you."

Then she sank down to the floor, put her cheek against the cool wood, and curled up with her arms around her abdomen. Her child.

Not his.

60

Lillian was dreaming about her mother singing to her. She opened her eyes, feeling a joy she hadn't known in years, thinking about her mother's sweet smile. Just like in the locket. She finally had photos of dear Mama and Papa, photos she'd longed for for seventy years.

She reached into the pocket of her floral housecoat and took out the gold heart. She would have worn it around her neck, but the chain was broken. Graeber had broken it the day he brought her the radio. She'd meant to have it fixed, but had never gotten around to it. And then she had to leave without it.

Graeber must have rifled her room after she left Berlin. He would have found her mother's letter, then taken the doilies and the locket.

Lillian felt a shrill fear, the joy gone.

And now Graeber was returning them. Letting her know at any moment he could come for her. For the painting.

For Kali.

Lillian slipped the locket back in her pocket and looked around her bedroom with a start. Where was Kali? Then she remembered. Kali running down the stairs, horrified by the truth. The front door slamming. She had left before Lillian had a chance to explain who Graeber was. How he followed her to Jersey. But Lillian had escaped with Harry and a new identity on the *Normandie*. And Graeber had lost track of her. At least he had until she foolishly lit all those candles.

She shifted and something moved across the blanket. The tiny painting. Kali had found it hidden in Dorothy's portrait, but now it was out for anyone to see. Had Kali locked the door when she left?

No. She had been too agitated.

So Graeber could walk in at any moment, take the painting, kill Lillian, and wait for Kali to return.

Lillian had to stop him, but how could she get down the stairs and lock the door? She needed to hide the painting first. Without the painting and the apparent physical resemblances to it, Graeber had nothing to tie Lillian or Kali to Hitler. Lillian had kept up with the news. There was no confirmed DNA of Hitler, but the likeness in the little painting could work as a link. Then, God only knew what Graeber would use it for.

She got out of bed and hurried across the room with the painting in one hand. It was only when she got to the door that she realized she'd forgotten her walker. Well, she'd have to manage without it.

Lillian put the painting in her pocket with the locket and used the walls for balance, crossing the hallway to Dorothy's bedroom. There was no furniture on this side of the room to support herself with, so she took several quick steps and practically crashed into the bed.

She let out a little laugh. Not bad for a ninety-three-year-old who had recently had a stroke. Leaning against the side of the bed, she worked her way around to the side by the rocking chair.

Dorothy's portrait was on the floor, leaning against the wall. Lillian picked it up with some effort. It was heftier than she imagined, or perhaps it was because she'd lost so much strength.

The brown paper backing was detached from the frame at the top. So that's how Dorothy had hidden it. Lillian took the little painting from her pocket and slipped it into the opening in the back of the frame.

Supporting herself against the wall with one hand, she held the heavy picture frame with the other and tried to hook the wire hanger onto the nail. The picture banged against the wall, but the wire wouldn't catch.

Her arms and legs trembled, tiring from the effort.

She let go of the wall and attempted to hook the picture with both hands. She lost her balance and swayed, but caught herself on the side of the bed.

Must do this. Can't let him find the painting.

She straightened herself up and went toward the wall taking small steps while holding Dorothy's portrait high in front of her. She aimed for the nail and brought the picture down toward it.

She could feel the wire catch.

She reached for the arm of the rocking chair and eased herself into it. She needed to lock the front door, but she had to catch her breath first. At least he'd never find the tiny painting.

She looked up at Dorothy's sweet smile. Just like her dear mother's. Her hand closed over the locket in her pocket and she rocked back and forth, thinking about the happy days of her childhood, the smell of challah baking, her mother singing.

> *Oyfn pripetshik brent a fayerl,*
> *Un inshtub iz heys . . .*

A noise from downstairs, like a footstep. Lillian tensed. It had come from the dining room just below her. Had Kali come back?

Lillian remained absolutely still. She would have heard the front door opening. Even when she slept soundly, the acoustics were such that the sound of the front door opening or closing carried through the living room fireplace up through the one in her bedroom. So Graeber couldn't have gotten in.

Yet—

She eased herself up from the rocking chair, held the edge of the bed for support to get to the other side of the room, then used the momentum from several quick steps to reach the doorway without falling.

Made it. She took another deep breath and balanced herself against the hallway wall until she was able to touch the banister. She clung to it with both hands. She brought her right leg down one step, then carefully brought the left foot beside it. Her arms trembled with exhaustion.

It had been easier when Kali had helped her down the other day.

Lillian had had no fear of falling with her granddaughter bracing her.

But Lillian was on her own. She could do this. She had to do this.

She brought her right foot down to the next step, following with the left. Then she went down one more step. Then another.

She didn't know how much time passed. Her focus was completely on reaching the next step, so when her foot touched the cold marble floor, it took Lillian a second to realize she was down. She'd done it.

Now, she simply had to work her way around the foyer's circular wall until she got to the front door. Her legs were shaking, but knowing she was close gave her a second wind.

She took a couple of quick steps, arms outstretched, and touched the wall. She braced herself against it, working her way past the archway leading to the living room, then to the foyer table. She caught a glimpse of herself in the mottled mirror. An old woman with messy white hair and sunken blue eyes. Who would believe she'd once been a beauty? Lillian continued the next few steps and reached for the doorknob. She clung to it and turned the lock.

Safe. She was safe.

She leaned against the door and inhaled deeply. A heavy, musky smell filled her lungs. Like cat musk. She sniffed again. It was cat musk.

The hair stood up on Lillian's arms. A draft was coming through the hallway that led to the kitchen. The back door was open.

He was here, in the house. She had to stop him before Kali returned.

She started across the marble floor, but there was nothing to hold on to. She swayed, unable to keep her balance, and felt herself falling. She hit the marble floor hard. She remained frozen, afraid to move and discover she'd broken something.

Her breathing was too fast, too loud. A creak came from the kitchen, then a bang. The sound of the back door closing.

Nothing more. If Graeber was in the house, why hadn't he come for her?

She moved one arm, then the other, expecting to feel shooting pains, but there were none. Just the stiffness and joint pain from her arthritis. She wiggled her legs. Nothing broken, thank God.

She crawled down the hallway, a few inches at a time, expecting Graeber to jump out of the shadows at any moment.

She reached the kitchen and grabbed one of the chairs to pull herself up. Her body was shaking badly, her vision blurry. Holding on to the chair, she reached for the wall, then made her way to the étagère that blocked the door to the storage rooms. The smell of cat musk was very strong.

The cats would keep him away.

The room was pitching and rolling. Lillian held on to the étagère. Her fingers touched the bag of cat food. She turned it over, watched it pour out over the floor.

Wulfie was terrified of cats. She was safe.

Kali was safe.

Her head was spinning, shadows moving up and down.

A large shadow coming toward her.

The scream froze in her throat.

"Is that why you feed the cats?" the shadow asked. "Because you believe they will keep him away?"

Her hands grasped the étagère behind her. The shadow came closer. Not a shadow, a man.

She heard the click of a light switch and the room exploded in brightness. She covered her eyes.

Her legs could barely hold her up. He was so close that she could smell his cigarette smoke and sweat.

"Nothing can keep him away," the familiar baritone voice said.

She opened her eyes and looked into his pale green ones. At the distorted iris, like a keyhole to hell.

"And so we finally meet." He smiled and his lip jerked downward.

"Graeber," she whispered.

"You think my father's still alive, old woman?"

Not Graeber. Graeber's son. Of course.

"But don't worry. My father told me everything. I've come for his painting, Ilse. And for his granddaughter."

He was standing near the back door, leaving the hallway unblocked. She seized the bag of cat food and scattered it toward him.

He laughed. "I'm not afraid of cats, old woman."

She grasped the wall, propelling herself forward, toward the front door.

He made no attempt to stop her. Maybe he would let her go. An old woman. What use was she to him? But she had to warn Kali. She had to save Kali.

Get outside. To a neighbor, a phone.

She reached the front foyer, panting like a dying dog.

He strode past her and blocked the door. Just like Graeber.

But not Graeber. His son. And he wanted Kali.

She turned toward the stairs, falling forward, banging her knees against the steps.

Get him away from the door, up the stairs. Maybe Kali would hear the commotion and wouldn't come inside.

Lillian clutched the step and pulled herself forward. She felt him watching her as she climbed on her hands and knees, up, up, up.

Her arms and legs were about to fold beneath her, but she had to get him upstairs, away from the door. Away from Kali.

The upstairs hallway came into view.

A pain cut through her chest. Weak, so weak, she could hardly move. One more step. Her hand gripped the edge and she held on. Held on tight.

She could hear him climbing the stairs, getting closer, closer.

She clung to the top step.

He was behind her now, stepping around her trembling body like she was a sack of dirty clothes. In the next instant, he was standing at the top of the stairs. He looked like a monster that had risen from the blackest depths.

He stared down at her with his hellish eye. Then he smiled. "For you, Vati."

She felt his shoe slide under her chest. He flipped her.

Ilse flew through the air, then bounced down the stairs.

Shadows and light and angels and her dear mama reaching for her.

Reaching for her, singing,

Oyfn pripetshik brent a fayerl,
Un inshtub iz heys . . .

61

Kali had nowhere to go. Nowhere but her grandmother's house. She pulled into the driveway. Her arms ached and her fingers were blistered and bloodied from her rampage in her studio. But the physical destruction of her paintings hadn't changed who she was—a monster's granddaughter. Or the painful realization that her mother had killed herself when she'd learned the truth.

Kali hated Lillian for that. For her grandmother's role in this bizarre, inescapable nightmare. But then Kali thought about the bits and pieces she'd heard of her grandmother's story and wondered if perhaps Lillian, like herself, was a victim. All Kali knew for certain was that she hurt. And she didn't know whom to turn to for comfort.

She closed the door of her Volvo and glanced across the dark yard at the house next door. Neil's car was under the awning. He was back from visiting his mother. He'd been phoning Kali for the last hour, but she hadn't answered. She had made her decision to tell no one her secret, not willing to chance any latent hatred her admission might release. Kali wasn't worried for herself, but her baby had to be protected at all costs.

The lights in and around her grandmother's house were out. Kali stepped onto the portico and reached for her keys, remembering as she did that she had run out the front door earlier without locking it. How could she have left her grandmother alone? Then she calmed herself. The man Lillian was worried about would be in his nineties. He couldn't possibly still be around to hurt them.

Kali tested the knob. Locked. That didn't make sense. She stepped back from the house and looked around at the hedges, trees, cracked sidewalks. Out here, everything appeared quiet, ordinary.

She unlocked the door, noticing a rank smell as she stepped

inside the foyer. Cat musk? She flipped on the overhead light and gasped. "Oh no. Please, no."

Her grandmother was lying on her back, her floral housedress up around her waist, her neck and limbs twisted in unnatural positions.

Kali doubled over, as though hit in the abdomen with a powerful one-two punch. The room blurred, went black, then came back into focus. Kali straightened up as the dizziness passed. She breathed through the pain until it subsided. Until she felt nothing at all. Then she crossed the foyer and crouched down beside the crumpled shape.

Dead. Her grandmother was dead.

Kali stared at the open blue eyes, at the upturned lips that seemed to be smiling.

She waited for the grief to hit her. Tears, a primal scream. That's what had happened when Kali learned that her mother was dead. But Kali felt nothing. It was as though she had discovered a stranger's body.

In a stranger's house. Everything seemed off. The smells, the chill in the air. But even a stranger's dead body would cause some emotional reaction, not this feeling of dislocation.

Maybe she was in a nightmare. She'd wake up and all of this would dissolve. The frightful painting, unfathomable revelations, Kali's destruction in her studio, her grandmother's body lying here twisted and broken.

Kali squeezed her eyes shut. Let this all be a dream, and when I open my eyes—

A knock on the door caused Kali to practically jump out of her skin.

"Kali?" Neil called from outside.

Kali could feel her heart pounding against her chest.

Her grandmother was still lying on the marble floor.

Not a nightmare.

There was something in her grandmother's hand. Glittering. A thin gold chain. Kali eased the clenched fist open and took out the heart-shaped locket.

The knock again. "Kali?"

She slowly got up and put the locket in her pocket. Her body felt stiff and unfamiliar. She opened the door.

"Where did you go? Why didn't you answer your phone?" Neil took in Kali's face. "What's wrong?"

She stepped aside so he could see.

"Oh, my God." He rushed to the body. "What happened? Did she fall? Did you just find her like this?" He checked the body, then got back up and went to Kali. He rested his hands on her shoulders. "You better sit down. You're in shock." He led her toward the kitchen. "I was worried when you didn't answer your phone. Then I saw your car in the driveway, so I came right over."

The smell of cat musk and rotting vegetation became stronger. Her feet crunched on something on the hallway floor. Small brown pebbles. They were everywhere.

"What the hell?" Neil said. "Cat food? She was feeding the cats?" He pulled out a kitchen chair and guided Kali into it. She heard him turn on the sink water. "Drink this. He handed her a glass. "I'll call 9-1—" He stopped abruptly. "What happened to your hands?"

He took one in his own, and turned it over, examining the torn fingernails, the sharp cuts, the open bloody blisters from the scissors. "What is this, Kali? Did you go to see Seth? Were you fighting with him?"

She shook her head. She felt emotionally dead, but some part of her mind was alive and fighting furiously. The front door locked, even though Kali was sure she'd left it open. The smell of cat musk. Her grandmother's broken body at the bottom of the stairs.

Someone had gotten into the house while Kali was gone, she felt certain of it. The man Lillian claimed was after the tiny painting. Had Lillian come downstairs, trying to keep him out? She would have locked the front door, maybe poured cat food all over the floor so she'd hear an intruder's footsteps as they crunched down the hallway.

"Something happened," Neil said. "You wouldn't have left your grandmother alone. Tell me what's going on."

The house smelled like cat musk, so an intruder had likely gotten in through the back door. Had he found the key beneath the planter?

Kali got up and went to the back door. She unlocked it and went outside.

"Where are you going?" Neil asked.

"I need to check something."

The smell of cat musk was very powerful. If the door had been left ajar, the smell would have gotten inside, permeating the house. Maybe the smell had roused Lillian from her bedroom. Kali bent over and shifted the planter away.

"What are you doing, Kali? If you think someone broke in, then we need to get the police out here. You can't go around touching things."

She slid her fingers under the planter. Gone. The key was gone.

"Come on, Kali. You're not yourself. Get in the house. You're making things worse for when the police get here. They're going to ask questions."

She followed him back inside. Thoughts were shooting around in her brain like stray fireworks. She could see everything clearly, like a picture she was composing in her mind. Someone coming in through the back door. Her grandmother, alarmed by a sound, terrified that he had come for the painting. The painting lying on top of the blanket where Kali had left it. Her grandmother panicking, thinking where to hide it.

Kali's footsteps crunched as she stepped through the hallway toward the stairs.

"Now what are you doing? Talk to me."

She continued into the foyer.

"Damn it, Kali. I have no idea what's going on here, but the police will think you and I have been up to something."

Against the yellowed marble floors, a floral housedress, a puff of white hair, arms and legs in a Picassoesque pose. Kali caught it in her peripheral vision as she averted her eyes from her grandmother's body and climbed the stairs. Not her grandmother. Just a stranger.

"Kali?" Neil called from the hallway.

Kali could see it in images—the layout for a montage. A looming shadow at the top of the stairs. Her grandmother struggling past it. A push. Her frail body flying backward, bouncing down the stairs, smashing against marble, her neck twisting and breaking.

"I'm calling 911 now," Neil called.

Kali was on autopilot, some part of her brain in strategic-survival mode, calling out instructions. Find the painting. Hide it. Protect the baby. No one must know the truth.

At the doorway to Lillian's bedroom, Kali felt a shift in the air and a foreign smell, as though someone who didn't belong had been here.

Find the painting, the voice in her head said.

Kali crossed the rug to her grandmother's bed and ruffled through the blanket, sheets, and pillows. No painting.

Lillian would have hidden it when she heard someone in the house. But where?

Kali had a pretty good idea. She went through the hallway into her bedroom. Something off. Her bed was pushed over a few inches and the white bedspread was crumpled. She checked if Lillian had stuck the painting beneath the mattress, but there was nothing there.

Kali straightened up. She sniffed the air. The strange, unfamiliar smell was in here, as well.

And then Kali noticed her mother smiling at her from her customary place on the wall, not on the floor where Kali had left the framed portrait. Kali let out a breath of relief. Lillian would have put the small painting back in its hiding place, so that Kali could find it, but no one else.

She listened for sounds, hoping that Neil hadn't decided to follow her. No footfalls coming up the stairs.

She took the portrait off the wall and turned it upside down, expecting to catch the postcard-size painting. But nothing came out.

Gone. The painting was gone.

Kali hung the portrait back on the wall and sat down on the rocking chair.

The frozen feeling spread.

Her mother was dead. Her grandmother was dead. The tiny painting was gone.

There was no one and nothing to connect Kali to her genetic roots.

Except for Kali herself.

And whoever had the painting.

62

Javier watched from behind a tree as his son packed up his paintings and folded the easels. Most of the other artists had already cleared out, leaving behind the empty booths, their canvas sides flapping in the breeze.

There were people milling about, children racing to-and-fro with their faces painted like clowns, balloons bobbing behind them, but Javier had planned it this way. He thought it less likely that Gabriel would make a scene in public. And that would give Javier more time to explain.

The smell of steamed hot dogs wafted toward him. Javier remembered a day in the park with his own father, eating hot dogs with sauerkraut. *Soon, Vati,* he thought. *Very soon now.*

Gabriel was almost packed up. He jogged the canvases into alignment, then zipped them into a portfolio case. There were several framed oils leaning against the side of the booth. Javier doubted Gabriel would flee and leave his precious paintings behind.

He stepped around the tree and slowly approached his son, feeling a bit like a fox sneaking up on its prey.

Gabriel spun around, his blond hair flying across his forehead. "What the fuck!"

"I won't stay long," Javier said, holding up his hands. "I promise. I just wanted to tell you that I found the old woman. I have the painting."

Gabriel's head turned wildly from side to side, as though he was searching through the passersby for a cop.

"Don't worry, Gabriel. We're out in the open. I don't know what you fear, but I obviously won't do anything to hurt you."

Gabriel went over to the framed oils and started stacking them up. They were ugly modern paintings with angry bursts of red and black.

"Please, just hear me out," Javier said.

"I have no interest in anything you have to say."

Gabriel's movements were fast and jerky. It would take him several minutes to gather up his paintings and clear out. Javier started talking.

"First of all, I want you to know," Javier said in a soft voice, "I am not a kook. I have nothing in common with those puerile neo-Nazis who parade around like children on Halloween. My goal has always been to right the wrongs of a society that has unfairly condemned an entire race for crimes they never committed."

"Go away," Gabriel said, trying to tie a rope around the paintings. The rope kept slipping out of his shaking fingers.

"Millions of good, loving, innocent Germans like your grandfather have been spat upon and treated like lepers. It isn't fair." Javier's voice rose as he smacked the folding table. "It isn't right."

Gabriel turned to face him. "They weren't innocent. They knew what was happening. They should have intervened."

"Really? What exactly was happening, Gabriel? Do you know for certain? There was a war going on. People were dying from disease and starvation."

"They were murdered."

"Some were. But weren't the Russians murdering plenty of their own? Why weren't they persecuted after the war?"

"I don't want to listen to this."

"What they teach in history books is all wrong. The victors have a way of making up lies to benefit their own purposes."

"Oh, and you know the truth?"

He'd gotten his son's attention. Javier held back a smile. "I believe I have found it beneath the ocean of lies we spend submerged in every day. I believe that the world has cast Hitler in the role of the murderous, ruthless devil as a means of uniting the masses in a common fraudulent cause."

"He was the devil."

"Really? You're an artist, Gabriel. You understand how one's paintings are an expression of what we're carrying inside ourselves." He gestured toward the slashes of red and black on the canvases. "Can you tell me that your work doesn't reflect your anger and hatred of me?"

Gabriel took in a deep breath. His shoulders went back and his nostrils quivered.

"Let me show you something," Javier said, reaching into his pocket and taking out the painting. He slid it out of the velvet sheath he'd put it in. "Does this look like the work of some maniac?"

Gabriel turned away. Javier pushed the painting in front of his face. "Look at this, I said." He'd raised his voice and realized that people had stopped and were staring at him. "Please, Gabriel," he said quietly, "can't you see the compassion and humanity of the man who has been vilified?" He moved in front of Gabriel. His son's face was contorted as though he was in pain.

Javier touched his shoulder. "Won't you join me in spreading the truth?"

For a long moment, Gabriel didn't move.

His son. He'd won his son back.

Then abruptly, Gabriel flung off Javier's hand. He picked up the portfolio, gathered the oil paintings clumsily under his arm, and started to walk away.

"We've been wrongly accused, Gabriel, you along with your forebears," Javier called after him. "But that's changing now. You hear me?" he shouted. "With or without your help, the hatred ends now!"

63

Kali blocked out the rabbi's words and took in the endless expanse of greenish brown grass, indented by headstones that were laid flat, rather than upright as Kali was accustomed to seeing. A battlefield with fallen soldiers, vases of wilting flowers, and empty marble benches. Before her, in the shadow of an underdeveloped oak tree, was the gaping rectangular hole into which her grandmother's coffin had been lowered.

Although her non-Jewish grandfather had been cremated ten years before, Kali felt that such a burial would be inappropriate for Lillian and had chosen a Jewish cemetery. Jews did not believe in cremation as a suitable means of getting to the afterlife.

The rabbi was reciting a prayer Kali had learned in her conversion class just a year before. Her lips moved in rote, but nothing penetrated her core of ice.

Kali hadn't come to terms with the implications of what her grandmother had set into motion over seventy years ago, but the former Ilse Strauss was still her grandmother, still her blood. Perhaps here, surrounded by other Jews and the prayers of their families and friends, her grandmother would finally be at peace.

At peace. Something Kali might never know again. A stab of fear shot through her abdomen as Kali's mind touched the danger she was in. Someone had broken into her grandmother's house, killed her, stolen the painting, and was very likely waiting for the right opportunity to strike Kali down.

But how could Kali protect herself? Whom could she tell who would understand? The police would probably think she was a crackpot if she started talking about her relationship to Hitler. But worse, what if it got out to the media? Instead of being protected, Kali would be exposed to hatemongers. No—not the police.

Kali glanced around at the crowd, all in black, wearing hats, yarmulkes, or other head coverings. Camilla was here, and a few colleagues from her publisher, but mainly friends and business associates of Seth and his parents. Standing with several lawyers from Seth's firm was Jonathan, his red hair sticking out around his black yarmulke. He kept his eyes on the rabbi, not on Seth.

Seth was beside Kali, chanting along with the rabbi, head bowed. He was meticulously dressed in a black suit and shiny wingtips. But although she recognized the closely cropped dark hair and squiggly eyebrows, he looked like a copy of an original painting. No longer her Seth, but an imperfect replica.

Mitzi and Al stood on Kali's other side. Mitzi's arm was around Kali, her fingers pressing reassuringly into Kali's hand. Both Mitzi and Al had been wonderfully supportive, especially after learning about Lillian's Jewish heritage. How could Kali shatter them with the revelation that their grandchild was descended from Hitler?

She looked over and caught Neil's eye. He gave her a little nod. He was wearing a brown tweed sports jacket and tie. He probably hadn't expected to need a dark suit while packing up his mother's house. There had been an awkwardness between them since Lillian's body had been found two days earlier and the police had questioned both of them extensively.

Kali realized the rabbi was speaking to her, pointing to a small bag of dirt and a shovel. She took the shovel and scattered the dirt down into the yawning hole, over the coffin.

The ceremony was over. People surrounded her like maggots clustering on rotting meat. "So sorry for your loss," they said. Kali nodded. She felt nothing. She noticed Javier Guzman standing at the periphery of the group wearing sunglasses and a dark hat.

"Ready to go, angel?" Mitzi asked. "You should ride with Seth. I'm going to see if anyone needs directions to your grandmother's house." She brushed something off the shoulder of Kali's black dress

and leaned in closer. "I can still call the caterer and have them de-
liver the food to our apartment. It's closer and not so—" She glanced
around the cemetery as though looking for the right word.

Kali relieved her. "I think my grandmother would have preferred
her house."

"Okay, then. Whatever you say." Mitzi gave Kali a reassuring pat.
"I'll go find Al and start moving the troops out." She disappeared
into the crowd, the black lace doily on the back of her head fluttering like an injured sparrow's wings in her auburn moppet curls.

Kali touched the lace doily in her own braided hair. She remembered the white doily that had so upset her grandmother.
Where had it come from?

"How are you holding up?" asked a baritone voice.

"I'm okay, Dr. Guzman. I appreciate your coming."

"Of course, my dear. I read about your grandmother's passing in
the obituaries. I'm so sorry for your loss."

"Thank you."

Seth was heading toward them. Dr. Guzman touched his hat.
"Again, my condolences, Kali." He turned and walked briskly toward the parking lot.

"Who was that?" Seth asked.

"A geriatric specialist. He was advising me on how to cope with
Lillian's depression."

Seth nodded, though he didn't seem to have heard Kali's response. "My mom said I should drive with you. Do you mind?"

"It's not really necessary."

"I'd like to, Kali."

"Okay, then."

They walked side by side, close, but not quite touching. For an
instant, she saw images of a movie rewinding. Back to the moment
they stood outside Seth's parents' apartment joking about Bucephala.

Then she saw Seth's head turn toward a group at the edge of the
parking lot. An elfin young man with red hair nodded at him, and
the vision evaporated.

❧

Kali stood behind the banister in the foyer, hoping to blend into the shadows so no one would notice her. She was able to see black shapes darting through hallways, in and out of rooms. Cockroaches converging around the dining room table, covering white discs with assorted shapes and colors.

She was relieved that Mitzi and Al had taken charge of things. Mitzi seemed to be everywhere, encircling and guiding small groups of people like an Australian shepherd herding black sheep, while Al held court in the formal living room with a group of men and women who sat on sofas and chairs that had rarely been used. She could hear his voice booming above the others, a deep chuckle in response to one of his own witticisms. How ironic that now that her grandmother was dead, the house seemed to come alive.

"A heart attack," a woman separated from Kali by a partial wall was saying in a low voice. "That's what the autopsy found."

Kali tuned in.

"I heard she'd become completely demented," another woman said.

"That's right. Mitzi told me that apparently the old woman went downstairs to feed the cats and make sure the doors were locked. Then she climbed back upstairs and had a heart attack from the exertion. That's when she fell back down and broke her neck."

"Where was the granddaughter in all this?" the other woman asked.

"Where were you ladies?" Neil asked in a clear voice.

Kali saw two slim, well-dressed women scuttle past her.

Neil appeared from around the wall carrying a mug. He'd taken off his sport jacket and his white shirt was slightly wrinkled, tie askew. "Hot tea." He handed Kali the mug. "And you should probably eat something."

The mug warmed Kali's fingers. "Thank you."

"I hate gossipers," he said.

"They're just curious."

"Yeah, well." He pushed his glasses up on his nose.

"I miss you," she said.

He ran his finger over the worn banister handrail, not meeting her eyes. "I'm sorry I stayed away. It just seemed like the prudent thing with the cops asking so many questions. I didn't want to give them an opportunity to dream up a scenario that we were in cahoots orchestrating your grandmother's death."

"Well, the medical examiner's satisfied that her fall was triggered by cardiac arrest."

Neil tilted his head as though he picked up something in her voice. "Aren't you?"

"Sure." She wondered if Neil had noticed the locksmith coming by yesterday to change the locks, then later the alarm company's truck.

Neil leaned closer and lowered his voice. "Why did you leave your grandmother alone that night? You still haven't told me."

"We had an argument."

"About?"

"Now you sound like the police."

"Fine. We don't have to talk about it."

Kali watched the cockroaches swarming into the dining room. She desperately wanted to unburden herself. To have someone to lean on, but could she trust him?

"It was about my mother," she said finally. "Lillian told me some things about the day my mom died and I realized my mom had committed suicide. I was very upset."

Neil nodded. "You've always been in denial about what really happened that day, even with the news reports about how fast her car was going. I guess it's good you've accepted the truth, but I'm sorry it hit you so hard."

Several people were leaving. They came over to say goodbye and express their condolences.

"We'll talk later," Neil whispered in her ear. "Remember. You're not alone."

He slipped away. When she looked among the shadowy cockroaches a minute later, there was no sign of him.

Not alone. And Kali felt a little crack in the ice. Not quite like it was melting, but at least a fissure.

64

Kali watched Mitzi usher out the last of the guests, then lock the door. Her mother-in-law kicked off her heels and extended her arms toward Kali. "Come here, angel."

Kali obliged, resting her face against Mitzi's shoulder. Fragrant-smelling curls brushed Kali's cheek.

Al stood in the archway to the living room. He had taken off his tie and jacket and opened the top buttons of his shirt. His white hair was ruffled, as though he'd walked through a windstorm. "Why don't you girls come in here and put your feet up? I can make you some tea, or would you prefer a glass of wine, Mitzi?"

"Wine would be great," Mitzi said, leading Kali by the hand into the living room. Although it was afternoon, the drapes were drawn and the room dimly lit.

"Just water for me, thank you," Kali said.

Mitzi gave Kali a gentle push toward the goose feather sofa and Kali sank into the pillows. Mitzi sat down on the opposite end. She patted the cushion. "Come on. Shoes off, feet up. Before the doctor gets back and scolds you."

Kali slid off her shoes and brought her legs up. She was startled when Mitzi took one of her feet and began to massage it.

"Shhh. Relax. You've been under too much stress."

"Way too much stress," Al said, coming into the room with a tray. He set it down on the coffee table, handed Mitzi a glass of wine and Kali a tumbler of an amber-colored liquid. "You're not looking well, Kali, and I'm worried about you. Drink the apple juice and eat this." He gave her a thick roast beef sandwich on a roll.

Kali inadvertently gagged at the sight of the red meat.

"What, are you crazy, Al?" Mitzi released Kali's foot and took the sandwich out of Kali's hand. "She's a vegetarian. You know that."

"Geez, honey. I sure do. I'm sorry, Kali. You just look so pale, I'm worried that you're becoming anemic. Tell you what. Try this." He took a sandwich of hummus and flatbread off the platter and gave it to Kali. "Better? And I'll get you some mixed bean salad from the dining room."

"Al," Mitzi said, "stop hovering and sit down."

Al looked confused and ran his fingers through his mussed white hair.

"Kali's tired," Mitzi said. "And you're not going to fatten her up in one sitting."

"Ha." He let out a booming chuckle and sat down in an arm-chair. "Look who thinks she's the physician here."

Mitzi leaned back against the sofa and resumed rubbing Kali's foot. "It's because we both love you, Kali, you know that, don't you?"

Kali nodded and took a sip of juice. She could feel the ice slough-ing off her shell.

"We know all about Seth," Mitzi said. "About what's happened."

"He's confused, that's all," Al said. "Probably the pressure of his job and a baby on the way. But it's not real. Seth loves you. This is just his way of escaping, for now. But he'll be back."

Mitzi's fingers were kneading more strongly. "I don't know if what Seth is going through is real or not. Maybe he is gay. Maybe he's not comfortable in a relationship with a woman. I don't think we should be giving Kali assurances about something we don't know." Mitzi held Kali's foot tightly. "But I know how hurt you must be, Kali, and I feel for you, angel. We both do."

"Mitzi's right," Al said. "Some things are beyond our control. If this is what Seth wants. Or I should say, what he needs, then we can't change that."

"But we have control over other things," Mitzi said. "You're like a daughter to us, Kali."

"That's right. We love you like our own."

Kali sucked in her lip and bit down, trying to hold back the tears. "And you've been the family I never really had."

"Oh, Kali," Mitzi said. "I'm so glad you said that. You must feel very lost and alone now that your grandmother's gone."

Al leaned forward on the armchair. "We want you to know that no matter what happens, we're here for you. It doesn't matter if you and Seth get back together or not, you'll always be our daughter and the baby, our grandchild."

Kali took in a deep breath. Tell them or not tell them?

"What's wrong?" Mitzi said. "I feel so much tension in your feet."

"I may be in trouble." She could hear the tremor in her voice.

Mitzi squeezed Kali's instep. Al clenched his fists.

"My grandmother told me some things about her past. Things that may have led to her death."

"What things?" Al asked.

Tell it slowly, so they can absorb it. Don't drop it like a bomb.

"You already know my grandmother was born Jewish and hid her true identity to become an actress."

"Many Jews did that," Al said. "It was a matter of self-preservation."

"Yes, well, my grandmother had a benefactor in Berlin. An older man who helped her get into films. Apparently he was very kind to her."

Mitzi stopped massaging. "She had a relationship with him?"

"Yes."

There was silence. Kali became aware of the clock ticking on the mantel.

"Did she have a child with him?" Mitzi asked.

Kali nodded. "He didn't know she was Jewish."

"And he was German?" Mitzi asked.

"Yes."

Al and Mitzi looked at each other.

"I assume this man is your real grandfather?" Al asked.

"Yes." Kali's heart was pounding.

Al leaned back in the armchair and steepled his fingers, tapping them together thoughtfully. "So you have some German blood. Not a big deal."

"Was he a Nazi?" Mitzi asked.

Kali opened her mouth to answer, but Al broke in. "And what if he was? We used to believe Lillian might have been. That has nothing to do with Kali. We still love her."

"You said you may be in some kind of trouble," Mitzi said, ignoring her husband. "That you think your grandmother's death is somehow connected to her past. Why is that? Had your grandmother aided this man in some way?"

"Not intentionally." Kali felt the ice fall away in large chunks, but beneath were burning hot embers and flashes of fire. A couple of tears slid down her cheeks.

"So why would someone want to hurt her, or you?" Mitzi asked.

"Because the man was very dangerous. And there are people who would want to destroy anything associated with him. Especially his offspring."

Al sat up very straight in his chair. "And who exactly was this man, this grandfather of yours?"

Kali took a deep breath, but she couldn't say it.

"Who, Kali?" Mitzi said.

"My grandmother believed it was—" The name stuck in her throat. She tried again, but this time the name came out too loud, like a shout from hell. "Adolf Hitler."

Mitzi put a hand over her heart and looked at Al. He hadn't budged and his gaze seemed fixated on something on the rug. Then he inhaled deeply and caught Mitzi's eye. "That's certainly quite a story your grandmother told you. I understand why you're so upset."

Mitzi was rolling one of her curls around her finger and jerking at it. Her charm bracelet made a soft, chinking sound.

"You've been under a lot of stress," Al said. "First with Seth, then your grandmother's passing. It's not unusual to blow things out of proportion. To start imagining."

"You think I'm making it up?"

The sound of chinking charms continued along with the ticking of the mantel clock.

"I think," Al said, "your grandmother was mistaken or maybe you misunderstood."

"It's the truth. My grandmother didn't know he was Hitler. He was wearing a disguise. And she thought about having an abortion, but she'd just lost her parents. Don't you see, she was a victim? And now someone has killed her!"

Mitzi got up from the sofa. She wiped her hands on the skirt of her dress as though they were dirty. "Come on, Al. I can't stay here."

"Relax. Let's help Kali upstairs to bed. She probably hasn't slept in days."

"Help her? Are you crazy?" Mitzi pulled Al by the arm. "Let's go."

"Come now, Mitzi. You're not taking her seriously, are you?"

"Didn't you hear what she said, damn it? She's Hitler's granddaughter."

Al jerked his arm out of Mitzi's grip. "Calm down. Kali doesn't know what she's saying. She's under a lot of stress. I'd give her a mild sedative, but that's not advisable at this stage in her pregnancy. She should go lie down."

"Listen to me," Kali said. "I'm not going crazy and I don't need rest. I'm all alone and I'm scared. Scared that whoever killed my grandmother will come back for me. To kill me so that Hitler's blood won't be perpetuated."

Mitzi and Al stared at her.

Kali realized she'd been shouting. She lowered her voice. "Please. I can't do this all by myself. I need you to believe me. To help me. Your grandchild is in danger."

"Our grandchild?" Mitzi said. "OUR GRANDCHILD? How dare you?" She went toward Kali swinging her arms, but Al held her back.

"Stop it, Mitzi."

"How dare you?" Mitzi said, ignoring her husband. "How dare you come into our lives, acting like a good little Jewish wife? Acting like a sweet little daughter-in-law. First you do God-knows-what to our son and turn him into a freak. And now this? You despicable creature, you."

Al held Mitzi around the waist and she struggled to pull free.

Kali pressed against the sofa, bracing herself against a physical attack. But she couldn't leave things like this. "Please, Mitzi. I know how you feel. It was a shock to me, too. But you have to help me. Help your grandchild."

Mitzi held her hands over her ears and shrieked. "NO. Not our grandchild. You get rid of whatever you have growing inside you. We want no part of it. No part of you. Do you understand? Stay out of our lives, you devil, you. And stay away from our son."

"Shhhh, shhhh." Al patted his wife's back. "Come on, Mitzalah. Let's go. Let's go home."

They backed out of the living room into the foyer, Al supporting Mitzi as though she was an old, crippled woman. He bent over and picked up Mitzi's shoes from the yellowed marble floor. Then he opened the front door and they stepped outside. He was still holding the shoes in his hand as the door closed after them.

65

And so it continues, Javier thought, as Beethoven's powerful *Appassionata* reverberated through the room. The sins of the fathers are visited upon the sons. He was dismayed by Gabriel's reaction, but what did he expect? The truth would come to his son in its own time, just as it had to Javier. In the meantime, Javier had to carry out his own destiny. His father and the German people had waited too long for redemption.

The painting lay in a black, velvet-lined box on his desk, a single ray of brightness from his flashlight caressing each curve, every rise of the thick paint. Despite the smudges of white and the damage caused by removing the outer layer of paint, the image was still vibrant.

Her tiny red lips were parted and he was certain he could see the tip of her tongue, the glisten of her saliva.

She had been as beautiful as her granddaughter now was. There was the strong, exquisite bone structure, the glossy blonde curls, the grace that his father had described to him. And in her four, sculpted, perfect arms she conveyed the future of the world, embodied in an infant—their Savior.

He had wanted so much to tell his son how everything had finally fallen into place. How two days earlier, he had watched Kali running from the house, backing out her car as though in a panic. Although she hadn't locked the front door, Javier used the key he'd found under the planter and entered the house through the back so the old woman wouldn't hear him.

He'd waited downstairs, listening to Ilse's footsteps as she crossed into Kali's bedroom. He recognized the rolling of a rocking chair, but the banging and scraping sounds against the wall had mystified him. Until he had gone into the bedroom after the old woman had taken a backward swan dive to the bottom of the stairs. That's when he noticed the portrait hanging askew on the wall opposite the rocking chair. The memory of the noise connected, and, as though led by an invisible hand, he went directly to the portrait and found the tiny painting inside.

He didn't linger, fearing that Kali could return at any moment. From the top of her chest of drawers, he took a hairbrush filled with long golden strands.

For the moment, he had everything he needed.

The notes on the recording were pianissimo, softly tinkling in the background.

He moved the flashlight back and forth, settling the light on the reddish brown initials in the corner of the painting. AH. Written in his very own blood. Javier had removed a small sample with a pair of tweezers and sent it off to a lab for DNA comparison with the follicles from golden strands of hair found in Kali's hairbrush.

There was no other known sample of the Leader's DNA in the world. There had been false speculations about a skull found by the Russians at the site of Hitler's bunker and burial chamber, but that had been recently dismissed as the remains of a female.

But Javier knew from his father that this signature was the real thing. His father had told him that Hitler always put a little of his own blood in his signature. So after the experts analyzed the style and strokes of the painting itself, there would be no doubt that Adolf Hitler had been its creator and the blood in his signature, Hitler's own. Then, it would be an easy step to make the connection to his granddaughter's DNA.

The testing and confirmation would take weeks, but Javier was ready to release the moment the results came through.

Hundreds of thousands of contacts were on the list server and would receive an e-mail and a link to Hailstorm. The website was primed with photos of the miraculous painting, of Ilse Strauss as Leli Lenz, and of her pregnant granddaughter. Javier had written down the entire story, just as his father had told him, starting with the meeting between Leli Lenz and a benevolent "art professor" who called himself Dr. Altwulf. Javier had described Leli's theatrical rise, the love affair, the conception of his child, the separation, and the temporary loss of the painting.

He hid nothing, explaining how the Leader had chosen a Jewess, Ilse Strauss, just as Mary, another Jewess, had been chosen by God. To be purified and reborn.

But Javier had been unable to complete the story. He did not yet know if Kali Miller would embrace her destiny as the new Madonna and stand by his side nurturing her soon-to-be-born child—the hope of the future of humanity. Though Javier's ultimate dream was that someday Kali would bear his own child, who would then assume the mantle.

He had, of course, considered destroying the seed that was growing inside her and planting his own, but as much as he would have enjoyed that prospect, Javier was practical. There was no assurance that Kali would conceive by Javier, and even if she did, months of precious time would be lost.

No, he would continue as planned.

Javier flashed on the parted red lips in the painting. Fortunately, whether or not the granddaughter was a willing participant, Javier could still have the joy of sowing his seed in the fruit from the Leader.

The music became faster, frenzied, building to a powerful crescendo.

How proud his father would have been of him.

66

Kali padded in her bare feet in the now-empty house, past the dim dining room, across the marble foyer floor where her grandmother had lain like a broken doll, then into the living room where her mother-in-law's scent still hung in the air and Kali's shoes lay discarded on the Oriental rug by the sofa.

After Mitzi and Al left, Kali had locked the front door and set the alarm. But how safe was she here, where whoever had killed her grandmother knew to find her? She should run away and hide. Like her grandmother had done for the last seventy years. Lillian had spent those years remote and guilt ridden. Afraid to share anything of herself with her daughter, then her granddaughter. Living a secret was not living at all, and Kali wasn't going to do that to herself and her own child. Problem was, someone out there knew her true identity, had the painting, and wanted Kali dead. Until Kali eliminated that threat, it would be impossible for her to live without fear.

But how could she, a pregnant woman alone with no idea who her adversary was, protect herself? Seth's parents weren't going to help her and now, after revealing her grandmother's secret, she felt more exposed than ever. Fortunately, it was unlikely they'd repeat what Kali had told them this afternoon, not wanting to either acknowledge that their daughter-in-law had gone off the deep end, or worse—that there was some truth in her story.

She needed to tell Neil. She felt like a bloodied boxer, knocked to the ground, then dragging herself up for potentially more abuse. But she had to do this. If her relationship with Neil couldn't withstand this, then maybe it wasn't meant to be. But she had to give it a try. She found her cell phone and dialed his number.

Ten minutes later, she let him in through the front door, then locked it behind him. He'd changed out of the clothes he'd worn to the funeral into jeans and a T-shirt, but he hung back from her, like he used to so many years ago before they'd become friends.

"Thanks for coming over," she said, her hand hovering by the alarm pad.

"I told you, I'm here for you." He glanced over at the bottom of the stairwell as though expecting to see Lillian's ghost, then back to Kali's hand. "I see you're planning on living here for a while."

"Why do you say that?"

"The alarm system."

She input the code. No reason to take chances. "I don't know how long I'm staying, but while I'm here, I feel safer with an alarm."

"But you still won't tell the police you don't believe your grandmother's death was accidental."

"We'll talk about that later. There are a few things I need to tell you first."

He took in her black dress, shoeless feet. "You haven't thrown your dress into the garbage." His voice had softened.

"What do you mean?"

"Like you did after your mother died. Remember? You told me you threw it away, so you could make believe she wasn't really dead."

"That's right." Kali looked down at the yellowed marble floor. Neil's sneakered feet took a step toward her bare ones. Two large feet. Two small ones. He would protect her.

"I guess you accept that your grandmother's gone."

The big feet moved closer to hers, almost touching the tips of her toes.

Neil took her into his arms. He kissed her hard as she pressed herself against him.

"I'm glad you called," he said into her ear. "I'm glad you decided to trust me with whatever's been eating at you."

She looked up into his fogged eyeglasses. "I'm sorry I waited so long."

"You haven't been yourself and I haven't known what to say to you."

She slipped her hand in his. Hers so small in his large one. He would protect her.

She led him down the hallway.

"Where are we going?"

She stopped in front of the door to the storage rooms. The étagère was back in its original place against a kitchen wall, no longer needed to block the door.

Neil pushed his glasses up as he cocked his head. "Up there? Who are we hiding from?"

"No one. It's just the place I associate with secrets and I'm tired of keeping them."

She went up the creaking stairs, grit sticking to the bottoms of her bare feet. She flicked on the light. The cot was open from a few nights before and she thought she could still smell their lovemaking mingled with the mildew.

Neil sat down on the edge of the cot, his elbows resting on his thighs as he watched her.

She remained beside the old oak icebox and picked at some white paint with her broken fingernail.

"So talk to me, Kali."

"You know, it's strange," she said. "My entire life has been built around so many lies and secrets, I'm not clear who I really am."

"You're Kali," he said softly. "The rainbow gypsy. The sad-eyed girl who sees Bruce Springsteen's music in primary colors."

She took in a deep breath, then slowly let it out. "Something happened back then that I never told you about."

The cot groaned as he shifted. "Why not?"

There was something beneath the white paint. A spatter of red paint. "I was afraid you'd be angry. That you'd reject me."

"Come here." He patted the cot. She sat down next to him and he put his arm around her. "Haven't you figured out yet that I love you? That nothing you tell me will make me feel any differently about you?"

"I hope so. I really hope so."

"Trust me, Kali."

She took in his scent as she rested her head against his arm. "I got pregnant."

"That's pretty obvious." He put his hand on her belly.

"I'm talking about fourteen years ago."

He pulled back. "What are you saying?"

"When you and I made love that first time fourteen years ago, I got pregnant."

"With my baby?"

She nodded.

"And you didn't tell me?"

"I was afraid you wouldn't want it."

"Damn, Kali." He sucked in his lips. "What happened? Do I have a kid somewhere? A fourteen-year-old kid that I never got to know? Tell me—do I have a son? A daughter?"

She shook her head. "I lost it."

"You had an abortion?"

"No, I miscarried. Just after my first trimester."

He looked down at the dusty floor and pushed his glasses up on his nose.

"I'm sorry I didn't tell you. I was young and scared."

"It's okay." He put his hand on the back of Kali's neck and brought his face around toward hers. "That was a long time ago." He kissed her. "Right now, I'm looking forward to being a father to this little guy or girl, and to having a few of our own."

She pulled out of his embrace. "There's more."

"I see." He straightened up.

"It's about my grandmother. I finally understand why she hid the truth."

"About being Jewish?"

"Being Jewish, an actress—everything about the last seventy years was a lie." She picked off a long gold hair from the skirt of her black dress and noticed her knees were shaking. "There was a painting she'd hidden in the pocketbook in the attic."

"In the handkerchief?"

"That's right. I found the painting in my mother's room and

showed it to my grandmother. I asked her to tell me the truth about it."

The cot creaked beneath them. "And?"

"She told me." Kali's broken thumbnail caught on the black fabric of her dress. "It was terrible, Neil." She looked into his eyes, hoping he'd see her pain and not make her relive this, but he just stared back at her, his brow creased.

"I didn't want to believe her," Kali said. "But this time I knew she wasn't lying. I'm sure she was killed because of it, and the painting stolen."

"But, Kali—"

"No, listen to me. The painting's gone and whoever took it will be back to kill me."

"Kill you? You're serious?"

"Yes."

"Then we're calling the police right now." He reached into his pocket for his phone.

"Wait."

"Wait for what? If you're in danger, we have to get the police involved."

"I'm afraid of what might happen if anyone finds out the truth."

"What truth?"

Trust him. He's not like Seth's parents. He loves me. He'll take care of me.

"What my grandmother told me. The man who made the painting was my mother's real father. My real grandfather."

"Okay. And why is that so terrible?"

"My grandmother didn't know who he was. He wore a disguise. And he didn't know she was Jewish. It wasn't until it was too late that she realized who he was. And that's why she felt responsible for everything. For *Kristallnacht*, for the Holocaust."

"You're not making any sense."

"Because he was so angry when he found out she was Jewish."

"What are you talking about, Kali?"

"And now there's someone out there who knows who my real

grandfather was. Who stole the painting and wants me dead. So there's no proof. No connection." She was breathless.

"No proof of what?"

"That he had Jewish offspring."

"Who, Kali? Who the hell are you talking about?"

"Hitler."

"Hitler? What about Hitler?"

"He made the painting."

Neil stared at her. "I don't understand."

"I'm his granddaughter."

"No, you're not. That's crazy."

"I'm not crazy."

"She lied to you."

"I saw the painting. My grandmother's story makes sense. Everything fits."

"You can't be Hitler's granddaughter."

"Oh, God, Neil. You have to believe me."

He got up from the cot and paced the small room in his large sneakers. He didn't speak for an uncomfortably long time. The stagnant air coated her lungs, making it difficult to breathe.

"You're Hitler's granddaughter," he said, finally, like he was repeating a phrase in a foreign language, without comprehension. He looked around the room, at the icebox, the broken chairs, the cushions from the lawn furniture, the cans of paint. "You are Adolf Hitler's granddaughter."

She nodded.

"Adolf Hitler, who tried to eradicate the Jewish race."

"Yes."

"My grandmother was in a concentration camp." His voice was a monotone. He stood by the icebox, picking on the same section of paint that Kali had chipped away at. The white had given way to a large blob of red. "She didn't like to talk about it, but it would come out in bits and pieces. The starvation, the abuse, the fear. She was young and pretty, so she survived, but she lost her parents, brothers, aunts, uncles, cousins, everyone in the Holocaust."

"My grandmother's family all died, too," Kali said.

"I've spent a lifetime hating this man, detesting him above everything else. He's the incarnation of evil. His name makes me cringe."

"That's how I feel."

"You're Hitler's granddaughter."

"Yes. I have his blood, but I'm Jewish, just like you. I share your heritage, your deep-rooted abhorrence for Hitler and all he did. But Neil, please, please don't turn away from me." She got up from the cot and took a step toward him.

"No." He held out his hand to stop her. "Don't look at me like that, Kali. Damn it—what do you expect me to do?"

"Hold me. Tell me you still love me. That who my grandfather may have been has nothing to do with who I am."

He closed his eyes and shook his head. The bruise on his forehead was practically gone, only a trace of bluish-green remained.

"Don't you understand?" she said. "I'm not asking you to forgive Hitler; I just want you to accept me." She took another step toward him and the floorboard creaked.

Neil opened his eyes, but his jaw remained clenched as though he was in excruciating pain.

The scent of their lovemaking seemed to engulf the room, or maybe she was just imagining it. Could he smell it, too?

She touched his hand. He didn't pull away. "Please, Neil. The sins of the fathers can't keep being thrust upon the next generation, then the next. It has to stop somewhere. At some point, civilization has to move forward."

"And do what?" he asked. "Forget? I'll never forget."

She shook her head. "Not forget. But maybe it's time to forgive the innocent."

He looked at her hand in his.

For a moment, she thought he would squeeze it. But he didn't. He released her fingers and turned toward the door. "I'm sorry," he said. "This is too much to process. Maybe you thought I was a bigger man than this, but I'm not. I want kids of my own someday, but the idea of propagating his—" He bit down on his lower lip. "I'm so, so sorry, Kali, but I can't do this."

He started down the stairs, his big sneakered feet echoing in the stairwell.

She felt a chill. Anger, frustration, rage.

She called after him. "So what exactly does that mean that you wouldn't propagate his? What would you have done if I hadn't miscarried? What would you be doing now if I'd given birth to your child? Would you still walk out on me?" she shouted. "Would you walk out on your own flesh and blood?"

She heard his footsteps quicken, then stop as he pushed open the back door.

And then the alarm began to scream.

67

Kali turned off the alarm. She felt eerily calm, as though muffled in silence.

She was completely on her own. No one to depend on, no support system.

Why wasn't she panicked and gathering up her things to drive far, far away where she and her unborn child couldn't be found? Because the reality was that there was nowhere to hide. She didn't know who her adversary was or how he might come after her, so how could she protect herself from him? Even if she locked herself away in the house, he'd find another way to come after her. Maybe run her over in the street, or shoot her from a distance with a sniper's rifle.

If she was meant to die, there was little she could do to prevent it. And so, she would simply try to live.

On her own.

She went up to her bedroom and got the heart-shaped locket out of the drawer where she'd put it after finding it in her grandmother's cold hand. The thin gold chain was broken. Kali rummaged through a small box with pins and buttons and fasteners. She found only one safety pin—a large one, but it would have to do. She put the locket around her neck, closing the chain with the safety pin. She caught her reflection in the mirror above the chest of drawers. The heart settled at the center of her breastbones just above the rounded neckline of her black dress. Her blue eyes looked back at her from a pale face, her braid coming undone.

Kali reached for her hairbrush, then remembered it had been missing since the day her grandmother had been murdered. The thought that the killer had taken it made her shudder. She plaited her hair quickly, slipped on a pair of flip-flops, then went downstairs.

She left the house after setting the alarm and locking the door, and got into her car. The Rabins' house was quiet and the thought of Neil's rejection broke her calm. Then she settled herself. She would depend on herself. It was what she'd been taught to do, first by her mother, then by her grandmother.

All those years of self-sufficiency had to be worth something.

She drove south on Alton Road and turned onto Dade Boulevard, then onto Meridian Avenue. A looming bronze hand covered with clinging, desperate figures reached toward a gray sky tinged with tangerine from the setting sun. The Holocaust Memorial.

Kali parked the car. The street was quiet. It was early evening, too late for groups of schoolchildren or curious tourists. A sculpture of a mother huddled with two frightened children stood at the entrance. Kali looked beyond the palm trees at the cars passing in the street. Had she been followed? The symbolism of this place for Kali's own murder was hard to resist, and yet she felt safe here. As though some force would keep the evil out.

Kali entered an arbor of white bougainvillea vines supported by stone columns and black granite slabs etched with photographs of a tortured Holocaust history.

Just beyond was the Garden of Meditation. Kali sat down on a bench in front of the water lily pond. The dark, still water was tinted with red from the setting sun and reflected the stone plaza, semicircular colonnade, and the soaring outstretched arm of love and anguish. Tormented bronze figures—mothers, fathers, children—were caught in perpetuity, frozen as they attempted to climb the arm to escape the horrors Kali's grandmother had believed she'd caused.

Seventy years of guilt had distorted her grandmother, making her remote and unlovable. But her grandmother had once loved and been loved.

Kali clasped the gold heart around her neck. She could feel it warm and pulsing.

Her grandmother was dead. And Kali had never told her she loved her. Never realized that she loved her until now.

Had stopped calling her Grandma.

She stood up and walked through a dark, repressive tunnel illuminated by slats of fading sunlight in pomegranate red. Around her came the haunting voices of children singing. In the distance, at the end of the tunnel, Kali could see a hunched child, whose sobbing grew louder and louder as Kali approached.

Kali ran the last few feet, the child's sobs reverberating in her ears. She threw her arms around the bronzed statue, clinging to it with all her strength. Soaking up its pain and tears.

She looked up at the red, red sky and realized the pain, tears, and cries were her own.

In that moment, she understood the depth of her grandmother's burden. That her grandmother knew her daughter and granddaughter would always be tainted and unloved because of her.

For seventy years, her grandmother had carried that guilt, unable to hug, to love, to be loved. And no one had ever released her.

Kali rested her head against the child's cool one, the gold heart pulsing in her hand.

"It's okay now, Grandma," she whispered. "I forgive you."

She heard a voice humming the now familiar Yiddish lullaby.

And she felt her grandmother hug her back.

68

The sun had set by the time Kali pulled her car into the driveway of her grandmother's house. Despite the glow from a couple of street-lamps, the color was drained from the street and neighboring houses.

Kali got out of her car and crossed the lawn to the front door. Something was moving at the house next door. A shadow by Neil's car.

She froze just as a dog began barking and she heard the slam of a car trunk.

Neil, holding a sport jacket, was standing beside his car in the dim light. The barking came from Gizmo, whose leash was attached to the doorknob of the Rabins' house.

It took Kali a second to grasp what was happening.

Neil put the jacket inside the car and waited by the open door as Kali approached.

She glanced up at the ornate balcony, where she'd once imagined being Juliet to Neil's Romeo.

"So you're leaving," Kali said.

"Everything's pretty much packed up." He pushed his glasses up on his nose. "I called one of those estate disposition companies, and they said they could take it from here."

"Oh." She could think of nothing more glib or meaningful to say.

The headlights from a car went down the street, brightening the poinciana tree. The lacey leaves seemed naked without their red flowers.

"So you're flying out tonight?"

He glanced at his watch. "Yeah."

Gizmo was pulling toward Kali, restrained by his leash.

"I was hoping you'd get back before I left," Neil said.

"Why's that?"

Neil went to the front door, untied Gizmo's leash, then returned. The dog barked and wagged its tail as he licked Kali's hand.

"I can't take Gizmo with me."

"You want me to keep him?"

"I thought you might want him. But it's okay if you don't. I can bring him to—"

"I'm happy to take him."

Kali started to take the leash out of Neil's hand, but he put his other hand over hers. "I'm really sorry, Kali. I've tried to understand what I feel. It's just— This is not a path I can take right now."

"You don't need to explain." She tried to pull her hand away, but he gripped it more tightly.

"Maybe over time I'll be able to handle this. Like with my mom—her Alzheimer's came on slowly, so I could adjust. First, she'd forget little things I had recently told her. Then bigger pieces of her life got erased. But it was a gradual process. It didn't totally rip my heart out when I realized she was no longer the bright, witty woman I'd always known."

"What are you saying? That I'm not still Kali to you? That the rainbow gypsy you said you loved doesn't exist anymore?"

"Oh God, Kali. It hurts so much to look at you."

"But I'm still me."

"Are you?" He shook his head. She could hardly make out his eyes in the darkness. "My whole life, all I've heard about is the Holocaust, the atrocities. It's part of who I am. I can't just disconnect from a lifetime of beliefs."

"But I'm not the Holocaust."

"No, but every time I'd look at you, or any children we might have, that's what I'd see."

Kali pried her hand out of his. "We see what we want to see."

"No, Kali. We see the images that have been permanently implanted in our hearts."

"Then I'm sorry for you."

And she walked back across the lawn with Gizmo at her side, noticing the rusty brown trunk of the poinciana, the pale green web of leaves, and a single red flower dangling from one of the branches.

69

Kali brought Gizmo into the house, took off his leash, and set the alarm. She felt numb and sad. And very, very alone.

"Well, it looks like it's just you and me, boy."

The dog looked up at her with its one good eye.

"Do you like cat food?"

The dog cocked its head.

"Just kidding. We've got some great roast beef sandwiches in the fridge."

Gizmo followed her into the kitchen. It was almost seven and Kali had no appetite, but she took a sandwich from one of the platters left over from the funeral and set it out in a dish for the dog.

Gizmo wolfed it down.

"Good boy." She bent down and buried her face in his soft chestnut fur. He smelled like nacho chips.

Just the two of them, and hopefully someday soon a baby. Seth, Neil, her grandmother—everyone she cared about—were gone. There was no one to love her, no one to hold her, just when she'd learned how lovely it felt to hug.

Gizmo licked her face and she realized she was crying. "It's okay. We'll be fine." She wiped her cheeks. "We'll be great. You, me, and Bucephala."

She went into the TV room and curled up on the sofa. The afghan her grandmother used was lying across the back. Kali shook it out and spread it over herself. Gizmo lay down on the shaggy rug beside the sofa, close enough for her to stroke the back of his head. She closed her eyes, hoping to block the images of the last couple of days, searching for a happy memory.

Her mother smiling, hair in a ponytail, dark wispy curls around her face, blue eyes sparkling. Holding a big chocolate cake with burning candles.

Happy birthday to you, happy birthday to you.

Grandma and Grandpa singing with her. Clapping their hands. A cigar at the corner of Grandpa's mouth. Grandma so beautiful with her high cheekbones and long neck, her blonde hair in a bun. Pretty as an actress.

Happy birthday, dear Kali, happy birthday to you.

Twelve candles and one for good luck.

Her last birthday with everyone there. Everyone happy.

It was possible. Happiness was possible.

Kali took the afghan and cried into it, inhaling the damp wool, a trace of lavender. She rubbed her belly as the sobs wracked her body.

Happiness was possible.

The doorbell rang. The dog's head shot up.

Who in the world? Neil changing his mind? Seth?

Gizmo barked.

"It's fine, Gizmo. The murderer isn't going to ring the doorbell."

She wiped her wet cheeks, then went down the hallway, the dog at her heels.

Through the peephole, she could make out Javier Guzman's bald head.

Damn. Not him. But she didn't want to appear rude.

She input the alarm code and opened the door. "Dr. Guzman."

The dog emitted a low rumbling noise.

Guzman remained outside, eyes on the dog. He was wearing the dark suit he'd had on at the funeral and holding a large black briefcase.

"Gizmo, be good. Sorry, Dr. Guzman. He won't bite."

"No, of course not. I hope I'm not intruding. I've come to pay my condolences. I didn't realize everyone would be gone."

"That's okay. Please come in."

"You sure it isn't too late?"

"It's fine."

"Thank you." He stepped into the foyer. Gizmo growled.

"I'd better put him in another room." She took Gizmo by the collar and led him into the TV room. She closed the door to the kitchen and then went through the TV room to the doorway that connected to the living room. "Stay here and be good." She pulled the pocket door out from the wall a few inches. It rattled as she slid it closed behind her.

Dr. Guzman was where she'd left him, still holding his briefcase. It was as though he'd come on business. Please, please don't stay too long, she prayed.

"Your grandmother lived here a long time," he said, glancing around the room.

"Seventy years."

"And you? You think you'll stay here?"

"For now."

Kali felt awkward standing in the foyer with this man she didn't really know. "Would you like something to eat, Dr. Guzman? There are plenty of leftovers."

"That's very nice of you, Kali, but I don't need anything. And please, call me Javier. I'm not here in my professional capacity. I just wanted to make sure you're okay. I know you don't have a lot of support right now and there are some things I'd like to show you that may help."

"Would you like to sit down?"

"Thank you. I would."

She led him into the living room, turning on a lamp, then going across the room to turn on another. Kali had been keeping the drapes closed the last few days, paranoid about someone looking in.

"Do you mind leaving that one off? Too much brightness hurts my eyes."

"No problem," she said, remembering his dark office.

Javier sat down on one of the wingback chairs. Kali chose the edge of the sofa, the coffee table with his briefcase on it between them. There was something disconcerting about the way he looked at her with his pale-green distorted eye. She wished he would get on with his purpose and leave. She wanted to return to her afghan and the sweet memories.

"You said there was something you wanted to show me?" she asked.

He smiled, his mouth tugging down at the side. "Yes. But first, if you'd bear with me, I'd like to give you a little background."

"Sure." There was something off in his manner. Something that made her uneasy. Her hand clasped the gold heart around her neck.

He took off his suit jacket and laid it across the arm of the chair. "You see, Kali, you and I have been thrown together by destiny." He unbuttoned his cuffs and started rolling up his shirtsleeves.

A tattoo became visible.

"Your grandmother, my father."

Four right angles in a pinwheel shape.

All of Kali's nerve endings lit up. Oh, no. Oh, God, no.

"Ah," he said. "I see you have some idea what I'm talking about."

A swastika on his arm.

He smiled again. "My father was a military man, a dedicated soldier. He was the personal attaché of one of the greatest human beings in history."

Please, God, this couldn't be the man.

"One of my father's jobs was to facilitate any liaisons of, let's just say, a personal nature, that his Leader desired. One such liaison was with a beautiful, young actress named Leli Lenz."

Kali felt the heat in her face. Graeber. This was Graeber's son.

He leaned over and snapped open the briefcase.

She jumped.

"I'm sorry." He looked at her with his hellish eye. "I didn't mean to startle you."

He stuck his hand into the briefcase. She expected to see a gun, but he was holding out some papers. "Please. Have a look at these."

She took the papers from him, her hand trembling. They were photos of Leli Lenz, an old letter on thin paper written in graceful letters, but in German. The signature. *Mama.*

Javier was watching her. "I sense from your reaction that you already know a great deal of the story. About the painting. Perhaps even about your own lineage?"

Kali was breathing too hard and it was impairing her ability to think. Slow down. Keep calm. If he'd wanted to kill her, he would have already done so. He'd had plenty of opportunities. "What do you want?"

"All in good time. But first, it's important that you know the entire story. That you base your decision on information, rather than on hateful lies and propaganda."

"What decision?"

"You, my dear, have the opportunity to change the course of history and save the human race in the bargain."

Gizmo was scratching at the pocket door. There was no one who could help her. Not Seth. Not Neil. She was on her own.

"When your grandmother fled Berlin, our Leader sent my father to find and kill her, and recover a very special painting."

Kali's hands tightened around the edge of the sofa.

"No, no. Please don't worry. No one's going to hurt you. Quite the contrary. You may not know this, but my father was in love with your grandmother. The choice he had to make—obey his Führer or his heart—was agonizing. And to tell you the truth, had he apprehended her, I'm not sure what he would have done."

She could hear Gizmo growling through the door, occasionally emitting a sharp bark.

"My father followed her to the English Channel Islands. Unfortunately, Leli Lenz got a new identity and slipped away. The war intervened and my father was unable to continue his search for several years. He never completed his mission, but he told me everything he knew. For most of my adult life, I have been working toward turning my father's dream into a reality."

"And what exactly was his dream?" Her voice sounded amazingly strong to her ears. Keep him talking. Maybe she'd figure something out.

"That he and the German people would be vindicated. That society would once again embrace the core values of love of family and country that our Leader advocated."

"How was that supposed to happen?"

"Through the miraculous painting. A painting that displays the humanity that was always in the Führer's heart."

Kali shook her head. "Humanity?"

His lips contorted into a smile. "But my father never knew there was a stronger link that could inspire lost generations. He never realized that the Führer had planted his seed."

Kali tensed. "There's no proof."

"Oh, but there is. You see, our Leader left something else behind for posterity. Once your DNA has been matched with the blood from the signature on the painting there will be no doubt."

Hitler's DNA? She touched her braid. Was that why her hairbrush was missing?

"You will be revered, Kali, as the true descendent of the great Leader."

Revered? What was he talking about? That he was going to turn her into some kind of freak show?

"How could you believe that I'd ever condone the most monstrous mass murderer in history?"

"I know you've been brainwashed your entire life. I went through a similar experience when I was growing up, so I completely understand. But I hope I can persuade you to listen to me." He got up from the chair and came around to the sofa.

Her insides felt as though they'd liquefied. She started to get up. He pushed her down.

"Please, Kali." He sat down next to her, squeezing her into the corner of the sofa. "Hear me out."

She could smell cigarette smoke and sweat as he pressed against her. The same smell she'd picked up in the house the day her grandmother had been killed.

"You're alone now," he was saying. "You believe no one wants you, but that's not the case. Millions will want you. Want your child."

Her child. The word brought her terror to the next level. She tried to push around him. "Get away from me."

Gizmo snarled and barked on the other side of the pocket door.

Javier tightened his grip on her arm. "Be reasonable." With his other hand, he ran his fingertips up and down her neck. "I'm the best option you have. I can protect you."

His fingers closed around the gold heart. She felt the chain dig into her neck, then release as the safety pin popped open.

"Everything's in place," he said. "One click on my computer and hundreds of thousands of the Führer's followers will know all about you. You and the child will reign over the greatest kingdom on earth with me. Together we will restore the world to the glory that the Führer envisioned."

"You'll never have me or my baby."

He pressed his hand against her abdomen. "I know you'll be a wonderful mother, that's why you have to think about what's best for the little one. When word gets out on Hailstorm, there will be those who will try to destroy you. There are many who believe the Führer's blood to be evil."

She could hear Gizmo furiously scratching at the door.

"But you're pure and beautiful, Kali. You have his eyes and his spirit. All I want is to be one with you, and together we will lead our people."

He pushed her against the arm of the sofa and climbed on top of her as she writhed and kicked. He was breathing hard, his cigarette breath foul in her face, his mutant eye too close. She could feel his hand slip between them and he fumbled to open his pants.

"Get off me," she screamed, flailing her arms, clawing at his vile eye.

He grabbed both her wrists.

The banging against the pocket door became frantic.

She craned her neck to the side and dug her teeth deep into his arm.

"Bitch." He released her wrists and smacked her hard across the face.

The room went white, then black. There was a pulsing pain in her nose, as a warm metallic-tasting liquid ran into her mouth.

Javier pinned her shoulders against the sofa, his face contorted. "Stupid bitch. I would have treated you like a queen. Now, I'll lock you away until the child is born, and I'll fuck you like the cunt you are." He held one hand around her neck, so she could hardly breathe. With the other, he pushed up her dress and ripped off her panties.

His breath hit her face in short, fetid gusts.

She struggled, but his full body weight pressed against her. Something pricked her side. The safety pin from the necklace. Her hand closed around it. It was large enough to do some damage. With her fingers, she manipulated the pointed side straight, then gripped it in her fist like a tiny ice pick.

She was dizzy from the lack of oxygen, the room swirling around her. His red face was inches from hers.

She had to save her baby.

Like a vicious cat, she swiped the sharp pin at Javier's face. One, two, three rapid slices across his cheek.

He roared in pain, releasing his hand from her neck.

She lunged forward, this time jabbing the end of the pin into his hateful iris.

"Fucking bitch." He lurched upright and covered his eye.

Gizmo was baying like a crazed hyena.

She squeezed out from under Javier and threw herself off the sofa to the floor. No way could she overpower him by herself. She crawled between the sofa and coffee table, then scuttled across the Oriental rug on her hands and knees toward the TV room. Toward Gizmo.

She reached the end of the rug and her raw knees felt the cold marble floor. A few more feet. Almost there. Her fingertip grazed the pocket door, just as Javier's hand clamped down on her ankle.

"Noooo." She kicked at him with her free leg. He gave her a painful chop across her calf, then flipped her over on her back. Her head banged against the hard marble.

"Where the fuck are you going? Do you think you'll be able to get away from me?" He sat on top of her, holding her down with his hands and fingers splayed across her chest. Below his rolled-up shirt-sleeve, she could see a circle of red puncture marks across the swastika tattoo where her teeth had penetrated his skin.

She squirmed and managed to free her left arm. The pocket door was less than an inch away. She reached toward it. A little more. A little more. The door rattled and shook as Gizmo flung his body against it.

Javier was pressing down so hard, she feared her chest would collapse beneath his weight. He looked at her with his left eye. His right was squeezed shut, something oozing from the closed lid running down his torn, bloody cheek. "You'll never escape from me," he grunted.

Her arm felt like it would pull out of its socket as she strained. A little more. A little more. Had to save her baby. Her fingers touched the crack between the door and the doorway. She clawed at it with her fingertips and broken nails, burrowing into the narrow opening as Gizmo scratched against the other side.

A little more. A little more. The door slid open slightly.

"Gizmo, come," she shrieked.

Gizmo forced the narrow opening and rushed through, filling the room with hysterical barking.

Kali saw the brown form dive through the air, hurling itself against Javier. The big man fell to the side of her. He grabbed the dog's flanks in an effort to keep him at bay, but Gizmo's bared teeth clamped down on Javier's throat. The man let loose a muffled yelp as Gizmo swung his head from side to side, tearing flesh, flinging blood. Javier tried to pull open the dog's jaw, to no avail. Blood gushed from the gaping hole in Javier's neck, spewing over Kali's face and arms. Still Gizmo held on, shaking his head in a frenzy.

Javier toppled over into a puddle of blood on the marble floor and lay motionless. Only then did Gizmo release his grip.

"Oh, God." Kali was shivering uncontrollably as she pushed herself up to a sitting position and wrapped her arms around her abdomen. Gizmo crawled beside her, panting. His fur was bloody and matted.

But they were safe. Safe.

And then she saw the dead man's body twitch.

She screamed.

Javier's arm trembled as he reached toward her, his eyes wide—one pale green, the other a dripping black hole.

"Madonna," he gasped. "My Madonna."

And then he fell still, hand extended, the swastika tattoo visible beneath the spray of red.

Like four arms entwined in a gory embrace.

EPILOGUE

The little girl sat at the kitchen table, gripping a red crayon. She bit down on her lower lip as she dragged the crayon across a piece of blank white paper. The line was wobbly.

She frowned and pushed the yellow curls out of her eyes. Then, she held the crayon with both hands and made another line. Not so wobbly.

The smell of burning candles hung in the air. The little girl liked when her mother lit candles. It reminded her of happy birthday.

She drew another line, then another. Each one a little straighter. Pretty lines. Like hugging arms.

"Ilse," her mother called.

"Coming, Mama."

She counted the arms on her beautiful fairy. One, two, three, four.

Then she slid off the chair and skipped down the hallway, the skirt of her pink pinafore flying out around her.